INFINITE
DOUBLECROSS

The South of France:
Art theft, art forgery and
artful duplicity

Michael McGaulley

This is a work of fiction. Names, characters, places and incidents either are the products of the author's imagination or are used fictitiously, and any resemblance to actual persons, living or dead, business establishments, events or locales is entirely coincidental

The title, *Infinite Doublecross*, is a trademark of Michael McGaulley.

For more detailed copyright, legal and other issues please refer to the end of this book.

ISBN-13: 978-0692710265 (Champlain House Media)

ISBN-10: 0692710264

Author's main blog and website: http://michaelmcgaulley.net/

The image on the cover is adapted from the painting, "Antibes, Afternoon Effect," by Claude Monet in 1888. Of this painting, Monet wrote, *"I am painting Antibes as a small fortified town glistening golden in the sun, and standing out against the beautiful blue and pink mountains."*

The Château Grimaldi is at the center of the painting. Picasso lived and worked in the Château for a while after World War II. It is now a used as a museum, mainly for the works of Picasso, where an early scene of *Infinite Doublecross* takes place.

The font used on the cover is Matisse, styled on the work of Henri Matisse, 1869-1954, who, like Pablo Picasso, worked in the south of France. *"When I realized that every morning I would see this light again,"* Matisse wrote when he first came to Nice, *"I couldn't believe how lucky I was."*

PART ONE

Picasso

EMILY'S FINGERS closed on the icy metal of the pistol. She was surprised at how heavy it was. Surprised, too, at how naturally her fingers found their way around the handle to the trigger.

"*No!*" she screamed to herself. "*No. Don't do it! Leave now! While you can!*"

"Linda and I, we were just hanging out together, nothing serious, just having a little fun," Porter said. "Besides, you're never here, always working."

Everything seemed to be happening in slow motion. She turned. Porter saw the gun in her hand and tried to dive under the bed. He was naked. No surprise, the woman had been naked, as well.

Her finger twitched on the trigger once, twice. His body jerked as the bullets hit, then slid to the floor.

She backed away, stunned at what she had done. He lay still, his lifeless eyes staring at her. She threw the pistol back into the drawer and ran out of the apartment and down the endless flights of stairs.

Fingerprints! She raced back up the stairs and into the apartment. Already his body had gone pale, as white as the sheets. She yanked open the dresser drawer to wipe the gun. A giant black snake sprang at her. She screamed, but her feet wouldn't move.

SHE JOLTED AWAKE, heart pounding, mouth dry.

She had no idea where she was. She swung her feet onto the floor, then yanked them up, away from the snake.

Then it came together. She was in France. In the old town of Antibes. On the Mediterranean.

All that with Porter was weeks past now—that awful Saturday: First the scene at TAG, then finding Porter and the woman.

But still the nightmares kept coming.

Not nightmares so much as alternate versions of reality, a might-have-been only a nerve-twitch from coming true. She had held the gun in her hand, feeling the cold and the heft, then—thank God!—had dropped it back into the drawer. She'd grabbed her things and run out of the apartment.

She had not spoken to Porter after that. She sent back the engagement ring by FedEx, and deleted his calls when he tried her answering machine in the days before she left Chicago.

He'd even called her mother, pleading for her to "talk sense into Emily." Her mother, bless her romantic heart, had told him, in no uncertain terms, who had been lacking sense.

It still hurt to think of how she'd been played for a fool. It turned out that he'd been playing around not just with this one, Linda, but with a half-dozen others, maybe more. Whenever she was out of town, which was most of the time.

It would be a very long time before she could trust anybody again.

SHE CHECKED THE CLOCK: a little after 1 A.M. The only sound was the gentle splashing of the waves onto the shore below.

She got up for a sip of water, and found herself drawn to the window and the view of the sea and the fortress.

It was hard to believe this was real, not just another dream. That really was the Mediterranean rolling in to the shore just below, and that really was the Château Grimaldi, the castle, hundreds of years old, where for a few months after World War Two, Picasso had lived and worked in Antibes and had left some of his paintings behind as a kind of rent. Over the years, benefactors added to the collection, and the Château had evolved into a Picasso museum.

A special exhibit had been running this summer, a three-month festival of Picasso and contemporaries, with the Grimaldi Museum's own holdings augmented by works on loan from around the world, covering all periods of his work over a long career.

Emily had never had much time, or, for that matter, much interest in art. But she had resolved that this trip was a time to break out of old ruts, to expand horizons, to reinvent herself. Coming here seemed a good idea, a chance to try something new, then spend some time on the Riviera beaches.

She left the exhibit wondering why Picasso was considered such a big deal, thinking maybe his real talent had been in manipulating the media into making him larger than life, over-rated and over-paid. People paid millions for these: a news article she'd read before coming here noted that one of the Picassos on display had sold for $150 million, and two others for over $100 million each.

Absolutely incredible, she thought. How can any painting be worth so much money? But of course value is set by what people will pay for it.

At the museum shop, bought a memento of this day, this journey: a reproduction of the Monet painting, *Antibes, afternoon effect*. It had appeared here on loan a few years ago, Monet's image of this very place, the Château Grimaldi.

Monet was definitely more to her taste than Picasso.

Beyond that, the Château and the area around had been built on the foundations of the ancient port city of Antipolis, first founded by the Greeks in the Fifth Century, BC. So she was spending the night on the spot where people had been living for 2500 years, maybe longer.

Life-ending

Chicago, six weeks earlier

THE END OF HER OLD LIFE began with a Saturday morning staff meeting following a red-eye flight back from San Diego. Bridges' words snapped her alert: "Morgan will be managing the new CommerBank project, so she and I flew down to Atlanta Monday to finalize things."

Morgan! CommerBank! That's my project! I brought it in!

Bridges is double-crossing me! Again! Bumping Morgan up to take it over!

She glanced around the conference table. The others were in T-shirts and sloppy blue jeans. She wore a crisp pink sport blouse and creased slacks: this was business, she felt, and for business one should dress like a professional.

She knew they were watching. They knew the game Bridges was playing. Here at TAG you had co-workers, not friends. That was the way he set it up–a constant Zero-Sum Game. For someone to get ahead, someone else had to get shafted. It made for constant competition. And it made it easier for him to control by fear and manipulation.

It was TAG's ritual Saturday morning staff meeting, "the only time we can all get together," as he explained at least once each month. Bill Bridges was the managing partner of the Chicago office of TAG, originally The Alexandria Group, a consulting firm specializing in custom software for banks and mutual funds.

Take some deep breaths. Be sensible. Think it through.

But I've always been rational, I've always thought things through!

Maybe thought too much, been too sensible!

And where has always being sensible gotten me? Taken for granted—that's where it's gotten me!

She stood. The room went still. "There's an old saying," she said, struggling to keep her voice calm. "Fool me once, it's your fault. Fool me twice, it's my fault."

SHE PAUSED by a window with a view across downtown Chicago to the rich blue of Lake Michigan. Sixty-six stories up, the effect was dizzying.

She stepped back to look at the person reflected in the tinted glass—a very tired-looking person. A hair less than 6 feet, still lean despite the seven pounds she'd put on this year from a diet of machine snacks and late-night pizzas to fuel the string of 16-hour days.

Her hair, shoulder-length chestnut with strands of natural copper, glowed in the morning sun, and her eyes Wedgewood blue—the gift of her father's Scandinavian genes. Back home, in Minnesota, most of her female cousins had the same look, some flaxen blond, others chestnut.

She saw, all too clearly now, that she was no longer the bright kid just out of college. She'd be 28 next month, practically in the shadow of 30—as her mother made a point of reminding in their weekly phone calls. Her life was slipping away.

Slipping away while she was sealed in offices like this, working on other people's crises.

Lake Michigan was azure blue and inviting. A bank thermometer down on the street level read 72 degrees. A perfect late-summer day, a summer that she'd been too busy to enjoy, and now another weekend cooped up in the office

My life is passing me by. And I'm letting it happen.

She felt sudden vertigo, and rocked forward involuntarily, as if pulled outward. She drew back and saw the imprint of her forehead on the glass.

She flicked on her laptop. It only took a couple of minutes to type the letter, print it out, and sign it.

THE DOOR OPENED; Bill Bridges stormed out. He was 41, thick and stocky, a college linebacker now 30 pounds over his playing weight, but still as aggressive as ever.

He jerked his thumb toward his office, grabbed another cup of black coffee along the way, then dropped into the big leather chair behind his desk. He didn't invite her to sit. That was fine: there was nothing to talk about. The letter said it all.

"So you walked out of my staff meeting to gaze out the goddam window? What the hell was that little performance of yours supposed to mean?"

"Thanks for asking, but no, I wasn't taken ill, just overtaken by a bout of reality."

"The hell're you talking about?" He knocked back some coffee. The grey rings around his eyes were even darker than usual, and the veins stood out on his neck as they did when he was stressed—which was most of the time. Stress was always in the air at TAG. She almost felt sorry for him. Almost.

He slammed the cup back onto his desk. "The bottom line is, don't you ever do that to me again. Don't *ever* walk out of one of my meetings."

"It'll never happen again, I promise you that." She slid the letter onto his desk. He ignored it.

"Better read it," she said, now even more sure it was the right decision.

He scanned it quickly, and it was almost funny the way his scalp drew back across his head as he slumped back into the chair and reread it.

Then he stared at her, his face blank. "What do you think you're doing? CommerBank really wants you for the project. You're not on it, they'll walk. They're expecting you in Atlanta on Monday morning. They– we–I–the firm really need you there." He threw the letter onto the desk.

"That's your problem, not mine. Not anymore. As the letter said, I'm giving four weeks' notice, but since TAG already owes me the six weeks of vacation time you never let me take, I'm gone as of now."

He stared at her, and she saw the pressure inside slowly deflate, leaving him somehow shrunken. Then he nodded. "Okay, looks like you got us by the balls, so go ahead and squeeze. What is it you want? You're upset because—"

"What I want? What I want is to get away from being manipulated and double-crossed."

"I've always been good to you, brought you along," he said, his hands spread wide.

"You know very well that it was my work that brought in the CommerBank business: a referral from Jerry Anders at Western Savings. Larry Cooper asked for me, *specifically* asked for me, and you know it."

"Hey, you'll be on the team, you need a little more seasoning, it's just that—"

"On the team? Not good enough. We went through this before, back in April, with the Continental Fund project. You told me then–you *promised* me–that I'd manage the next one. Well, next time has come and gone, and you double-crossed me again."

9

She paused at the door to add: "Fool me once, it's your fault. Fool me twice, it's my fault."

Cold Metal

EMILY DROPPED the box of office stuff at her apartment, then changed into shorts and running shoes and headed out to walk the parks that stretched for miles north along Lake Michigan–the parks she'd been too busy to enjoy.

Now, out in the sun and air, away from the claustrophobia of the office, she felt a last-day-of-school kind of freedom.

She was still shocked at the way she'd reacted this morning. "The Ice Princess"–they'd called her that in school because she'd always come across as cool, rational, analytical.

But I hadn't been cool and rational this morning.

What's happening to me?

Tired, very tired. Too much stress, for too long.

Tired of being taken for granted.

Tired of being manipulated and used.

Tired of being betrayed.

SHE REACHED FOR HER PHONE to call Porter, then remembered: she didn't have a phone any longer, she'd turned it in when she left TAG.

She walked along the lake-front, on the look-out for a pay-phone.

It'd blow his mind, hearing from her this early on a Saturday. She'd had a total of two totally free weekends since New Year's, and one of those had gone to visiting her family over Easter.

The wedding was now only five weeks away. Five weeks from today.

Maybe it was just as well that she'd quit TAG. Now there would be time to get things ready . . . and a lot less stress..

She finally found a pay-phone. Porter's line was busy. Of all times. She didn't leave a message.

His apartment was in a high-rise along the lake, another half-hour's walk, but today was perfect for walking, and for once she had the luxury of time. The fresh air and exercise felt good, and it felt even better to be free of the office and deadlines and pressure and squabbling and double-crossing.

SHE FOUND another pay phone a block away from his place. The line was still busy. At least that meant he was home. She really needed someone to talk to.

Not just someone, Porter.

From the lakefront, she cut through the parking area to his building. It was a safe area, but you could never be sure. Porter kept a pistol in the bedroom, in case of a break-in.

She rode up on the elevator with a mother and a baby in a carriage. They hadn't talked about children: that was another of the topics he always seemed to back away from.

She paused at his door, wondering if this was such a good idea. Maybe she should forget about surprising him. She'd never dropped in like this before.

She slid the key into the lock.

But Porter wasn't sitting at his computer, and the living room blinds were drawn. His land-line was off the hook.

Something smelled wrong as she stepped inside. Smoking! Somebody had been smoking.

Odd. Very odd. He loathed smoking. He was an account manager at an ad agency, and had even refused on principle to work on a campaign for one of the tobacco companies. It would have been a big promotion, a chance to work in Asia. It was one of the things she admired him for.

Then she knew what it meant, and she wanted to run away, to let things be as they were.

You can't run from it! Confront the reality!

She moved softly toward the bedroom. They were asleep in the bed.

She stood, frozen. The woman stirred and opened her eyes. She gasped when she saw Emily, then bolted for the bathroom—naked. Very big on top.

Porter rolled over and saw her. She couldn't read his expression in the dim light. He pulled himself up in the bed. "So you finally took a Saturday off."

She reeled back against the doorframe. "How long . . . how long has this been going on?"

"You're never here. You're always working, always rushing out of town."

"I can't believe you could do this to me! I thought . . . I thought you loved me."

"Look," he said, pulling on a robe. "Linda and I, we're just friends, just hanging out together, nothing to get bent out of shape about."

"You call this 'hanging out?' With a wedding in five weeks?" She turned so he wouldn't see the tears welling up in her eyes, blinding her.

She groped for the drawer she used for the things she left there: a sweater, a pair of slacks, a bathing suit. She would take them and never come back.

But this was the wrong drawer, and her hand closed on the cold metal of his revolver.

Assault team

EMILY BLINKED AWAY the memories, and forced her attention to what was here and now.

The floodlights had been turned off, and the Château and the fortifications seemed as shadowy and mysterious as if this were a night centuries ago. She wondered about the battles that had been fought here, and about the men who had died trying to scale these walls.

A shadow moved. At first it seemed a trick of the eyes, or maybe another nightmare. Men, dressed in black, moving in the shadows. Ghosts of the soldiers killed here?

Then one of the men swung a rope with a kind of giant fishhook attached to the end; the hook caught the edge of the stone wall with a grating crunch. He tugged on the rope, then pulled himself up the wall like a mountain climber.

She fumbled in her bag for the camera. There might be enough light.

Two more men ran across the narrow street and pulled themselves up the rope, and she snapped a half-dozen quick shots.

She grabbed for the room phone, not leaving her spot by the window. No dial tone. She jiggled the cradle. Nothing.

"*Qui? Q'est que c'est ca?*" It was the old man at the desk, his voice thick, as if he had been sleeping.

"*Police! Vite! Vite!*" she said. He wanted to know if there was a problem. She said no, just tell the police a robbery is in progress at the museum. He hung up, and she wondered if he had understood.

BERTIE DERHAM headed the assault team, his cell-phone linked to a headset so he could stay in instant contact throughout the job.

The woman on the other end—Stoddard told Derham he had no need to know who she was—spoke English with an accent that mingled French with a tinge of snooty British upper-class. She was out there somewhere safe, supposed to be monitoring the police radio frequencies, just in case something went wrong.

Derham didn't like that, he didn't trust a woman to stick around if trouble developed. But he didn't have the choice. She was French, monitoring the police radio calls.

"We're in," Derham whispered into his microphone. She was clocking their elapsed time.

Vern Billy—leave it to the bloody Americans to come up with a name like Vern Billy—was tasked with getting through the only window that wasn't wired into the alarm system.

The window was nine feet up, and looked impregnable. But whoever set up the security system didn't understand that what was impossible to everybody else was just an inconvenience to a team of commandos.

Vern Billy, a wiry guy all arms and legs, piggy-backed on California's shoulders, grabbed hold of the window ledge with one hand, and cut through the glass of the window to reach in and unsnap the latch.

Once he scrambled through, he dropped a nylon line, and California—another of those stupid damned American names—pulled himself up.

The night remained quiet, no police klaxons in the distance, not even a passing car. Derham hauled himself up the rope and went through the window, head first.

"We're in," he whispered into the phone. "Confirm you're there."

"Where else would I be?" Vera snapped. She held a handkerchief over the mouthpiece, hoping it would disguise her voice if the police were taping this.

The clock was ticking; the team moved fast to get the job done and get the hell out of there.

The three members of the assault team had gone through the museum as tourists earlier in the week to get a sense of the layout. They knew exactly where to go and what to grab, because somebody had worked out which of the paintings were worth bothering with and which not. Derham wondered if that was the work of the French woman, whoever she was.

He had made a point of reading up on the museum, and had a good sense of what was on display there, and what it was worth.

It puzzled him at first why they weren't taking the really valuable pieces, the ones that were supposed to be worth $10, $20, $100 million and more.

Then he got it: the really valuable pieces were too well known. They could never be sold, not even for a tenth of their value. They could only be ransomed back to the insurers. But that was risky. In a ransom operation, every communication was a danger point.

The more Derham saw, the more impressed he was at how bloody well this had been planned. It had been set up by somebody who was obviously a hell of a lot smarter than Stoddard.

He figured he'd play along for a while, find what other operations were in the works, then cut himself a better deal. Maybe grab the whole thing.

"Get out! Get out!" he heard the woman screaming in his ear. "Someone saw you entering and called the police. "Take what you have and leave now!"

"Christ!" Derham muttered. They hadn't even been inside a full minute. "Are you certain of that?"

"Yes I am certain. Are you insane? Get out while you can! Police are on the way!"

He moved fast, grabbing the key paintings now, just cutting the wires, not worrying about disabling the alarms.

"You listen to me now," he said into the phone as he moved. "One, don't you ever, ever call me insane. Two, you stay on the line, because if you don't, if you run and let us down, I'll hunt you to the ends of the goddam earth, you understand?"

"Just move! *Vite! Vite!* They're taking it seriously. Now at least two police cars have been dispatched and are on the way. Get   moving!"

17

A couple of shots

EMILY THREW CLOTHES ON, keeping watch by the window, camera ready in case the men came out.

The night remained still, no sound of police klaxons. Had the old man at the front desk understood what she'd said? Or had he set the phone down and dozed off again?

She fumbled in her bag to find her cell phone. Then she thought: This is Europe, 911 doesn't work here! What *is* the French code for emergency calls?

Still no sound of police.

She grabbed the phone and camera and ran down the winding staircase to the hotel's back door, the door she had used in bringing her things in from the car.

She stepped through that door into the dark alley, feeling suddenly vulnerable. Now she wasn't just a watcher, now she was part of it, now there was no going back.

Something appeared at the top of the fortress wall, a head silhouetted against the night sky.

She snapped a couple of shots as a man scrambled over the wall and rappelled down the rope. Another form appeared at the top and lowered a large black bag on another line.

The man already on the ground grabbed it and raced to the van parked, nose out, across the narrow road. He ran with an odd, rolling stride. Had he hurt himself in the fall, or was one leg shorter than the other? Was that a blond pony-tail? But it was a man, no question of that, a man with a blond pony-tail and a definite limp. He'd be easy to identify.

He threw the bag into the back, fired the engine, and pulled out of the parking spot. Now, in the better light, she saw it was a Mercedes SUV. The police will want to know that, she thought, zooming in for a close shot of the car's license plate.

The two other men were down; she got a couple of shots of them as they scrambled into the car. She heard the hee-haw of police klaxons converging from two directions.

SHE CUT THROUGH a labyrinth of medieval alley-ways and emerged on the square in front of the museum, lit now by the flashing blue lights of a half-dozen police cars.

She spoke to one of the officers setting up a line around the front of the museum. He was 40-something, with a broken nose and a black walrus moustache. He shooed her away.

"You don't understand," she tried to explain in French. She was rattled, and it was hard to come up with the right words. "I saw the whole thing! I was the one who called the police! I can describe the men!"

He shook his head and turned away.

She circled and tried to approach from another direction, but another officer ran over to block her way. "I need to speak to someone! I saw the whole thing! I have photos!"

He waved her away. "Get back, or you'll be arrested."

"You aren't listening. I saw the whole thing. I have photos."

"I warned you, yes?" the policeman said. She saw his face twist with anger, and slipped away before he could grab her.

Someone appeared at her side. A young man, wearing a white shirt and black vest–the uniform of French waiters. "You say you have photos, yes?"

"Yes," she responded, suddenly wary.

"I have an uncle. He will listen to you. He's not like these. Pfft! These are stupid street cops. My uncle, he's a detective, you can talk to him."

He led the way to a café. She was surprised that it was still open.

"Sit, please," he said, indicating a table by the door. "I am Jean-Paul. I will make the quick phone call, and be back in a little instant."

He snapped his fingers, and in a moment a waiter brought her a mineral water. It helped, her throat was dry.

Jean-Paul returned in a couple of minutes and sat with her. "My uncle, he is on the way."

Ten minutes later, a Citroen station wagon pulled up in front of the café, the logo of *Nice-Matin,* the local newspaper, painted along the side. Two men jumped out. One ran to the police lines, the other headed to the café.

Jean Paul stood and hurried over to talk to him, a man in his 40's, silver-haired, paunchy. He looked at Emily, then turned back to Jean-Paul and nodded.

"This is my uncle," Jean-Paul said, bringing him over "Monsieur Sabitaille."

"But you told me your uncle was a detective. This is a journalist."

"*Nice-Matin* is the best newspaper here," Sabitaille responded. pulling out his press card. His ID photo seemed to have been taken ten years and thirty pounds ago. "I will listen to your story, then I will pass it on to my friends in the police."

"I should tell this directly to the police."

"You have photographs, so I am told," Sabitaille interrupted. "Of the robbers caught in the act, yes?"

"A dozen or so shots, as well as some in movie mode."

"Let us be reasonable. Suppose you do talk to the police. They have already turned you away, even threatened you with arrest. But now suppose they for once have the intelligence to listen to you. Then what? They will thank you by confiscating your camera, and then you will end up with nothing."

He paused, then added, "But if you sell your pictures to *Nice-Matin*, we can be very generous. And of course we will immediately pass the pictures on to the police."

"How generous?"

Sabitaille took her elbow and guided her to the car. Jean-Paul followed. Sabitaille peeled off some bills. Jean-Paul took the money and disappeared into the night.

"Now we can do business, you and I," Sabitaille said, opening the door of the station wagon. The photographer squatted and snapped a series of shots of her talking to Sabitaille. She caught a glimpse of herself in the car window and wished she had taken a bit more care with the brush.

SABITAILLE DIALED a number on his cell phone, spoke rapidly, then turned back to her. "For your photos, and your story of what you saw tonight, we can pay you €200. That is perhaps, what? Around $250 American, yes? But now we must talk quickly, so I can make the deadline for the morning's paper."

She almost said yes, then paused. She didn't want to be taken advantage of again. "That's not enough. I need twice that. Plus the cost of my hotel room, since I'm not getting any sleep."

Sabitaille nodded, "Yes, okay. €500. But now we must talk."

Police Judiciare

IT WAS AFTER FOUR when Emily got back to bed, and nearly eight before she woke to find that someone had slid a copy of the morning's *Nice-Matin* under her door.

ART THEFT THWARTED AT ANTIBES PICASSO MUSEUM
Thieves Escape with Minor Pieces, Under €2 Million
Eye-witness Alerted Police

Three of her photos were splashed across the front page, but the men were unrecognizable, their faces squashed by nylon stockings pulled over their heads.

Sabitaille had written up their interview as her eye-witness account, and got it mostly right.

But some bad news: there were a couple of photos taken of her negotiating with Sabitaille, and she looked dreadful—hair askew, eyes wild.

Dreadful.

And recognizable.

Madame, the owner, caught her as she entered the small breakfast room. "Ah! I was just calling your room. It is nothing to be concerned about, but two detectives are here to talk to you about what you saw last night. I know both men. It's nothing unusual. You are not a suspect, of course, merely a witness, and they need to have on record a statement from you."

"That's really ironic. I tried twice to talk to the police on the street last night, but they shooed me away. If they'd only listened then, they might have caught the men."

"I am not surprised," Madame shrugged. "Those last night were street police, not always the smartest of men. Their job was to maintain order, and that is all they thought of. These men today are from the national police, men of quite a different order. They are PJ— *Police Judiciare*, Judicial Police— the elite. Like your FBI."

THE POLICE INTERVIEW took less than ten minutes: there wasn't much to say beyond what they had already read in her account in *Nice-Matin*, and the detectives were eager to get on to other things.

At the door, one of them turned to say, "I understand you took some photos of the men you saw last night. But rather than turning them over to the police to assist the investigation, you sold them to a journalist."

He let that hang in the air.

Was that supposed to be a question?

"As I told you: when I tried to make a statement last night, one of the officers threatened to arrest me. Someone, a waiter I think, overheard me, and introduced me to the reporter from *Nice-Matin*. He bought the photos that the police weren't interested in."

"Do you still have those on your camera?"

She nodded. "He said he would pass the photos on to the police, but if you want to download copies now, that's fine with me."

WHEN THE POLICE LEFT, Madame brought fresh hot croissants, then insisted on scrambling some eggs. "I know how you Americans love your eggs for breakfast."

"There is the matter of the television people," Madame mentioned as she poured a second glass of orange juice.

"Television people?"

"Ah yes, there are three crews outside waiting to interview you."

"Interview me? But—I don't have anything to say for television, especially not in French. My French is not very good. I was hoping to improve it while I'm here."

Madame smiled. She was perhaps 55, with a thin face and a long narrow nose. "You will do very well with the news people, I'm sure, an intelligent young woman like you. And your French is very good . . . good for an American, that is. But perhaps you would do me a small favor? When you talk to the television, perhaps you would stand so that the hotel's sign is visible in the background, yes? We are a small family hotel, and the publicity would be very helpful, you understand?"

MOST OF THE QUESTIONS echoed those asked by Sabitaille of *Nice-Matin* last night. Then one reporter asked, "Would you recognize the men if you saw them again, perhaps on the street?"

"Not likely, as they were wearing stocking masks."

Then she remembered a detail: "Actually, one of the men was quite distinctive. He had a blond pony-tail, and he ran with a very distinctive stride, his head bobbing. Maybe one of his legs was shorter than the other."

As she said it, she realized that was something she had neglected to tell the two detectives.

When she came back inside, Madame looked troubled. "I wonder, should you have said that you could recognize that one man? He might consider you a danger, don't you think?"

Beach bums

THE DRIVE from Antibes to Nice was only a few miles along the coast, but the traffic was stop-and-go once she passed the airport and entered onto the highway that ran alongside the bay.

The sun was bright in an intensely blue sky, the sea an even richer deep blue. No wonder, she thought, that the French called this the *Cote d'Azur*—the blue coast—with a sky like that and a sea to match. Tall palms waved in the breeze; banks of multicolored flowers radiated color as if lit from within.

THE HOTEL EMINENCE was a small, family-run place on a side street between the railway station and the sea. The building, she guessed from the style, dated from what they termed *La Belle Époque*, the end of the 1800's when Nice was being discovered as a resort.

Madame checked her in with a smile—a pleasant change from the dour semi-tolerance she had experienced at some other French hotels. She even spoke English well, but deferred to let Emily practice her rusty French.

The inside seemed little changed in design over the decades, with a curving marble staircase to the upper floors, and narrow halls with slightly sagging floors. The old-fashioned flowered wallpaper left no doubt that she really was in France.

She quickly unpacked, then stepped onto the small balcony for a look, determined not to waste a moment of a day like this. The balcony overlooked the hotel garden, compact and formal in the French style, with distinct places for each type of flower, and with each shrub neatly trimmed. There were two orange trees, and four small palms. The fronds of one of the palms brushed against the wrought-iron railing of her balcony.

25

The garden, sheltered on each side by four and five story stucco buildings, was an oasis in the heart of the bustling city— the warm sunshine glowed on the pastel stucco buildings, and it was as if the colors radiated from the walls into space.

She forced herself to take a deep breath and stay still long enough to enjoy the experience. It had been nearly a month now since she left Chicago, and it still took effort to slow down and readjust to a life not dominated by the crush of one impossible deadline after another.

She paused a moment, tempted to call her mother back in Minnesota, maybe even e-mail a quick photo to show her where she was. She was staying at the Eminence because her mother had recommended it . . . after a quick look through her souvenirs from the European trip she had taken between college and marriage.

But France was seven hours ahead of Minnesota time. Mother would probably still be asleep. She'd call tonight for sure.

SHE HAD A QUICK LUNCH—a *Pan Bagnat*, a Nice specialty, a sandwich of *Salade Nicoise* on a crusty roll liberally sprinkled with olive oil. Before the first bite, she took a picture to send her mother.

She went back to the hotel and locked her phone, camera and wallet in the room safe, changed into swimming gear, and headed for the Mediterranean.

The brilliant sun streaming out of a cloudless sky charged her with energy, despite the lost sleep. She walked slowly, letting the salt-tanged breeze blowing up from the sea balance the warmth of the sun on her skin.

She paused in every block to drink in the sight of the flowers and hedges along the way, glowing with surreal color in the brilliant sunshine, the warm rays bringing out the heavy perfumes.

She savored the sights and smells of the tiny shops she passed. *Epiceries* exuding the scents of ripe fruit and pungent cheeses. *Boulangeries* marked by the clean odors of crusty bread. A newsstand. A garage. A toy store. A *patisserie* heavy with the thick sweet aromas of cakes and delicacies. Restaurants broadcasting the aromas of soups and sauces that had been simmering for hours.

THE BROAD EXPANSE OF THE BLUE MEDITERRANEAN came almost as a surprise after the blocks of shaded streets, and she paused in the shade of a palm tree to take it all in.

The beach curved in a giant arc around the bay—the Bay of Angels, it was called—extending from the airport at one end of the bay to the remains of an old fortress perched on a pine-strewn knobby hill above the sea. The mountains behind marked the way to the Italian border.

The traffic light changed, halting the flow of traffic along the *Promenade des Anglais,* and she crossed with the throngs to the broad, palm-lined promenade above the beach.

As far as she could see, there was an unending flow of strolling tourists and bumper-to-bumper strings of cars and buses.

Some sat on rental deck-chairs reading in the sun, or gazing at the sea. Others peered back at the apartment buildings and hotels across the street, ornate structures gleaming in the bright mid-day sun like sugary wedding cakes.

A few late risers took lunch on the apartment balconies, or sat over coffee and newspapers on the garden terraces of the hotels and cafés, gossiping and watching the young people pass on their way to the water.

She moved along with strolling crowds, enchanted by the beauty of the day and the multi-colored sea: rich azure blue farther out, then green, silvery closer to shore.

Holiday excitement crackled in the air, an excitement generated by the interaction of the sun, the sea, and the crowds.

The strollers seemed to make up a cross-section of the world.

Sailors in whites.

Dusty young travelers with backpacks and sleeping bags.

Couples walking hand-in-hand. Some were young, others into their 70s and 80s.

Families of two, three and sometimes four generations. Older people dressed for a different era—the men in coats and ties, the women in dresses and hats, and some even wearing gloves.

Others, older still, in wheelchairs.

There were petite, style-conscious French. Casually dressed Germans. Loose-gated Americans, bigger still, and even more casually dressed. Precise British. Raucous Australians. A smattering of swarthy Mediterraneans—Greeks, Algerians, Arabs, Israelis. Sleek Orientals. Groups of Arab women in black *djellabahs*, some with their faces covered by veils, one woman even wearing a gold mask in place of a veil.

Africans in tribal robes sold hand-carved wood and ivory pieces. Local photographers cruised with instant cameras and a baby monkey or snake to use as a prop.

A continuous stream of humanity . . . all affecting to be unaware of the others, yet watching those others, and watching as well to see whether they in turn were being watched.

THE FOCUS OF ATTENTION was on the beaches below; from them radiated a perceptible sensuality. Bronzed bodies baking in the sun. Couples stroking sun cream on each other in long erotic strokes. Topless girls in monokinis. Tanned beach attendants strutting among sunbathers on mattresses.

The shore was divided every couple of hundred feet by fences, alternating public beach areas with elaborate, privately-operated beaches that offered food service and showers, and rented mattresses and umbrellas.

Renting an umbrella seemed like a good idea. With her fair skin, she couldn't risk a sunburn the first day here.

Most of the private places seemed to be filled with an older crowd, forty-plus, and most of them couples. Others had music going, and she didn't want that: she had come for the sea, not for a night-club in sunshine.

She settled on a place that seemed quiet, the patrons not so pompous. Most of the women were topless, but she wasn't ready for that now. If ever.

She began with a swim. The water was cool, but pleasant enough, and she got in 20 minutes swimming back and forth along the shore.

Later, a wizened little woman in red passed along the beach peddling the afternoon paper, the *Nice-Soir*. The headline story was still last night's art theft, so she bought a copy. There had been no arrests yet. This paper was apparently not affiliated with *Nice-Matin*, as it was not using her photos. There was a photo of *Commissaire Principale* Bertrand Bourchette, who had flown down from Paris to take over the investigation. He was a short, squat man glaring at the camera.

She read a little until the sun, the swimming, and the salt air made her eyes heavy. She turned on her stomach and dozed under the shade of the umbrella.

"YOU JEOPARDIZED THE MISSION, you put us all at risk because of your stupid goddam hair," Derham said. "And your goddam limp!"

The four of them—Derham, California, Vern Billy, and Jorgensen—had gathered in the warm sun at the beach in Nice after getting some sleep. It stretched for miles around the broad bay that framed Nice. The shoreline was made of pebbles, not sand, and the water hissed through the rocks when the waves receded. They were off by themselves so they could talk without being overheard.

"Did you bloody well hear what I said? You jeopardized the mission, you put us all at risk, you dumb shit, because of your stupid goddam hair," Derham said.

His voice was soft. Derham didn't need to talk loud to get respect from the other three, because they had all seen the type. You had to be a little crazy to be a commando, but some guys went over the edge and became really crazy. Derham was one of those, and they tried to stay out of his way.

They didn't know, nor had Stoddard learned before he recruited him, that Derham had spent a year in a psych ward while the British military decided whether or not to prosecute him for what he'd done on a mission in Afghanistan.

He was British, with sandy hair and a plain, pale lumpy face. It was the kind of face you'd forget almost at once—an asset in undercover operations, and one of the reasons he had been selected for SAS service.

But the eyes were unforgettable: icy blue, expressionless, slightly out of focus, never blinking.

"Yeah, I heard," California said, "but I been wearing my hair long like that most of my life, since I got outta the service." He was 41, with a pot-belly, and, until a couple of hours ago, a sun-bleached pony-tail that reached to the middle of his back.

Even with the sunglasses he wore day and night, he looked a little crazy, and had the dreamy, formless way of speaking that said he had burned away a lot of brain cells over the years.

The limp was a reminder of the time, floating on a cocktail of drugs, he had climbed out of a van going 60 on a freeway to do some push-ups on the roof.

"I don't care how many years you had that hair," Derham said, "the point is you were ordered to get it cut off, and you didn't, and now this little blond dolly has seen enough that she might recognize you, and that puts all at goddam risk."

Derham looked around at the others and shook his head. A bunch of misfits. None of them swift, just the kind of dumb grunts who filled out armies. Not commando material, any of them. Maybe California had been, years back, when he was a SEAL, but since then he'd doped away a hell of a lot of brain cells.

Michael McGaulley

PART TWO

Galerie Vera

Washington. Noon. Five weeks earlier.

Vera de Cochin-Jessup closed her checkbook, glanced at the nearly bare walls of her gallery, then slipped to her office in the back and fixed herself a vodka on the rocks.

I'll have lunch soon, she told herself. She hadn't brought anything to eat, though. She never did. But she never forgot to bring a bottle.

It was so utterly depressing to see how everything had crumbled again. This time there seemed no way out, no way at all.

Her gallery, *Galerie* Vera, occupied half of the ground level in a brownstone on the fringes of Georgetown, in an area the developers hadn't discovered yet. For a couple of wonderful years, it had been *the* significant gallery in Washington, and the money flowed.

But then the troubles began. Troubles always seemed to follow her.

Now there wasn't enough to pay next month's rent, not for the gallery, not even for her flat. She'd been down before and managed to bounce back. But never down this far. Now all her bridges were burned– not just in Washington, but in New York, London, Paris. There was no one anywhere she could touch up for a little loan. Now the important people wouldn't even speak to her any more, the bastards.

Only a miracle could save her now, and she didn't believe in miracles. The closest thing to a miracle she could hope for was the jar of sleeping pills she'd hoarded . . . a painless way out when the time finally came. Probably soon.

She heard the chime as the front door opened. Hardly anyone visited the gallery these days, only occasional tourists looking for cheap posters. It seemed pointless now, but she had nothing else to do, and the apartment was even more depressing.

She took a couple of quick swallows and felt the reassuring warmth of the icy vodka, then peered through the one-way mirror that gave her a view of the display rooms. A man, early 30's, tall and lean, wandered around the gallery. She'd spent her life sorting out those with money from those not worth bothering with, and his lumpy suit told the story.

But he looked interesting: rugged good looks, a strong chin, dark curly hair. She went for strong men, when there weren't any rich ones around. These days, everyone had credit cards.

She checked herself in the mirror, pleased with what she saw: a white Ungaro dress, set off by a red, blue and gold Hermes scarf—both old, but still exuding class and quality. She still looked prosperous, despite everything. It paid to buy quality.

She was 46, but looked a decade younger. She'd had the sense to stay out of the sun after reaching 20, so her skin was still fresh, with the peaches-and-cream complexion of the Jessups, the English side of her family. She was 5'2" and still barely over 100 pounds, with flowing blond hair.

Despite everything, despite the hangovers, despite the pointlessness of it all now, she spent an hour every morning exercising to keep her figure, and she still spent a fortune on her hair. From long before her arrival in Washington she had made a point of buying only designer clothes—until her credit cards were all maxed out For her, it was part of the game: if you didn't look the part, you definitely had no hope of playing it.

She took another quick swallow, then another, hoping it would calm the desperation she was feeling. She couldn't afford to let the panic show.

Then she made her entrance, pausing at the top of the little staircase.

ROGER STODDARD handed her a business card. It identified him as David Thompson, a partner with a large Baltimore law firm. It was modeled on one he'd picked up a couple of weeks ago.

He saw the interest in her eyes, but missed seeing her finger run along the back of the card to check whether it was engraved. It wasn't.

"We just got a new case, my law firm did," he began. "We're looking for a consultant to work with us, somebody that really knows the art business. Your name was suggested to us."

"Really?" She tried to keep the excitement out of her voice. Perhaps there really were miracles! "Suggested by whom?"

"One of our clients, somebody I can't name. Question's this: suppose I came to you with a bunch of really top-quality paintings to sell. Think you could find a buyer for them, somebody with ready cash?"

"How much cash? What kind of paintings?"

"That's what I need your input on. Let's just say we're talking a lot of money, maybe seven figures."

She turned away, hiding her excitement by pretending to straighten a picture. Someone was liquidating a collection! And this bumpkin of a lawyer was handling it! Sheep ready for a shearing!

"Please," she smiled, gesturing to one of the easy chairs at the back of the showing room. She hurried up to her office and got a bottle of her best wine and two glasses, pausing long enough to rinse her vodka glass and set it out of sight.

She wished now she hadn't had the vodka. She needed her wits about her on this one. I'll hold back on the wine, she resolved.

"Let me just ask you this," Stoddard said when she returned. "What I need is some buyers that've got real money to spend on paintings— say a million or so. That's what I need, any ideas?"

She smiled and took a sip of wine. One mustn't seem too eager. "I trust you won't repeat it to a soul, but several very prominent people have recently asked me to handle their art investments. They have immense sums, truly phenomenal amounts of money ready to invest, waiting in banks, ready to move after the right pieces."

He stared at her for a moment, and she wondered if he would fall for it.

He let the silence hang in the air, let her wonder, before saying, "I think you're exactly the person I'm–I mean my law firm – is looking for. Let's talk about it over lunch."

"But the gallery. My clients–"

"Forget the damned gallery. Close it and throw away the key. We're talking about more money than you'd make here in a thousand years. Come on, I'll buy lunch."

STODDARD FOUND A CAB, and named an Afghan restaurant in Georgetown.

Vera knew the place. The food was quite good, but she'd hoped for something more upscale, a place where she'd be seen by the people who mattered, let them to know that she was on the way back up again.

She decided not to push it. This was an opportunity she couldn't let slip away.

The waiter led them to a secluded booth in the rear, and she realized that it had all been arranged in advance. How could he be so sure I'd come with him?

"There's something I'm curious about," Stoddard said as soon as they were settled. "Probably you know the answer."

"Perhaps," She was feeling the combination of the wine on top of the vodka. It slowed her down, now of all times when she had to be on the top of her form.

"I hear about these big art thefts every so often," he said, "millions of dollars worth. All those paintings that get stolen – what happens to that stuff?"

"Stolen art?" She fingered the silk of her scarf. What an odd question. Was he trying to test her? She shook her head. "I have no idea. In any case, you were asking earlier about people with money to—"

"No," he cut in, "let's talk about this. You're in the art business, you must hear rumors. It seems every month or so there's a big art theft, a couple million bucks worth taken here, ten million or fifty million there. These guys aren't taking these pictures to hang over the mantelpiece. So what happens to the stuff? Who buys it all?"

Vera took a deep breath. She wanted to get on with things, not chatter on about stolen art. If he was representing an estate, then she wanted to lock herself into the deal as soon as possible.

"Some stolen pieces pass under-the-counter, so to speak. A good bit of it is quietly ransomed back to the insurance companies, which are usually willing to pay a certain percentage, no questions asked."

"What percentage?"

"How would I know?" she snapped, then caught herself and smiled. "After all, my business is selling art, not stealing it. I believe it's ten or twenty percent."

"You're telling me there's no underground market for stolen paintings? That's not what I've heard."

Would he ever get to the point!

"Oh, there definitely is a market for stolen art, most definitely. A very sizeable market, as a matter of fact. Measured in dollar volume, the traffic in stolen works of art ranks in international crime behind only drugs and arms! And perhaps money laundering! I find that absolutely incredible!"

"Yeah, I've heard that, too. Probably we read the same article. But what I want to know is, who buys it? After all, if it's stolen property, they can't display it or sell it, can they?"

The waiter—small and wiry, with a huge black moustache—brought their drinks. Stoddard had ordered a light beer. Vera forced herself to take only a token sip of the vodka-tonic, then put it back: she needed her wits about her on this one.

"Who buys stolen art?" she repeated when the waiter left. "One does hear rumors in the trade. It's said that certain collectors don't mind stolen art. All they care about is possessing the paintings, and have no interest in selling. One of those collectors, so the story goes, is a certain Russian Oligarch who has cash to burn. But I think it's more likely that the Columbian cocaine lords are behind some of the thefts. There are rumors, too, that the trade in stolen art, the drug trade, and the trade in illicit armaments are intertwined."

"Why's that?"

"It varies. Paintings would be useful as collateral. They're compact, portable, and incredibly valuable. A top painting, a Picasso, say, or a Van Gogh, is far more valuable, ounce for ounce, than gold. Then, too, these drug dealers may want them as toys, as status symbols. They all have their mansions and their dozen Mercedes and private jets and helicopters. Perhaps they feel that a personal collection of Picassos or Van Goghs is the only way left to show off."

"Nah, forget the drug people. The arms dealers, too. They're too dangerous to get mixed up with."

That puzzled her, but she let it pass, and said, "There are rumors that the Mafia, and the Japanese equivalent of the *Mafia*, the *Yakuza*, may be holding stolen paintings with the view that they will be even more valuable in the next century. And not to forget the Russian Oligarchs and the Russian crime gangs."

"No, stay the hell away from the *Mafia*. The *Yakuza*, too. And definitely out of sight of the damned Russian crime gangs—they're real trouble, too."

Now she was baffled. She indulged herself in another sip of the vodka-tonic. "Oh, David," she said, forcing a smile. "Surely you're not interested in buying stolen art."

THE SMILE, coupled with the macho way he leaned back in the chair, told her that she had very seriously misjudged him.

"Let's quit dancing around," he said. "I'm not really a lawyer. That was just to test you out. What I'm really looking for is somebody with the right contacts to help me sell some paintings."

"If you're not a lawyer . . . Are these paintings from a private collection?"

"Yeah, you could call it a private collection. *My* collection."

"*You* have paintings to sell?" The thought of this bumpkin in his cheap suit having significant paintings to sell was ludicrous. His type would only be interested in pictures of naked women silk-screened on black velvet.

"I'll be getting them. Good ones. But I'll need some buyers with big money to spend, really big money, millions. Maybe some rich Arabs, or one of those Russian Oligarch guys—they're tough, what I hear, but they've got money."

"You'll be getting the paintings? From what source?"

"I'll be stealing them. With your help."

IRA Redux

The Limerick Pub, Washington.

When Johnny McDevitt heard the question, he took a sip of lager, his mouth suddenly dry.

"The IRA?" he echoed, forcing a laugh despite the panic he felt. Was this it, the way it ended? "For the kind of IRA you're looking for, it's a stock-broker you'll be needing."

Stoddard slipped a folded $20 bill from his shirt pocket and stuck it under a salt-shaker. "IRA—Irish Republican Army."

"Ah, those lads, they're all out of the business these days, don't you keep up with the news? Truce with the Brits, some years ago. Years and years."

Stoddard shook his head. "I hear they're still around, still accepting contributions."

McDevitt scanned the mirror over the bar for unfamiliar faces that might be moving in around him. Things seemed normal enough. "Suppose," McDevitt said, groping his way, "just suppose I did come upon someone from the IRA. What is it you'd be wanting?"

"You don't want to know," Stoddard said, now upping the ante by sliding another $20 to join the $20 under the salt-shaker. "Make the call, and I'll make it worth your while."

McDevitt shook his head and forced a smile, stalling for time to think. He was a tall, beefy Irishman in his early forties, a big sandy-haired guy with the look of a football player 20 pounds above his prime. He worked part-time at the Limerick as a bartender.

He'd seen the fellow around the Limerick a few times recently, but all he knew was that he'd been a good tipper.

It wasn't unusual for customers to ask him if he could find a few minutes to give some advice on what to see when they visit

Ireland. They usually made it worth his while, so he usually took a break and brought a couple of pints of Harp lager to loosen them up and make them more generous.

Now he wondered what in hell he'd gotten himself into by agreeing to talk with this one. McDevitt had an American passport and an American driving license, but if the authorities ever looked too deeply into them, the truth would come out: they had belonged to an American from Boston who went to Ireland to die of AIDS so he could pass on his papers for the sake of the Cause.

McDevitt took another long swallow of lager, studying the fellow over the rim of the mug: tall and lean, with thick, dark hair and the kind of boyish face that women seemed to go for. But there was something about him that bothered McDevitt, an arrogance in the way he moved and spoke that made him think of soldiers. And cops.

McDevitt rolled around in the chair, scanning the mirror over the bar again. "Why me? Why come to me with this? What makes you think I'd know the IRA?"

"You're Irish." He slid a third $20 bill under the salt shaker, beside the bills that McDevitt hadn't touched. "I figure you know a lot of people."

"I don't even know your name," McDevitt probed, wanting to know more, but reluctant to get in too far.

"Sullivan. Jack Sullivan," Stoddard said. He reached into a different pocket and come up with a $50 bill, and put it with the others.

McDevitt looked at the bills on the table. He looked up at Stoddard again, then at the money again. He took another swallow of lager. When he set the mug down, he picked up the bills and stuck them into his shirt pocket with practiced ease. "I'll make some phone calls, but no promises."

43

McDEVITT SLIPPED OUT of the Limerick by the back door, and went down the block to use a pay phone at the hotel. He couldn't use his cell, and the phone at the pub might be tapped for drug deals. He couldn't afford to make a mistake. He'd done time in a British prison, and had no intention of going back inside.

Things had settled down in Ireland now, but the Brits were still looking for him for his part in bombing an Army barracks. The amnesty didn't cover that. If they found him, he'd go away for life.

"There's a fellow here asking some questions I don't like the sound of," McDevitt told Matt Gilligan when he reached him. "Get over here, fast as you can. Follow him when he leaves. Find out what you can— his car license number, where he lives, that sort of thing."

"You can count on it, Johnny," Gilligan replied. Matt Gilligan was also wanted by the British. He was earnest and reliable, but dumb as a post.

McDevitt went back to the Limerick and worked the bar until he saw Gilligan slip in and take a table by the door. Gilligan was a little fellow, with milky white skin and carrot-red hair.

The red hair made him too noticeable. "Wear a hat when you're operational," they'd told him time and again. But Gilligan usually forgot. Or didn't give a damn. Which was the trouble with most of them, McDevitt thought: dim-witted romantics with a death wish.

McDEVITT PUNCHED OUT for the night, then stopped to fill a couple of fresh mugs of Harp to bring back to the table.

"I found someone for you, Mr. Sullivan. A friend of a friend." He glanced at the salt shaker and the pile of bills. Stoddard took the hint and slid another $50 onto the table. McDevitt didn't reach for it.

This time Stoddard had to dip into his wallet for another bill. He hadn't expected it to take this much. "What did your friend say?"

"He's a suspicious sort. He thinks you're asking strange questions. He's thinking you're a federal agent." McDevitt laughed, but his eyes stayed hard. "But I don't think you're FBI or ATF. They wouldn't be daft enough to try your approach."

Stoddard shook his head. "I'm not FBI, ATF, nothing like that. I just want some information."

"That's easy enough to say. Anyway, the person I reached says to find out what you want," McDevitt said. "The thing is, he doesn't understand what it is you want of the IRA."

"I'll deal with him directly."

"You won't get the chance. He won't talk to you until he knows more."

Stoddard hesitated, then leaned forward and said softly, "What I want is weapons, small arms. Delivered in Europe. I'll pay cash."

"What's that to do with the IRA?"

"The IRA's been running guns to Europe for decades. From what—"

"That was a long time ago. Things have changed. In any case, you can go just across the river, into Virginia, and buy all the guns you want. So why are you talking to me?"

"You're missing the point. I need them in Europe, not Virginia. You—the IRA—have the kind of expertise I need, to deliver them where I want them. I'll make it worth your while."

"Before they'd deal with you, they'd surely want to know what you'd be using the weapons for."

Stoddard shook his head. "Nothing that can ever be traced back."

McDevitt emptied his glass, staring at Stoddard over the rim. "You're asking me to violate federal law, and that's something I don't do. I don't like the idea of prison. I don't deal nose-candy, and I damned well don't deal guns."

He reached over and picked up the fifties that Stoddard had tucked under the shaker. "But if you were to stop back, say a week from tonight, who knows? You might just find someone wanting to buy you a beer."

Mr. Slash

THE EVENING'S RAIN had given way to a light mist by the time Stoddard left the Limerick. The mist reminded him of the umbrella he'd been carrying earlier, and he went back in for it, nearly bumping into a little guy with milky-white skin and carrot-red hair just coming out the door.

Back outside, he left the umbrella furled, and headed for his car, a couple of blocks away on a side street. He was sleepy now from the beer, his ears ringing from the music in the pub.

He came alert when two shadowy figures stepped out from behind a van, blocking his path. "Got some change, man?" A knife glinted in the light of the street lamp.

He sensed a third moving in from behind. In his time in the Army, Stoddard had spent endless hours in unarmed combat drill, and the moves were automatic. He pivoted, and chopped upward with his elbow. The blow broke the mugger's jaw-bone, and he fell, grunting in pain.

The other two moved in fast. Tyrone Roberts, known in the streets as Mr. Slash for his skill with a blade, came in low, hands gyrating in a slow, hypnotic rhythm. Mr. Slash had been on the streets since he was 14, except for the five years, off and on, in on various jails and prisons.

Mr. Slash waved his brother Curtis to close in from the other side. Curtis had his own knife out now. He was only 13, but useful sometimes.

Stoddard feinted left, drawing Curtis off balance, then punched the long point of the umbrella into his face. Curtis yelled and clutched at his eye, his knife clattering away on the wet street.

Stoddard grabbed Curtis's elbow and swung him into Mr. Slash. It happened too quickly for Slash to turn the knife away, and the shiny blade cut through Curtis's jacket to enter his chest. Curtis fell, a pink froth forming on his lips and chin, the sign of a punctured lung.

Mr. Slash backed away. This wasn't going at all right.

Stoddard drove the umbrella at his face, but Slash swept it aside with his left hand, then drove in with the right, the silver blade flashing in the dim light.

Stoddard danced aside. But his foot caught on a piece of broken sidewalk, and he fell onto the wet pavement. He tried to roll away. A parked car blocked his way, and he was trapped.

Slash, grinning, came in fast, and drove his knife at Stoddard's heart.

Stoddard kicked, and his foot caught Slash under the chin as he dove in for the kill. Slash's head jerked back hard, and the base of his skull snapped his spinal cord. He was dead before he hit the pavement.

McDEVITT WATCHED it with Matt Gilligan from half a block away, and was very damned impressed with the performance. A man who could handle three muggers that easily knew what he was doing.

That, added to the fact that he had doubled back into the Limerick checking for a tail, convinced him that he was a professional: leaving the umbrella behind was the sort of thing pros were trained to do.

But he couldn't understand why in hell a pro would have come to the Limerick looking for guns in the first place. It was a daft idea. Guns could be arranged anywhere in Europe, given the right contacts, so why fiddle around in a bar with someone you don't know from Adam?

Something else going on, that was obvious enough. But what?

It didn't sound like an FBI or ATF set-up—the approach was too clumsy for them even at their worst. But someone who would put out money like that to get an introduction wasn't just playing bar-room games.

He couldn't afford to take anything for granted. He had no intention of making a mistake that would put him back into a British prison for the rest of his life.

But there just might be an opportunity here.

He left it to Matt Gilligan to follow the man back to his car, a battered old BMW, and got the license plate. That was all they needed for now, enough to trace who the hell the man really was.

The Leadership

THE NEXT DAY, McDevitt took the information about the man he knew as Jack Sullivan and his interest in guns in Europe to his Control Officer.

The Control Officer's name was "Joe." McDevitt guessed, from the fussy, prissy way he handled himself, that Joe was probably either a priest or an undertaker.

Joe was an undertaker in an Irish neighborhood in Baltimore.

Joe passed the license plate number to one of his connections in a network of first and second generation Irish who still sympathized with The Cause, and were willing to do whatever they could to help.

From the plate number, they learned Jack Sullivan's real name: Roger Stoddard, and got his address in Northern

Virginia, as well. He was renting in a complex of garden apartments that had seen its best days.

The Leadership fed the information to some of the sympathizers around the area. A police detective in Baltimore ran the name through the FBI computer network: Stoddard had no police record other than a handful of speeding tickets over the years. A private detective in Washington tapped into his sources: data from credit bureaus, from Stoddard's government personnel file, and from some discreet interviews posing as an executive recruiter.

With the information that came back, they pieced together a picture of his life.

Roger Stoddard, they found, had been born around Boston. He hadn't been much of a student, though he was a pretty good quarterback on a second-rate team. After college, he went into the military, where he found his niche. Beginning with Officer Training, he finished every school at or near the top of his class. He made it into the Rangers, and earned outstanding ratings, even though he was a little too independent to suit his commanders.

Stoddard's main interest from the start was in commando operations, and spent three years with the Rangers. But he broke a leg in a night operation. That ended his Army career, and he was released on a medical discharge with 20% disability, and explained the slight limp. Now he was 31, and divorced.

It seemed that all he had ever wanted to be was a soldier, and that was all he was ever good at. He drifted for a year.

Finally, an Army buddy helped him get started as a stockbroker. People liked him because of his clean-cut All-American appearance, and his friendly, confident manner. But he pushed his luck, churning customer accounts to boost his commissions. At the first downturn, it caught up with him, and his clients found themselves stuck with junk.

He moved on to another brokerage, but the same pattern followed. "You don't really give a damn what happens to the client once you have their money, do you?" his manager asked as he was firing him. One of Stoddard's clients, a widow, 73, had lost $53,000 to his bad advice.

Stoddard laughed. By now there was no reason not to tell the truth. "You got it."

But he hadn't expected to get fired again, at least not so soon. He was in hock up to his ears with car payments on his old BMW, the lease on his apartment, and the clothes and furniture that he had bought on credit.

He'd tried selling cars on commission, but the market just wasn't there.

He took his last paycheck and drove up to Atlantic City. He'd been going there to play the tables for a weekend every couple of months. Having every cent riding on a roulette wheel wasn't quite as much fun as going out on a night commando operation, but it was the next best thing. Stoddard loved risk, and never felt as alive as when he was right on the brink.

One weekend he got lucky, and the numbers wouldn't stop coming right for him. He cleared $50,000, and got out when he sensed the power leaving him.

JOE CARRIED THAT INFORMATION to the Leadership, and in 24 hours got back to McDevitt with $1,000 for expenses. "We want you to follow up on Mr. Stoddard. You've been trained. You know what to do. Find out what he's up to. Perhaps we can let him do the work for us, then move in and take it away from him."

A COUPLE OF DAYS LATER, Stoddard led them to his next step: his recent contact with Vera de Cochin-Jessup. Joe took that lead to another supporter of the Cause, a small-time lawyer in downtown Washington, and asked him to check out Vera and *Galerie Vera.*

It took a couple of days, and when the information came back, it told him everything about Vera—except how she fitted into Stoddard's plan. And what that plan was.

Working Dinner

VERA WAS THE ONLY CHILD of a French mother (the de Cochins had crossed the Mediterranean from France to Algeria in the 1850s), and an English father (Jessup) who had first passed through Algeria during World War II.

The de Cochin family had developed one of the better vineyards in Algeria and lived very well, in the colonial fashion. But Algeria was the first focus of the wave of Arab nationalism that followed the war, and after 15 years of escalating terrorism and fighting, French President de Gaulle finally made the decision to pull out in 1962.

Along with the other *colons*, the de Cochin-Jessups lost everything. Vera's mother and father, and nearly a million others of French ancestry who had colonized Algeria over the previous 130 years, had left Algeria that summer of 1962, allowed only one suitcase each after days of heated misery crowded together at the docks, waiting for boats to take them back to impoverished lives in mainland France.

Her family settled in the mountains behind the French Riviera and tried without much success to re-establish the vineyards. That was where Vera obtained her early education . . . along with her ability to project a French or an English background as the circumstances shifted. As the child of former colonials, she was a *pied-noir*, never fully accepted back into French society, yet inheriting the stinging anger of the others who had been forced away from their homes and sources of wealth.

But there had still been the Jessups, her father's family. The money on that side was all gone, but at least they were able to arrange a good education in art and art history in England and France, thanks to old family connections.

The same connections had gotten her into the right circles in London and Paris, and opened doors for work after she got her degree. First at the Courtauld in London, then at the Louvre. That had enabled her to run in the right circles.

She enjoyed living well too much to be satisfied with museum wages, so moved on for a spell at Sotheby's, the auction house, until she hooked up with a rich, married, male "friend," who got her a good apartment and a wardrobe of the latest fashions.

But that arrangement didn't last long. Two marriages came and went, and she got good settlements from each. She moved to New York with her second husband.

When that marriage ended, she came to Washington. With a little help from her friends she set up *Galerie* Vera on the fringes of Georgetown, adding the small touch of spelling it in the French style, with one L, to convey that certain *je ne sais quoi.*

The gallery thrived, and Vera became a player in the Washington social scene courtesy of introductions by her male friends. A particular friend was Jerry Strong, society accountant, who created some miraculous tax-sheltered schemes, along with some clever methods of avoiding sales taxes.

Then it went wrong for Jerry Strong and his clients, and soon for Vera. The tax shelters that Strong created fell under IRS scrutiny, and his clients were hit with whopping penalties. In exchange for her testimony against Jerry Strong, the charges against Vera were dropped.

But Washington neither forgot nor forgave. The corporate clients quietly dropped her, hoping that the shareholders wouldn't learn how much of their money had been squandered on overpriced second-rate stuff. The important people in Washington art scene stopped coming to her openings. The promising young artists who'd been in her stable moved to other galleries.

She had stuck it out, stubbornly determined to survive. Even then she made it even then she might have made it had she not talked to a *Washington Post* reporter when she'd too much to drink at a party, saying, "I quite agree with Andy Warhol, or was it Marshall McLuhan? Art truly *is* whatever you can get away with."

Now she was down to her last few hundred dollars, and was months behind on her apartment rent, gallery rent, and credit card bills.

STODDARD LET VERA STEW for a few days to let her worry that she'd lost the chance, then phoned her at the gallery on Wednesday.

She invited him to dinner at her apartment that night. She could control things better on her turf. She lived on the second floor of a Victorian brownstone near DuPont Circle, a big step down from the flat in Spring Valley she'd had to give up when things started going bad. She'd managed a good deal on the lease here by sleeping with the agent, but he was gone now, and she didn't have enough for next month's rent.

Something would have to break soon. Soon. Or never.

SHE STOPPED AT Sutton Place Gourmet for dinner—he was a beef man, she was sure of that. The tab took a big bite out of her remaining cash.

When Stoddard arrived, she was wearing a silk blouse and skin-tight slacks from a little shop in Paris, shoes by Ferragamo, and perfume she'd brought back from Paris when she still had money.

Stoddard—though she still knew him as David Thompson—arrived wearing a checkered sport shirt, tattered blue jeans, and running shoes. Just about what she expected from him.

She fixed him a drink. She made her own weak, for once. Tonight she needed her mind absolutely clear.

"I get the sense you're military," she probed.

"That so?"

"You seem very military in your bearing, your manner."

"Let's keep to business."

"I just want to get to know you."

"Why?"

"So I can understand you, work better with you." She took a sip of her drink and held his gaze over the top of the glass. "Besides, to be quite frank about it, you seem . . . you seem like a very fascinating man."

"We've got business to talk about."

"At least tell me how you found your way to me."

"I read about you in an old *Vanity Fair* at the dentist's."

"That horrid magazine. They—the media—are vultures, always looking to see who's up, so they can drag them down."

It had been a gossipy piece that painted Vera as a scheming, manipulative, snobbish social climber who made a point of knowing the important people, and wasn't shy about using them.   When Stoddard read it he knew immediately that she was perfect for what he had in mind.

He invested $500 on a private detective to dig up some background on her. It turned out that she was even better than he could have hoped.

HE GOT TO BUSINESS AFTER DINNER as Vera served an apricot liqueur.

"The idea's this: we hit the best museum around, whatever it is, you tell me. Basically we pull a raid on a cache of art, just like it was a military objective. Work with a bunch of ex-commando types, go in fast, accomplish the objective, then haul ass out and dissolve into the environment."

In the days since their last meeting, Vera had researched the major art thefts of the past few years, to get a sense of what had been done successfully. Museums were quickly being forced to tighten security. The days of the amateur art thief were past.

But a fast commando raid on a museum—that had not been tried, not by people who really knew what they were doing. It sounded insane, but she had nothing to lose. If it worked, wonderful. If not, there was still that little jar of sleeping pills.

But if it did work, then he was thinking too small. If it worked with one museum, why not three? Why not a half-dozen?

But she would lead him there step by step.

"It's perfect, absolutely perfect," she said, her mind already generating other possibilities. "I do so want to be part of it."

She touched her glass to his. "To our success."

Then she said, "And you want me to suggest a possible target, yes?"

"Right. But not Washington, not anywhere in the U.S. From what I've been picking up, most American museums put guards everywhere, keep the bastards off welfare, I suppose. Also all sorts of electronic security. I was thinking of Europe."

"I know the perfect spot."

"Tell me."

"How can I be sure you won't just use my information and cut me out?" Most of the time she spoke with an upper-class

British accent, but now she let her French accent come through. Men found that sexy, and stopped thinking clearly.

"You're part of it, you can count on that. Provided you come up with something useful."

She clasped his hand momentarily. A little touching always worked wonders with men. "It's such a fabulous opportunity! I'm so glad we'll be working together!"

She reached over and quickly kissed his cheek, then backed away to refill their glasses. When she was in the kitchen, she loosened another button on her blouse. She hadn't worn a bra.

She brought some books over to the walnut coffee table, and sat beside him on the sofa, leaning forward. She had planned this out earlier, so that moving closer to him would flow naturally. She was wearing the last of the perfume she had brought from France.

The books were folio-sized, containing color reproductions of Impressionist and Post-Impressionist works. In the next ten minutes, she pointed out several paintings that had recently sold for at least a million dollars each, and some for as much as $100 million and more. "These very paintings, or others by the same artists, are all to be found on the *Cote d'Azur*. Ours for the taking."

"*Cote d'Azur*? The French Riviera?"

She watched his response over the next few minutes as she expanded on his original idea. His expression told her he'd had no idea of the real possibilities. Now he was dazzled.

With a little finesse she could end up with most of it for herself, and he'd never realize the difference! It was so far beyond his expectations that he'd be as happy as a pig in wallow, whatever he got.

She leaned back and snuggled herself into the L of the sofa. She sipped from her glass, holding his eyes over the rim. Her tongue slid along her upper lip. "After this, the hard work begins for both of us. But now we must celebrate our accord, yes?"

STODDARD DIDN'T HEAR her slip out of bed in the middle of the night and move softly into the living room where they had left their clothes—as she had planned.

His wallet told her everything: his real name, his address, even where he worked, and, thanks to an ATM receipt, how much he had on deposit—$47,412. Interesting. A lot of money to keep in a bank account.

She got the number from his Virginia driver's license, and copied the numbers and expiration dates and security codes from his Visa and Master Card. If nothing else, she could charge some things to him, and he'd probably never know how it happened.

His pay stub told her that he was a salesman at a used car dealership in the suburbs. She phoned there after he left the next morning.

"Mr. Stoddard is no longer employed here," the receptionist said. She had some kind of accent Vera couldn't pin down.

"No? When did he leave?"

"A while ago, a month or two. I don't know."

From that point, she locked her gallery, and spent her time working her Rolodex, phoning anyone who might be able to help her connect with the right kind of buyers.

Not many would even take her calls. For those who would talk, she developed the story line that she was closing her gallery to assist in liquidating some major European collection. If they could introduce her to potential buyers, "a very generous share of the commission" would be theirs.

Several laughed in her face and hung up. None had any worthwhile ideas.

But there was plenty of time; she would find good buyers yet. It was one of the lessons of her life: there were always fools with more dollars than sense.

And if none turned up, then at least she would milk Roger Stoddard for enough to carry her a while, until something else came along.

Things were definitely looking up.

Kinky Old Girl

"KINKY OLD GIRL, she is that," McDevitt said when he first played the CD for Joe, his control. They had managed to get into her apartment before Stoddard's visit and set up recording apparatus borrowed from a private detective in the group Joe knew. "That horny bastard doesn't know what he's up against with her. She's already leading him with a ring through his nose."

"Not exactly his nose, eh?" Joe responded. It was the first time McDevitt had ever heard anything like humor from Joe.

They were meeting in an apartment they borrowed from time to time from a supporter, in one of the anonymous high-rises just across the District line in Silver Spring. There were a couple of hundred flats in the building, and underground parking, so no one noticed who was coming or going. The apartment was swept for bugs each time it was used, and there had never been a sign of interest.

Joe snapped the CD out of the machine. "Do you have what you need off this? I want to keep it."

Was Joe kinky? McDevitt wondered. He did look like the sort who kept a collection of dirty books. "I don't want it, it's incriminating. Better to burn it in case the federals ever get interested in us."

"Don't worry, I'll get rid of it, but I want some other people to hear it first. I think you're onto something very significant. I want to get you some more funds to work with. I think this may prove to be worthwhile for us — for the Movement."

"THERE IS SOME POTENTIAL FOR TROUBLE," Joe added before they separated. "You need to know about Vera's history.

Our people—loyal supporters of the Cause—did some checking on her. She's got a reputation for milking the people around her, the men around her. She can't seem to leave well enough alone. She tends to be a little too greedy, a little too smart for her own good. There's a chance, a very strong chance, she may try something like that with Stoddard. If it blows up, you need to be prepared to get out fast."

"Stoddard does sound like a babe in the woods, compared to her."

"He also gives himself credit for being a great deal smarter than he really is. To be sure, he's over his head with Vera. If she follows her usual pattern, she'll use him, then try to push him aside."

McDevitt recalled seeing Stoddard in action against the three muggers that first night. "I think Stoddard's a hard bastard. If she plays games with him, and he catches her at it . . . "

He left the sentence hanging in the air unfinished. Then he said, "I get the feeling it wouldn't bother him a bit to . . . "

"To do what?"

"They make a matched pair. If it's true, what you suggest, that she's looking for a chance to cheat him, and it strikes me it's his intention to kill her in the end, so he gets it all and so she can't talk."

Reconnaissance

OVER THE NEXT COUPLE of weeks, Vera closed her art gallery and apartment, generating enough from a final sale of the paintings and antiques to catch up on her back bills, and even clear a couple of thousand.

Knowing that Stoddard had $47,000 sitting in cash in a bank, she told him she needed $20,000 in expense money, but settled for half that. She flew to Nice via Paris, glad to leave Washington behind her.

She settled on a big chain hotel in Nice, one filled each night with different bus-loads of tourists. That way, she would be less likely to bump into anyone she knew from her years in France, and the staff wouldn't pay her any attention. If things went wrong with Stoddard's plan, she didn't want there to be anyone who could link her with the thefts.

She picked up a rental car, and spent the next five days visiting the museums and collections along the coast.

She had known from the start that the Picasso Exhibition in the Grimaldi Museum in Antibes would their first priority. It was housed in an old fortress overlooking the Mediterranean, a place where Picasso had lived and worked for a while after the War. This year, the museum was hosting a special exhibit with works by Picasso and some of his contemporaries and predecessors on loan from museums and collectors around the world. It was a treasure trove, ripe for the taking.

Stoddard agreed, but insisted that she set up some Plan B operations, just in case the Picasso fell through for them.

But as she visited other collections, she realized that she had created a problem for herself. She had told Stoddard that the Riviera was packed with multi-million dollar paintings. It seemed reasonable at the time.

But once she got to France and looked around, she realized how few really first-rate paintings these museums held. There were some very good pieces in private collections, of course, but those were hard to locate. And the security systems would be far better.

What the museums did have were plenty of secondary works—works by lesser painters, or the less-important pieces of the major artists. A lot of these were valuable enough, with open market values ranging from $500,000 to $1 million or more.

Actually, it came to her, these lesser pieces were even better targets. They would be much more marketable, as stolen works, than the major paintings. For every $10 million painting, there were hundreds worth $500,000 to $1 million.

A major Picasso was easily recognized around the world.

If one were stolen, everyone in the trade would know it. In a sense, it would be worth less than nothing: no one, other than a cocaine lord, would buy it because it could never be resold on the open market.

But it was different with the less valuable, less known paintings. Because there were so many of them, they could be sold relatively easily, even though stolen.

She had promised Stoddard multi-million dollar paintings. Would he accept anything less?

IT TURNED OUT TO BE A NON-PROBLEM. He flew in the following weekend, and they spent three days revisiting the museums she had targeted. Vera wore a dark wig, sunglasses, and floppy straw hat that hid her face; he got the point, and bought himself a big hat and big sunglasses. Together, they looked like any other couple there on holiday.

He was interested in the art collections only as military objectives. He didn't give a damn about the paintings themselves, other than a curiosity about how these little pieces of colored canvas could be worth so damned much money.

His focus was on practical things: How to get into the museums at night without setting off alarms. How many guards there were, and where they would be positioned. What kinds of security devices were in place. What escape routes were available. How and where diversions could be set up to confuse and delay the police.

He went through the Grimaldi Museum on the sea in Antibes a couple of times, scouting out the security. The Museum was based in the castle where Picasso had lived and worked for a while in the 1940's.

"We can do it," he reported back to Vera.

He looked at the dozen museums and private collections which Vera targeted as back-ups. He narrowed it down to six which he felt they could pull off without too much risk. One was excellent, three others were okay, they'd hit the other two only as a last resort.

AT DINNER on their final night in France, Vera accepted his decisions on the places he targeted as priority, and on those he decided to pass up. "This would be the first target. If all goes well, no others would be needed."

"It's best not to be greedy," she agreed. "After all, the items I've pointed out in just these six collections have a market value of perhaps $50 million. The buyer will pay five to ten percent of value. Therefore, if we hit all six museums, we can count on as much as two million dollars for each of us, after expenses. I think it's far better to be content with that than to take the risk of losing it all, and going to prison as well."

"Yeah, I can make do with a couple million, no problem there."

How naive he is, how low his sights are, she thought. In reality, if the paintings she had targeted could be sold on the open market, they would be worth at least $150 million. At least.

But that was on the open market. One obviously couldn't bring these stolen paintings to be auctioned at Sotheby's. Still, she was confident that buyers could be found who would be willing to pay significantly more than the 10% of market value the insurance companies would offer.

Perhaps as much as 20%. Twenty-percent of $150 million would leave her quite comfortably fixed, thank you.

She would be in no rush to sell the paintings. All she needed at the start was someone willing to buy one or two of them, yielding enough cash now to pay Stoddard off and be rid of him. And enough for a comfortable life for herself, of course.

Then she would be patient, spreading the sales out over years, getting the best price each time, minimizing her risks.

LATER, IN BED, she played one of her cards: "There's so much about you I don't understand, Roger. You were a stock-broker for a while, then you were doing very well with the car dealership, you made a very nice–"

"Hey, hold on! What's this Roger stuff," he interrupted, sitting up in the bed, suddenly alert. He hadn't told her anything about himself. Not Roger. Not his job. Nothing. The less she, the less anybody, knew the better.

She gently eased him onto his stomach and began massaging his back. "Of course I know about you, Roger Stoddard, I checked. I'd have been very foolish if I hadn't. You know who I am, so I need to know who you are. That way, we remain balanced, so we protect each other."

She wanted him to know that from the start: Don't walk away from me, don't sell me out . . . or I'll do the same to you.

AS HE WAS LEAVING the next day, Vera said, "You must swear to me that there will be no violence. The French are sometimes a strange people. They will find it amusing when the art is taken, *très drôle*. Most will rather enjoy the idea. They'll envy you the money you make, but they'll also be pleased to see someone finally besting an insurance company. They'll like that. But it will be quite a different matter if anyone is killed or seriously injured. Then they'll turn against you. Do you understand?"

"Yeah, sure, don't worry, no violence." He wasn't planning any shoot-ups, but if he got into a tight spot, he sure as hell had no intention of standing still to be arrested.

Michael McGaulley

Gawbi al Senour

AFTER LEAVING NICE, Vera passed through Switzerland. She chose Geneva, as it was in the French-speaking part of the country, where she was comfortable with the language.

She opened a pair of numbered bank accounts, one to feed into the other as insurance against the money ever being traced.

She wondered if the two layers offered enough insulation if anything went wrong, but there was no one she could ask. And if she did ask, someone might remember her later.

It would have surprised her to know that Stoddard had been smart enough to figure the same system for himself.

After a day in Geneva, she flew on to London. Her priority now was to find a buyer for some of the art, someone who could come up with a million or so at this point. Enough to bankroll the rest of her plan. Enough so she could pay off Stoddard and be rid of him.

A day passed, then two, then three, and she found herself no closer to finding a buyer for the paintings.

She began by working her old contacts, but few of them would even take her phone calls. Even if there had been interest, she had no real idea how to approach the subject she had in mind. How do you ask someone if they want to buy some stolen paintings—even worse, paintings *to be* stolen?

She had been too eager, had spoken too fast with Stoddard, she realized now. Even if the art were clean, not stolen, finding buyers with millions to spend would not have been easy. But for stolen paintings, who, other than drug dealers, would be interested? For that matter, who could she trust not to turn her in to the police? She had enemies, she knew that.

AT LAST, SHE GOT A BREAK. She phoned back to Washington for messages, and found that an urgent call had come in from Abdullah Rakeh. He was the pathetic little vice-consul at one of the Arab states' embassies.

Not worth a trans-Atlantic call, she felt, then changed her mind. There was just a chance that he had come up with someone worthwhile, after all.

Abdullah was at first disappointed to hear that she was in London, because a friend was in Washington whom he very much wanted her to meet, Gawbi Al Senour.

THE NAME AL SENOUR catapulted the project into another order of magnitude.

Gawbi Al Senour's father was Sheik Rafik Al Senour, one of the Arab "consultants"—men who shuttled between the Gulf States, Europe, America, China and Japan, making introductions, setting up deals.

Deals for drilling rights, deals for hundred-million-dollar projects for prefabricated factories, schools, hospitals, even whole cities to spring up in the desert.

But most of all for armaments deals, opening the doors for the salesmen of fighter planes and high tech missiles. Fees in the tens of millions, sometimes more, were not uncommon, according to the newspapers.

Al Senour had referred to himself as an "investment consultant," but in fact he was a middleman, a fixer, working on commission. He made the introductions . . . and the payoffs for the western companies who wanted the business badly enough. Tens of millions of dollars, split among four or five influential families, could easily be hidden in the costs of a new city being built from scratch in the desert.

Sheik Al Senour tended to operate quietly behind the scenes, so the media could only guess at his earnings. Some articles pegged him at a modest twenty to thirty million annually in fees; others speculated that his take was perhaps ten times that, or even more.

Over time, he found ways of tapping in on the oil wealth flowing from the mid-east, and even more on the dollars flowing back.

He had three sons and five daughters. The oldest son died at age 6. Before Al Senour died—of throat cancer at 61—he provided for the daughters, then divided the balance evenly between the sons. The amount was shrouded in desert secrecy, but the most-likely estimates figured that the sons split around $100,000,000.

A grave mistake, as it turned out. The oldest son, Motar, inherited the canniness and financial skills of his father. Gawbi inherited only the money, but none of the intelligence and savvy. To his face, his older brother referred to him as a stupid playboy.

That stung, and Gawbi set out to make a name for himself, which he did—as a stupid playboy so desperate to make a name for himself that he could be conned into one losing investment after another. Between those investments and high living expenses, he had managed to turn his inheritance into around half of what it was at the start.

VERA IMMEDIATELY OFFERED to fly back to Washington to meet Gawbi Al Senour, but Abdullah said he would check on Gawbi's plans and call her back. "We will fly over tomorrow to see you, Gawbi and I," Abdullah told her an hour later, pleasure and triumph in his voice at having arranged a trip for himself.

Abdullah was a scavenger, Vera realized, trying to attach himself to Gawbi. As soon as she got Gawbi's confidence, she would show Abdullah up for what he was. That would better cement her own position.

GAWBI AND ABDULLAH arrived in London the next day in time for dinner, and picked her up in a chauffeured Rolls for the ride to an overpriced French restaurant in Mayfair.

How characteristic of them, she thought. So much money, so little taste.

Gawbi Al Senour was a small man, not much taller than Vera. Though his face had the dark, craggy hawk-like good looks she had seen in the photos of his father and brother, Gawbi's eyes betrayed his insecurity. A moustache and goatee made him look younger than he was: 25. His suit was Saville Row, but badly in need of a pressing.

She had spent a few hours on-line reading up on Gawbi and his father. Gawbi's passions seemed to be chasing blond movie starlets and collecting expensive cars. A couple of years ago, he and some of his friends had taken to racing their Ferraris and Lamborghinis around some of the staid squares in Kensington, managing to smash up their cars along with those parked in the area. The problem was solved by writing a few checks.

Because of the low profile that his father had kept, there was only rumor and gossip, but the stories generally agreed that Gawbi had a trust fund, administered by a London bank, that supposedly paid him five million per year. If he needed more, he called his brother Motar, who was usually willing to pay to keep this embarrassment of a brother out of his sight, and out of the newspapers.

Gawbi had a collection of cars, mostly Ferraris and vintage Corvettes at the home he kept in California. Now it was said he was beginning to build another car collection in Europe.

Good. Very good. First, it showed he was into collecting: she would just change him from collecting cars to collecting paintings. Second, the cars could be converted into cash. Some he could sell quickly, others he could take loans on.

GAWBI HAD LITTLE TO SAY at the start, so Vera kept up the conversation with a flow of stories of how she had helped clients invest wisely in art, and how quickly those paintings had doubled and tripled in value. The stories were all lies, but he'd never know the difference.

As he drank more wine, though, Gawbi opened up, and she realized just how accurate her first impression had been: his intelligence matched the dullness of his eyes. That opened up a whole new range of possibilities.

She recognized, too, that Gawbi was also particularly insecure—natural enough, she felt, for a son dwarfed by the shadow of a world-class father. That would make things much easier for her.

AT THE END OF THE EVENING, as the Rolls was bringing her back to the hotel, she mentioned that she would "of course need operating expenses to get the project moving."

"Yes, yes, of course," Gawbi said, pulling out a thick wad of bills. He handed her half, and the other half to Abdullah "with gratitude for bringing Vera and I together."

Abdullah took the wad, but the expression beneath his smile showed that he had been hoping for a partnership.

She counted the bills as soon as she got back to the hotel. It came to just under $15,000. The next afternoon, a messenger arrived at her hotel with a thick envelope containing about $100,000, spread among dollars, pounds and Euros.

GAWBI AL SENOUR got back in touch with Vera a couple of days later, while she was still in London. "I have some good friends who might be interested in joining in our little investment."

She had suggested the first evening that he might want to bring a few "very trusted friends" into the venture with him, "discriminating people with a good bit of venture capital."

She put the names he gave her with a private investigations agency. She explained that she was writing a book for an American publisher on the lives of the very rich young Arabs, and paid in cash.

She rejected two of the names Gawbi suggested. The trust account of one was too closely watched: she didn't want to raise anyone's suspicions. The other was being sued for divorce after a six-month marriage to an American actress. The wife's attorney would be watching his financial dealings.

Gawbi came up with three more names: she took two of them, but rejected the third because the report on him indicated he was too intelligent. She didn't want anyone who might ask questions.

The five potential partners she settled on were of a type with Gawbi: playboy sons from the Middle East, young men whose interests focused on fast cars, fashionable drugs, women, and gambling. "Gawbi and the Five Dwarf-brains," as Vera thought of them.

Vera programmed Gawbi with the things to say in convincing his friends to make an investment that would not ripen for years. Given their life-styles, the odds were that none of them would live twenty years. That was crucial, as it would be very awkward indeed if they were around to realize what she had done to them.

Four of the five agreed to join the partnership at once, and the fifth joined when he learned the others were in.

"WE MUST HAVE THIS set up in a legal, businesslike manner," she said when they met next. To accomplish that, she suggested the name of a solicitor, an old lover of hers. She knew him well enough to be sure he wouldn't mind doing something a little on the shady side, and who could be counted on to keep his mouth shut.

The solicitor drew up the papers for an investment partnership. They based it in the Bahamas, where the authorities keep their nose out of the financial affairs of international firms. Gawbi wanted to call the firm Art Investments International, Ltd., but the solicitor suggested discretion—"a lower profile"—so it became AII, Ltd., with its headquarters a file drawer in the office of another solicitor in Nassau.

AII, Ltd. then opened a numbered Swiss account with a bank in Geneva. Codes were set up so the funds could be transferred by telephone to another Swiss account. This second account would be Vera's. From that account, she would channel payments to Stoddard and one other key person—a Frenchman, his name yet to be determined. And of course she sent all that remained to her own account in Geneva.

Opening capitalization of AII, Ltd. totaled just over $2 million, which the five partners scraped together from various sources: gambling winnings, cash on hand, loans from friends and cooperative banks, the sale of cars and jewelry, mortgages on their various houses scattered in resort areas, London, Paris, Hollywood, the Riviera. Under no circumstances were they to approach their fathers or trustees for additional money: "We must be discreet," she told Gawbi, "we don't want the press to get any hints."

The solicitor passed the $2 million through accounts around the world before it came to rest in the primary account in Geneva: that way, he assured Vera, it would be so well-laundered that no one could ever trace the money back to its sources.

She talked the partners into advancing her $1,000,000 immediately, then another $500,000 before the first art theft. For "expenses," she told them.

She paid the London solicitor was paid $20,000 for a couple of days' work, along with the promise of a weekend with her in the Cotswolds.

VERA DIRECTED PAYMENTS to the accounts of Stoddard ($200,000), and to a French person she'd found by tapping her old contacts ($100,000, with double that to come when all was wrapped up).

She put the remainder into the numbered account, supposedly double-insulated, she had set up in in Geneva, apart from $100,000 in a readily-accessible account for daily expenses.

VERA MET with Gawbi every couple of days in London while the details were being worked out. She found him loathsome, but this was too important to let feelings get in the way, and there were details to attend to.

She made a point of radiating charm for the couple of hours they were together. Normally they met over lunch, never going to the same place twice. She didn't want to be remembered by any restaurant staff as the woman who was having an affair with a young Arab.

As she expected, Gawbi eventually got up his nerve and made a pass: "You want to make love in bed with me now? Many women have said how good I am." But she was able to pass it off, with no hard feelings.

Most days the meeting was brief. She programmed him with the tasks he needed to attend to, and dealt with any difficulties that had arisen since their last meeting.

SHE WAS CAUGHT OFF-GUARD when he began one luncheon with, "There is a very big problem."

"Yes?" she smiled, overcoming the sudden sick feeling that the whole operation could fall apart.

"One of my friends, one of the partners, asked me how we are going to get our money out of this investment. Since the paintings will be stolen, how can we sell them without going to jail? Who will want to buy them?"

She smiled, warmly, reassuringly. "Do you have any idea of how many pieces of art are stolen in France in a typical year?"

He shrugged. "A hundred? Two hundred? Maybe a thousand."

"Between six and seven thousand pieces. And, mind you, that's in France alone. England loses at least another five thousand in a year. In Italy, the figure is even higher: in some years, 10,000 pieces disappear. Of the art that is stolen, less than ten percent is ever recovered."

A wide, vulpine grin broke across Gawbi's face. "Good odds, yes, very good." Then his face darkened again. "But still, how do we get our money back?"

"Several ways. First, there will be collectors who are desperate for what we have. After all, there are only a limited number of Picassos and Cezannes and Matisses in existence, and since the artists are dead there will never be any more. Most of the very best have already been taken out of circulation by museums and large private collectors, and are not for sale at any price. Yet there are collectors who absolutely must have a first-rank Picasso. Regardless, they are willing to buy, at any price."

"Do you know some of these people?"

"Of course," she lied.

"Perhaps some of them will be prepared to buy soon?"

"I am certain they will. It would not surprise me at all to find that you have offers within a few weeks that *absolutely dwarf* the money you have invested with me!"

"That would be very good if we can begin making our profits soon. It would be difficult for my friends and I to continue making these sacrifices for long."

She smiled, and nodded sympathetically, hoping the contempt didn't show. She would be very surprised if Gawbi was living on less than $20,000 per week. There was plenty more there, and she would be back for the rest as soon as things got under way.

"A PRIVATE PURCHASER drawn by the publicity is one possibility," she continued, "and I will, of course, be putting out feelers to find these offers if they come. But there are other ways of marketing, as well. When the time comes, I'll help you get the paintings to Switzerland."

"Why Switzerland?"

"The Swiss are pragmatic people. It's much easier to deal in art there. Under Swiss law, if you hold a stolen painting that has since passed through someone else's hands, you are considered an innocent purchaser and would not be prosecuted as a receiver of stolen goods. Thus all you need to do is appear to buy the paintings in Switzerland."

Was that still true? she wondered. It didn't matter.

Gawbi frowned, overwhelmed by so much confusing information. "But we will already own the paintings. Why would we then want to buy them again?"

"To launder them."

"Launder them? You mean clean them? But why?"

"No, launder the trail, so you appear to hold them as an innocent purchaser."

His blank expression told her he still wasn't getting it, so she broke it down further. "Keep in mind how many paintings are stolen each year—thousands upon thousands, of which only one in ten are ever recovered. Thus each year there are more and more stolen paintings floating around. You can see that it becomes an impossible task for the authorities to keep up with the flow. There are gallery owners who, for a fee, will take a painting, and resell it to another dealer, who'll sell it again, and so on, until you can buy it back safely in a phony transaction. That is, no real money passes at any point. Each dealer in the chain could say that he failed to recognize it as stolen, and there would be very little risk to them, even if they were caught. And as for you and your friends, so long as you appear to be innocent purchasers, you would get good title."

"You mean our title would be even better–*stronger*–than the persons they were stolen from?"

"Exactly," she lied. "So long as the paintings stay in Europe, continental Europe. But you must never bring them to England or America."

He grinned rapaciously, finally comprehending. "Then once I have bought it from myself, then I can sell it again for full price. Wonderful!"

She nodded. "You're very quick, Gawbi. You have a nose for these things."

Actually, he had overlooked the key point, as she expected. His clear title would depend on appearing to be a good faith purchaser. Each hand they passed through in making his purchase look legitimate would also be a hand expecting payment– and would be attached to lips that could tell secrets.

BUT LET HIM BELIEVE how rich the paintings were going to make him someday. It would be decades before he could safely hold the paintings openly. Once she had his money, then she would point out the risks in selling early.

Playboys tended not to live long lives. The odds were that Gawbi and all of his friends would be dead through car crashes and drug overdoses long before they dared show the paintings.

If they did survive and try to sell the paintings?

Then there would be a problem. She would have to go underground, change identities, hire a bodyguard. It would be an inconvenience, but well worth it for the millions at stake. Gawbi's two million was only a starting point: the real money would come on her side deal, the one behind Stoddard's back.

In any case, if there were a problem, it wouldn't ripen for twenty years. At least.

The Artful Forger

THE FOLLOWING MORNING, as Vera was putting on her make-up, she realized how Gawbi's blissful stupidity opened up another dimension of opportunity.

Stunned by the possibilities, she dropped back onto the bed to think it through. It *could* be done! She *could* pull it off!

And she wouldn't need Stoddard for this part!

Though it was not yet ten in the morning, and she was wearing only a dressing gown and half of her make-up, she called room service to have a bottle of champagne sent up for a celebration. This was going to be very, very big, indeed!

Very big indeed! Gawbi Al Senour took care of one part of it: finding a fool with enough money to get the enterprise going, enough to allow her to pay off Stoddard and get him out of the way.

But there was a limit to what she could get from Gawbi.

The real potential would come if she could manage to sell the same paintings twice, maybe three times. That would bring the big payoff.

THE NEXT STEP was obvious. She took a taxi that evening to a wine bar just off the King's Road, Chelsea. Nothing had changed in ten years: Peter Edleigh was at his usual spot, tonight chatting up what seemed to be a pair of Swedish au pair girls.

Peter still dressed the part, just as in the old days. Pleasantly seedy in a distinguished way, the calculated image of a painter: flowing hair, a loose-knit baggy sweater stained on one cuff with a touch of oil paint.

But he had put on weight. The once sharply-chiseled angles of his face had filled in, and now he had a bit of a paunch. He, too, had become middle-aged.

Still, she thought, he might be as creative as ever in bed. After the business was arranged.

She took one of the side tables, and waited for Edleigh's eyes to meet hers in the mirror. When she saw the flash of recognition, she smiled and beckoned a finger at him, once.

The girls went off to the loo before long, and he walked over to say hello.

"Kiss the little girls good-by, Peter. Tell them you'll ring them tomorrow, but now you have some important business to tend to. They'll understand, and come visit you tomorrow night instead."

He laughed and helped himself to a glass from the bottle on her table. It was one of the better Algerians. "Drinking from the old country, eh?"

"I do resent giving those thieves my good money. Algerian is hard to find in the States."

"What brings you back, old girl? It's been years."

"Get rid of your little friends, and then we'll talk. I have a lucrative proposition, potentially *very* lucrative, to share with you."

"Better still," Edleigh said, "why don't you come along with us? You were always kinky. Pleasure before business. We can always talk later."

PETER EDLEIGH had three rooms in a red-brick row house in Baron's Court. Vera had forgotten how grim London housing could be.

The third room was his studio. At least it was bright, thanks to the big window looking out over the garden of a house across the way.

After the Swedish girls left in the morning, Vera took a few minutes inspecting some of his works. "No more 'Legends,' I see."

A decade earlier, at the age of 37, Edleigh had finally come to the inescapable realization that as a creative artist he was a failure. Ironically, that recognition was the breakthrough to his first real money from painting.

In his youth at the Academy, the teachers had praised his "technical competence" and assured him that the rest would come with experience and maturity.

He believed it, because it was what he wanted to hear. He believed it though his twenties and into his thirties, and he scrimped and hustled and did what he had to in order to support his "work." He taught painting, he did some stretches with commercial art houses and even ad agencies.

All the while, he spent his Sundays, summer and winter, at the artists' row along the Bayswater Road by Kensington Gardens. Along with a couple of hundred other hopeful artists, he strung his works up along a spot on the park fence that he rented for a few pounds each quarter.

THAT STRETCH OF FENCE on the Bayswater Road was Peter Edleigh's gallery, his show-place, his chance to be noticed.

But in a decade and a half no one significant had ever noticed. Each Sunday he made just enough from sales to tourists to scrape by until the next week. In time, it became obvious even to him that he was never going to make it. But by then he had gone too far down the art track. There didn't seem to be anything else he could do in life.

But it was at his little stretch of the Bayswater Road that he discovered his real talent. He found himself one week too fed up to do anything creative: he was burned out, depleted, facing the undeniable fact that he had invested his life in a quest that was never going to pay off. As a finger exercise, he dashed off a couple of canvasses in the style of Picasso, signed them "Pierro." To his surprise–and annoyance–they both sold in the first hour that Sunday. The tourists went for his quick little copies, and ignored his real work.

The hell with it, he decided. If that's what the fools want, let them have it. It was time to start cashing in.

The next week, he did nothing but "Pierros," and again sold out. In the following weeks, he did some "Legends" in the style of Leger, a "Basque" based on Braque, and a couple of "Duffanys" that attempted to capture the vibrancy of Dufy. He decided to be creative in the signatures, not push his luck, though it would have been just as easy to forge the signatures, as well.

These were, technically, not forgeries in the eyes of the law. He didn't attempt to pass the works off as genuine, nor did he try to replicate any particular painting. From his days at the Academy, he had been a superb copyist. But now he went beyond mere copying and tried to get inside the mind of the artists, spring-boarding beyond what they had actually painted to create new works that they might have done.

The new approach paid off, and before long, he was able to trade his old Mini for a Thames van that made it easier to transport the canvasses each week. He still brought along some of his own originals, but he usually had to carry most of those home again on Sunday evening, while the Pierros, the Legends, the Duffanys sold out.

By then he was facing the truth about himself: his only real talent was as a mimic, a copyist of others' works. Somehow, in a way he couldn't really understand, he had a facility for reading what the original artist had been trying to do, and then replicating that original—not just to copy, but to go beyond to what the artist intended. In some cases, he could even springboard from what the artist actually did to what he might have done, had he thought about it.

THE TURNING POINT for Peter Edleigh came when he spotted one of his "Basques" on display in a gallery in Kensington. It was selling for £1500 pounds. He had gotten £50 for it and considered himself very fortunate indeed. A couple of days later, when he passed the gallery again, the Basque was gone. "Some Americans bought it," the clerk told him.

The following Sunday, a man stopped by his stand at the Bayswater Road with a roll of £100 notes. From that point, Edleigh's paintings were signed "Picasso" and "Dufy", and not "Pierro" or "Duffany." From that point, too, he no longer spring-boarded to create the paintings that his models might have painted: now he copied, as exactly as possible.

And from that point, he began tasting the joys of prosperity without spending his Sundays on the Bayswater Road.

THE GOOD LIFE lasted two years. He traded the Thames van for a second-hand Volvo, and then that for a new Mercedes. He found a nice cottage in Kent, and took holidays in Ibiza, Sardinia, the Greek islands.

It all came to an end at three in the afternoon one September day. He answered a knock at the door, and found a pair of Detective Inspectors from Scotland Yard, along with a couple of uniformed officers, and a search warrant.

He was lucky: he got off with a few weeks in the lock-up, and a warning: no more forgeries.

Unfortunately, at that point he was £20,000 in debt, having taken for granted that his golden goose would live forever. By the time his creditors finished with him, he was lucky to afford another old Mini, some paint and canvas, and a month's rent on a cheap bed-sitter.

But in the process, he had become a cult hero. *The News of the World* paid him for an "as-told-to" story.

He got the press clippings of his arrest and trial framed, and hung them on the fence beside the paintings as a kind of pedigree. He changed his signature to "Pierro" Edleigh, and found that people now were willing to pay £400 or £500 for his own originals–paintings that previously he had barely been able to sell at all. No longer was he a forger, now he was an artist in his own right—based on his press clippings as a master forger.

He was comfortable enough again, but the taste of the big money had spoiled him. Thus he was primed for Vera's proposal when it came.

IT WASN'T THAT Vera trusted Peter Edleigh. She trusted no one, just as others had learned never to trust her.

It wasn't trust, rather it was that she had a kind of confidence in him. Not because of his honesty; honest he was definitely not.

She was confident she could trust him—up to a point— because his horizons were as narrow as those of an old dog by a warm fireplace. Peter, she was convinced, now wanted only to be comfortable. He had taken his risks and gotten burned—which cost him time in a British jail. Now he would be content to do her work and bank his share, and not be greedy for more.

After the Swedish girls had hurried off in the morning, they sat over a pot of tea while she told him her plan, though leaving out names and details.

He let her talk, and when she was done, he laughed and said, "Well done, old girl! You are a genius, indeed—a genius of the lucrative double-cross."

Then he turned away quickly, pretending to make a fresh pot of tea, hoping that she hadn't seen the idea that flashed in his eyes. Her plan was insane: one couldn't do what she was asking, certainly not in that kind of time-frame.

But it opened the way for something that would work, something he could pull off, on his own. Play her game for a while, bring her along, then cut her out. With any luck, she would never even realize what had happened.

Totally impossible

EDLEIGH SIGHED, then said, "It's a wonderful idea, *mon cher*, but, alas, impossible to bring about, totally impossible."

"Impossible? Why? You are one of the most talented, most prolific ... copyists in the world?" Copyist sounded more flattering than forger, she thought.

He shook his head. "It's quite apparent that you have no idea what goes into my ... my special little 'tributes' to other artists. First of all, there is the creation—paint to canvas to match the originals, brush-stroke by brush-stroke, each perfection positioned, each precisely as the master did. That cannot be rushed."

"You have weeks to work before the operations begin. I'll see that you have travel money, you can go to the museums, take your photos—I know how you work, you get a good color photo and project it as your template, and —"

Edleigh waved his hand, as if brushing away her error. "Yes, I do that. But that is only the start, only the start. Then comes all the other. You apparently have no idea how long it takes for painter's oils to dry, to harden, to crackle. We're speaking not of days, not even months, more a span of years, and the more the better. So I suggest—"

"I'm not stupid, Peter," she snapped. "I know very well that you don't wait years to sell your other forgeries. I looked around while you were still sleeping. I saw the oven you use—"

"Ah, my artist kitchen. Yes, true, I do speed up drying by that process, but that's only adequate for run-of-the-mill copies, sold to unsophisticated people. But for what you propose, well, that quick bake won't begin to—"

She smiled, her you-have-no-idea smile. "You are correct, in one sense. My clients do have a great deal of money to invest, they are not like the run of your usual clientele But they are not at all sophisticated. They are ignorant, stupid people."

"But with that money at stake, won't they want authentication? Surely, *mon cher,* they will want more than just your word for the authentication."

She shook her head. The sigh that emerged was more like a hiss. "First of all, Peter, I am not your *mon cher.* Your ignorance of things French is appalling. *Mon cher* is a plug of chewing tobacco. You meant *ma cher:* 'my dear', a patronizing term. But I am not that, I am your employer."

"Employer?' To whom I also serve as your sex slave, as earlier? *Va bien,* that's fine with me. A nice roll on the sheets sharpens my brush, in a manner of speaking."

"You can be amusing, Peter. And satisfying. I like that in a man. But to get back to the issue at hand, you need not be concerned with the matter of authentication. Just turn out your usual quality, and all will be well."

Authentication. That was a concern, she knew. So far, neither Gawbi nor any of the others had insisted on an outsider's opinion. If they did, somewhat later along the route, that could be a problem. But once it starts, it will all be happening so fast.

A FEW DAYS AFTER Vera's visit, when Peter Edleigh was in Paris scouring the art shops and flea markets looking for vintage canvasses, an idea dropped into his head. "What the hell, in for an inch, might as well be in for a mile," he told himself. "She'll never know the difference."

He phoned Vera's number in the States to tell her that he had done the preliminary research, but had found he would need to have the originals in his possession for a few days after each operation.

"Why?" she objected. "We agreed that you'd do up the copies in advance."

"I need to have the originals in hand to double-check that my copies are totally accurate," he lied, hoping she wouldn't think it through.

She resisted, saying that it was an absurd request, that it caused impossible risks in delivering the stolen paintings to him and then getting them back. But he held firm that he absolutely had to have the originals, and finally she gave in and agreed to find a way of getting them to him. For 48 hours after each theft, no longer.

That was fine, he agreed. Forty-eight hours was more than enough time.

Trouble

IT WAS NIGHT on the other side of the world as Gawbi's brother, Sheik Motar Al Senour, climbed aboard his Gulfstream G650 at Hong Kong International Airport

Increasingly the plane was his refuge from the difficulties that surrounded him these days, most of them compounded by the global slowdown that seemed endless.

Al Senour and his clients had built up enormous cash reserves over the years, and had leveraged that cash into investments around the world that at the time had seemed interesting speculations with the potential of returns averaging 500%. It was the magic of leveraged investments: a small investment of your own could be multiplied many times over by other people's money, and when it was time to cash out, the little people would be content with what they got, leaving the big returns to those like Al Senour and his friends who'd had the big vision to create the opportunity.

But no one had counted on the global slowdown, and no one had counted on all the speculations becoming troubled at the same time, nor troubled for so long.

Motar Al Senour had managed to keep his house of cards standing for years, further enhancing his reputation as the financial wizard who never failed, the smart son of the legendary Sheik Rafik Al Senour.

But now he was in trouble, weeks away from the puff of wind that could blow down his house. Ironically, it was only a small puff–a $50 million note due by the end of November. Pocket change in the flush days.

If he could somehow get past this, if he could somehow come up with the $50 million in time, there was a good chance he'd make it. But if he couldn't meet the note, then that would crack his aura of financial infallibility.

That's all it took: one crack, and then the vultures all over the world would be upon him, ready to tear him and his holdings to shreds.

HE HAD COME TO HONG KONG hopeful that one of his old contacts there would advance him the $50 million. But Chen had laughed at Al Senour. "You are leveraged to the hilt. You hold much on paper, but own nothing. All of it is mortgaged to others. The truth is, if the papers were called you would not have enough left to buy yourself a meal. Come to me then, and I will buy you a very good dinner for old times' sake. But I can give you nothing now. You have no security to offer me, so anything I advanced you would be gone forever."

What Chen said was true, Al Senour, knew. Indeed, it was even worse. He was not only over-extended, but over-extended several times over. Thanks to the sharpest lawyers around the world, he had found ways of borrowing two and three times against the same properties.

Even his plane, his refuge, his most indispensable working tool, was at risk. Al Senour had felt a rare moment of pity for his father's old rival, Adnan Khashoggi, when his plane had been taken away from him for unpaid fuel bills. An American creditor had obtained a judgment, then sent a team to the Bahamas with it when they learned Khashoggi was overnighting there. The team included pilots, and while Khashoggi slept, they presented the judgment to local officials and flew the plane away, leaving him stranded.

Now that same kind of total humiliation could happen to him.

"WHERE FROM HERE?" the pilot had asked when Al Senour returned from his meeting with Chen.

"It's not clear yet," Al Senour replied, determined to keep up the facade. The reality was, he was out of ideas. There was no place else, no one else, that would advance him the money he needed without security of some sort.

There was no one who would loan him the money he needed. But there was one person from whom he could *take* the money: his stupid, profligate brother, on the other side of the world.

He spent an hour in his office in the back of the plane, then told the pilot, "London."

A DAY EARLIER, when he arrived in Hong Kong, his first move had been to set his lawyers looking for ways of finding a way to recapture what was left of the money in Gawbi's hands. that his father had set up for Gawbi. He had given Gawbi a share equal to that given to Motar, but for Motar it had been outright—a vote of fatherly confidence in his ability. Half of Gawbi's share had been locked away in impregnable trusts to protect Gawbi from his stupidity, extravagance, and unerring knack of falling under the spells of the wrong people.

Now, for the sake of the Al Senour family honor and fortune, there had to be a way to get that money away from Gawbi.

Within 24 hours, the lawyers were back with the news that only days earlier Gawbi had cleaned out his reserves for the year. He had borrowed against himself . . . for what possible purpose?

"Three days ago? But why? How could he spend it all?"

"That will take time to find out, given bank secrecy."

Within hours, the lawyers were back with the news that Gawbi had sold his nearly-new Ferrari the previous week, and had taken out a $1,500,000 mortgage on his California house.

"Trace the money. Trace it quickly."

As soon as he was off the phone with the lawyers, he contacted the security firm in London he and his father had dealt with for years.

"There is the matter of our outstanding billing," the firm's Managing Director said. He had heard recent rumors of trouble around Sheik Al Senour, and had no intention of losing money, even for such a good client.

"An oversight," Al Senour said. "I will personally see that a check is delivered to your offices within a few hours. I would bring it myself out of personal regard for you, but am in Hong Kong as we speak."

Al Senour explained what he needed done. The Managing Director, who had been in the British diplomatic service in his early career, said, "Gawbi is a very trusting young man."

"He is also, to be frank, a very stupid and naïve young man, and has suddenly drawn large amounts of money, large even by his standards. I need to know where that money has gone. Move quickly, but be discreet. Be *very* discreet."

Recruiting Derham

WEEKS BEFORE he contacted Vera, Stoddard invested in a couple of ads in a blog that catered to would-be "security consultants"—a euphemism for mercenaries and soldiers-of-fortune. He was still forming an idea, and wasn't yet sure he would go ahead with it, but it seemed worth spending a little to have people lined up, just in case. The first ad read,

> *Building a crack commando team to fight international terrorism. If you were Delta Team, Special Forces, LURP, SEAL, SAS, etc., and still have what it takes, tell us why you think you're good enough to be part of it.*

The second ad was much the same, though calling for a helicopter pilot with combat experience.

He got 43 responses. That surprised him. It told him there was a buyer's market for this kind of talent.

He put the letters aside until he had met Vera and was reasonably sure the project would be a Go. Then he phoned a secretary he knew from Navy BUPERS—Bureau of Personnel—and suggested a drink after work. The drink stretched on to dinner and breakfast, and she got him printouts of the top American candidates' service files.

By the following evening, he had pared the list down to three pilots and ten commando types, all of whom had combat experience in Iraq or Afghanistan. He wanted guys who had been proven, and wouldn't crack under pressure.

Phone calls over the weekend further winnowed it down, as he cut out any who sounded drunk or stupid. Or too intelligent. He didn't want any of them poking around and asking questions.

Two of the most promising were Europeans, one French, the other British. He hadn't expected responses from Europeans, but they raised interesting possibilities. The Brit looked very interesting.

ON HIS WAY BACK from the trip to the Riviera with Vera, he stopped off in London to meet the Englishman, Albert "Bertie" Derham.

In his e-mail response to the ad, Derham claimed that he had spent four years with the British Special Air Service, the SAS. That impressed Stoddard, as the SAS was generally considered the best commando group in the world, the model for most of the teams that had been set up in the 1970's and later to combat terrorism.

Stoddard had been through commando training with the U.S. Army Rangers, but was in awe of the British SAS. He had gotten hold of a bootleg video of the original BBC coverage of the recapture of the Iranian Embassy in London back in 1980. He'd watched it dozens of times, marveling at the speed and precision with which the SAS team had carried off the operation while working in the center of London in broad daylight.

Even now, every time he watched the tape, he got chill-bumps from seeing such a fantastic piece of work: Black-hooded figures rappelling down from the roof of the Embassy, tossing "flash-bang" stun grenades through the windows to disorient the terrorists, then bursting through the windows and walls to rescue two dozen hostages from the armed fanatics holding them. All this within seconds.

If Derham had been SAS, Stoddard figured, then you could be sure he knew his stuff and could be counted on. Besides, he'd probably have some good ideas, SAS techniques that could strengthen the operation.

He met Derham in a pub near Piccadilly Circus.

Bertie Derham, at 5'10" and about 180, was shorter and heavier than Stoddard but he was solid, and walked with the confident springiness of an athlete in prime condition. His hair was sandy, his face unremarkable, one you'd forget almost at once. That was a definite plus, as Stoddard had read that the really prime commando groups, like the American Delta Force and the SAS, selected partly on the basis of ordinariness of appearance, so they could blend into civilian environments without being noticed.

Derham's eyes, though, were unforgettable, chilling even to Stoddard: pale icy blue, expressionless, slightly out of focus. They put Stoddard off at first. Then he decided, what the hell, you had to be a little crazy to be a commando.

They got a couple of pints of ale, and found a corner in the back of the pub where they could talk freely. Once he got used to the eyes, Stoddard decided Derham was okay. He sure as hell had been around. He told of joining the Grenadier Guards at seventeen, then at twenty-four being accepted into the Special Air Service. That was a distinction in itself; he'd heard somewhere that only one in twenty managed to make it through the SAS screening and training process.

"How come you got out of the service so young?" Stoddard asked when they were working on their third pint.

It seemed, in that first instant, that Derham was going to come across the table at him. "Hey, mate, that's none of your—"

Then he caught himself. "Right, I guess maybe it is your business, under the circumstances. Fact is, I got in a little trouble. With a woman. She made a fuss, the Major decided the SAS didn't want the publicity, and they wanted to transfer me back to my old regiment. Well, I wouldn't be having none of that, it'd be a real come-down after SAS, don't you know. But the SAS takes care of its own. They let me out with a medical retirement, not as good as what I'd have gotten if I'd stayed in my full time, but comfortable enough."

Somehow it didn't ring true to Stoddard. Soldiers were always knocking up the local women, and he didn't see the SAS demanding celibacy. Besides, from what he'd read of the SAS, it was normal to go back to the regiment after a few years. No one could sustain the SAS pace indefinitely.

Most suspicious of all, no government gives away medical retirements as a gesture of kindness. But there was no way of checking on it: he knew that the records of former SAS types were permanently sealed for reasons of national security.

A lot of Derham's other stories were lies, as well, Stoddard realized as he talked on. He really had served in Afghanistan -- those stories all rang true. But the rest were second-hand adventures, full of the kind of mistakes that someone who had really been there would not make.

Still, Stoddard felt, what difference did it make? War stories were like fishing stories—you had to expect a little embellishment here and there. So what did it matter if the guy wanted to build himself up a little? It only showed how eager he was to be part of the operation.

Stoddard had no way of knowing that Derham had been given a quiet discharge from the SAS and the service for psychiatric reasons midway through his second tour of duty in Afghanistan.

Stoddard suggested a base pay of $2,000 per week, with a $2,000 bonus at the end of the operations. Derham laughed in his face. He sensed that Stoddard was impressed by his SAS experience, and had no intention of selling himself cheaply. In the end, Derham got it up to $5,000 per week, plus a $20,000 bonus.

Besides, in his SAS training, Derham had learned to speak fluent French, and that might come in very handy.

IT WAS EASY ENOUGH AFTERWARDS for Derham to follow Stoddard back to his hotel at Russell Square. A couple of £10 notes to a bellman got him Stoddard's name and home address from his registration, and he began working out how he could cut himself in for a bigger piece of the action, maybe even cut Stoddard out of it altogether.

Crazies, liars, and misfits

AFTER SIGNING ON BERTIE DERHAM, Stoddard flew back to Washington and took another look at the replies sent in by the Americans who had responded to his ads.

They were a sorry lot, he felt, either young kids who'd never seen any real combat, or old farts who'd been in Iraq, Afghanistan or even way back in Desert Storm, and turned out to be losers and misfits once they got back to the World.

He made some calls, and found the guys he wanted were free to meet any time. That meant they didn't have anything else going and would be desperate enough to work cheap and not ask questions.

He caught a morning jet from Washington Dulles to San Diego. He checked into a hotel, then drove over to meet with Eric Jorgensen, the copter pilot with the best credentials.

Jorgensen had suggested they met at a cocktail lounge overlooking the bay. That was a bad choice, Stoddard realized as he walked in. It was only early afternoon, and Jorgensen was already staggering.

Jorgensen was tall and lean, with prematurely grey hair and rugged Scandinavian good looks. Except for his haunted eyes, he could have been an actor in afternoon soap operas.

But the eyes reflected too much of what they had seen. Jorgensen's eyes made Stoddard uncomfortable. Looking in them, you saw fear, guilt, self-loathing, despair.

Jorgensen had flown AH-1 Cobras, little 2-man attack helicopters, in the operations in Iraq and Afghanistan. Since then, he'd flown in Alaska on the pipeline, had done a lot of work with drilling rigs in the Gulf of Mexico, and had been on a couple of extended assignments with oil companies in the Middle East.

Stoddard didn't need to ask why, with his experience and contacts, he had to be looking for another job: Jorgensen's drink was vodka, neat.

But he was the only chopper pilot with real combat experience who had responded to the ad. Stoddard signed him on, figuring he could keep him dry for a couple of weeks–that was all he needed.

They agreed on $1,000 per week, plus a $5,000 bonus. Stoddard was surprised at how cheaply he was willing to work. But there wasn't much of a job market for alcoholic pilots.

THE NEXT MORNING, Stoddard drove up to Redlands to meet with another prospect. His name was Jack Rafferty, but he said he hadn't been called anything but "California" since he joined up at 19, a kid who talked about nothing but his home state.

He was a beefy guy, 6' and 220, middle-aged and paunchy, with a significant limp and sun-bleached pony-tail reaching to the middle of his back, along with an ever-present pair of mirrored sunglasses to hide a pair of drug-ravaged eyes. He arrived on a beat-up Harley.

California said he had been farming up in the mountains, skipping over the fact that his farming consisted of growing marijuana in remote areas of the mountain national parks.

He looked a little crazy, too. But he'd been a Navy SEAL. To Stoddard, that was evidence he could handle himself in a tight spot. Besides, he'd been cross-trained as a medic, as well as in demolitions and electronics. Stoddard figured those might be useful skills to have on the team, and hired him on.

He seemed to be desperate for cash, so Stoddard offered only $1,000 per week, plus a $5,000 bonus. California took it without haggling.

STODDARD CAUGHT A RED-EYE back to Washington, got a couple of hours sleep, then drove out to West Virginia to check out Vern Billy Blodgett. They were to meet at a McDonald's. Vern Billy was an hour late, as he'd had to hitch a ride after his old pick-up blew a tire and he didn't have a spare.

He was short, lean, and wiry, with stringy black hair that looked like it hadn't been combed for a week. His moustache was ragged and thin, like a teen-ager's, even though he was over 30. He wore a dirty red Valvoline baseball cap, a battered Army fatigue jacket, dirty blue jeans and ankle-high work boots. His big metal belt-buckle read, "Viet-Nam! I served my time in Hell!"

His eyes were small and mean, like snake eyes. Not intelligent, but crafty.

Stoddard had known dozens of good soldiers like him, products of the Appalachians, slow learners but good shots, men who could go all day without tiring, who didn't ask questions, and who could climb like monkeys. Stoddard took him on at the same rate as the other Americans, $1,000 per week, plus the promise of $5,000 at the end.

"You weren't in 'Nam," Stoddard said at the end, indicating the belt-buckle.

"No, but my Daddy was, and I learnt a hell of a lot from him, from what he done in 'Nam."

HIS NAME, Stoddard told them all, was Colonel Thompson. He led each of them through a secrecy oath that implied they would be working for the U.S. Government, then got them to sign an employment contract with Deltarms Corporation.

He'd made up the company name, and copied the contract out of a book. He figured that, if they even thought about it, they'd assume that Deltarms was a CIA front and not ask too many questions.

Someone to make things happen

VERA HAD BEEN PHONING Stoddard from early morning onward, but he hadn't picked up. She refused to meet him face-to-face now that the operations were under way, so they bought pre-paid cell phones, paid for in cash. If the police listened in, there wouldn't be any way to trace who was on the line. Nor would the police be able to trace her even if they arrested him and got his phone.

She sat on the hotel balcony, overlooking the busy *Promenade des Anglais* and the sea beyond. With the traffic noise and the sound of the waves she wasn't concerned about being overheard.

Stoddard finally returned her calls just before three.

"I am very disappointed," she said. "What you got was almost insignificant. You missed the really good items, the very ones I pointed out to you as most worthwhile."

"Too bad, but that's the way it is. So we move on to Option B."

"Your Option B, as you call it, is settling for second best. In any case, now there will be more risk. Now they'll be on guard everywhere along the coast."

"My guys are flexible. We'll cope."

"That American girl, the one who saw your people, she has moved to a small hotel in Nice."

"Why are you telling me that?" he asked.

"Didn't you see her interviewed on television? She said she could recognize one of the men from his strange walk."

"Shit! She said that? I didn't see that, don't speak French, you know that."

"She is staying now at the Hotel Eminence in Nice, a small hotel in the Musicians district, near the rail station. I leave it in your hands."

"How do you know that? Any case, what's this about leave it in my hand? The hell you mean by that?"

"I simply called the hotel in Antibes and told the woman I was a reporter wanting an interview. I do speak French like a native, keep that in mind. It seems that the American—Emily—had already made a reservation at the place in Nice . . . at someone's recommendation, the lady said."

"I don't understand why you're telling me this. What's your point?" Stoddard was standing in the afternoon sun, and it was hot in the glare against the stone wall behind him. The flow of traffic made it hard to hear.

"The point is obvious. She is a danger."

"Danger? Hell, it was a fluke. She happened to look out a window. A chance in a million."

"She saw your men. That makes her a threat. She can identify them. That puts us all in jeopardy."

"You still haven't said: Just what is it you're suggesting?"

"I have told you where she is staying. Need I say more?"

"You were the one who said no violence."

"I meant nothing overt—no shoot-outs, nothing of that sort. But accidents happen, especially to tourists."

He laughed. "You're tougher than I gave you credit for."

"If that's a compliment, *merci*," she replied, thinking, You have no idea how tough I really am, you foolish little man!

"When're we going to get together? Just talking to you I get turned on."

"It's the same with me, of course," she lied. "Soon. When all the work is finished. Then we will go away together for a few weeks, yes?"

"That's too long to wait."

"You will take care of her soon, yes? Today? For my sake?"

"I'll check her out."

"Do more than just check her out. Deal with her. She is dangerous to us."

"Maybe she'll just move on, go to Italy or someplace."

"That would be the best thing. For her. But we can't count on it."

VERA HUNG UP, FRUSTRATED. Maybe he wasn't going to be as easy to manage as she had expected.

She switched to her second cell-phone and dialed a number.

If Stoddard wouldn't get the girl out of circulation, then there was someone who would, someone who could make things happen here in France, someone to whom she'd already advanced $200,000.

Michael McGaulley

PART THREE

Dining alone

EMILY HAD DINNER at *L'Etoile d'Argent*—The Silver Star—
a small, family-run place a few blocks from the hotel.

She got a table outside in the balmy evening air, and the *prix-
fixe* dinner was at least as good as most of the hotel meals on her
business trips in the States. *Soupe de legumes, pommes vapeur,
epinards, boeuf*—it sounded better in French than vegetable
soup, boiled potatoes, creamed spinach and roast beef.

But she felt lonely, and wondered what she was doing
roaming around Europe. She had called her father before
leaving the hotel, catching him on the golf-course—or, more
likely, from his slurred speech, in the club-house. "I still can't
believe you quit your job to go playing hippie."

"I needed a break, some time off to get perspective."

"That's nice, if you can afford it. But jobs aren't so easy to
find these days, you should know that." He was in the club-
house, no doubt of that now. He was tight by nature, the grim
Scandinavian blood in his veins. He'd never been demonstrative,
never really affectionate when she was growing up. But not rude
like this.

A lot of it, she understood now, was that he'd been a Child of
Children of the Depression. His parents had been through the
bad times in the 1930's, and they had drilled into him the
insecurity and rigidity that had come from growing up in those
uncertain times. He had internalized their anxieties, never
feeling secure, forever avoiding risk, driven on an unending
quest for stability and security.

Which was why his first real job after college and a short stint
in the Army Reserve had been with a bank, and why he'd stayed
with the same job for all those years: it was safe, stable, secure.

Secure until the merger-fever came along, and he was pushed into early retirement. And that crushed him: managing the bank had been his life, his security. Suddenly gone.

He'd gone off the rails then, taken up with a woman barely older than Emily. Then the divorce.

Looking back, maybe the divorce was the best outcome for them both, Mother and Dad. They had never been suited for each other. He, the dour Swede; she the romantic. Never in accord, and each bringing out the worst in the other.

THE PRIX FIXE menu included a small carafe of house red wine. She finished it, telling herself it would help her sleep without the nightmares that had been plaguing her for all these weeks.

She was finishing *le dessert*, a cup of yogurt, part of the Prix Fixe, when the French ladies at the next table—a mother, 50ish, and daughter maybe 20, both down from Paris—invited her to have an *apres-diner cognac* with them. That cognac became two, as she felt obliged to reciprocate.

And she learned something French: if the cognac is less than the best, which this was, then hold a cube of sugar in your mouth as you sip, and that works magic.

SHE GOT BACK to the hotel later than planned, tired after losing so much sleep at Antibes last night. But she did want to call her mother to tell her that she was staying in the Hotel Eminence.

"Emily!" her mother exclaimed. "Thank God you called! I've been trying and trying to reach you all day!"

Her breath caught. "What—What's happened?"

"You're famous! Those pictures you took, the ones of the art thieves, they were on all the networks today—the robbers of course, and some pictures of you, as well. You looked as though you'd just rolled out of bed. Had you?"

"It was the middle of the night, Mother."

My photos on all the networks? So Nice-Matin passed them on, syndicated them, probably got big money for them. And I got barely enough to pay the hotel bill!

"You said you tried to phone me all day? What number were you—"

"Oh, *Emily*! Can you believe it! I was phoning your old number, the one in Chicago. I completely forgot your new phone, your Europe phone. How silly, how absurd of me."

"Moving on, Mother, you'll never guess where I'm staying in Nice."

"I most certainly hope you're at the Hotel Eminence. How wonderful. I wish . . . I wish I were there. No, take that back! I don't want to intrude. It's just that, well, that is a wonderful part of the world. Such a romantic spot, the sun, the sea, the flowers."

"Romantic? You're making me wonder if you had a romantic interlude here, Mother," Emily said, then immediately wished she had not. Too much cognac.

"*Moi*? Your mother having a romantic interlude in France? How can you even think such a thought! In any case, it was a very long time ago. Just enjoy yourself. Enjoy it for all it's worth, and then you can come back and get on with the rest of your life."

TWO MINUTES LATER her phone rang. It was her mother calling back. Emily clicked on, hoping it wasn't again going to be the biological clock sermon.

"I forgot to tell you— No, that's not true. I didn't really forget, I just didn't want to say it, but it is your life, and I should . . . well, whatever."

"Sorry, Mother, but I have no idea what you're trying to tell me."

"Porter has been calling again. Several times, actually. He wants me to talk you into, as he put it, 'listening to reason.' He acknowledges he made a 'little slip,' that's the way he put it, and wants you to give him a second chance."

Emily forced a deep breath, then another. "He's wasting his time, and yours, Mother. Next time he calls, if he calls and I hope he doesn't, just hang up."

"Maybe it was just a last little fling before the marriage?"

"I found out later that was by no means his only so-called 'little slip'. You know the saying, 'Cheat me once it's your fault; cheat me twice it's my fault'. That's where I stand. No second chances."

Upper Corniche

HE PAUSES on the climb back down to his car parked on the side of the road. The Upper Corniche, a quiet, twisting, historic route that followed the jagged mountain outcroppings from the Italian border to Nice.

The coastline of the Riviera stretches out, a thousand feet below. Clusters of colored lights shimmer on the dark waters of the Mediterranean. Triangles of light outline the riggings of the yachts moored in the bays.

Directly below, at the tip of the peninsula of Cape Martin, the lighthouse flashes its beam across the water.

The heavy warm aromas of the flowers drift up to mingle with the cool scents of the pines and shrubs. His tension dissolves into the gentle evening air.

Then he sees the flashing blue lights of three police cars weaving along the twisting coastal road and onto Cape Martin below, the sound of their klaxons faint up here on the mountain.

This Upper Corniche road is deserted at night, narrow and remote as it winds around the jagged red rocky mountainsides. His mood shifts, and he suddenly feels vulnerable in an eerie world of jutting rocks and windswept trees. He scrambles back down the slope.

A car rounds the blind curve fast, breaks hard, then backs up to pull in behind his BMW.

Two men climb out and shine flashlights into the open convertible.

He ducks behind a scraggly pine, not sure how to play this. A rock gives way under his foot, starting a gravel slide. Beams from their flashlights stretch out and find him.

He runs, trips on an outcropping, and falls.

The men are upon him before he can scramble to his feet, and he feels the barrel of a pistol jammed hard into the base of his skull.

"Police," one says, flashing a badge. Handcuffs snap on, pinning his arms behind his back.

They drag him to their car, frisk him, then shove him into the back seat.

"*Votre nom, Monsieur?*"

Night Manager

EMILY BACKS AWAY until she's trapped against the windows. She cries for help, but no one hears.

He runs at her, yelling, "You'll never get away, never!"

"Help me! Please! Somebody help!" she screams.

He flicks a lighter and touches the flame to the letter he's holding. The paper flares up, and he tosses it at her.

She pulls back to escape the flame and feels the glass dissolve behind her. She grasps for the window-frame, for the edge of the building, for anything, but her fingers miss, and she tumbles into the air 66 stories above the streets of Chicago.

"Help me! Help me!"

An arm reaches out and she grabs for it. A man. She throws her arms around him, desperate. But he loses balance and he's tumbling out the window with her.

Now she's not in Chicago, not hanging over the edge of skyscraper. Now she's in a room somewhere, and a man stands in front of her, gripping her shoulders. He is bare-chested.

She lashes out. Her knee hits his leg, and he stumbles back against the armoire and slides to the floor.

"Who are you! Get out!" she screams. "Help! Help!" She's wearing only panties in the warm evening, no top. She pulls the sheet up around her.

"Are you okay?" he asks.

"Who are you? Why are you in my room? Get out!"

"You were screaming for help. I climbed across —from my balcony to yours. I'm in the next room."

Knocking at the door. "Mademoiselle! It is here the night manager. Is something all right–not all right, that is?"

She hesitated, looking at the man still sitting on the floor where he had fallen. "I . . . I had a dream, a nightmare."

A babble of outraged voices in the hall. "Mademoiselle, I should — I must come in to see that all is really . . . really safe with you," the manager said through the door.

Now the man on the floor was laughing. He rolled to his feet. He was lean and muscular, and wore only a pair of boxer shorts.

"I tell you I'm fine," she called back to the manager. "There's no need to—"

"But I must come in and see for myself. A man—he could be holding you with a knife to your throat. It is for your own protection."

She waved to the man in her room, pointing back to the open door to the balcony. "I need a moment to put on a robe," she called to the manager.

The man in the room blew her a kiss, still laughing, and disappeared out the balcony door.

She saw the shadow as he climbed back over the balcony railing, then pulled on a long T-shirt before opening the door.

The night clerk was a friendly old man with silver hair, a big white moustache, and a large red nose. Now he wore bed slippers.

"See?" she said. "I'm fine. I was having a nightmare, that's all."

A dozen people crowded behind him, trying to get a look into her room. "Thank you, everyone. I'm sorry if I . . . if I woke you." *Just go away!*

The door next to hers opened. It was the man. "What's happening?" he asked.

He's American, Emily realized. It was coming back to her now, the nightmare of Bill Bridges throwing the burning letter at her, the sense of falling off the window ledge.

"All is well, *pas de problem*," the night manager said, "everyone back to bed. *Bonne nuit.*"

Morning

EMILY WOKE to the sound of palm fronds swaying softly in the breeze. She threw on a blouse and shorts, and stepped onto the small balcony.

The balcony overlooked the hotel garden, compact and formal in the French style, with each flower and shrub neatly trimmed. Four small palms marked the corners, with a pair of orange trees symmetrically placed between them. The garden was sheltered on each side by five-story stone buildings, an oasis in the heart of the bustling city.

Today is the first day of the best part of my life, she told herself. It had been her mantra since arriving in Europe.

And it is a perfect day to be starting a new life. The morning sky was intense blue—no wonder the French called this the Cote d'Azur, the Blue Coast—and warm morning sunshine glowed on the pastel stucco buildings across the garden.

The scents of the flowers blended with the salt air and the aromas of fresh bread and coffee drifting up from the hotel's kitchen. Time to get out into this beautiful day.

Then she remembered last night, and stepped back, a wave of embarrassment washing across her at the thought of the crowd in the hallway last night, babbling on after the nightmare.

They must have thought I was a psycho, screaming in the night like that.

Maybe I'm going psycho. The nightmares, night after night.

And that poor guy who tried to help. What a scene I put on!

She looked across at the next balcony. It wasn't that close, a gap of a good three feet. He risked his neck climbing over to help me. And I accused him of—of what? Of coming in to attack me.

What an idiot I was! The others, the other guests, will be laughing into their coffees when I go down to breakfast.

Michael McGaulley

I've got to get away from here! ASAP!

Howdy

I'M PROCRASTINATING. Let them laugh. Get past it. Then get out of here, ASAP.

Emily went down the circular staircase to the ground floor, feeling she was making a grand appearance in a drama she wanted no part of. She'd grab something to eat, then move on, ASAP.

Somewhere else, anywhere else!

Someplace where people wouldn't be laughing about the fool she'd made of herself.

Breakfast was served in the hotel's garden. The man who'd climbed into her room last night was already there, finishing a call on his cell-phone.

He waved and smiled when he saw her. Or was he laughing?

"I really owe you an apology," she said, suddenly flustered. "I'm sorry about what happened. I over-reacted. I was having a nightmare. About work."

"I probably shouldn't have climbed across to your room like that, but it seemed . . ." He broke off and chuckled.

What a nice smile he has, she thought, and found herself smiling, too, as if they shared a private joke.

It is a private joke. And I'm the butt of the joke.

He gestured at the empty seat across from him. She sat, yet felt awkward being close to him now. No telling how much he saw when he came into the room last night.

He looks like a Viking, with that beard and his sunburned nose. Or like one of those hearty types in the L.L. Bean catalogs.

"That was quite a nightmare."

"Things were very stressful before I— before I decided to take a vacation."

"Been here long?"

"Since yesterday afternoon. And you?"

"How long are you staying?"

She shrugged. "I was planning—" *He looks very interesting. Maybe a change in plans?* "I was planning to move on today, but the sunshine, the weather here is so wonderful, maybe I'll stay another day or . . . who knows?"

He smiled. "Maybe we can spend some time together."

"I'm Emily." *I should have said that's a nice offer and I'd like that.*

After a moment, she added, "And you are?"

"Howdy."

The memory of last night. Grabbing for his arm in her dream, pulling him onto the bed, then waking up and kicking him. Not a good start.

"I am sorry about last night. I made a . . . made a real scene. You were kind to come and try to help. And I'm Emily. Emily Cederquist." She held out her hand. He took it. It felt good.

"Cederquist? Sure and begorrah , but that's a fine Irish name."

"Irish? That's not—" She broke off, realizing he was joking. "Actually my mother is Irish–third generation. Cederquist is from my father's side. Swedish."

"I'm told you're a celebrity."

His eyes were twinkling, and she wondered if this was another joke.

"Celebrity?"

"The night manager at the front desk showed me the *Nice-Matin* with your pictures on the front page. You broke up the art theft, single-handedly, he says. They seem very honored to have you staying here."

"Not after the scene last night. I must have seemed—"

She broke off that line, and said, "In any case, I'm Emily. And you are?" She noticed his shirt; not only did he look like somebody from an L.L. Bean catalog, but his shirt was L.L. Bean, she was sure of it; her father had one just like it.

But this shirt was—not really shabby---just tired-looking, around too long.

"Howdy." He reached out and shook her hand again. "Nice to meet you, Emily. Again. You have nice hands."

"So do you. But your name is?"

"Howdy."

She felt it flaring up again, the stuff that kept bubbling up inside ever since that awful Saturday in Chicago. Anger. Fury.

She pushed her chair back abruptly and stood. "Howdy yourself, and I'm out of here."

"But that *is* my name. Howdy. How—as in 'I'll show you how,' comma D."

She stared at him, then sat again. "I thought you were putting me on." He laughed.

"Maybe a little bit. I have been known to use that joke before. But that really is my name."

"So your last name is Howe? What does the D stand for? What name do you go by?"

"I don't really use the D. It was my mother's family name, Darnton. My late mother, sadly. But I don't use it."

"No?" she replied, still not sure whether he was putting her on again.

"The other kids in school abbreviated it to 'Darnit.' My brother was Andrew, Andy, and they'd see us coming and start chanting, 'Here they come, Darnit and How!'"

She nodded. "So what name do you go by?"

"Jeremy."

"Jeremy. That suits you, yes."

"But it's not my real name."

She took a deep breath, feeling there was still a joke she was missing. "Then what is your real name? Or is that secret?" That last bit sounded snotty even as she said it, and she wished she could take it back.

"Jeremiah. But not as in Jeremiah the prophet. Jeremiah is my middle name, but I go by Jeremy."

"Well, that clears it all up, I guess. Darnit, Jeremiah Howe, you sure can make things complicated."

"Got anything planned for today? Maybe you'd like to—"

The waitress came to the table and cut him off, whispering in Emily's ear: "There is a telephone call for you. In the lobby."

"For me? I don't know anyone here. Who could be calling me?"

"It is the police. You must hurry."

Passport

EMILY TOOK THE CALL in the small booth just off the lobby, frustrated that a call had come just at that particular moment. A day with Jeremy—or whatever his name really was—might have been very interesting.

Then it struck her: How did the police know I'm at this hotel?

"*Commissaire Principal* Bourchette will see you in 30 minutes," a man said when she identified herself. "Be prompt. Come to the PJ office at Avenue Foch and Dubouchage."

"PJ? I don't understand."

"*Police Judiciare*. Judicial Police. Identify yourself to the officer at the front desk."

PJ—the French equivalent of the American FBI—that was what the lady at the hotel in Antibes had said yesterday.

"What's this about?"

"You must be here in one-half hour, on time."

"But I already talked with two Judicial Police officers yesterday, back in Antibes. I gave a full statement then."

"I know nothing of that," the officer on the phone said. "Report here in a half-hour, no later. And bring your passport."

"My passport? Why?"

"Bring it."

THE CLERK at the hotel front desk gave her a map, then traced the route to the headquarters of the Judicial Police. "The Judicial Police are part of the national police force, like the FBI in your country," he told her.

Alibi

EMILY FOUND the police headquarters, a boxy concrete building, stuck incongruously in a pleasant tree-lined residential section not far from the old part of Nice.

She gave her name to an officer at a desk in the lobby, and he pointed her to the worn marble steps leading to the second floor. The walls were a dirty mustard yellow that seemed to have been ripening for decades.

Another sergeant was waiting at a desk at the landing. When she said that she was there to see *Commissaire Principale* Bourchette, he took her passport, jotted her name on a card, then got up from his desk and escorted her to the tiny elevator, barely bigger than a phone booth.

They rode to the top floor along with two plainclothesmen smoking thick-scented *Gauloises* and talking about a soccer game.

"*PJ ici*," the sergeant said when they stepped into the hallway. "PJ. *Police Judiciare*. Judicial Police. Like your American FBI, the big-timers, the elite. It's much more pleasant up here, yes? Bigger offices, bigger budget."

Interesting, she thought. That's the third person who's linked the PJ to the FBI.

But why would the French FBI want to talk with me?

THIS FLOOR WAS BRIGHTER than those below, with walls freshly painted in a cream color, a nice change from dirty mustard yellow. The only sound was a typewriter clicking away in a slow, two-fingered rhythm. She wondered when she had last heard an old-fashioned typewriter.

The sergeant led her down the corridor, then paused before one of the doors. It was slightly ajar.

As he knocked, she heard a fragment of a sentence: *"Qu'est ce que lui l'American German?"* What a strange question, she thought, it makes no sense at all. What do you know of the American-German something or other?

"Oui? Entrez!" snapped the same hoarse voice, obviously irritated at the interruption.

The sergeant stepped through the door and came to attention. "An informant for *Commissaire Principal* Bourchette," he announced in French. "Mademoiselle Emily Cederquist, from the United States of America."

He mangled her name, but Cederquist got mangled in English, too.

But 'informant'—the word caught her ear. *An informant is a snitch. I'm a witness, not a snitch. Why am I here? Why this command performance?*

Two of the men were sitting, and the other stood by the window. "That's all, sergeant," said the man sitting at the head of the table, taking the passport. His voice was a deep, throaty rasp, and she knew that he was the one who had spoken the curious sentence.

He looked at her and attempted what might have been a smile, but his face contorted as if he were in pain, and his eyes disappeared beneath the hood of dark eyebrows. The effect was chilling,

"I am *Commissaire Principal* Bertrand Bourchette," he said, flipping quickly through her passport. She wondered why the passport was relevant.

She recognized his name from yesterday's *Nice-Soir*. He had flown down from Paris to take over the investigation of the art thefts.

He was even more ugly in person than in the news photo, a squat, powerful man in a rumpled black suit. The curly black hair on the back of his hands was so thick that she could barely see through to the skin beneath.

The same curly black hair circled his head, and grew unnaturally low on his forehead. His eyes were dark, alert, predatory.

He reminded her of a bear.

Bourchette handed the passport to another man, then sat back and studied her for several seconds without speaking. He did not invite her to sit, although there were two empty chairs.

The air was dense with the thick, cloying smoke of French tobacco. Non-smoking rules had not arrived in police stations, so it seemed. Or the police didn't follow the rules. Her eyes burned, and she felt nauseous.

The second detective was copying information from her passport onto a white card. She had a sudden urge to snatch the passport back and run out of the room.

"You were an eye-witness to the robbery at Antibes, yes?" Bourchette said. He spoke in French. She hesitated, wondering whether to ask for a translator, then decided to be as cooperative as possible and get it over with. She had spent her junior year in Grenoble, so her French was good, but rusty.

"Yes. I did see the men from the window of my hotel."

He stared at her; she wondered if he had heard her response.

"But you were more interested in taking photographs for the press than in calling the police."

"What? No. That's not true," she said, her mouth suddenly dry. "It's not true at all. I tried, almost as soon as I saw the men, to call the police. It took me a while to get an outside line."

"An outside line, you say? But the fact is, it was not you who made the call to the police, yes?"

"Well, not exactly. I told the hotel's night manager to call the police. He was the one who actually made the call, but I alerted him."

"If you didn't make the call, then how do you know how long it took to get an outside line?"

"What I meant was—"

"But what you just said was incorrect, yes?"

She shrugged. "Technically speaking."

Bourchette snorted, and stared at her. The silence hung heavy in the room.

Finally he said, "Yet even after the police arrived, you made no attempt to come forward as a witness."

"That's also not true. I did try, I tried with two, I think it was—with two different officers and they all shooed me away. One even threatened to arrest me if I pushed it any further."

'You contradict yourself. Was it three officers, or two . . .or none?"

"It all happened so fast. I know I talked to at least two, though there were others standing—"

"Now you are claiming that you tried to give a statement to three officers at the scene?"

What is going on here? "I'm not just claiming it, I *did* try. They threatened to arrest me."

"Arrest you? Perhaps you can tell us the names of these officers?"

"Names? How would I know their names? It was night, everybody was excited. I was trying to help the police, not build an alibi."

Bourchette smiled, and again his eyes receded behind their slits. "So you believe you need an alibi for your actions that night?"

"Not at all!" Her teeth stuck to the side of her dry cheek, and she had to pull the skin free. "You're treating me like a criminal, and yet I was the person who reported the crime."

"But, conveniently, you were unable to get through to the police until the men were safely away."

She took a couple of deep breaths, then said, "Look, I don't know what your point is, but the fact is I did try to help. I called the police, or passed the word. I tried to give a statement of what I saw to the officers on the scene. I already gave a complete statement to two of the detectives yesterday."

"Did you in fact tell them all you know?"

"Of course," she said, wondering if there was something she was overlooking. Why was he was treating her like this? "Of course I've told everything. Why not? What could I possibly have to hide?"

"That is the question, is it not?" Bourchette said, and stared at her. She felt naked. "What are you hiding? Why? Who are you protecting?"

The silence hung, then Bourchette said, "It has come to our attention that you were not completely honest in what you did, finally, tell our officers yesterday."

"That's not– I don't know what you're talking about."

"You were interviewed on television yesterday, yes?"

"Yes. I didn't ask to be, but they were there, waiting outside my hotel."

"You told the television people that you could recognize one of the men, even though his face was covered."

"That's true." What's he getting at? she wondered, a sense of foreboding building.

"Why were you so certain you could recognize that man?"

"It was the way he moved, as if he was trying to walk on a waterbed. I think one of his legs might be shorter than the other. And he had long hair, a ponytail that—"

"The unusual way he walked, you say now. But you didn't tell the detectives that yesterday. Why not?"

"I thought of it only later, when the TV cameras were running, and then I didn't know how to get back in touch with those men."

"Who am I to believe, the written report of police officers, or the account of someone who keeps changing her story?"

Bourchette picked up a typed report and read it for what seemed a very long time.

Then he looked at her. Again he smiled, incongruously, and his eyes disappeared behind the lids. "You are at the Hotel Eminence?"

"Yes."

"You will notify me first if you should decide to move from there."

"But I'm only a witness."

"At this point, yes, you are only a witness. But that may change. We need to know how to reach you." He looked down and began shuffling through the papers on his desk.

"Is there anything else?" she finally asked.

"You are free to go. For now."

Free for now! What is he saying?

"But you have my passport."

Again his eyes receded as he smiled. "Ah yes, your passport. Are you aware of the danger of pickpockets in a resort area? An American passport is very valuable to them. Perhaps it would be a good idea to leave it with us for safekeeping."

"Are you saying that I'm, I'm– " She cut off, not wanting to use the word. Detained.

He shrugged. "Very well, then, take your passport." He flipped it to her, spinning. It bounced off her hand, forcing her to bend over to pick it up . . . as he intended, she was sure.

SHE WAS AT THE DOOR when Bourchette stopped her. "Tell me the truth now: Are you certain you could you recognize that man with the limp if you saw him again?"

"If I saw him walking, then, yes, I'm sure I could."

"And the other men?"

She shook her head. "There was nothing distinctive about them."

Bourchette nodded slowly. After a moment he said, "It surprises me that you have the courage to remain here in Nice."

"Courage to remain? Why should I leave? I've done nothing wrong."

"When I called you here, I wondered if you were part of the team, the art-theft team. I still wonder that. But if you are not, then you could be in great danger."

"Danger? Why?"

"Because you are a threat to the man you claim you can identify. You have your passport now. If you have any sense, you'll get away from this area as fast as you can—before he finds you."

Suspicious

WHEN EMILY LEFT the room, Commissioner Bourchette repeated the question he had been asking as she arrived. *"Qu'est ce que lui l'American?"* What do you know of the American?

"As we told you earlier, he was observed climbing down from one of the outcroppings above the Upper Corniche road, not far from Cape Martin last night," *Commissaire Principal* de Castaret replied.

De Castaret held the same rank as Bourchette, though he was nearly two decades younger. De Castaret handled the *Departement Alpes-Maritime,* this was his turf. Bourchette was an intruder, from Paris. "This was about twenty minutes after the first call on the break-in arrived."

"As for his background," de Castaret continued, "at this point, we know only what was available from the papers he presented last night . . . assuming, of course, that they are legitimate documents. He's American, 29 years, unmarried. The address in his passport is a suburb of Boston, in the state of Massachusetts, while his driving license lists an address in Virginia, near Washington. He was driving a new BMW, which, according to the records, he picked up at the factory in Germany about two weeks ago."

"But the passport he showed last night was Irish. If he is American, then why is he traveling on an Irish passport?" Bourchette asked.

"American citizens can obtain Irish passports, provided a parent or grandparent was born in Ireland. It is the same for those with ancestors born in France."

"Legal, perhaps. But very odd. Why would an American use an Irish passport?"

De Castaret shook his head. Could Bourchette be so uninformed? "An Irish passport simplifies border crossings within Europe. It is not at all uncommon for American business people to use a European passport for the sake of convenience."

Bourchette asked, "Again, that Irish passport. Could he be a terrorist? IRA? INLA? Real IRA? Have you checked him with the British?"

That had not occurred to de Castaret. "We are awaiting their response," he said.

"IT IS INEXCUSABLE that your Inspector Le Blanc released him last night," Bourchette said.

"His papers were in order. The officers searched his car. They found nothing suspicious."

"His *behavior* was suspicious. He was parked on a lonely road in the vicinity of a theft. What could be more suspicious?"

"He said he stopped to relieve himself. The officers couldn't arrest him for that. In any case, he was some distance, more than five kilometers, from the crime scene."

Bourchette smiled, his eyes again receding behind the folds of flesh. The effect was intimidating even to de Castaret.

Bourchette walked over to the aerial photograph that had been pinned to the wall. "Again, I point out that the *Autoroute* to Italy lies only a few dozen meters from the point where he was picked up. He could climb the last few meters, a car could pause beside the *Autoroute* for a few seconds, long enough for him to throw the paintings over the fence, and within moments, the car and the paintings could be across the border into Italy."

"Those few meters are up the side of a very steep mountain."

132

"From what Inspector Le Blanc has told us, he is an athletic young man quite capable of such a climb."

Bourchette smiled again, his eyes receding once again behind the folds of flesh. He knew the chilling effect his smiles had on others, and smiled often. "It was stupid to let him go. Now we have no trace of him."

De Castaret shrugged. You couldn't hold everyone on suspicion. In the old days, in Bourchette's prime, yes. But things were different now. But it wasn't something he was going to argue with Bourchette.

"It was a mistake to let him go. There are other ways of following up. You know them as well as I. We can cable the FBI for information on him. Talk to our informers. Put out an alert for his car. Tell us what you think should be done."

Bourchette walked to the window and stared out at the parking lot below.

Then he turned and said, "No, don't do any of that. No request to the FBI, no bulletins on him here. We don't want to alert him to our interest. The name is almost certainly an alias. Wait until we have more specific evidence. Understand that: we do not want to alert him to our interest."

Michael McGaulley

The Black Bear

COMMISSIONER DE CASTARET walked back to his office, puzzled by Bourchette's treatment of the American woman. It was as if he had truly seen her as a suspect. Absurd, of course.

De Castaret held the same rank as Bourchette—*Commissaire Principal*, Principal Commissioner.

But he was a generation removed from Bourchette in age and mindset. De Castaret was one of the "New Wave" of younger, better educated police who were gradually replacing the old line, the men they privately referred to as the "Neanderthals"—people like Bourchette, people who should have been retired years ago.

De Castaret was 37, and headed the elite *Police Judiciare* in the D*epartement Alpes-Maritime,* a territory that comprised most of the Riviera and the area behind. It was the first time the post had been held by one so young, but de Castaret had both the right connections and the right schooling. He was from the north of France, and was blond and lean, a tennis player. He had attended university at one of the *grandes ecoles,* breeding-ground for the elite in French politics and bureaucracy. He had a law degree, and came from a family that, despite some losses during the French Revolution, could trace itself back five centuries.

Bourchette was nearly twenty years older, and had worked his way up from the uniformed ranks. The two had clashed from the moment Bourchette flew in from Paris at dawn yesterday, hours after the Antibes raid.

Bourchette was the son of a Paris butcher, had not attended an important university, did not play tennis, resembled a bear, and had no social graces whatever.

De Castaret was annoyed at the way Bourchette had intruded into the case without invitation, flying down immediately from

134

Paris after the first art theft. The *Departement Alpes-Maritimes* was de Castaret's turf, and he didn't like Bourchette moving in.

Bourchette had been effective in his time. But his time was past. Now he was months from retirement—and nearly everyone from the Minister on down was pleased by that prospect.

Somehow it amazed de Castaret and most of his generation that Bourchette had been appointed Operations Advisor for Art Theft by the Minister of the Interior, a liaison post, based in Paris, which gave him scope to do as he chose on art thefts. Bourchette was an odd choice for the job. One of de Castaret's friends in Paris had said that Bourchette "wouldn't know the difference between a Picasso and a postage stamp."

Bourchette's nickname within the *Police Judiciare*—the PJ— was *L'Ours Noire*, the Black Bear. It was appropriate not just because of the pelt of black hair that covered his hands and so much of his head, but equally because of his the heavy, direct, brutal way he moved in resolving cases.

But de Castaret's concern was not just territorial. Bourchette was clearly up to something, treating the girl the way he had. It made no sense to alienate her, especially since she already had a contact at Nice-Matin.

And then there was that charade about keeping her passport. There were rules and regulations on that, and what Bourchette had done—even suggesting that he keep it for "safekeeping"— was out of line. It was a bizarre thing to do, threatening to hold her as a witness. The photos she had taken that night told all she had to tell.

Still, Bourchette might be brutal, but he was not stupid. The Black Bear knew something, something he wasn't sharing.

De CASTARET FOUND A MESSAGE WAITING on his desk: Inspector Galoir needed to see him immediately.

Galoir was one of his best people. De Castaret had managed to keep him off the Special Brigade that Bourchette had drafted to deal with the art thefts.

Instead, De Castaret had instructed Galoir to work independently in investigating the thefts. Bourchette would be outraged if he found out, but Galoir was shrewd; he wouldn't let Bourchette find out. With luck, they could close the case on their own and leave Bourchette looking like the old fool he was.

Galoir closed the door, and handed de Castaret a copy of yesterday's *Nice-Matin*, folded to the photographs of Emily Cederquist.

"Yes," de Castaret said. "I just met her. Bourchette called her in."

"I know," Galoir said. "I saw her arrive. That's when I made the connection. Regard these." He opened a manila envelope and handed de Castaret a half-dozen glossy prints. They were grainy, made from surveillance videos.

"My God, it's her!" De Castaret said. "But where were these pictures taken?"

Galoir grinned. "It surprises me Bourchette and the others didn't make the connection when they saw her."

"You didn't answer. Where were these taken?"

Galoir was young and husky, an athlete in his school days, now 28. He laughed, and de Castaret recalled what it was to feel that kind of boyish delight over a police matter.

"The photos were pulled from the video security cameras of the Picasso Museum in Antibes. The Grimaldi. The afternoon before the break-in."

"At the Grimaldi! That afternoon! *Merde*! That is something!" De Castaret said. "But of course it's no crime to go to the museum."

"True. But look more closely at the photos. "It's strange what she's doing looking out the window, walking slowly, looking up at the motion detectors. It does appear that she is checking the security arrangements on the window. This window, let me point out, is the very window that the thieves entered."

"The same window? You're certain?"

"The very window."

"It could be perfectly innocent. That window overlooks the sea."

Galoir shrugged. "Some coincidence, yes?"

De Castaret shook his head. "So you think she is one of them, one of this 'Gang of Connoisseurs,' as *Nice-Matin* now calls them? But if she were one of them, then why would she take the photos and sell them to the press?"

Galoir smiled. "As always, you ask the hard questions. I don't know the answers. Not yet."

De Castaret patted him on the shoulder. "I want you to find out for me. But do it discreetly, yes? We need to work around Bourchette."

"Le Gang des Connaisseurs"

EMILY LEFT the police station drained and troubled. From the start, Commissioner Bourchette had been unreasonable, twisting things as if she were guilty. But why? Was he just annoyed that she had made the police look bad?

Still, he did have a point: it had been stupid of her, very stupid, to have said on television that she could recognize the man with the strange way of walking.

Especially when she hadn't mentioned that to the police.

Maybe Bourchette was right: Maybe it would be prudent to move on, to get away from this area. To get away from the man with the limp. And from Commissioner Bourchette and his bizarre hostility.

She stopped at a small newsstand on the Avenue Durante for the *International New York Times*. But the eyes were caught by the big black headlines that dominated the morning's *Nice-Matin*:

ART THEFT AT CAP MARTIN
Ten Paintings Taken From Home of Investor
Loss Includes Two Picassos, Matisse, Renoir,
Others
Second Major Theft in Two Days
"Gang of Connaisseurs" Suspected

At first she thought it was old news, something on the robbery she had witnessed. Then she realized this was a *new* art theft, just last night.

Gang of Connoisseurs. Interesting name for them

She bought a copy, and found a spot in the shade of a palm tree.

The robbery had occurred shortly before midnight, while the villa's owners, British financier Robertson Bosforth and his wife, Juliana, a former actress, were attending a charity dinner in Monaco. A map showed the place: on Cape Martin, a peninsula about twenty miles to the east, close to the Italian border.

The paintings taken were unofficially valued by a local art expert at "perhaps €40 million." That was how much? Around 50 million dollars, maybe more. Not a bad night's work.

Not as pricey as the ones at the museum in Antibes, but then the thieves did get these.

The article pointed out that both this Cape Martin operation and the Antibes theft, the one that she had thwarted, followed the same pattern: well-planned, executed rapidly with military precision by a team of several men.

The article had been reported by Jacques Sabitaille. It was Sabitaille who had bought her photos in Antibes.

Bought the photos, and cheated her on their true value.

Then again, he didn't know they'd be sold to media around the world.

It was Sabitaille who had dubbed the team the "Gang of Connoisseurs."

SHE WAS NEARLY BACK to the hotel when it struck her: *Given that this new theft had taken place last night, then why had Commissioner Bourchette called me in this morning to talk about the Antibes theft? Antibes was yesterday's news.*

Maybe, just maybe, this wasn't really an interrogation.

Maybe it was Bourchette's way of warning me. You're a threat to the man you can identify. If you have any sense at all, you'll get away from this area as fast as you can—before that man finds you.

Maybe Bourchette meant well. Maybe gruffness was just his manner.

Yesterday, after that TV interview, Madame at the other hotel had said almost the same thing: "I wonder, should you have said that you could recognize one of the men. He might consider you a danger."

She had brushed that off.

But what if?

What if they were right?

She was a threat, a potential threat, if she could recognize one of the men.

A sudden chill: last night, the man in the room. It might not have been Jeremy. It could have been someone there to silence her. A big man with a ponytail and a limp.

It really would be smart to pack up and leave France. The Italian border isn't far, I could be across it in a half hour's driving.

She checked her watch: still plenty of time to make the noon check-out.

Pay on delivery

VERA HAD SLEPT RESTLESSLY, wired after the Cape Martin operation.

She kept a bag packed so she could slip away quickly if there was trouble. It would be nice to be working with a second passport, one in another identity, but there hadn't been time or money to arrange that.

Her tension eased when she saw the headlines in the morning's *Nice-Matin*. Good news: they'd gotten away with it, no arrests. Wonderful news. She could finally relax. A little. She fell asleep in a chair. Stoddard's call jolted her awake, heart pounding. "Mission accomplished," he said.

"Where are— Are things in place for me to pick up yet?"

"Not yet, better to let things cool."

"Then when? The client will pay only on delivery. Now we are two projects behind in delivering to him. He is very anxious."

The truth was she hadn't been able to contact Gawbi Al Senour: he was supposed to be here in France, but days had passed and he hadn't arrived at the hotel.

But it wasn't for Gawbi that she needed the paintings quickly; Peter Edleigh needed time to do his part.

"Tell your client this: No pay, no delivery. Any case, I'm busy today, and working tonight."

"Working? You mean another—" She cut herself off before saying operation. A cell-phone was more secure than taking calls through a hotel switchboard, but still you never knew.

"Yeah, working, as in working."

"That person I mentioned to you yesterday. Have you taken care of that situation?"

"I don't know what you're talking about."

141

"The woman, the one who caused the trouble. She said she could recognize one of your people. Have you dealt with her?"

"Yeah, yeah, I'm working on it."

"I wish I could believe you," she said.

"I'll handle my side of things, you handle yours."

VERA HAD BEEN TRYING to reach Gawbi Al Senour for days. Now he was four days late in checking into the Hotel Martinez in Cannes. Had he lost his nerve?

She called the Martinez again, desperately hoping that he had checked in overnight. "Mr. Al Senour will not be staying with us this time," the hotel operator said.

"Not staying there! But I must speak—"

"However, he has left a number where he can be reached."

Vera called that number, a woman answered. From the sound of her voice a young, stupid thing. She said Gawbi was "resting."

"You must wake him and call him to the phone," Vera said. "Tell him it's regarding an urgent business matter."

"What's your name?"

"Just tell him I'm the lady from London."

When the girl finally returned to the phone, she said, "Gawbi says to call him back in a couple of hours, about six o'clock tonight."

"Six o'clock! That's more than a couple of hours! I must speak to him now!"

"Call him then," the girl said, and hung up.

Cape Martin

THE HOTEL EMINENCE lay tucked away on a small cul-de-sac not far from the railway station, a quiet oasis in the midst of the unending bustle of Nice.

Emily was staying there at the suggestion of her mother. It was where she had stayed "way back once upon a time," as she put it—on her own tour of Europe after college. She had kept the postcards of the Eminence and Nice all these years, and asked Emily to take a lot of photos, if she went there— the implication: Please do go there, for my sake.

The Eminence seemed to have changed little over the years. Despite the elegance of the name, it was a pleasant, *Belle Époque* three-star hotel, by no means eminent: no fancy doormen, no pretentions. But it was comfortable and clean, and the staff friendly.

Emily had taken some pictures yesterday, and planned to take a few more today, before checking out. Maybe she could come back some other year, when it wasn't risky.

As she shot the view from up the street, she realized she had included Jeremy in front of the hotel, washing his car. A convertible, metallic blue, with a white top. A BMW, she saw as she got closer.

He looked up and smiled. "Solve the case?"

"Not quite," she said, suddenly feeling better just seeing his smile. He was one of those people who seemed to project energy. Just being around them made the world seem a brighter, happier place.

"As you see, I'm washing the car in the hope you'd like to take a ride down the coast."

"I was just about to—" She cut off before saying she was just about to check out of the hotel and leave France and get away from Bourchette and all of that. She hesitated only a moment. "That sounds like fun."

Is this really a prudent thing to do? she wondered as she walked up to her room for a bathing suit and sun-visor.

Do it! For once in your life do the fun thing, not just the prudent thing.

Besides, even if—a very big if—the guy with the limp really did want to hurt me, what could he possibly do while I'm with Jeremy?

JEREMY FIRED THE ENGINE and wound through narrow streets shaded by tall old apartment buildings.

They emerged into the brilliant sunshine at the *Promenade des Anglais*, the broad boulevard that ringed the bay, and drove east along the wide road, shaded by palms.

The beaches were spotted with sunbathers and swimmers, and Emily again was captivated by the blue Mediterranean breaking onto the shore in long, slow waves, the sun dancing like diamonds on the water. How wonderful to be here, she thought. No wonder Mother loved this place.

They passed under the rocky cliff that held the remains of the fortress of Nice, then circled around the old harbor and took the *Corniche Inferieur*, the lowest of the three roads to Menton, a winding, curving route which clung to the coast through a succession of bustling resort towns. Traffic was heavy, with impatient drivers tailgating, then cutting around against oncoming traffic to gain a few yards.

After Monaco, the road curled around a wide blue bay, the far side marked by a green peninsula. She checked her map. That was Cape Martin, where last night's art theft had taken place. Was it a coincidence that Jeremy came here?

AFTER THE FRANTIC TRAFFIC of the busy coastal road, Cape Martin was like a time warp into the serenity of a country drive in the twenties.

The road was narrow and bumpy, twisting through pines and banks of flowers, fragrant in the warm sunshine. Olive trees cast cooling shade across the roadway. Nearly hidden behind the shrubbery were the houses. Most were in the Mediterranean style of beige stucco walls and red tile roofs.

A helmeted motorcycle policeman stood in front of the Bosforth estate and waved them on when Jeremy slowed. She got a glimpse of a flower-strewn garden and a large villa standing above the sea.

The road at the end of the cape angled down a hill to the blue sea. They parked beside a restaurant and took the hiking trail along the shore back toward Monaco, a city of skyscrapers across the bay.

The paved trail followed the shoreline, shaded by tall sea pines. Gentle waves washed steadily against the jagged white rock, worn and mottled as a lunar landscape. Puffs of wind carried the salt spray against their faces. Sea birds wheeled overhead, crying and shrilling.

A six-foot wire fence, capped with barbed wire, guarded the shore side of the trail. In the space between the fence and the white cliff grew an assortment of pines, cactus, fragrant hay, wild geraniums, and bougainvillea.

The Bosforth villa leaned over the cliff, by far the largest of the houses in the area. A uniformed policeman peered down at them, then wandered out of sight. A concrete stairway led down the cliff-side to a locked gate in the fence.

Emily studied the lock on the gate, but it showed no signs of tampering, though there was a warp in the fence a few yards away, twisting it backward at one point.

"Look at this," she said, pointing to a pair of fresh scratches on the pavement. "Isn't that Just about the width of a ladder? My guess is that the thieves came in and out by boat, and used a ladder to get over the fence."

"So?"

"So, the police are wrong. Didn't you read the article in *Nice-Matin*? The police said they had set cars on fire to block the road on and off the peninsula. But it didn't say anything about them escaping by boat. The police were wrong. Or not telling the whole truth."

He looked at her with what she felt was an odd expression. "It wouldn't be the first time that's ever happened."

THEY FOUND A CLUSTER of small shops and bought bread and cheese and cold drinks, and Emily picked up the afternoon paper, *Nice-Soir*.

They pulled into a shady area to have lunch. She flipped through the paper while they ate. There were additional photographs of the Bosforth villa, this time including the door the burglars had forced in entering.

She scanned the article and summarized it for Jeremy. "There are only two entrances to the Cape. The robbers set stolen cars on fire at each end of the road to keep the police from getting through."

She nibbled on some bread. "Yet the police theorize that the paintings were taken up the mountain and passed to a confederate waiting on the toll road, then whisked across the border into Italy."

"Makes sense," Jeremy said, stuffing more cheese into his baguette.

"Sorry, but it doesn't make sense at all. It's ridiculous. It doesn't tie together. If the robbers blocked both ends of the road, how would they have gotten off the Cape? Those burning cars were decoys. My guess is they came and went by boat, and we just saw where they went over the fence."

"You seem very interested in this stuff."

"I suppose because I witnessed them at work that first night. I almost— I could have caught them, *helped* catch them, if only the police had moved faster."

"The one with the bad leg. Do you really think you could recognize him if you saw him again?"

"Bourchette— he policeman in charge of the investigation. He asked me that today. Yes, I'm sure I'd know him, from his walk."

After a moment, he said, "It's not my business, and I'm enjoying your company, but . . ."

"But what? That I should get away from here? Bourchette implied that, but no. I'm prudent. I'm careful. That's my nature."

Absolutely must have

VERA SPENT AN HOUR in the hotel's health club, working through her exercise routine. That calmed her. Now she could think clearly.

Gawbi would arrive in France, sooner or later.

And if he didn't? There were always other fools with money. As her mother had told her so many times, "You don't have to fool all the people all the time . . . just one person at a time . . . for just long enough."

The priority at the moment was to make sure Peter was doing his part.

SHE WENT BACK UP to her room and rang Peter Edleigh's cell-phone. He didn't pick up.

She showered, then tried again. Still no response.

What did that mean? He had gone to get food? Was he sleeping off a hangover?

Or had he lost his nerve and run back to England?

It was noon now, and there was nothing she wanted more than a drink to soothe the tension she felt returning. But this morning she had sworn off drink for these few days, until this was all over.

She had a salad and tried Peter again. This time he answered on first ring.

He'd rented an isolated old cottage in the hills behind Nice so he could do his work without the risk of a neighbor smelling the paints.

"You heard the news?" she asked. "The new operation last night, at Cape Martin?"

"When do I get the pieces? I need to get to work on them."

"I expect to take delivery tomorrow. You need to be ready."

"Ready? Hell, I've been ready for days, but as I told you, I need the originals."

"I still don't understand why. Why can't you just work from photos, the way you always did?"

"We've been over that, old girl, as you well know. These aren't just to be hung on the Bayswater Road to catch some tourist's eye. These need to be perfect. To bring that off, I need the originals."

"My client—he won't pay until he takes delivery. If we could reduce that delay—"

"Forty-eight hours, I made that clear. I need the originals for forty-eight hours, no less. That was what we agreed to, and that's what I absolutely must have."

Mutiny on the beach

THE FOUR MEN Stoddard had put together as his team—
Bertie Derham, the former British SAS commando; Jorgensen,
the helicopter pilot; California, now shorn of his pony-tail, but
still wearing his trademark mirrored sunglasses; and Vern Billy,
the mean-eyed little West Virginian—again got together at the
beach in Nice after lunch.

The Colonel had called this morning: they would be
operational again tonight—the third time in three nights, and
they were ragged with nerves and lack of sleep. They weren't 20
years old any longer; it was harder than hell to pull an operation
and then go back to the hotel and get to sleep without being
wired till dawn.

Only Derham seemed to manage sleep. Derham loved action.

For the first half-hour they traded stories about last night's
operation at Cape Martin. At least that one had gone off
according to plan—though Derham pointed out the ways he'd
have run it differently.

A beach vendor passed, and they bought all the beer he was
carrying, then sent him back for more. The hell with the No
Booze rule. A little beer wouldn't slow them down.

Tonight they'd be operating down the coast at Le Trayas.
Three operations in three nights was a grind, but better to get
the jobs over and done with and get the hell safely out of France
before the Fuzz got organized.

JORGENSEN FELT A CHILL PASS OVER him when he'd
gotten the call today.

Le Trayas was his big job, the only reason he'd been brought
onto the team, and he'd had a bad feeling about it from the start.

But he didn't have a choice: this was the only work he'd had in months, and he was flat broke.

He knew the others were watching him, especially today, and again he passed up the beer. He'd be flying the chopper tonight.

Never mind, he told himself, keep them happy. He didn't need the beer, he had three bottles of vodka stashed in his room. That would take care of his nerves, quiet the dread that had been gnawing at him since he'd gotten the Colonel's call. The vodka would give him the courage to climb into the cockpit and do what he had to do.

There were a lot of things about his life he regretted, a lot of bad damned mistakes—letting the booze take over was the worst of them, but signing on to this crazy venture held second place in that list of bad choices.

It wasn't until he got to France that he'd learned what was expected of him, the day they took a drive out to the airport in La Bocca a few miles down the coastline beyond Cannes.

By then there was no going back. "It's damned insane," he'd said. "Trying to steal a copter is crazy enough, but that's just the start of it. Fact is, what I see here are all European aircraft, nothing I've ever flown."

"A car's a car, whether it's a Chevy or a Ferrari. Can't be that damned much different with copters."

"You don't know what you're talking about. I'm not qualified on these types, don't know where the controls are located, don't—"

"Just take a flashlight so you can see the controls. All we need is about 10, maybe 15 minutes of flying time. You can hold it together that long."

"I'm trying to tell you it *is* a problem, a *big* problem. It's not just finding the controls under pressure, while I'm in the air, it's knowing flight characteristics, what it can handle, speed, that sort—"

"I don't want to hear that crap. You signed on, you took the money, now it's time to perform. You do your job, or else I'll come looking for you . . . for the rest of your life. You can't hide, just remember that."

That didn't scare Jorgensen—let him come, he'd deal with him. What he couldn't do is let the other guys down. If he bailed, then they'd be sitting ducks for the cops.

And if he screwed up in the air? Then they'd all be dead, charred meat.

Crap! What a mess!

THE TALK ON THE BEACH shifted to griping. Griping about why they were dumped into crummy hotels where nobody spoke English. About never having a night off to spend with the women they saw all day on the beaches—most of them topless.

Griping most of all about the fact that their work last night at Cape Martin pulled in $50 million worth of art, while they were taking all the risks and getting paid peanuts.

Sure, he'd promised big bonuses, but promises were easy to forget. It was easy to disappear before time to pay arrived.

"We're getting shafted, that's what," California said. "Me, I think it's time we spoke up. Hell, without us they wouldn't get nothing. They owe it to us, that's what I feel."

"Suppose you were to complain," Derham responded. "Who would you talk to? What would you say?"

"Hey, gimme a break, shitdamn! To the Colonel, who the hell else? First tell him nice, then if he don't go along, say we're going on strike, something like that, the whole nine yards."

Derham raised his hand, signaling to hold down the volume. Here on the beach there were likely to be people who understood English.

"Tell him you're going on strike, and I'll lay you odds you find an Uzi poking in your stomach before you can blink. Military discipline, he'll tell you, does not permit strikes."

"I beg your goddam pardon, but it's four of us against one. We can take the sumbitch, we work together."

"No way," Vern Billy put in. "He's got control of the weapons. That changes the odds a whole lot."

"Not if we catch him off-guard."

"You guys are talking mutiny, you know that, don't you?" Jorgensen said. It was the first time he had spoken. Until then, he had been in his own world, staring out to sea.

Jorgensen's mood had been bothering California—he'd seen guys go suddenly quiet like that. That was usually just before they bought it—and tonight he'd be riding with Jorgensen in a goddam helicopter. But he made himself forgot about his worry for the moment.

"My old man, he was in 'Nam," California said, his eyes even more unfocused than usual. "Used to tell me about a crazy lieutenant they had, real gung-ho West Point type, always pushing the guys into these real wildass situations. Didn't give a shit how many grunts got wasted so long as he looked good to the brass, the whole nine yards. Well, pretty damn soon ol' Daddy and his buddies'd had enough of that crap, so they fragged the bastard. Next time they got in a firefight, somebody just tossed a grenade the lieutenant's way when he was busy shooting Charlie. End of problem."

"Are you suggesting that here?" Derham asked, his watery blue eyes impassive.

"I ain't suggesting nothing," California said. "I'm just telling what happened one time."

"Suppose we did that, offed the Colonel?" Vern Billy said. "Then what? How do we get paid? We don't even know what the hell he does with the paintings."

"Insurance companies generally are willing to pay for the return of stolen paintings, no questions asked," Derham said.

"How much of a reward?"

"I don't know," he lied. He had researched it all out before leaving England. "Whatever you can bargain for, I expect."

"Jesus," California said, "Suppose we could get them to pay half. What's our total so far, just from last night's operation—$50 million, plus another two mill from Antibes? Half of that's, what? Ten, twenty million or so, split four ways, what's that come out to? Maybe four million for each of us? Not too shabby, right?"

"It's something to think about," Vern Billy said.

Bertie Derham grunted, not letting his annoyance show. From the start, he'd been looking for a way to cut the Colonel out and take the operation over for himself. He was going to do it when the right time came, and he sure as hell wasn't going to share it with this bunch of losers who couldn't even get it right doing simple arithmetic.

Presence

FROM CAPE MARTIN, Jeremy drove to a sandy beach in Menton, the last village before the Italian border. The clear water was refreshing after the hot sun, and they swam in the gentle waves, getting rid of the kinks from the time in the car.

There, walking on the sand, she noticed for the first time that he had a slight limp.

He saw her looking, and said, "Sky-diving, years ago. A gust of wind hit as I was coming in to land, and I bounced off a tree."

After a swim they lay on the sand in the warm sunshine.

There were people whose presence drained you of energy, but there were others who seemed to radiate energy, and Jeremy was a definite energy projector, definitely charismatic.

People like that were great to be around.

But they were also magnetic, even addicting.

She was surprised at how comfortable she already felt with him. She was usually slow to warm up to people, but it already seemed as if she had known him for years.

And he seemed interested in her—asking questions about herself and listening, really listening, to what she said. That was a novelty, to be with a man who was interested in her and what she did. Porter had talked only of himself and his problems and his career, and never asked about hers.

Jeremy's interest in her, his fascination, even, seemed almost too good to be true. There was something about him, his sense of humor, his energy, the way he seemed to give his total attention to their conversation, to be "there," with her fully in the present moment, that made her wonder if this was the chance meeting of a lifetime.

155

Even despite that embarrassing episode in the hotel last night.

"So, what do you do at home?" she asked.

"*Do?*" he laughed. "Who cares? Now, here, I don't *do*. I *am*."

"I mean, when you're not driving around Europe in your convertible, what do you do for a job?"

He laughed. "Why? What difference does it make?"

"A way of getting to know you better, that's all."

"Typecasting me into a job category? We are who we are, not what our job happens to be."

Surprised by his response, she dug into her beach-bag and pulled out a sun-visor and a tube of sun-block. She spread the cream on her face, neck, arms, stomach and legs, then said, "My father's parents came from Sweden, and most of my mother's were from Ireland, so from both sides I inherited skin that wasn't made for Mediterranean sun."

"We don't have to stay—"

"No, no, I love the beach. I'm glad we're here. As long as I have my sun-blocker. You're laughing at me, aren't you?"

"Not laughing. Just hoping you'll ask me to spread some of it on your back."

She stretched out on the beach mattress, and luxuriated in the feel of his hands massaging her back. "It feels so good. I guess I've been very tense." Many of the women on the beach were going topless, and she wondered if he'd try to unsnap her bra. The idea gave her a tingle. But he didn't try.

Finally he snapped the top back on the tube and stretched out beside her. He reached over and squeezed her hand. She squeezed back, feeling very happy.

"What about you? Maybe you'd like some cream on your back?"

"Sounds good. Then let's just close our eyes a bit—the salt water made my eyes sleepy. But promise one thing?"

"Promise what?"

"No nightmares this afternoon?"

"You'll never let me forget that, will you?"

"It is a unique way of luring men into your room."

SHE FELT A PRESENCE looming over her. Commissioner Bourchette. He held her passport in one hand, a lighter in the other. "No, don't!" she said, but he smiled, his eyes again recessing into his face. He touched the flame to the passport and threw it at her. "No!" she yelled, twisting to escape the flame.

She snapped awake. She was sprawled onto Jeremy on the next beach mattress.

"When you throw yourself at a man you are not subtle about it," he laughed. "You're cute when you're having nightmares."

He kissed her, lightly, then let go. "But you have them a lot, don't you?"

"A lot of what? Men? Or nightmares?"

"It's your story, you tell it."

She told him about that Saturday in Chicago. The double betrayal: first at the office, then finding Porter with the woman.

"So you really didn't really pull that trigger? You're really not a fugitive from justice?"

She forced a smile. "I think over here . . . I think we're all fugitives in one way or another. All running away from something, all looking for a fresh start."

Immediately she wished she hadn't said that: it told him too much. Too much to someone she barely knew.

THE DREAM brought back what she had felt in the police station with Commissioner Bourchette that morning: fear, definitely that. Bourchette was an intimidating presence.

But even more, she felt anger, a sense of outrage at the way he had treated her. Not only was she innocent, but had tried to help the police, and they had rejected her help.

It was obvious enough now: Bourchette had lashed out at her because she had made the police look bad. That was why he had been playing games with the passport.

Police whistles

DERHAM HAD BEEN DOZING when something hit his head. A couple of locals, maybe 20, skins tanned to mahogany, were playing beach tennis, bouncing a hard black rubber ball back and forth on the crowded beach.

He let it pass the first time. The ball hit a little boy on the back, and he went crying to his mother. Derham let that pass.

This time the ball hit Derham on the shoulder. It was what he had wanted. He sprang over and grabbed it.

"Them sumbitches been doing that for twenty minutes," California said. "Hitting it hard. With them rackets they got, the ball probably goes sixty miles an hour."

"They don't give a shit, stupid bastards. Hit a lot of people here before you."

One of the players sauntered over and held out his hand for the ball.

"You speak English?" Derham asked.

He shrugged. "A little. Why you ask?"

"So I can tell you this, you stupid frog bastard. If you hit anybody else on this beach I will personally stuff this ball down your throat. *Comprenez-vous* what the hell I'm telling you?"

The boy snickered and walked away with the ball. A minute later, the ball smacked the topless woman sunbathing on the next blanket.

The same boy came for it, wary this time.

Derham let him bend over, then sprang off the ground and slammed a fist into his solar plexus. He fell back onto the beach, gasping for breath. Derham forced the boy's jaws open with one hand, then shoved the ball into his mouth.

159

After a few seconds of stunned silence, a cheer rose from the others on the beach. *"Bravo, Monsieur! Bravo!"* Derham smiled and waved.

"Sure is a nice feeling when you do something good for humanity, ain't it?" California said. "Shoulda just killed the bastard while you're at it, ask my opinion."

As he spoke, California realized this was the first time he had ever seen Derham smile.

But he'd also seen what was in his eyes as he'd been working the boy over, and he knew then that Derham was far more dangerous than anyone realized.

THE IRISH TEAM had been tailing California for two days, since Liam Clancy spotted him. California had led them to Jorgensen, who was staying at the same hotel.

None of them had any experience in surveillance work, so they would have been easily spotted . . . though neither California nor Jorgensen had thought to look behind.

They hated the work. It was boring, sitting for hours waiting for things to happen. Uncomfortable, too, as their delicate Irish skins were easily scorched crimson by the blazing Riviera sun. Their first day here, Liam, enchanted by a sun he had never experienced in the northern cloudiness of Belfast, sat unprotected in a lounge-chair on the Promenade. By evening, he was in agony. Now he wore a floppy straw sun hat, carrying an umbrella to shield his still-painful skin.

He knew the bastards were laughing at him and his portable patch of shade. They took him for a crackpot, one of the loony ones who flocked to Nice. But he told himself, The hell with what anyone thinks.

But now the work was paying off. Now he had all four of the team in sight, and it was just a matter of waiting to follow them back to their hotels. He had phoned McDevitt, and he'd sent Theresa Mullarvey to help.

THERESA AND LIAM froze at the sound of police whistles. Years as fugitives had frazzled their nerves so they lived in a state of constant paranoia.

They relaxed when they saw a pair of blue-shirted cops racing down the steps from the Promenade, nightsticks ready. "*Votre papiers*, your papers," the cops demanded of Derham and the others with him.

It was all over, Theresa figured, when the cops asked for their papers. That stupid Derham, the blood-thirsty bastard, would have to botch things up.

At that point, several people on the beach—older French people—came up and told the officers the story of what had really happened. The officers looked at each other, then put away their notebooks and went after the two boys with the tennis rackets. But the boys were too fast, and got away down the beach.

Derham and the others packed up and got out fast when the cops left.

Liam stayed with Jorgensen and California. Theresa and Matt Gilligan teamed up to follow Derham and Vern Billy as they walked back through the afternoon crowds.

Now they had a line on every member of Stoddard's team, and knew the hotel where Vera was staying. Only Stoddard's whereabouts was unknown.

Pickpocket

DERHAM AND CALIFORNIA, coming back from the beach, were walking up the *Avenue Jean Medicin*, the main shopping street.

It was late afternoon, and the street was crowded with shoppers. They had stopped for a coffee at a sidewalk café. Another operation was planned for tonight.

"Don't mind telling you, I just about shit my pants when those cops came running at us," California said. "I tell you, I just want to get this work over and get the hell out of here. If we screw up, just once, we'll be in jail for the rest of our lives. That don't turn me on, spending years in a French prison."

"If you don't—" Derham broke off and spun around on the street, his arms moving fast.

California turned in time to see a small, dark-haired man slump to the ground, his mouth open in a silent scream. He hit on his knees, then rolled back, his hands clutching at his midsection. Thick brown snakes tumbled out of the open torso. California had seen it before, in Iraq, and knew what the snakes were.

Derham grabbed his elbow and pushed him down the street. People behind screamed. "Don't look back," Derham said, "just walk on as if you didn't see a thing."

"You goddam knifed that poor bastard? That's his guts, they was falling outta him right there onto the sidewalk!"

"He was a pickpocket," Derham said, looking straight ahead. "The bloody bastard was trying to grab my wallet. The hell with him, he got what he deserved."

"But an open wound like that, in the torso— That's real bad. He'll die unless they're real good at the hospital."

"Then the bastard shouldn't have tried to lift my wallet."

162

California froze in place. "My God, you're fuckin' crazy, aren't you? You're a psycho! I didn't sign on to be part of no murders!"

Derham grabbed his wrist and squeezed at a sensitive spot. "Shut your mouth and move on. You're part of it now, you're in it."

MATT GILLIGAN vomited in the street when he saw the guy on the sidewalk, his stomach sliced open, his intestines flowing in a river of blood. Theresa Mullarvey swallowed hard to hold it back, then carried on tailing Derham and California, realizing even more just what a dangerous bastard Derham was.

Special moments

JEREMY ROLLED THE TOP BACK to catch the soft evening air. As they left Menton, he turned off the coastal road, they wound up around the side of the mountain until they arrived at the Upper Corniche road, and the coastline lay spread out far below.

She wondered how he had known about this road. Hadn't he said he only arrived here last night?

They rode in silence, awed by the beauty of the landscape. In the soft light of early evening, the region took on a different aspect, gentled from the hard brightness of the Mediterranean sun. The sea below was silver now, the shoreline marked by the first strings of colored lights. The stark outlines of the mountains seemed smoother in the gentle light of day's end. Fragrant soft air, filled with the scents of flowers, pines, and the salt of the sea washed over the windshield.

This is one of those very special moments in life, she told herself. Pay close attention, soak it all in and store it away

She couldn't remember ever being happier.

HE FOUND a parking space on the Promenade, overlooking the bay, and they sat for a while, just taking it in.

Then they walked, hand-in-hand, through the old part of Nice, nestled under the mountain that had housed the fortress in centuries past. With its narrow streets and overhanging antique buildings, the area seemed little changed in 400 years. They sat on the seafront balcony of a restaurant where the specialty was fish that earlier in the day had been swimming in the Mediterranean.

It was the energy he seemed to project that attracted her, she realized. His vibrancy and zest, were infectious.

What would it be like to live around that energy full time?

Wonderful! Absolutely wonderful!

He reached across the table and took her hand, and she squeezed back, trying to communicate via touch the incredible sense of joy she was feeling.

I could marry this man! she realized. *He's everything I've ever wanted: intelligent, funny, positive. And tall enough for me.*

But is he feeling it for me?

THE WAITER brought an open carafe of house wine. "With our compliments," he said.

Jeremy poured a little into his glass, sniffed it, sipped it, swirled it around in his mouth, filled her glass and pronounced, "Light and fruity with just a hint of bass and treble."

She sat frozen in place, holding the wineglass, thinking, *He doesn't have a clue what he's talking about! Is that wine jargon supposed to impress me?*

She sipped, then said, "Yes, exactly. I suppose."

He laughed. "Gotcha! Your face is an easy read. That description fits you, too: Just a hint of bass and treble, and a knack for spotting what's phony."

They walked along the Promenade above the beach later, and settled in deck chairs to watch night descend over the sea.

A pastel mood settled along the coast, and the day's intensity gave way to a calmness, an acceptance of another day gone, but well-spent.

The sea moved through a spectrum of colors. First the white of the gentle surf breaking on the pebbles of the shore. Beyond, the water was aquamarine for a couple of hundred yards before becoming dark blue. A half-mile out, a band of violet began, and merged into the solid blue that ran to the horizon.

"I'm really happy that we met," he said, reaching across to hold her hand.

"I'm glad, too. It's been a very nice day. And night-- I mean nice evening."

They talked, oblivious to the flow of strollers behind. It still surprised her that he seemed so interested in her life and ideas . . . and that he said so little about his own. So many men wanted to talk only about themselves.

"YOU . . . you don't talk much about yourself," she finally said, cutting off before adding, So many guys, that's all they want to talk about—themselves and their achievements, never asking questions about others.

"What would you like to know about *moi*?" he smiled, that smile that projected energy, fun, enthusiasm for life.

"Whatever. Tell me about yourself. What do you do? What's your family like? Any siblings?"

He laughed. "What do I *do*? You mean for work? What does that matter? You asked that earlier. The way I look at it is life's about who I *am*, not what I happen to be *doing* for a living at any point in time."

"What about when you're at home? What's your ideal way of spending a perfect day away from the job?"

He laughed again. I don't *have* a job—that's why I'm over here. And before that?" He shrugged. "I'd run every day, at least till I hurt my leg. How about you? Do you run? What about exercise? Swimming?"

"Why do I get the sense you're very good at changing the subject?"

"I suppose because I find the best to get to know somebody is to spend time with them, then as they are at the moment. The person in the *present*, not the person in old patterns."

Emily nodded. *Is he very profound? Or very evasive?*

Curving marble staircase

JEREMY PARKED in the reserved area in front of the Hotel Eminence, and they picked up their room keys at the front desk. It was the first time she had seen the night manager, *Monsieur* Rocoquillon, since she had made such a fool of herself last night. She wondered if he recognized her as that crazy woman screaming in the middle of the night.

She wondered, too, what he was thinking when she and Jeremy picked up their room key-cards at the same time, for rooms side by side. Ah, but this is France. The French are open-minded about these things.

Jeremy stepped aside and let her lead the way up the wide curving marble staircase.

Lead the way: to what?

It's been a wonderful day, Jeremy. . .but I'm not into . . .

I've really enjoyed today, Jeremy, but . . . but I hope we can get to know each other better.

It's been . . . but I'm not into . . . into vacation romances.

What romance? He hasn't made any moves. Except to check his watch a couple of times. Why? Was he bored?

"It's been a fantastic day," he said, pausing at the door. "If you're going to be here, well, maybe we can do something again tomorrow."

He put his arms around her, and her face seemed to move of its own volition closer to his.

Her phone rang in her bag.

"Beethoven's Seventh! That's your ring tone? I'm impressed."

"I'm impressed that you recognize it," she responded. It's always been a favorite of mine," she said, checking the phone quickly, ready to ignore it. "Uh oh, it's my mother calling from home. I really should take it."

He nodded. "I understand," he said, giving her a quick kiss on the forehead before going into his room.

"Oh good, you're there," her mother said. "I was just sitting here, thinking of you on the Riviera and . . . I suppose I called just to have you send some of that sunshine over to me where it's been cloudy and rainy all day. What did you do today?"

Of all times to call! "Today I just took it easy, did some sightseeing, went to the beach for a very nice swim. Just came back from dinner in Old Nice."

"Fresh fish, I hope you had the wonderful fish fresh out of the Mediterranean."

"As a matter of fact, yes, we had fish, as good as I've ever had."

"Broiled? I hope you had it broiled, they really do that well there. Oh! You said 'we.' Are you still at the restaurant? Are you there with friends?"

"Just one person."

"One person? Oh, I see. A young man? I hope you met someone really nice. I met someone in Nice, a long time ago. I think you know that. Tell me about him, is he just a friend, or something . . ."

"Another time."

"Oh dear! I think . . . is he there with you?"

"Not exactly, not just now."

"I'm thinking maybe I'd better let you go for the moment. Is that correct?"

"Uh, more or less. I'm glad you understand." As she spoke, she heard Jeremy's door close and his footsteps going back down the staircase. *He's going out again?*

"You will call me with news, developments, won't you? Maybe even send some photos?"

"I took a lot of photos today, I'll email them."

"I certainly wouldn't want you to do that now." She giggled. "Maybe you'll even send me a picture of your new friend. What's his name?"

"Yes, mother, I will for sure. Tomorrow."

SHE OPENED her smartphone and typed "Jeremy Howe" into Google. She hesitated before clicking Search., then stepped onto the balcony for some fresh air.

Definitely Google any new guy you meet—that was wisdom she'd grown up with.

But did she really want to do that now? It seemed like an intrusion. Jeremy, who seemed so . . . so interesting. So charismatic. Why spoil it? Another day or two and they'd be going separate ways, so what did it matter? Why throw a shadow over whatever magic there might be?"

Interesting development

"AN INTERESTING DEVELOPMENT," Inspector Galoir said when he phoned Principal Commissioner de Castaret at home that evening, waking him. De Castaret had lost most of the previous night's sleep after being called out to the Cape Martin break-in.

"I traced the American girl back to her hotel," Galoir said, "and got there just as she climbed into very nice new BMW convertible, and drove off with a young man, maybe 30 years."

"The BMW was metallic blue, with tourist plates? And the man was driving?"

"*Merde*! Yes. How did you know?"

"I have my sources." Maybe Bourchette was right about the young American. He confirmed the license number with Galoir, then told him that this same BMW convertible had been spotted by a police patrol on the Upper Corniche road not long after the theft from the Bosforth villa on Cape Martin.

Still, it didn't make sense. The girl seemed an unlikely art thief. Things didn't tie together. Yet the links were there.

"Where did they go?"

"That's the strange thing. They drove back to Cape Martin, and wandered the area around where last night's break-in took place."

"Then what?"

"They swam at Menton, then headed back to Nice by the Upper Corniche road."

"The Upper Corniche? Really! That's where Le Blanc stopped him last night. Perhaps there is something to the old saying that the thief always returns to the scene of the crime."

"I tell you, it is all very strange. They took dinner by the sea, then back to the hotel in Nice, the Eminence. They're there now, for the night, I expect."

"You've had a long day, too, my friend," de Castaret said. "Time to go home and get some sleep."

"You're sure?"

"Don't you think that's what the Americans are doing—sleeping?"

Galoir chuckled. "Not for a while, I think. There is one other thing: I checked with the Eminence. They are both staying there. In adjoining rooms."

"Adjoining rooms? Interesting," de Castaret said, realizing that already he was pulling ahead of Bourchette. "Then it seems they did not just meet here."

PART FOUR

At the end of a string

THEY HEARD THE WHOMP-WHOMP OF the chopper, and saw it slipping in low and fast across the bay.

California jumped out to signal it with the flashlight, but Derham pulled him back. "It could be the coppers."

"That's not a police chopper. It's got no running lights." He flashed the signal, three shorts, and the copter swung left to center on the light.

It came in fast, then the nose pulled up and it drifted slowly to earth, the blades whipping up the gravel and sand of the parking lot, flooding them with hot kerosene exhaust. It felt like old times. But this wasn't a big Blackhawk, this was some kind of dinky little toy, with pontoons, no less. What the hell was Jorgensen thinking?

They saw the headlights of the police car now, as it bounced along the bumpy entrance road to the museum.

California tossed the four bags of paintings in, then pulled himself up and squeezed in behind the seats. Derham jumped into the co-pilot seat.

Jorgensen gave it full power, but the copter rose slowly, too slowly, and the police were already in the parking lot.

Looking down, they saw the flash of guns in the dark, and heard the plink-plink of bullets hitting the copter. It wasn't armored. They hoped to hell that none of the bullets hit the gas tank.

Derham stuck his Uzi out an opening in the bubble window, and emptied the magazine into an empty corner of the parking lot. It would keep the cops' heads down without doing any harm.

Jorgensen threw the nose forward, and the copter rose slowly. He pointed it at a clearing in the trees. It squeezed through, the tips of the blades whipping the outer branches.

He dropped lower, and they shot across the water, barely skimming the tops of the waves. That low, they wouldn't show up on radar.

But at 120 miles per hour, the water would be as hard as concrete if they hit. One unexpected gust of wind, and they'd be debris bouncing across the tops of the waves.

Jorgensen headed toward St. Raphael, crossing onto shore in the open area west of the city. They stayed low, following the contours of the land until they came to the drop-point where Vern Billy was waiting. His role was to grab the paintings and secure them in a hiding place overnight. That was why his code was "Snatch."

THEY WASTED A COUPLE OF MINUTES circling before they spotted Vern Billy's signal light. Static from the chopper's engine made the cell phone useless.

It was a wooded area, with no place to land. Jorgensen hovered while they lowered the four bags of art on the end of a rope. They lowered the weapons in a separate bag. They were vulnerable without the guns. But at least they would have nothing incriminating on them if stopped. Nothing . . . except one stolen helicopter.

That done, Jorgensen pulled up and flew another few minutes to the second drop-point where the assault team would exit. The escape car was hidden in the trees a minute's run away.

The terrain was again too uneven to risk a landing, so Jorgensen hovered a couple of yards off the ground, and they jumped free, choking in the dust stirred up by the downdraft.

When they were out, Jorgensen saluted, then lifted off. He would head back to the coast, gaining altitude to make himself visible to the radar at the airport. That way, he'd draw the police west toward St. Tropez while the others headed back east to Nice.

Jorgensen would set the chopper down in a remote area outside Toulon, where they had hidden a stolen motorbike. He would blend into the traffic of the city, then catch a train back to Nice.

THE CLOCK WAS RUNNING for the guys on the ground. They knew they should be sprinting for the car. But something kept them watching the copter.

They saw it lift, then pivot to go forward and out over the valley. They yelled when they saw the power lines that Jorgensen did not, and they watched in stunned silence as one of the pontoons snagged the wires.

Sparks lit the sky like lightning as the wires snapped free of the poles, and they thought maybe he was going to make it after all.

Then the slack was used up, and the wires jerked the copter like a yo-yo at the end of a string. It had been rising fast at full power, and the sudden jolt yanked the nose forward.

The craft somersaulted, and the wires hanging off the poles wrapped into the rotor blades.

The copter twisted again, another slow somersault, the motor off pitch, the blades madly flailing for purchase.

It began another turn, but lost its momentum and rolled, slowly gyrating, into the valley, its sick motor still trying desperately to pull it out.

Seconds later, an orange fireball erupted on the dark hillside.

THEY STOOD frozen in place, knowing their clock was running, but unable to look away from the ball of roiling flames down in the valley.

Finally California said, his voice breaking, "Jesus, but I'm so damned tired of seeing people die!" As he spoke, he swayed, then fell to the ground.

"Dammit, get–" Derham started, then cut off when he saw the blood soaking California's pants leg and shoe. "Goddamit! He got shot, he's bleeding like hell, he needs a tourniquet, fast!"

Liquid peace

THE MUSEUM stood on a rocky promontory above the sea, near the village of Le Trayas, a few miles west of Cannes.

The road along the coast here was narrow and winding, bounded on one side by the massive red-rock mountains, and on the other by cliffs falling to the sea. That made it disastrous as an escape route, but perfect for hindering the police response from the *Gendarmerie* a few miles down the coast in La Napoule.

The raiding party would have plenty of time to do their work, then be plucked to safety while the police plodded along that slow road.

The "assault team," as they were calling it, consisted of Derham and California. Vern Billy dropped them off in the village next to Le Trayas, then headed up to wait for them at a spot in the mountains.

They had already targeted a fast Zodiac rubber boat, the tender to a yacht where no one was aboard. Snip-snip and it was theirs to use.

Their radio-code was "Fish."

Vern Billy's was "Snatch."

STODDARD PLANNED his part in each of the operations so he was never in the raiding party. That's what he was paying these guys for, to take the risks. If anything went wrong, he wanted to be able to cut out fast.

He was carrying a false passport so he could slip across the border into Italy without any delay.

After dropping Jorgensen, he parked on the open stretch of beach east of Cannes, by the airport at La Bocca, where his was just one in a string of cars left there by night fisherman, strollers, and lovers. Away from the city and from the mountains, cell phone reception would be clear, so he could coordinate the messages among the three groups: "Fish," "Birdman," and "Snatch."

JORGENSEN, HIDING in the darkness outside the La Bocca airport, recognized the cold feeling within him.

It was not fear. He knew what fear felt like, had lived with fear day in and day out through his tours in Iraq and Afghanistan This was something else, something almost mystical, something beyond fear, a sense of acceptance, almost of peace.

He'd seen people go like this; loud, outgoing guys who, one day, abruptly drew in on themselves. Suddenly silent, thoughtful. But peaceful, detached, as if they knew their number was coming up that day. It usually did.

Now it was happening to him.

He crouched in the shrubbery outside the airport fence debating whether or not to go through with it. He could walk back to the train station in Cannes and hop on a train to somewhere. Get the chance to live another 20 or 30 years.

But he knew he couldn't do that. There were guys depending on him. He couldn't let his buddies down. If he didn't climb in the chopper and go for them, they wouldn't have a chance. They'd be stranded at the museum, sitting ducks for the cops.

Besides, he told himself, it didn't always happen. Some guys got this feeling then came out without a scratch.

He took a couple of swallows from the plastic vodka flask he'd strapped to his leg. For Jorgensen, vodka had become as essential to flying as gasoline. It was aviation fuel for the pilot. Liquid peace to banish the memories. Memories of friends blown away in a flash when a stray shell hit their copter. Images of fireballs on the desert sands, the funeral pyres of other pilots, guys he knew.

THE SIGNAL CAME on the cell phone. Time to move.

Jorgensen pulled himself over the wire fence, and ran twenty yards to the hangar used by the helicopter charter company based there.

He'd posed as a tourist and taken one of their orientation rides along the coast to check out their operation, mentally working the controls along with the pilot to get a sense of how it handled. It wasn't a real check-flight, but it was the best he could manage.

He'd gotten there for the ride early enough to see where they kept the keys to the choppers—hanging on a wall rack, and not in a safe. Dumb thing for them to do. But damned lucky for him.

He paused in the shadow of the hangar to phone the code that he was in place, ready to go.

Then he took another couple of swigs of vodka, climbed aboard the chopper, and began running through the pre-flight checklist. The checklist was in French, but he figured he could figure out most of it.

His radio code was "Birdman."

Marchand goes to the mountain

FREDDIE MARCHAND left the club early, leaving Gregoire to close up for once.

He took long-legged Danielle, one of the dancers, with him. He had a little house at the northern edge of Nice, back from the sea. It was quiet and private there, and no snoopy neighbors.

Having his pick of the girls at the club was one of the fringes of running the place.

The other was the chance to skim off a little for himself. But not too much. He had been in the *Milieu* long enough to know the risks of being greedy. Just enough to make life a little more comfortable.

A couple of hours later, he snapped awake, a strong flashlight searing his eyes. Danielle tried to scream, but one of them clamped a hand over her mouth. They snapped cuffs on Marchand's hands, and dragged him naked to their car.

The road up the mountain was unmistakable: rough, winding, an endless series of hairpins. He had been up that road for his first "settling of accounts" when he was 20, and new to the life.

That first time it was a chemist who had been caught sneaking heroin out of the laboratory. There had been a dozen others since, but Marchand would never forget the face of the chemist, a chubby bald man with huge frightened eyes, pleading to be spared. He was Marchand's first.

Marchand wouldn't plead. He wouldn't give them that satisfaction.

But his knees were rubbery when they dragged him out of the car. Two of them caught him under the arms and pulled him across the rough ground. He was still naked.

It was the top of a mountain above Nice, *Mont Chauve:* Mount Smoke, from the perpetual cover of cloud and haze that hung over it. It had been an artillery site in the First World War, then again in the Second when the Germans held the area. The mountain top was honeycombed with tunnels, used by the military to store cannons and men. It was used now by the *Milieu*–the underworld–as a place to hide cars, refrigerators, TV sets. And bodies.

The locals stayed away from the place. So, for the most part, did the police.

The face of the chemist wouldn't leave Marchand's vision. Now he was not pleading any longer. Now he was smiling, triumphant. He was waiting for Freddie to come over and join him on the other side.

They stopped. The men let go of Freddie's arms. He collapsed for a moment to the rocky ground, but forced himself up, determined to go out strong. He wanted to be remembered for that.

He felt a presence behind him. So it was to be the *garrote*, the cord that choked life away. They used the when they wanted to prolong it, when the punishment called for something more than merely death. They could stretch it out a half-hour, loosening and tightening it so there was never enough air to live, but too much to let you die and get it over with. It was not sadism, just a different sense of justice.

He had been an expert at the *garrote*, but he didn't like it: it was too personal. You had to get too close to the guy: you felt the heat from his body, and smelled the sweat of fear. If you weren't careful when the guy lost control of his bowels and bladder it could splash over you. That was the worst, to get your shoes wet and stinking.

He waited for the leather cord to sear into his flesh, straining to control his sphincters. Get it over with, for God's sake! JUST DO IT! he wanted to scream.

"Freddie," a voice whispered in his ear. He grunted in shock, and his bladder let go. The men around laughed: that was always funny.

It was the Director. Why him? He never came to the settling of accounts.

"You've been cheating us, Freddie, we know that. Now it's time to pay us back."

"I can't pay you back if I'm dead," he replied. His own voice surprised him: it was the whine of a frightened child.

"You're the best man I've got, Freddie, the most intelligent."

Marchand had attended university for a time, had considered even becoming an *avocat*, a lawyer, but it didn't work out. He was bright enough, but could never get much interested in books. Besides, his father had died in prison, a known member of the *Milieu*. His professors made it clear that he would not be welcome in the legal profession.

He had tried a couple of things, then one of his father's friends asked him if he would like to be a private detective. It was mostly running down guys who had skipped out on the debts they owed the organization: gamblers, small drug dealers. He had a talent for it, and they moved him onto bigger things, checking out potential wholesalers in the States for the heroin they rendered in the laboratories scattered around Marseilles, finding lucrative legitimate operations to move in on.

The job in the club was just a resting-place, a spot to let him get back on his feet after four years in an American prison.

"It pains me," the Director continued, his voice still a whisper, intimate, reassuring, the voice of a sad, disappointed parent. "It pains me to think of seeing such a talent as yours lost, snuffed out."

Marchand knew then that this had all been a sham. They had done it to fire him up, to scare him so thoroughly that he would walk on nails to do the next job. This was a foretaste of what he could expect if he failed. Whatever it was had to be very, very big.

Rage coursed through him as he realized how he had been tricked, but even stronger was the gratitude that he would be spared. He would do it, do whatever they wanted.

"You read the newspapers, Freddie? Those paintings that have been stolen. If anyone profits from them it should be us, yes? This is our territory. We want you to find them. Will you do that for us?"

"Yes," Freddie said. "Yes, but of course. Yes."

Bad and worse

WHEN THEY GOT THE SIGNAL that Jorgensen was in the copter ready to take off, California swung the nose of the rubber Zodiac around and drove fast for shore, the craft skipping over the gentle waves. They pulled it onto the rocky shoreline and hid it in the shrubbery.

It would be there as a backup in case something went wrong with the chopper. Not much of a backup, but better than nothing.

The museum grounds were at the top of a fifty-foot cliff. They scrambled up the red rock, then spread out, keeping to the cover of the shrubbery in the formal garden.

California was the first to spot the guard, and he caught him from behind. While he held him, Derham bound and gagged him, then moved on to the museum.

California took cover while Derham knocked at the door. He'd learned some French while in the SAS, and he talked his way in, pretending to be the outside guard. When the door opened, he shoved it wide, and California raced in behind him. They were wearing stocking masks to distort their features.

The two guards inside froze when they saw the Uzi. California herded them into a closet and locked the door.

JORGENSEN COULDN'T GET the damned chopper to fire. He jumped out and phoned Stoddard to abort the mission.

"Too late," Stoddard replied. "They're already in. You've got to go for them. Try another chopper."

186

Jorgensen ran back to the hangar for the keys to the other helicopter.

That was going to be trouble. It was French-made, one he'd never checked out on, never even ridden in. Worse, it was only a two-seater: would it have the lift to carry three guys? Even worse, it was set up with pontoons for landing on water: that slowed it down, made it harder to handle. A hell of a spot to be learning a new aircraft.

When he stepped out of the hangar with the keys, a spotlight flashed in his eyes. *"Police! S'arret!"*

He dove back into the hangar, wishing he had a weapon.

The cop was dumb and eager, and came in after him. Jorgensen let him step through the door, then slammed his head with a computer keyboard. The keyboard shattered, but stunned the cop long enough for Jorgensen to grab his handcuffs and cuff him to a pipe.

DERHAM AND CALIFORNIA had finished their work in the museum and were outside in the pickup zone with the paintings a couple of minutes ahead of schedule, so the absence of a copter's whomp-whomp did not worry them.

Derham punched in Stoddard's number on the cell phone. "Job finished, ready to go home."

"I heard from Birdman. Slight delay, but not to worry."

"Slight delay? Bloody hell, what does that mean?"

"He's in progress, not to worry."

Two minutes later Derham tried again. "Where the hell is he?"

"On his way," Stoddard lied.

In the first backup plan, the team at the museum were to use one of the guard's cars to get away. But tonight there were no cars in the parking lot, just a couple of battered old motorbikes. Scratch Backup One.

The Zodiac boat was their second backup, but they knew they wouldn't have a hope in hell in the raft. Once the cops knew they were out there, there'd be no place to go. The fuzz would just sit back and wait for them to run out of gas, or for first light. Whichever came first.

Minutes ticked by. They heard, faintly in the distance, a police klaxon. It was coming from the east, from the village of La Napoule, the nearest *Gendarmerie*. Seconds later they heard another coming down the coast road from the west.

Derham hit the redial button. "Where the hell is he? Dammit to hell, we need transport, fast."

"No information. Maybe the phone doesn't work from the chopper. Hold tight another two minutes, then take an alternate measure. Your option."

"Our bloody option! Shit! The bloody hell with waiting," Derham snapped. "We should get out of here now. While we still have a chance."

"The boat's hopeless," California said. "Why don't we let the cops run into the museum, then steal their car?"

"Not a bad idea. If we can do it without killing any flics," Derham agreed. "Then they'd really come after us."

When they spotted the flashing blue lights of the police car a half-mile away along the coast, Derham waved them into position. There was no need to explain that he was setting up clear fields of fire both toward the museum and the entrance road. Other cops might be arriving before they could get out. Killing *flics* was bad, but getting caught was worse.

Trust

EMILY REACHED for the phone by the bed.

"It's me, Jeremy. I'm just calling to say I love you."

"Love me? That's a very nice word."

"Technically speaking, it's two words."

"Do you *mean* it? *Really* mean it?"

"From the moment we met."

"Can I really believe you? Can I trust you, Jeremy?"

"You know you can trust me as much as you can trust yourself."

"You won't betray me, ever? Do you promise?"

"I do. And can I trust you?"

"Know that you can *always* trust me, Jeremy. *Always.*"

A DOOR CLOSED SOFTLY. She woke.

It had been such a nice dream.

"You can trust me, Jeremy, as much as you can trust yourself."

Suspicious

VERA WOKE at six after a restless night's sleep, and rang room service to order her usual breakfast of orange juice, coffee, and the morning's *Nice-Matin*.

"Oh God!" she exclaimed when she saw the headline:

ANOTHER ART THEFT: LE TRAYAS
Helicopter Snatches Thieves to Safety
Copter Crashes in Flames. Pilot Killed.

She stumbled back into a chair, oblivious of the waiter. "Now it's out of control!"

"*Pardon, Madame?*" the waiter said, wondering if she would recover in time to give him his usual tip.

"Nothing, nothing," she replied, pulling herself to her feet. "I was just shocked by the headlines. Another big theft, when will they ever end!" She fumbled in her purse for money, her hands quivering almost uncontrollably.

As he took the money, the waiter looked at her with new interest. She wasn't what he had taken her for, not just another divorcee hanging around to meet a new sugar-daddy. There was something going on with her.

Definitely worth watching.

SHE CARRIED THE TRAY out to the balcony. There were already early walkers and joggers along the *Promenade des Anglais*, and even a few swimmers along the long bay.

The morning sun was all that she allowed herself: she had no intention of becoming brown and prune-wrinkled like so many of the women along the *Cote d'Azur*.

She was staying in a suite at the *Hotel Palais-sur-Mer,* the Palace of the Sea, the newest hotel on the beach front in Nice.

She had talked the manager into giving her a corner room, so she had a view both across the Promenade to the sea, and to the Palm Garden on the side. The Palm Garden, the size of a couple of city blocks, was one of the few tranquil spots in Nice, a haven of green grass, flowers, pines, fountains and stately palms.

But there was no tranquility for her.

She had failed to anticipate just how nerve-wracking these days in Nice would be, wondering hour by hour whether Stoddard or one of the idiots he'd hired would make a blunder.

If only she could be safe in London or Washington or almost anywhere except here. But that was out of the question. She had to be here to receive the paintings from Stoddard and pass them through the chain. That couldn't be done from a distance.

Even in the warm morning sun, she felt chilled. It was stress.

I will not, she told herself, I will not drink before mid-day.

She forced herself to read the article on the Le Trayas operation, and to reread it, looking for details that might make all the difference in the world to her. There was no mention of what paintings were taken, nor any estimate of the value of the take.

Then it hit: The helicopter pilot was dead, but what of the paintings—did they burn along with the plane?

And the body: Had the pilot left behind any clues? Could the body be identified and traced?

She went back inside and poured a jigger of vodka into her glass of orange juice. Just one, absolutely just one.

Memorial service

DERHAM WAS FIRST to bounce back from the shock of seeing Jorgensen crash. He pulled California into the car and got under way before the cops could get roadblocks organized.

California's bleeding had stopped after he rigged a tourniquet. After a while the flow eased, and he could loosen it. But there was still the risk of infection; they'd have to deal with that later, somehow.

He'd been too charged up on adrenalin to notice when it happened; now there was pain, but nothing he couldn't handle.

Once back in Nice, they drove around the city to pass the time till dawn, too wired to think of sleeping.

Along the way, Derham realized the smart move would be to check Jorgensen out of his hotel. Sooner or later the cops would identify the body, and trace it there, so best to get his luggage out of reach in case it had any connections with them, or his life back home.

Jorgensen and California had been staying at the same place. California hobbled in, despite his leg, and picked up the keys for both rooms. He went up to change out of his blood-stained pants and pack his own things, while Vern Billy took over packing Jorgensen's. Derham stayed outside in the car.

Vern Billy's first priority when he got to the room was to look for hiding places, maybe find some money that he could tuck in his wallet before going downstairs. There was none, but he did come upon a stash of vodka bottles hidden under the bed. Party time! he thought, wedging them into a suitcase with Jorgensen's dirty clothes, so they wouldn't rattle.

HE PRODUCED Jorgensen's vodka once they were safely in the car. They had gotten no sleep, and their nerves were still on edge. A drink sounded like a good idea, even before breakfast.

"Good a time now as any," California said, so they drove past the airport to the beach at *Cros de Cagnes.*

"The Eric Jorgensen Memorial Service," California dubbed it in the car on the way out. They couldn't just go on as if nothing had happened. Jorgensen was a boozer, a strange guy, but one of them. They felt they owed him something.

They bought coffee to go and some plastic cups for the vodka at a beach-front stand, then sat on the beach where they could talk freely.

They toasted Jorgensen with the vodka he never got to drink, then sat staring at the waves for a while.

California broke the silence. "I tell you, man, seeing that chopper blow brought back some real bad memories, y'know what I mean?"

The others nodded and said nothing. "We coulda been in it, just luck that he hit them wires after dropping us off, coulda just as easily done it on the way in. We'd all been Crispy Critters now, too, just like him. I'm getting too old for that kind of crap, man. I mean I know the Colonel says his organization will get us out if–"

"WE NEED TO TALK ABOUT SOMETHING," Derham cut in. "Question is, why are we the only ones risking our necks? Where is this so-called 'Colonel' in these operations?"

"Back where colonels always are, back where it's safe," California said, his words slurred. The booze was hitting hard after the blood loss.

"The fact of the matter is it's lies, all of it," Derham said. "And we need to face that fact, and watch out for our own skins."

California took another long swallow from the bottle, not bothering with the cup any longer. "You're probably right. All that stuff he told us about the CIA—we don't really know diddly-squat about what's really behind all this."

"It's been bloody obvious to me from the start, I'm surprised you're just now realizing it," Derham said, "He's having us all on, there's no organization behind him, it's all his own doing. He's paying us $5000 for each job, and—"

"$5,000! You're serious? He's paying you five thousand dollars?" California cut in. "I'm getting $2,000, and I had to fight my ass off to get that. You're getting more?"

Derham laughed. "Two bloody thousand? And you agreed?"

"Plus a bonus at the end. $5000. But I didn't have a hell of a lot of choice," California admitted. "The fuzz was after me for growing a little pot up in the mountains, and I'd kinda been on the run for a while, the whole nine yards, y'know."

"What about you?" Derham asked Vern Billy.

"Same. One thou. Still, it ain't too bad. It's sure a hell of a lot more'n I was making at home. Only thing I was ever any good at, being a soldier."

"Right, so you take whatever he feels like giving you, and then what? He walks away with millions from selling the paintings, and the rest of his life he laughs like hell at the dumb twits who took the risks for him."

"Frag the bastard," California said, his words slurring more. "Next mission, we just blow him away."

"I'd rather have the money, thanks," Derham said. "No, we don't frag him. Instead, I say we collect our pay, then take the paintings away from him. Cut him out of the deal."

"Right on, I like that," California said. Then he said, "But where we gonna go to sell the paintings?"

"Wherever he's selling them. We find out who his buyers are, then get to them directly and cut him out of the deal."

"How you gonna do that?"

Derham thought a moment, then drained his vodka glass into the beach and jumped to his feet. "We follow him. Or the art. Or both, if we're lucky."

"Follow him? How we going to do that? We don't even know where he's staying. Or do you?"

"We find out. We work at it. We get lucky. Then we grab it all."

"Sounds good on paper, but you ain't told us how," Vern Billy said.

"I've been thinking about it. Thinking about it a great deal. And we'll talk another time."

Disappointment

EMILY SLEPT through till dawn, for once untroubled by nightmares, and woke with the phrase *Qu'est ce que lui l'American German?* echoing in her head.

A nonsense phrase, she thought at first.

But it wasn't just nonsense, it was something she'd heard somewhere. But where?

What do you know about the American German?

IT WAS NEARLY EIGHT before she woke again. The day was slipping away. Time here was too precious to waste sleeping.

She jumped out of bed, splashed some water on her face, combed her hair, and dressed quickly.

She looked out to the garden, wondering if Jeremy was already at a table. Not yet. Or had he come and gone?

She brushed her teeth, realizing as she did just how much she had enjoyed the time with him yesterday. The weeks of traveling alone had been good therapy after the constant pressures over the three years at TAG . . . and the situation with Porter.

But now I'm tired of solitude.

I'm lonely, admit it. I've had enough of my own company. Now I'm ready . . . but ready for what?

Not ready for an involvement, not this soon, but something light. Maybe . . . maybe something like a flirtation. A summer romance.

She stepped out on the balcony, thinking Jeremy might be on his. He wasn't. She went downstairs: he wasn't on the front terrace, either, but there was a note in her mailbox at the front desk:

I have to go somewhere this morning, but maybe
we can do some more exploring this afternoon???
Jeremy

She was surprised at the disappointment she felt. She was almost 28, not some drippy schoolgirl, and yet . . .

And yet there was just something about Jeremy — his energy, his smile, his *joie de vivre*. Something very special.

Maybe there was something to the old saying: Maybe there really was such a thing as love at first sight. She felt comfortable with him, very comfortable. Far more than she ever had with Porter.

And she got the sense he was feeling some of the same thing.

Well, it would have been nice to spend the morning with him, but she'd use the free time to do some shopping.

Definitely a gift from Nice for her mother. Mom had always talked about how much she had loved her time in Nice on her trip to Europe when she was 22 or so, the year before she married.

Well, if Jeremy wasn't going to be here, then she'd catch up on her French. She walked down to the little newsstand on the corner for the morning papers. It was part of a promise she had made to herself: wherever she was on this trip, she would read through the local paper to improve her French.

ANOTHER ART THEFT: LE TRAYAS
Helicopter Snatches Thieves to Safety
Copter Crashes: Pilot Killed, Others Escape with
Paintings

Absolutely astonishing, she thought as she scanned the article. She followed the story to its continuation on page 9, and there the headline of a sidebar article caught her eye:

Victims of Cape Martin Art Theft Increase Reward

Robertson and Juliana Bosforth, owners of the paintings taken in Cape Martin the night before, had immediately offered a reward of ten percent of value for the return of their paintings. Now they had extended the reward to cover the items stolen from the museum in Le Trayas, as well as their own.

SHE SETTLED at the same garden table as yesterday. The waitress, who doubled as a chambermaid, smiled and signaled that she would be along in a moment. Emily flipped through the pages to follow the cover story. A related headline caught her eye:

POLICE STUMPED
No New Leads
Bourchette Pressured to Show Progress

This article, apparently written yesterday, before the new theft, carried comments by several local figures.

199

The lack of progress was putting additional pressure on Commissioner Bourchette. "France is being bled dry of its national treasures," the owner of a major art gallery in Cannes said. "This must not continue. If the present police leadership is unable to stop this drain, then it should be replaced with others more capable."

Emily chuckled. That paragraph alone was enough to ruin Bourchette's breakfast. That would be wonderful! He deserved it.

But it also reminded her of that meeting with Bourchette yesterday, and his not-so-subtle warnings to get out of France, supposedly for her own good.

Well, too bad. She wasn't about to take off now, not after meeting somebody as interesting as Jeremy.

Even if he did wear worn-out shirts.

But they were *good* shirts, *quality* shirts.

Marchand's first lead

BY THE TIME FREDDIE MARCHAND made it back down from *Mont Chauve,* Danielle had left, taking with her all the money and jewelry visible in the house. She'd been around enough to know what a night visit like that usually meant, and figured he wouldn't be needing it again.

Never mind, he'd get it back from her. He couldn't wait to see her face when he showed up at her door, like a walking ghost.

But first things first. Get the job done for the Director. Make some phone calls, drop in on some people, get things moving. Then stop by and have the talk with Danielle. She'd sleeping till afternoon, anyway.

HIS FIRST LEAD came from an informant in the police, an unhappy sergeant with a taste for things his police salary could never buy. They met in the underground garage of one of the new hotels on the *Promenade des Anglais.*

"There's the young American Bourchette pulled in the other night. The word is, Bourchette's been after him from the start. No one else took it seriously. They thought he just wanted a scapegoat. Now they're beginning to think differently. The name he uses, they think it's a fake."

"The name hasn't been in the papers. Why not?"

"For the same reason Bourchette released him the next day: to let him run, see who he links up with. He has a girl-friend. Her name is Emily Cederquist, also an American. What I hear, she's the brains."

He passed Marchand an envelope. "That's a copy of the transcript of Bourchette's interrogation of her. No, not really an interrogation, just that she appeared in one of his team

201

meetings, and he went after her—so it was informal, but that got transcribed to paper along with the rest. For some reason, old Bourchette really went after her."

Marchand scanned the pages. Does he know something we don't, something about her?"

"There's photos of both of them in there, too. Emily whatever the name, and another American, someone they stopped up on the Upper Corniche only after a few minutes after the Cap Martin job."

Marchand counted out €500 and put the bills on the car seat. The sergeant slipped them into the pocket of his jacket.

"You think the American girl can help?"

The sergeant shrugged. "Who knows? But she's worth a try, yes?"

Before leaving, the sergeant hesitated, then said, "You're not the first from your . . . from your . . . organization asking these questions, you know that?"

It didn't surprise Marchand. The Director liked to set his people competing with each other. He'd play them off, use what one said with another, sow insecurity so they would work harder, make himself look infallible.

"How long ago?"

"A couple of days. When the art thefts first started. You're getting a late start, my friend."

Of course the *Milieu* would not have sat back and let outsiders come in and steal away the crime that should rightfully be theirs.

Marchand was glad that he had not been selected first, and wondered who had, and whether he'd been punished yet for failing.

ACTING ON THE SERGEANT'S TIP, Marchand put two men watching the Hotel Eminence around the clock, ready to follow Emily and Jeremy wherever they went.

He sent a third man to rent a room in the Eminence. It might be handy to have someone there on the inside, someone who could come and go past the front desk.

Warning

EMILY STROLLED through the back streets, pausing to wander through the farmer's market, taking in the variety of small shops and cafes. It was like walking through a travel calendar, only this was real, and she was really here, living it.

She emerged by the *Basilica of Notre Dame de Nice,* a massive stone church that seemed more suited to the grey towns of northern France than here in the sunshine and excitement of the main shopping street.

She entered, remembering her mother's Irish wisdom: Make a wish whenever you go into a new church, and that wish will come true . . . most of the time.

She sat, savoring the peace. A sudden pang of sadness passed over her when she thought of her mother: What wish had she made when she came to this church? Had that wish come true? Or had it been a case of, Be careful what you wish for . . . because you might just get it?

Her parents' marriage had been okay. Not perfect, maybe better than okay. Until the end. They were too different, never should have married. Mother a free-spirit; father a grim Swede, driven by numbers, married more to the bank than to his family.

But if they had not married? Then I wouldn't be here.

She thought about it, then made her wish: That Jeremy really as good as he seems, that he really is the one, and that we live happily ever after.

Even though we've only known each other for barely a day. But I couldn't be more sure of someone.

AVENUE JEAN MEDICIN was the main shopping street, and she sauntered along it, checking out shop windows and people-watching, looking for the block that held *Galeries Lafayette*.

That was where she'd get mother's main gift, a very special gift, a replacement for things she had bought so many years ago, when she was in Nice. Little things, but treasures to her ever since.

She was waiting to cross the avenue when her phone rang. Who on earth would be calling here, at this time? Certainly not Mother, it was the middle of the night back home.

Jeremy? Had he come back early? But how would he know this number?

"Yes, hello?" she said, ducking onto a side street away from the traffic.

"*Ca va, Mademoiselle* Cederquist," a man said in French. "I am Gerard Sabitaille, of *Nice-Matin*. We talked the other night, I bought your story and your photos of the burglary at the Château Grimaldi museum at Antibes, the Picasso museum. Do you remember me?"

"Yes, of course," she replied. *I also remember that you bought them from me and then sold them around the world, and I didn't get an extra centime.*

"The reason I am calling, I think we should meet."

"Meet again? Why? I have nothing to add."

"Ah, no no, of course. But I have some information for you, something that I think is very important, very serious for you."

"I can't imagine what that would be, I'm just a tourist, here in Nice for another day or two."-

"You are staying at the Hotel Eminence, *oui*?"

That surprised her. "How did you know that?"

"That is part of what we need to talk about. Are you there at the hotel now, as we speak?"

"No, I was about to go into *Galeries Lafayette.*"

"A*h, bon!* I am nearby. We can meet at a café for a few minutes, yes? Trust me, it will be worth your time."

Trust. She remembered last night's dream. Can I trust you, Jeremy? You know you can trust me as much as you can trust yourself.

And it's the same with me, Jeremy: Always know you can trust me. Always.

A SMALL COFFEE SHOP tucked away in a corner of the shopping mall on the ground floor of *Nice-Etoile,* part shopping mall, part office building on the Avenue.

Sabitaille was shorter than she had remembered him, and a little more aged. Or tired. And rumpled.

It struck her that this French café was modeled on the American Starbucks chain. *Incroyable!* The French, connoisseurs of the café, now copy American cafes.

But why did Sabitaille choose this place out of the mainstream? Because he was a journalist, and journalists cultivated their sources in privacy. But I'm not a source.

"Are you enjoying your stay here?" he asked after they'd settled at a table in the corner.

"Yes, very much. It's a wonderful place, highly recommended by my mother from her visit many years ago."

He nodded, "Good, good. You have seen today's headlines?"

"I have, and I saw your by-line. You're having an interesting week."

"As the Chinese saying has it, 'May you live in interesting times.' This week is too interesting for me, I've hardly slept since our first meeting, so much happening."

She was silent, wondering, *If he's that busy, why he was fitting this into his schedule?*

"You were helpful to me the other night, you gave me much good information. And I have spoken to management, and they have agreed to pay you more for the photos we used, as they were syndicated and we—the paper—received payment. I had not expected that when we met that night."

He handed her a sealed envelope with the *Nice-Matin* logo. She was tempted to open it, but held back.

"Is that why you wanted to meet? Is that the information you said you have for me?"

"Ah no. Or yes, rather. Part of it. The other part is . . . well, it is awkward, and you must promise to hold it in confidence. Do you agree?"

She took a deep breath, stalling to make sense of this. "I thought it was news sources that speak off the record, not news reporters."

A small laugh, "Yes, it is so. But this is different. Do you agree? I must ask for your word, as what I have to say comes by way of a source in the police."

"In the police? About me? Then, yes, I give my word."

"A certain young man with the name Jeremy . . . Hoge or Howe, I do not know how to pronounce the English. But I believe you know of whom I'm speaking?"

"Jeremy? Howe? Yes, of course I do. Why are you asking me?"

"May I ask how you happen to know him?"

"He and I happen to be staying at the same hotel, the Eminence. We met for the first time only yesterday. And, by the way, how did you know that I was staying at the Eminence? I find that very strange that you should know."

"I know because of what my police contact has told me. How well do you know Monsieur Howe--is that how you pronounce it?"

"As I said, we only met yesterday. He seems okay, a nice person, intelligent. Why are you asking me this?"

"You had never met him before, not in America?"

"No, never. But where are you going with this?"

Sabitaille leaned back in his chair, and slowly looked around. She guessed he was checking for eavesdroppers. "Were you aware that he was stopped by the police near Cape Martin soon after the art theft from the Bosforth estate there?"

It felt as if an explosion had knocked the wind out of her. "No, I didn't know that," she finally managed, trying to keep her voice calm. "But what would that mean?"

"That was a few minutes after the second art theft, the one on Cape Martin."

That was the night she had first seen Jeremy, when she had woken from the nightmare to find him in her room. What time was that? she wondered. Two o'clock, maybe three in the morning.

"I've seen the report," Sabitaille continued. "It seems he had pulled his car off the road on the Upper Corniche. When a police patrol stopped to examine the car, he came scrambling down the cliff-side. This area is just a few meters below the *Autoroute* to Italy."

She nodded, finding it hard to comprehend.

"The police speculate that it would have been easy enough for him to have passed the stolen paintings to someone on the *Autoroute*—that's a fast road like your interstate highways— and, if so, they could have been across the border into Italy in moments."

"If the police thought that—if it really did happen that way— why didn't they arrest him on the spot?"

"That is precisely what Bourchette is asking. *Commissaire Principal* Bourchette, the art theft specialist down from Paris."

She nodded again. Baffled by this whole conversation.

Sabitaille was silent, as if waiting for her to speak. Then he added, "I understand you have already had the rather dubious pleasure of meeting Bourchette?"

"You do have sources, don't you? He called me in and raised hell that I had talked to you, the press and the TV, about what I witnessed at Antibes, rather than to the police. I told him how the police wouldn't listen. He didn't want to hear that. He's not a nice man, not at all. I'm surprised that— I would not have taken him to be France's leading expert on art theft."

Sabitaille shrugged. "A matter of politics, so I understand. But getting back to the subject at hand, your friend Mr. Howe. What can you tell me about him?"

"I can tell you that I find all this very hard to believe. Again, if he really was at the scene, why didn't they arrest him then?"

"Believe it or not, as you will. But the event was documented." Sabitaille passed her a typed police report. She scanned it and found it was just as Sabitaille had said.

"Jeremy is no more guilty than I am," she replied, realizing as she spoke how badly she had phrased it. "Why are you telling me this? What are you suggesting?"

"I am telling you that Bourchette is under much pressure, and is desperate for arrests. He is watching your friend, and he is watching you as well."

"That's totally absurd," she said, her mouth suddenly dry.

"There is something you can do to help yourself. If you are willing."

"What is that?" she asked, already guessing.

"It would be helpful for you to cooperate with the police. To collect useful evidence. It would be a way of demonstrating that you are innocent.

"Collect evidence? You mean evidence against Jeremy? I can't. That would be betraying my friend."

"Ah, but is he truly your friend? Or is he merely using you as a cover?"

THAT STRANGE PHRASE echoed in her mind again-- *"Qu'est ce que lui l'American German?"*

Now she knew where she'd heard it: just before going into Bourchette's office. He'd said it. Something like, What do we know about the American German?

Now she understood what he'd actually said: What do we know ab out the American, Jeremy?"

Eliminate

VERA FOUGHT the urge for a little—absolutely just a little—more vodka.

She was sick with fear, she craved something, anything, to calm her. But she knew she had to keep her head clear.

Her special cell-phone rang a little after half-past ten. That was the phone that only Stoddard knew.

"Number three, ten minutes." Stoddard's voice.

"I've been waiting for your call. Is everything—"

"Damned right there's a problem. Number three. Ten minutes. Be there."

The French police routinely tapped telephones, often at random. Calls on the cellular system were particularly vulnerable, as anyone, police or private individual with the right equipment, could listen in.

That was no problem for routine conversations—they could speak in their own code and no one would understand.

For emergencies, and when they had something detailed to discuss, she'd worked out a system for her communications with Stoddard. They had picked out a half-dozen public pay phones—there were still a few, mostly for tourists—and would use those for any detailed discussions. Calls between two public phones were about as secure as anything could be, particularly if they didn't talk long, and didn't use names.

For her, phone number one was in the railway station, two in the bus station, three and four were phones in the Palm Garden, across the street from her hotel. Stoddard had his own list, for which she had the phone numbers.

She threw clothes on, realizing that it was foolish not to have dressed earlier, just in case of an emergency. Now the nerves were back, and her fingers fumbled with the buttons and zippers.

She allowed herself one more jigger of vodka with the last of the orange juice, determined not to seem nervous when she was talking with Stoddard.

She hurried across the street, realizing as she got to the phone that already twenty minutes had passed since his call. The phone rang as she walked up to it, and she wondered if he was somewhere watching.

"I just checked with my bank," he said as soon as she answered. "They told me you haven't made a deposit yet for that first delivery."

She still hadn't been able to locate Gawbi Al Senour. He was supposed to have been at the Martinez in Cannes since before the first operation, but had not checked in. "Things are happening so fast that my client hasn't been able to keep up with them. But he will, you can be sure of that. Besides, that first delivery was very small, not at all what we planned."

"The point is, I need my money. You've gotten a delivery, and I haven't seen a damned cent."

"I'm working on—"

"Don't just *work on* it, *do* it!"

"But—"

"No buts. I hired you to do a job. If you can't do the job, I'll find somebody else who can."

She was standing in the warm morning sun, yet still felt a chill. "Threats don't worry me," she lied. "I do my part, you can count on that. It's simply that there are some aspects I don't have complete control over."

"Then get control. Fast."

"THERE'S ANOTHER DELIVERY waiting for you at the drop," he said.

"Good, good," she said.

"To be very clear, this is the absolute last until I get paid. Is that clear?"

"Yes, yes, of course."

TO CHANGE THE SUBJECT, she said, "There is an interesting new development. The police are quite interested in someone."

She was pleased to hear his sharp intake of breath. She got his attention. Let him share some of the worries. "Interested? Who? One of my guys?"

"I don't know who your 'guys' are, but I doubt it. But I think it raises some very interesting possibilities."

"You mean like setting some other person as a scapegoat? That'd be good, take the heat off us."

"Precisely."

"How're you going to do that?"

"Leave it to me," she said, pleased that she had regained the upper hand so easily. "As for the American girl, what have you done about her? I've seen no mention of unfortunate accidents in the newspaper."

"I'm working on it."

"To use your own words, don't just work on it, do it. Get her out of the way. Eliminate her," Vera snapped, feeling the vodka, and hoping her words weren't sounding slurred. Immediately she wished she hadn't used the word "eliminate."

SHE WENT to another phone and called Peter Edleigh, telling him to be ready for a delivery from her in an hour or less.

She went to a third phone and called the Martinez in Cannes. Gawbi Al Senour had still not checked in, and the hotel had no idea how he could be reached, or when he would arrive.

Trail of evidence

EMILY LEFT the session with Sabitaille dazed, disbelieving what he had told her about Jeremy, yet afraid that it just might be true.

She needed to think things through, to compose herself before facing Jeremy. Despite what Sabitaille had told her, despite even reading the police report that he had been stopped that night so close to Cape Martin, she was still inclined to believe he was innocent.

But do I really believe he's innocent? Or am I just *wanting* to believe him?

Heading back to the hotel was out of the question: Jeremy might be back by now, and she wasn't ready to face him. Not yet. Would she ever be ready?

GALERIES LAFAYETTE occupied the whole of a city block on the Avenue, an ochre stucco relic of another era, complete with shaded arcades.

She spent some time wandering the floors, just getting a feel of the place her mother had talked about so often over the years. She snapped some random shots to send to send later.

But she couldn't blot out what Sabitaille had suggested. Jeremy might not be the person he seemed to be. He might be drawing her in, using her as cover.

Focus, she told herself. Focus on the task at hand: get Mother's gift.

From her long-ago visit to Nice, her mother had brought back several of what she called her "nice Nice washcloths"—washcloths that were doubled-over, sewn into terry-cloth mitts. Hers were worn now, threadbare from three decades of use.

215

There would be nothing, Emily knew, that she would appreciate more. Of all the gifts that she would bring, these would be Mother's favorite.

Clearly, those few days in Nice had been one of the high-points of her life. Why? Emily wondered, not for the first time. Was it just the sunshine and colors and flowers and sense of adventure? Or something more? A special romance?

She found the wash-mitts on the third floor, and bought a half-dozen in assorted bright colors, colors that matched the buildings that radiated the warm Riviera sunshine.

STILL NOT READY to go back to the hotel and risk running into Jeremy, she bought a *Pan Bagnat* from a little shop on a side-street just off the Place Massena and brought it over to eat at a bench in the Palm Garden, officially the Albert the 1st Garden of Palms. Curious, she thought, still trying to distract herself: Didn't the French Revolution wipe out the aristocracy? So who was Albert 1st?

"Pan Bagnat" was another of the French specialties she'd been hearing about from her mother since childhood. "It's just a sandwich, but what a sandwich! *C'est magnifique!"*

A round crusty loaf oozing olive oil and vegetables and tuna and anchovies. It was good. If a little messy.

She snapped a picture of it on her smart-phone before taking the first bite, something else to send to her mother.

WHEN SHE FINISHED, she wiped her hands to sop up the olive oil, then started dialing her mother's number in Minnesota. She caught herself before the first ring: it was midday here in Nice, but still only five in the morning there.

Phone in hand, it occurred to her that she had never Googled Jeremy.

Strange. She Googled everybody, people she worked with, sometimes just people she encountered on planes or along the way. Amazing what turned up sometimes.

But not Jeremy. There hadn't been time in these—what? Not even 36 hours.

Now she had the time she needed, and not a moment too soon. Maybe too late.

She hadn't seen it in print, but his name was probably spelled the usual way: H-O-W-E.

Jeremy Howe was on Google, pages and pages of people named Jeremy Howe, but nothing fit the one she knew.

Then she remembered: his real name was Jeremiah, Jeremy was only a spin-off. But again pages of Jeremiah Howe, and none fit.

Here they come, Darnit and Howe—what the other kids said when they saw him with his brother, Andy. And his name was Darnton, he'd said. From his mother's side.

She tried Andrew Howe—nothing useful. Darnton Howe— nothing useful.

She tried Linkedin, and then Facebook listings. Nobody matched the Jeremy Howe she knew.

SHE SWITCHED THE PHONE OFF to save the battery, then sat quietly, pondering what to do, taking in the passing scene.

A few businessmen with briefcases, wearing suits despite the warm sun.

Strolling tourists of all colors and nationalities.

Arab women covered head to toe walking behind their husbands.

Babies in strollers, some pushed by young mothers, others by older nannies.

And one man with a limp, a very distinctive limp.

Could it be? Could it possibly be the man she had seen before outside the Picasso Museum in Antibes the other night?

Now he was walking with the aid of a cane, and seemed to be having a very hard time moving, much more so than the other night.

But there was no blond ponytail.

That would have been easy enough to get rid of.

He passed close by, close enough for Emily to hear him speaking English into the cell-phone he held to his ear. American English.

She let him get a bit ahead, then quietly rose from the bench and followed.

Curious. He was walking slowly, but obviously intent on something. He came out of the Palm Garden, then turned to cross the *Avenue Verdun*, crossed again, and then again, heading now up the *Avenue Jean Medicin*, back toward the *Galeries Lafayette*. He seemed to be walking in a big circle around the square city blocks

He turned suddenly, heading east along the *Rue Gioffredo,* but his eyes were focused on the shaded arcade of the *Galeries Lafayette* across the street.

He still held his cell-phone to his ear.

At the end of the block he suddenly ducked into a shop doorway, phone still to his ear. She realized then that he wasn't just strolling, he was following someone. Someone who had suddenly cut back across the *Rue Gioffredo*, now headed back toward the sea.

A woman, a petite, blond, well-dressed woman was the only person in sight ahead at that moment.

Once the woman was out of sight, the guy with the limp emerged and hurried after her, half-jogging now despite the limp, his phone still to his ear.

Across the *Avenue Felix Fauré*, a zig-zag route through the *Espace Massena*, a park. Then the woman suddenly settled on a shaded park bench overlooking the six massive fountains. The guy kept going straight and disappeared behind the fountain spray.

After a minute or so, the woman stood and retraced her steps, scanning the area.

Now there was no sign of the man with the limp. Had he given up? Or had someone else replaced him?

STAY WITH THE WOMAN, forget about anything else.

The woman took a circuitous route, across the park to the *Avenue Jean Jaures*, then a detour down into the fringes of Old Nice, then back up again, pausing from time to time to turn and look behind. Without a doubt, she was checking for a tail.

But why? Who was she?

No sign of the man with the limp, no indication of anyone who might have taken his place.

Emily was blocked by a bus turning onto the street; and when she looked again the woman was gone. She was in front of a boxy concrete building overgrown with vines. A bus pulled around the corner; Emily realized this was the city central bus terminal.

She hurried inside. It smelled like a bus terminal for sure, with dead air and rows of drab plastic seats occupied by tired people with bags and suitcases.

But no sign of the woman. Emily hurried to check each of the gates. Still no woman.

She looked back in time to see the man with the limp hobble across the floor to take a seat in the corner. He looked weak, wiped out, as if he was struggling to keep going. The phone was still held to his ear. Now he snapped alert, eyes focused on the bank of lockers on the far wall.

Emily followed his eyes: a woman with flowing dark hair was pulling a large suitcase out of a locker. She wore a floppy straw hat and a garish blouse—a disguise thrown on in the ladies' room. But his was definitely the blond woman she had seen earlier, now with dark hair.

She rolled the bag along the tile floor to the taxi entrance. The limping man spoke urgently into his phone. Emily ducked out another entrance, then cut around the building to the taxi rank.

The woman climbed into the first cab waiting, an old red Mercedes diesel. She insisted on keeping the bag with her on the seat beside her, and not in the trunk. Interesting.

Emily hurried to the cab rank and jumped into the next car, pushing past a blond man with icy blue eyes. He started to speak, but she cut him off, "Sorry, emergency."

"Follow that cab," Emily said in French to the driver. "The old red Mercedes."

The driver turned in the seat to look at her as he drove, then grinned. He was sixtyish, grey-haired, with a three day stubble of beard and a dead yellow cigarette stump glued to the corner of his lips. Despite the day's heat, he wore an old brown leather jacket. "*C'est incroyable*," he laughed.

"Incredible? Why?"

"For twenty years I have been driving the cabs, yes? But never until now has anyone said 'Follow zat cab.' It happens in the films, but never before for me. You are a—what zey say?—a private eye?"

"No, not really. Just following a friend of a friend."

"Another woman, yes?"

"As a matter of fact, it is another woman."

He shrugged, making a clucking sound with his tongue. "Too bad. *Mais c'est la vie.* That's life."

Transfer point

IT WAS NOON, when offices and many shops were closing for a two-hour break, and traffic was heavy and slow. The midday heat, the glaring, sun, the thick diesel fumes from the busses, the explosive exhaust of the motor-bikes buzzing past, and the cacophony of a hundred shrill horns combined to push the drivers into a frenzy.

It took nearly ten minutes to go the few blocks from the bus terminal to the railway station.

Emily held back as the woman emerged from her cab, scanned the area briefly, then dragged the suitcase to the luggage storage room at the far side of the station.

The woman seemed nervous, on-edge, glancing around as she moved. Was that a sign that this was not just an ordinary suitcase stuffed with clothes?

Emily paid the driver and hurried over into the shadow, an idea forming. She had a shopping bag holding only the washcloths from *Galeries Lafayette*. She could buy more later if she had to leave these.

For the idea to work, she had to be next in line after the woman at the counter in the luggage room to be sure to get the next numbered ticket.

Then, when a different attendant was on duty, she would return to claim the bag she had checked. The attendant would take her ticket and come back with her beach bag. "No," Emily would say, "this isn't my bag. Mine was a big, heavy blue bag. There was another person checking a bag when I was there: perhaps the other clerk got the tickets mixed up? I can describe my bag."

But the woman—who she would later learn was Vera de Cochin-Jessup—upset the plan. Instead of going into the

222

luggage room, she went to the bank of coin-op luggage lockers down the hallway.

Too bad, nice try, Emily thought. *So what's Plan B?*

She walked through the storage room and got a glimpse of Vera lifting the bag into one of the lockers. It was on the end of the row, second level up. Easy to find.

She ducked into the next bank of lockers, and fumbled in her bag for some coins, just to have ready. These were the new kind of key-less lockers: they printed out a receipt containing a four-digit code.

She heard Vera's coins clink into the collection box, and the buzz of the master computer printing out the receipt.

Seconds passed. She didn't emerge. Emily walked past, and saw the woman writing something on the inside page of a newspaper. Peculiar.

Emily followed as Vera crossed the plaza in front of the station, and waited for the light to change at the *Avenue Thiers* crossing. She tossed something into a small trash bin on the side of a light pole. Could it be the receipt from the locker, the receipt containing the locker combinations? Had she been copying the combinations into the newspaper?

The light changed, and the woman crossed. Emily dug into the disgusting junk in the trash bin: cigarette butts, used gum, and other stuff she didn't even want to look at. But right on the top she spotted a little wad of white paper.

She opened it on the spot. Print-outs from the lockers, computer-stamped with code numbers and time of rental, two minutes ago. This had to be the one she'd tossed.

But why toss the receipt away? Why transfer the codes to a newspaper?

SHE FOLLOWED the woman through the twisting streets by the station, then saw her turn in at one of the big sidewalk cafes on the Avenue and take a seat on the back row.

Emily slipped in the side door of the café, and found an indoor table where she was partly shielded by a pillar.

The waiter brought the woman a tall glass of something. Emily realized how thirsty she was and ordered a coke.

The woman pulled a newspaper from her bag, flipped through it briefly, and set it on the table.

The newspaper on which she'd scribbled locker code!

After a couple of minutes, a man settled at the table next to the woman's. He seemed shabby. Not a street-person, just rumpled and shaggy-haired.

He and the woman didn't speak, didn't look at each other. Emily thought about the bag waiting in the locker at the railway station.

The way to play it from here seemed obvious: go back, use the combination, open the locker, make sure the bag really held paintings. There were rewards being offered. Phone Sabitaille with the tip, he would serve as her witness to be sure she collected.

She stood to leave. At that moment, the man turned to Vera and said something. Emily eased back into her chair. Vera nodded, and handed the man her newspaper.

Emily felt excitement swelling inside. *This was it! This was the transfer point! That was why the woman had taken the time to copy the locker code into the newspaper!*

But what was the man's role? Was he the ultimate buyer, or just another link in the chain? He didn't seem the type to have money to invest in art, stolen or otherwise. But that could be a disguise.

She left some coins on the table for the waiter, and hurried back to the railway station. If she moved fast, and with a little luck, she could secure the paintings, then get back to the café before the man and woman left.

With a lot of luck, she might even be able to follow one of them to the next link in the chain.

IN THE RAILWAY LOCKER ROOM, she punched in the numbers from the slip she found, and the locker clicked open, revealing the blue suitcase. It was secured by only a cheap lock.

She used a coin to spring the lock and peeked inside the bag: Paintings, some rolled, a few still in frames.

She moved the bag to another locker in a different row, slid in the coins, then hurried back to the café.

Slip

THE WOMAN WAS GONE when Emily returned to the café, but the man was still at his table flipping through the newspaper. The waiter brought him another beer.

Emily settled at the same table as earlier. After a minute, the woman emerged from the toilets, now dressed as she'd been earlier—a petite, well-dressed blond—before her earlier quick-change at the bus station into the straw hat and garish blouse.

A change from one persona to another, then back again.

The waiter arrived to take her order. "Sorry, I've changed my mind," Emily said. The waiter raised his eyebrows and shrugged.

The woman walked out the front entrance to the Avenue. The man at the table watched her, but she didn't acknowledge him. Emily followed as she headed back toward the sea. It was hard to tell her age. Flowing blond hair, good petite figure, confident perky walk.

Emily watched as men turned to catch another glimpse of the woman as she passed. She was striking, no question of that. What age? Around 40, plus or minus.

Emily stayed on her trail through the arcades before the Place Massena, then through the verdant, flower-bedecked Palm Garden. As they neared the Promenade, Emily closed the distance between them, guessing she was heading for the new *Hotel Palais-sur-Mer.*

She was right, and was close enough to hear the woman ask at the desk if there were any messages for her room: "*Quatre cent-vingt.*" 420.

"*Votre-nom?*" the clerk asked as a security check.

"Vera de Cochin-Jessup," she replied, obviously annoyed at not being recognized.

He handed her the room key, along with a yellow message slip.

EMILY DROPPED onto a soft leather sofa to get out of sight. Vera went directly to the elevator without looking back. While waiting for the elevator to come, she scanned the message slip, crumpled it, and tossed it into the trash receptacle.

As soon as she disappeared into the elevator, Emily hurried over to the receptacle and pulled a handful of message slips from that trash receptacle.

A bellman materialized. "May I help you?" he asked in French, his tone suspicious.

"I'm staying here," she replied in English. "A few minutes ago, I got a message from the desk and stupidly threw it away without keeping the phone number."

"*Ah, oui, oui,*" he said, and faded away. She waited until she was back out on the street before unfolding the slip:

Mme. Vera de Cochin-Jessup, Room 420.
Mr. Gawbi called and said he is eager to see the items.

Michael McGaulley

Urban surveillance

DERHAM CAME ON THE RUN when Vern Billy called, and caught up with them at the big café on the *Avenue Jean Medicin.*

He slipped in a side entrance, and spotted the woman they had been following at a table at the front. He settled at a table inside and ordered a coffee.

Out of the corner of his eye, he saw a tall woman stand from another table, then suddenly sit again. He turned to look at her over the top of his newspaper. Something about her seemed familiar, but Derham couldn't place it. Tall, flowing dark red hair—chestnut hair.

He walked over to the toilet, stayed in only a few seconds, then returned, catching a view of her face. He'd been trained in the SAS not to react to surprises, but this threw him off stride.

He'd seen her picture in the papers and on television, the American who'd screwed up the Antibes operation. What was her name? Emily something, Emily Cederquist, that was it. Sounded Scandinavian.

Now she stood again, this time hurrying out of the café. He followed her back to the railway station, and watched as she transferred the bag from one set of lockers to another.

But what the hell was she doing in the middle of this? He had assumed that she was simply what the news reports had said: That she just happened to be looking out the window at Antibes. But that had to be wrong; she was mixed up in, somehow. But how? A police agent? Not likely.

THE SAS HAD TRAINED Derham in urban surveillance techniques, but it didn't take skill to follow Emily and the woman she was following. Neither bothered to check behind.

He followed them both into the *Hotel Palais-sur-Mer*, but hung back as a precaution. He wasn't close enough to hear the woman's name when she asked for her room key.

He saw Emily retrieve the crumpled message slip, and was impressed. She wasn't a professional at this game– otherwise she'd have checked behind along the way. But she was smart. That made it interesting. Did she know enough already to make it worthwhile grabbing her?

She kept the message slip, didn't throw it back in the receptacle.

He followed her back through the pedestrian zone, and held back as she stopped for an ice cream cone from a vendor. She finally tossed the pink message slip in the vendor's trash bin.

Derham closed in fast behind her, and ordered a cone for himself, a double, and grabbed the pink slip out of the trash while the woman was scooping out his raspberry and lemon.

Vera de Cochin-Jessup. Room 420. Now he had a name. Who the hell was Mr. Gawbi? But he was "eager to see the items."

This was looking very good, very promising.

And the young American, Emily Cederquist—obvious enough that she was in it, involved somehow if she was following Vera de Cochin-Jessup.

Involved somehow, definitely worth keeping an eye on.

Disaster

PETER EDLEIGH lingered at the café, nursing his third beer, dreading the walk over to the rail station to pick up the next batch of paintings. That's where the risk was, at the transfer points. He'd done jail-time for his forgeries; that was bad enough in England, but a French prison would be living hell, he was sure of that.

It had been a royal pain that the first operation, the Antibes operation, had fallen through– damn the American girl! He'd had his work done, the key paintings from the Picasso retrospective copied and ready to deliver. Those weeks, preparing, working from the best copies he could find, had been the hardest he had ever worked in his life, up before dawn to get the good daylight, then going on sometimes till midnight cleaning up the details, even sitting for hours running a hair-dryer to harden up the paints.

And then the whole damned batch had been useless because some neurotic bitch got up to take a pee at the worst possible moment.

Good that he had done some of the back-ups, just in case.

VERA WANTED forgeries to pass on to her client: It was Edleigh's job to produce them. The client would think he was getting the real thing, of course, and would pay. But he'd get only the copy, and Vera would keep the original for herself, to resell later.

That had been Vera's plan.

But she had overlooked one factor: simply that two could play the same game.

That had come to him in a flash that first morning back in his flat in London: He could do the same to her, passing her one forgery for her client, and another copy for herself. That way, he would get to keep the original. It was a bit more work, but had the chance of taking care of him for the rest of his life.

The client would never know the difference, and—with any luck—neither would Vera, until too late. He knew Vera: So damned arrogant. The idea someone else might have half a brain would never cross her mind.

It seemed almost too good to be true. Vera had never been naive, yet she had handed over this opportunity on a silver platter.

THEY WEREN'T ATTEMPTING to copy every painting that would be stolen. There wasn't time enough for that, not with only few-weeks' lead time. They were focusing on the better, more marketable pieces, the comfortable lesser works that might sell on the open for market for somewhere in the under $1 million range. The big pieces were too recognizable; everyone was on the watch for them. Not so with the marketable items they were pulling out for their little scam within a scam.

EDLEIGH COULD POSTPONE IT no longer. He walked to the terminal, his knees so weak it seemed they were about to collapse. He strolled the length of the terminal, inside and out, alert for any signs of a police stakeout. All looked in order.

He walked past the bank of lockers and glanced in: nothing, other than a couple of back-packers trying to squeeze two big packs into a single cheap locker.

He took a deep breath, found Vera's locker, and punched in the code from Vera's newspaper.

The lock failed to snap open. He tried it again. Still nothing. He tried again, and heard an alarm sound somewhere.

He stood, his panic growing.

A man in workmen's blue appeared and said something in French.

Edleigh shook his head.

The attendant kept speaking in rapid French.

"I– I—" Edleigh responded. His voice sounded odd, and he knew he had never been as frightened since childhood. It felt as if he was going to lose control of his bowels.

An older woman who had arrived with a suitcase offered to translate. She listened to what the baggage clerk had to say, then repeated it for Edleigh.

"He is asking if you have a problem. You tried three times with the wrong code, and that set off a signal."

"Tell him," Edleigh said, trying to get his breath, "that I have a bag in this locker, and now the lock won't let go."

"When did you put it in?" she translated back.

"About an hour ago, maybe a little longer."

The attendant bent over and checked the locker. "No, this locker was only rented much more recently than that. See, there is still much time left."

"But I had a bag in this locker, I'm sure this was the one."

"You have the receipt?"

"I threw it away. I just kept the numbers." Between the breathlessness and pounding heart, Edleigh wondered if he was starting a heart attack.

"Then perhaps you have the wrong locker. Describe your bag."

"I can't. My— it was my wife who put it here."

"Then perhaps you should talk with your wife, yes? Perhaps she used a different locker."

Think first, drink later

"THAT IS THE LOCKER I tried," Edleigh said as Vera bent over to punch in the code. "And the same code. I'm sure I got it right."

She tapped in the code and pulled the handle. It didn't release.

"It's obvious enough that the lock is jammed." She walked to the luggage room next door, and asked for help. A different attendant come out this time, and brought with him a print-out of when the lockers in that bank had been rented.

He pointed out the time of her rental: at 12:17 P.M. "Yes, that is correct, that is when I put the bag in, I'm certain of it."

"And then you opened the locker and ended the rental at 12:43 P.M. the same day, not yet one half-hour later."

"Opened it! My God, no!" she said, stumbling back in her shock. "No, no, I did not take it out! It's impossible! You—Peter—you were still with me then, in the café. It's obvious that someone broke into this locker and stole my bag!"

The attendant shook his head. He was about 40, with a big droopy black moustache that made him look intensely sad. "No one could have broken in, Madame. Regard—there is no damage to the door. Most certainly, if anyone got into the locker, then they used the correct combination, of that we are certain. Then this locker was open for a few minutes and someone else rented it."

She saw herself, wadding up the little slip of papers that the lockers had printed out and tossing it into a trash can just before she crossed the street. That little slip held the combination for the locks.

"My God, oh my God!" she said, stumbling out of the station.

Peter Edleigh caught up with her, and put his arm around her to steady her.

"That was no accident, Peter," she said, her voice quavering. "Someone followed me. They knew what they were doing. Someone is doublecrossing us!"

"Who?"

"How would I know!"

"They may be following us now."

"Oh God, Peter, what are we going to do? I need a drink, oh God, I desperately need a drink!"

"No, old girl, this time we think first, drink later."

THEY SETTLED in the cheap buffet restaurant of the rail station to think. It was noisy and anonymous, and they could talk freely. She wished they had gone to a café. She desperately needed a drink to calm her so she could think clearly. All she could get here was beer or cheap wine. It would have to do.

"This is an utter disaster," she said. "These were all the . . . uh, all the items that came from Le Trayas. As you know, worth to us several million, and I just got a call from my client, and he's finally ready to take delivery, and he's counting on these, and his money is ready."

"He's only now ready to take delivery?" Edleigh said. "You told me yesterday that he'd already taken delivery of the first pieces, and payment was in process."

"Yes, well," she said, realizing she had blundered. She had told one set of lies to Stoddard, a different set to Peter, and now she was so stressed she couldn't remember which was which. "The point is I must deliver these paintings to my client.

Otherwise, he won't pay. You must have misread the numbers. You *must* have."

"Perhaps you wrote the wrong numbers, that's always possible. Do you have the receipt? That's what we need."

"I threw it away."

"Threw it! Why?"

"Because it was incriminating. Some numbers on a newspaper, they couldn't prove anything from that, but if I were caught with the actual receipts, well, it would be tantamount to be caught with the paintings."

"You say your client will pay as soon as he takes delivery? When will I get paid?"

"Immediately, of course."

"That's what you've been saying all along."

"This time I will see that you get paid as soon as I do."

"THERE MAY BE a way out of this," Edleigh said after a while.

"Tell me."

"But I haven't been paid yet."

"I said I'll see that you got paid in full. Tomorrow."

"The check is in the mail—is that the expression when you're stalling paying somebody?"

"I don't understand."

"I probably shouldn't, not until I see the money, but I'll tell you a secret. I already have a set of copies of some of these. We could delivery them to your buyer even though we don't have the originals, provided I get paid on the spot. In cash."

"But– but I thought you needed the originals for 48 hours to make your copies. That's what you told me. How could you already have the copies made if you didn't have the originals to work from?"

Still shocked by the turn of events, Edleigh hadn't thought it through before making the offer. He had insisted on having possession of the originals for 48 hours, claiming that he needed to have them to copy from. That was a lie. The real purpose was to get possession of the originals so he could make the switch, passing her back the second set of forgeries in place of the real paintings.

"You told me you needed the originals to copy from," she accused when he was silent.

"Well, rather, actually not this particular bunch–not as I knew them so well. I did some on my own. For practice, you see. It's simply that I haven't compared them, item by item, with the originals. I can have them to you within the hour."

"You're certain they're good enough?" Anything at all would pass Gawbi Al Senour's inspection. The risk was that the other investors he had brought in–people she had not met–might be more astute.

They might even be smart enough to have hired an expert to look the things over. Or have enough savvy to notice that the paints were not really dry, not through, only what could be done with a hair-dryer and a couple of hours in a low-bake oven.

"You know the quality of my work. I haven't let you down on these. Trust me," he said, hoping she was too stressed to think.

"But if these are so perfect without your having compared them with the originals, then why did we take the risks of passing the copies and originals back and forth each time? It was you who insisted on that."

She wouldn't let that go, the bitch! He nodded, groping for a response. "Don't you see? Isn't it obvious? I meant we can get away with not having the originals once, but we couldn't make a practice of it. Moreover, it's important for me to see the various markings on the back of the canvas, so I can reproduce that accurately, as well—the evidence of provenance."

He saw that she was accepting it, and added, "It's all in the details. Anyone can forge a painting. A professional, a master, goes the extra steps."

"Very well," she said at last. "I can pass the copies to the client, and trust there will be no problem. But that doesn't give us back the originals we lost. Rather, that were *stolen* from us."

"Forget about them," Edleigh said. "They're gone."

"No, no! I refuse to accept that! Someone stole them from us, and I'm going to find who that is, and make them very sorry they ever interfered."

She stood.

"Where are you going?"

"Back to the luggage room. There were video cameras up by the ceiling, don't you recall? I'll get the attendant to let me look at the tapes. That's what the security tapes are for: to catch the thief in the act!"

He grabbed her hand and pulled her back to the chair.

"How dare you! Let go of me!"

"Better think it through, old girl. Suppose you go out there and raise a fuss, and they call the police in, and suppose they do find the paint— That is, find the items. What then? If you complain again at the left luggage office, and they find what's in the bag, then you've made it very clear to them who you are. Then they can come and haul us off straightaway to jail."

She pondered a moment. Then nodded. "Perhaps you are right."

Cottage

EMILY SAT at a corner table in the railroad buffet, watching Vera and the rumpled man. He wasn't dirty, he was actually fairly well-dressed if you looked through the shagginess. Upscale scruffy. An artsy look, deliberately beyond casual.

Artsy!

An artist? An actual artist? Involved in an art-theft scheme? Hmm, interesting.

When the two parted, Emily elected this time to follow the man. He jumped in a cab the front of the railway terminal, and Emily took the next in line.

This time, instead of saying, "Follow that cab," she gave the driver directions, street by street, pretending to work from memory of another trip, while watching the cab ahead.

The route led to the edge of Nice, then up a steep hillside. Her driver dropped back without her asking. "You are following that other cab, yes?"

"Yes."

"Just tell me. It is no problem. It happens all the time, sometimes the woman, other times the man. You are American, yes? This is France."

Peter's cab pulled up in front of a small, run-down stucco cottage. It had been a cute little place, once upon a time, but now it was forlorn and shabby, isolated in the midst of a construction zone. The white stucco walls were cracked and dirty; the windows coated with dust. What remained of a garden was now brown and dying of thirst.

Her driver went past, but the street dead-ended at a construction site. High-rises were springing up all around the area here: very likely this and the other remaining cottages here would be gone soon, and next summer there would be a few hundred more apartments.

Why would he choose to live up here in this isolated area? How did he know Vera? Were they working together, or was he the buyer?

She memorized the route on the way back down the hill, then traced it on a map she picked up at the office of the *Syndicate d'Initiative* at the railway station. She had no idea how this man fitted in, but had the feeling she would be returning to this little cottage.

Follower

AS HE FOLLOWED Vera, and later Emily, Derham had for once slipped up, neglecting to look behind to see if he was also being followed.

If he had, he might have spotted the scruffy girl with long hair and a backpack who had walked into the bus terminal behind Vern Billy, or the young man with flaming red hair and a sunburned face who stayed behind Derham.

The scruffy girl was Theresa Mullarvey; the red-haired youth was Matt Gilligan. They were members of Johnny McDevitt's team, and had been following in the expectation they would lead them to Stoddard and the rest of the paintings.

Theresa put it all together within the first few minutes. Vera had apparently picked up the bag of paintings, probably planted in the locker by Stoddard. They knew who Vera was from tracking her and Stoddard back in Washington.

Theresa phoned McDevitt, and he met her at the railway station. Neither could figure out the new face, the tall woman with the chestnut hair. She was an intriguing new development.

But it was obvious that the woman was following Vera. So how much did she know? How did she fit in? Who was she?

They followed Vera and Emily to the café, but missed Emily's retrieval of the paper from the trash bin. From where they stood, it seemed she was tossing in a piece of gum.

THERESA SETTLED at one table in the café, and McDevitt sat outside, in the shaded sidewalk café. Neither picked up the significance of a man at the next table borrowing Vera's discarded newspaper.

But Theresa knew something was up when the younger woman stood and hurried back to the bank of lockers in the railway station. Theresa followed, and saw her transfer the suitcase from one locker to another. Why?

As she walked out of the station, Theresa got her first good look at the woman's face. "Good God!" she muttered, surprising an elderly lady who was passing. Emily Cederquist! So she *is* involved! It was not just a fluke that first night!

LATER Theresa and Matt followed Emily as she followed Vera to the *Hotel Palais-sur-Mer*, and spotted Derham following them both.

Theresa stayed with Emily and followed her back to the café and then as she went back to the railway station.

Now she recognized the man making the fuss at the lockers as the shabby bloke back at the café. But who was he, and how did he fit in? How did all these faces fit together?

McDevitt phoned her twenty minutes later: Vera had run out of the hotel and was in a cab headed back to the station. Derham was close behind.

Second thoughts

WHAT HAVE I DONE! Emily was asking herself as the cab arrived back at the railway station.

What I've done is stolen a bag of paintings! Now I'm in possession of stolen art!

At least I assume they're the stolen paintings.

Then she thought: *But what if it isn't stolen? What if the woman—Vera de Cochin-Jessup—is legitimate? Then it's even worse!*

But if she is legit, then why were those guys following her?

Maybe Vera was to be their next target.

But why would a genuine art collector be moving paintings from one rental locker to another? And then passing them—in a sneaky, roundabout way—to the shabby guy in the shabby cottage?

No matter, the bottom line is that I stole the bag! And, almost certainly, there are video cameras watching the locker area. So I'm on tape! On tape, pulling a luggage theft!

What on earth was I thinking!

SHE WAS HOT AND TIRED from running around all day, and craved a swim. Or a shower.

But she wasn't ready to go back to the hotel and face Jeremy.

That was another pending disaster. Was Sabitaille right? Was Jeremy really a police suspect? It didn't seem possible, and yet what reason would Sabitaille have to make it up?

And now, according to Sabitaille, Jeremy had pulled her into the police spotlight.

Which meant she was vulnerable twice over. As an associate of Jeremy, and now as the star of a surveillance video showing her stealing a bag of stolen art.

What a mind-boggling mess I've gotten myself into!

SHE WANDERED DOWN the *Avenue Auber*, avoiding the Hotel Eminence. This was the Musicians area of Nice, where the streets were named after composers: Paganini, Rossini, Auber, Berliz, Durante, Goudod.

She came on a small park built over an underground parking garage: the *Place Mozart*, and there was grass, along with and shade trees and a bench on which to sit and think.

She had tried phoning home a couple of times through the day, but got no answer. Now it was late morning in Minnesota, Mother should be home from shopping, or whatever.

Her mother's voice, a new message: "I will be away for a few days, so please leave a message."

Away for a few days! That was a surprise. Away where? She left her cell number, and asked for a call-back, at any time. Now it didn't matter if Mother called and interrupted Jeremy.

Which brought back the issue of Jeremy. What to do, what to say?

And what about the suitcase full of paintings in the locker?

The answer came in a flash: Sabitaille of *Nice-Matin*! Sabitaille was the key. Tell him about the paintings, tell him the whole story of how she stumbled on them. Give him the exclusive story and he could run interference with the police. His story could make it clear that she was . . . was what? Not exactly an innocent bystander, but something like that.

She punched in his number from the business card he'd given her at the café. After six rings, the message came in rapid

French. She was not about to leave a message, she had already incriminated herself enough.

She thought about that, then tried again in five minutes. If Sabitaille had been up most of the night getting the story on the Le Trayas job, then very likely he was catching up on his sleep. "*Monsieur* Sabitaille, it's Emily Cederquist. I'm calling to thank you for your information this morning. That was very kind of you. Something has come up, and we should meet again as soon as possible. I think you'll find it time well spent."

THAT DONE, she stood and headed back to her hotel, stopping off at a small shop to buy a cold drink. It had been a long, hot day.

She stepped out of the shop and nearly bumped into Jeremy. He was coming back from the beach, his hair still damp, a towel sticking out of his backpack.

He moved to hug her, but she stepped back out of reach. An odd expression passed across his face. She passed it off, saying, "I'm hot and grungy and you don't want to get close to me."

"I'm sorry we missed signals today. I got back before noon, but guess you took off for the day."

"I did some shopping. For my mother," she said, aware as she spoke that she held only one small bag from *Galeries Lafayette*.

He glanced at the bag, then said, "Well, maybe dinner tonight somewhere?"

She didn't know how to respond. "It's been a long day, I've been walking all over Nice. I'm really tired." That much was true.

"I'll drive. Or we can go someplace near the hotel."

"I'm also waiting for a call-back." Then added, "From my mother. She seems to have left home suddenly."

He smiled, and she again felt that energizing personality radiating outward. "I understand. Why don't you take a shower, do your calls, and then we can see about dinner. If you're up to it. If not," he smiled again, "if not, I'll miss you."

Visit to an old friend

AFTER LEAVING EDLEIGH, Vera stopped in an upscale café for a quick lift. The idea that someone had been following her, watching her carry the bag of paintings was terrifying. Bad enough that they stole it from the locker; they could as easily have killed her.

Then she thought, My God, what if someone is this very minute watching me as I sit here!

The waiter came with her drink—a vodka-tonic—and she told him she would prefer to take it inside, not out on the street with all the noise and passing crowds.

Protect myself! I need to protect myself! she heard herself mumbling. Then she knew what to do.

SHE FINISHED THE DRINK, then took a cab to the port of Nice. She walked up one of the side streets to a small antique shop. The window shone with brass and porcelain: ceremonial shields, crests, colorful vases and plates.

He was at a desk in the back, doing paperwork, and he didn't recognize her when he first looked up. Jean-Yves Vourquerre was her age, short, lean. His black wavy hair was styled so it nearly covered the bald spot on the top. He wore a silk smock, designer jeans, and sandals.

They had both been children of the *pied-noirs* group, children of parents who had been forced out of Algeria when de Gaulle pulled out in 1962, their families settling along the *Côte d'Azur*. They had run in the same social circles in their teen-age years, sometimes competing for the same boys. Their discovery

247

of a mutual love of art had drawn them together, and her approval made him more acceptable to the others.

His pleasure in seeing her again was evident, but so was his wariness. She had seen him a few times over the years since, and each time had borrowed money which she had never repaid.

She was prepared for that, and handed him an envelope. "A little thanks for past favors," she said, kissing him on both cheeks. It was only a fraction of what she owed, but enough to soften him up.

As she expected, since it was the end of the day, nearly time to close the shop, he suggested an *aperitif*, and took her to one of the outdoor cafes fronting the port. She controlled her impatience until the second drink. "Jean-Yves, I need a favor."

His smile froze. "But of course."

She dropped her voice. "I need a gun, a small pistol."

"A pistol! You are not serious?"

"I am. I'm here on a buying trip for a very wealthy client—an Arab—and sometimes I find myself carrying a great deal of cash. I feel the need for some protection."

"They're very strict about guns in France. You should know that. It's not like America. It's quite a serious crime here to have a gun without a permit, and permits are very difficult to obtain."

"I'm willing to take that risk. It's better than being killed. Besides, my client has connections, if anything should happen."

"Why do you think I can help you?"

"I think you know a lot of people."

He considered a moment, then finally took a small leather-covered pad and a gold pen out of his pocket, handed them to her, and dictated a phone number. "When you call, say Robert sent you. They'll be able to help, if they want to. But be careful. There's a risk that they may get curious. Then it would be bad for you."

248

"Who's Robert?"

"It doesn't matter. The name will introduce you. But don't use my name–promise me that."

"Of course. I won't use your name, I would never do that. I promise." She stayed another couple of minutes, long enough to finish her drink, then told him how sorry she was that she couldn't stay for dinner, there was so much to talk about, another time for certain.

TIME WAS CRITICAL NOW. She caught a cab back to the center of town, and called the number from a public phone in the back of a café.

The name Robert wasn't enough, so she gave Jean-Yves' name, as well, and that did it.

"It will take time," the voice on the phone said.

"But it's urgent, very important. I must have it now."

"It's not possible now. Give me your phone number, where you'll be tomorrow."

"But—" She couldn't let them know her name or where she was staying.

"No buts. If you want the gun, give me your number so we can find you when it's ready."

She gave him the number of the cell-phone she used with Stoddard.

Uneasy

LE PETIT JARDIN—The Little Garden—was recommended by Roche at the front desk as a quiet restaurant not far from the hotel. It was situated in the garden of what had once been a large old hotel, now converted to apartments, and the waiter led them to an outdoor table under an awning.

Emily really didn't want to be here, she had no idea what to say to Jeremy. Her mood had shifted from bewilderment to anger. She didn't let it show, but she was feeling betrayed, lied to– which churned up the emotions of that awful Saturday in Chicago: betrayed, cheated, double-crossed by both her boss and her fiancé.

Cheat me once, it's my fault. But you'll never get a second chance.

"Separate checks, please," she told the waiter as they sat.

"It's my treat" Jeremy said, "I invited you."

"I feel better this way."

"Are you okay? You seem . . . seem not like yourself."

"I am myself," she said, realizing that was abrupt. "Sorry, I'm tired. And concerned about several things."

"Your mother?"

"That's one issue, yes." She paused a moment, then decided to go ahead get it over with. They hadn't ordered yet, she could still leave. "And there is something else. I found out this morning that you were stopped by the police on the Upper Corniche road, the night of the break-in at Cape Martin."

He tilted his head in a kind of shrug, and she caught a flash of surprise in his eyes. "I'd stepped away from the car a moment. Call of nature. A police car stopped, asked some questions, then we went our ways."

"I understand that happened just a few minutes after the art theft."

"I didn't know that then, had no idea. I saw flashing lights, police sirens and such down on the lower road, but the cops who stopped me didn't say anything, just checked my papers and moved on."

"But you didn't tell me about this. That also happened to be the night we met, the night you climbed into my room."

"I didn't tell you that I'd stopped to answer the call of nature, no, that's true. Maybe because you were screaming and trying to kick me." He laughed, but she knew it was forced.

"Cute. But you never said anything later."

"Why would I?"

"You do read the news headlines, don't you? About the string of art thefts?" She paused, realizing she'd revealed too much of what she was feeling. "The police consider you suspicious, a person of interest, as they say. Now, because we've been spending time together, I'm under police scrutiny, as well. You should have warned me."

He leaned back in the chair and took a deep breath. "Whoa, let's take it step by step. You're saying that the police consider *me* a suspect? Who told you that?"

"I . . . I can't tell you that, but I can say it's someone who is well tapped into what's going on within the police."

He shook his head slowly. "All I can say . . . it's bizarre. I'm no more an art thief than you are."

That triggered the memory of the dream: *You can trust me, Jeremy, just as much as I can trust you.*

251

The waiter arrived then; it was too late for her to try to make an exit. They both took the Prix Fixe menu: tonight *boeuf bourguignon, pommes vapeur, une petite salade, et yogourt pour le dessert.*

JEREMY SAID, "I get the sense I've been there, seen the movie."

"What *are* you talking about? What movie?"

"*To Catch a Thief.* You're Grace Kelly, I'm Cary Grant, and you don't trust me."

"That happens to be one of my mother's favorite movies," she said, stalling for time to think. "She bought the tape as soon as it was available and wore it out watching. Then bought the DVD. She's always had a fervent love for this area, from her first—*only*—visit here back when she was 21."

Why am I telling all this? The less said to him the better.

"So, is life imitating art?"

"You haven't answered my question, Jeremy: Why didn't you warn me the police had stopped you that night?"

"It didn't seem important. I assumed it was just a routine traffic stop. I'd pulled off the road, I figured they stopped to check if someone was hurt in the car, or whatever." He held her gaze. "The point is, you've suddenly become very wary of me, correct?"

"I've never met anyone like you." *At first I thought that was wonderful; you seemed like one of the nicest, most interesting people I'd ever met. But now I'm thinking it was all an act, our way of manipulating.*

"Meaning? Should I take that as a compliment? Or the opposite?"

"You're very secretive about your background. About your job, or profession, or whatever it is you do."

"What I said was, I am not my job; I am who I am, and whatever work I do is incidental to that. It's the same with you: you are you, not what your job happens to be. Bottom line, if your life is in balance, you are who you are, and who you are shouldn't be defined by what your job happens to be."

He paused. Finally she nodded. It did make sense. It was actually profound, a very zen-like insight. Profound, that is, for an art thief.

"And, it seems we're both on holiday, extended holiday, so neither of us has a job, which makes that issue even more irrelevant."

"There's another thing. I looked back over the time we've been together—known each other here, and something interesting: you've been away each of the nights on which there was an . . . operation, an art theft. The night of the job at Cape Martin, that's the night you arrived, later. Then the next night, the night of the Le Trayas operation, the night my mother called, I heard you leave your room, and don't know when you got back."

"You're forgetting: There's also the night of the commando operation at the Picasso in Antibes. I wasn't in my room then, I wasn't even in France."

For the first time she noticed music soft in the background, old music. Then Frank Sinatra's "Strangers in the Night," and a wave of sadness washed over her. She blinked back tears, determined not to let him see.

"What is it?" he asked.

"That old song, that was one of my mother's . . . well, not a favorite, just one she'd play from time to time, and—" She paused to pull in a deep breath— "and she told me once it was one she heard a lot when she was here. It reminded her of the days she had been here, always a bright spot in her life. When I heard it just now it made me think of her, and . . ."

She dried her eyes. "For whatever reason, my mother is not answering her phone, which is very unlike her. So, yeah, there are a lot of things on my mind right now."

Party time

VERA WAS DOZING in a chair when the room phone rang. She picked it up, disoriented. She checked the clock: she had been asleep for over an hour, since she got back from having the drink with Jean-Yves Vourquerre. Was this already someone calling about the gun?

"Ah, Vera, you are there, so wonderful. It is here Gawbi Al Senour. You called me before, and said you would have the—"

"Gawbi, remember we must be very careful what we say on the telephone."

"Yes, I forgot. No matter, I am here now in Cannes, and I am having a party tonight to celebrate. You must come, and—"

"Oh yes, I would love to come, but—"

"I am sending a car for you, it is a very nice Rolls-Royce I have ordered for you, and it will be there at your hotel in one hour, and it will bring you back later. Tonight is very casual dress, you come as you are. It will be on my boat here in the yacht harbor in Cannes."

She hung up, her mind racing.

Stoddard and Peter Edleigh and her other contact were all demanding money now, so she desperately needed a payment from Gawbi.

But the originals had been stolen from the rail locker. Peter Edleigh had promised to bring her his practice copies, but he had not. Which meant she had nothing to bring to Gawbi . . . apart from another promise. Would he possibly be that stupid?

Then it struck her: Now he was staying in a boat in the yacht harbor. His own boat? Or one he'd chartered? Was it safe to go on a boat with him?

Phone calls

THEY PASSED JEREMY'S CAR, parked in the hotel's parking area, then walked silently up the stairs.

"Good night," Emily said, intentionally turning her back to him as she fitted the key-card into her door. She had the feeling she would never see him again, that he would slip away overnight, ahead of the police.

Once inside, she checked the room phone and her cell-phone: no messages, and there had been no messages waiting in the hotel's mailbox.

While she washed up, she tried to plumb just what it was she was feeling. Sad. Depressed. Angry. Frightened. Betrayed again by her naivete.

No matter. Time to move on. She closed the door to the balcony so he couldn't listen in, then dialed her mother's number, hoping against hope that this time she would pick up. Still the same message: Away for a few days.

She dialed her father's cell. It was mid-afternoon back there. He was probably at the golf course. More likely at the bar in the clubhouse.

"Hi, Dad, it's me. What's happening?"

"Just finished 18 holes, nice summer day, having a late lunch."

His voice tended to be louder when he'd been drinking, and now it was very loud. Bad news: that was happening more and more now. He'd been a very sober bank president—the job he'd focused his life on getting—until a national bank forced a merger, and he'd been pushed into early retirement. Now, without the job, it seemed he no longer knew who he was. He'd gone off the rails: the younger girlfriend, the divorce, now the drinking for want of something to do.

"Have you heard from Mother today?"

"No."

"I've been trying to reach her. There's a new message, that she's gone out of town for a few days. She hadn't said anything about that yesterday."

"It's news to me. Where are you?"

"France. The Riviera."

"Well, la de da. When are you coming back and getting on with a career? You're, what is it now, 29? 30?"

He had always been a good father, despite the fact that the bank always came first. "I'm 28, 28 next month, Dad, and I'll be home and back into a career all too soon."

Interesting, she thought after hanging up. Jeremy had a point: If your life is in balance, you are who you are, and that shouldn't be defined by what your job is. Dad had defined his life by his title, and now he was lost.

And then he fell apart when he lost that title. Or maybe his life was never in balance from the start: he let his job define his life.

SHE HEARD THE PHONE ring in Jeremy's room, then heard him leave and lock his door.

SHE TRIED HER BROTHER, Terrence, in California. "Please leave a message." She asked him to call, any time of the day or night, as she was worried about Mother.

She tried her mother's best friend, in Minneapolis. She was at home, but hadn't heard of any trip she might be taking.

She phoned another of her friends, and Mother's next-door neighbor. They had no news to offer.

PART FIVE

Bleak morning

"YOU TOLD ME I could trust you," Jeremy said. "You said I could trust you just as much as I trust myself." He was in her room; she had her back to the open door to the balcony. He moved closer to her, step by step, swinging a butcher knife in wide, fast strokes.

"That was then, this is now," she mumbled, waking herself as she spoke.

She was in her room, alone. She rolled over and tried to go back to sleep. But she knew sleep wasn't going to come.

It was just after dawn, and the sky was pale.

She splashed some water on her face, then dressed quickly and went downstairs. Jeremy's car was missing from its spot in the hotel parking area. No surprise: she'd expected that—he was gone for good, trying to get away before the police arrested him. She would never see him again.

She couldn't pin down just what it was she felt. Sadness—for one wonderful day he had seemed to be the perfect one for her.

A lot of anger that she had let herself be duped, again.

Yet a sense of hope—that Jeremy would get away. It would be very painful to be a witness against him at a trial, even more painful to think of him locked away for years in a French prison.

THE *PROMENADE des ANGLAIS*, so busy in the daytime, was all but deserted in the early morning. Only occasional cars passing. A few people strolling the beach. A couple of men casting lures into the water.

The sun was hidden behind a bank of fog, and the air felt cool, damp. Without the bright sunshine the city seemed bleak, forlorn.

She passed the *Hotel Palais-sur*-Mer and wondered if Vera de Cochin-Jessup was still there. Or had she panicked and left France when she found that someone had grabbed her bag of paintings?

She corrected herself: Not *grabbed* the paintings, *stolen* them— and she was the thief.

She bought a copy of the day's paper at the white wooden kiosk on the Promenade. No art theft overnight. So maybe Sabitaille had taken the night off to rest up.

But what if Sabitaille didn't call back? He seemed her only hope, someone who could put out the true story of how she came by that suitcase full of paintings. If he didn't call back, if he wouldn't take her calls, then what?

Maybe do what Jeremy did? Disappear. Jump in the car and get across the border, ASAP. In a few days, that locker would run out of time, the staff would clear it out, and then the police would have the paintings.

Case closed. Closed, but she had made herself the star of the security video, the electronic eyes watching her open Vera's locker and move the bag to the new one. Now her fingerprints were all over everything.

Case closed, suspect identified, bulletin sent to the American authorities to arrest and deport her back to France for trial.

She headed back to the hotel. The city was waking up. The rattle of shopkeepers raising the metal curtains on the front windows. Other shopkeepers hosing down the sidewalks. The increasing hum of traffic. Motorbikes buzzing past.

The Corsican

VERA WAS AWAKENED a little after seven by the ringing of her phone. It had been nearly five before she got back from Gawbi's party, and her head ached from the drinking.

After all that, the slimy little bastard still didn't have all the money ready to transfer. "Today, Vera, today I will arrange for the money to be paid to your bank," Gawbi had promised as she left. "That is the very first thing I will do this morning."

She cleared her throat and took a sip of water. Was this Gawbi calling now to say the money had been transferred. "*Qui? Allo?*"

"You wished to make a certain purchase," a man said. His voice was throaty, between a whisper and a grunt.

Her head throbbed, and she was slow to understand.

"Robert said you wished to make a purchase. Yes or no?"

"Oh yes, yes, of course," she said finally comprehending. Robert was the name Jean-Yves Vourquerre had said to use as an introduction in buying a gun. "My husband is insane, you see, and—"

"You know the *Marché aux Fleurs*? The flower market? Be there in one half-hour, not longer. Sit at the café at the east end, north side. When the bell at the church rings the hour, pin one red rose into your hair. A man will speak to you. Follow him. When it is safe, he will give you what you want. You give him €2,000."

"Two thousand! That's far too much. And besides, I can't be there in– "

"You want it, yes or no?"

"Yes."

"Then be there. And be sure the money is all there. We know where to find you if you try to cheat us."

263

She recognized the thick accent now. It was Corsican. Naturally enough. The Corsicans controlled the underworld here, the *Milieu*, the *Union Corse*, the Corsican Union, the French equivalent of the Mafia.

She felt a chill: it was getting out of hand. Now dealing with the Corsicans. Would it never end!

She made herself a Bloody Mary with canned juice from the mini-fridge. Well, with luck it would all be over in a couple of days and she'd be gone from here before the Corsicans had time to wonder why she needed a gun.

Later, once the vodka had done its work, she felt in control again. The *Milieu*, the criminal element–effective in their way, but stupid. No matter what, she would be able to handle them. Intelligence always won out over brute force.

She opened the wall-safe in the room, and counted out €2,000–a big part of her emergency reserve, too big a part–and sealed it in an envelope to bring with her.

Summons

EMILY FOUND a phone slip in her box when she returned to the hotel, a message to call a number "immediately."

It would have to wait. She was famished now, after her walk, and needed breakfast. She was nearly finished when the same chambermaid rushed out: "Mademoiselle, you have a telephone call, you must come at once. It is the police."

Deju vu all over again, she thought. The same chambermaid, the same message as—was it only yesterday morning? No, the day before. The only difference was that Jeremy was gone. Now Jeremy had betrayed her.

Again she took it in the small phone booth in the lobby. A woman's voice: "*Commissaire Principal* Bourchette will see you immediately. You must come at once. And again I must tell you to bring your passport."

That did not sound good, not at all. While she was in the booth, she dialed the number on the message. The same woman picked up. "I just got the message you left at my hotel."

"Yes, you must come immediately. You should not keep him waiting. He said it is good news for you."

SHE HURRIED across Nice to the police station, arriving sweaty and out of breath, eager to get there before Bourchette changed his mind and changed the good news to bad.

A uniformed officer escorted her to the Judicial Police offices on the top floor, and a young plainclothesman brought her immediately to the same conference room. Bourchette was

265

waiting at the table, sheaves of papers spread out in front of him..

Today the room seemed less oppressive. The window was open and there was no haze of smoke.

Bourchette looked exhausted. His eyes were ringed with grey, and his usual black suit was rumpled and stained. The pelt of wiry black hair that ringed his forehead and covered his hands was even denser than she had remembered it.

Despite his fatigue, he seemed almost glad to see her. She felt a surge of optimism. She felt a touch of sympathy for Bourchette: he had spent 30 or 40 years at this. No wonder he was tired. Crime never stopped.

He motioned for her to take a seat. "Have you any news for me? Any developments?"

She shook her head.

"No news for me, none at all? You are certain of that?"

Her mouth was suddenly dry, her heart pounding. He was after something. "Yes. I mean no, there is no news for you."

He opened a file folder, and scanned the contents for several long seconds. "It has been brought to the attention of the police that there was a certain bag, containing art stolen from Le Trayas. I thought perhaps . . ."

He smiled, his trademark rictus, and his eyes receded into their slits. He said nothing more, and the silence filled the room.

Her mouth went dry, and she had to peel her lip back from a tooth. *How on earth does he know that? Has he already seen the security video from the railway station?*

She was trapped. Admit that she had intercepted Vera's bag, and he would ask why she had not turned it in to him earlier. And was it still in that locker?

On the other hand, deny she had seen the bag, and he might well confront her with evidence linking her to it.

The silence was heavy in the room. Finally Bourchette said, "Then we move to another matter. You met again with Monsieur Sabitaille of *Nice-Matin*. Is that correct?"

She nodded, suddenly convinced that he had been bluffing about the bag. "Yes, he called me."

"And what did you discuss?"

"He told me, warned me, that the police were watching me, almost as if I were a suspect. I told him that was ridiculous."

"Ridiculous? Why do you say that?"

"Because I had nothing to do with these thefts. And the police—*you*—know that."

"We go by the facts. Fact number one: you were in the vicinity of the first in the series, at the Picasso Museum in Antibes. You were there, you claim you tried to alert the police. But conveniently just too late to do any good."

"We've already—"

"Fact number two: you have been consorting with a person who was seen in the vicinity of the second in the series. That, of course, is your fellow American, Jeremy Howe. Do you deny that?"

Bourchette pronounced the name as "hog" but it didn't seem the time to correct him. "We are *not* consorting, not in *any sense* of the term! He happened to be staying in the same hotel. We spent a day touring together. I had never met him before, and so far as I know he has moved on."

Bourchette stared at her, his eyes all but invisible behind the folds of skin and hair. "You are lying. Or mistaken."

"I'm not lying."

"He is still at the hotel. I am offering you an opportunity to save yourself. Do you want to do that?"

"I'm not sure what you're saying."

"You are a civilian, not a police officer, a friend of Mr. Hog. You can find out things and pass on the information to us. Discreetly."

"What kind of information?"

"I think you know that very well. If not, then you will recognize it when you see it."

"First of all, I don't think he's still in Nice. His car is gone, he's likely—"

"The hotel told me that he has not checked out. His things are still in the room. I leave the matter in your hands."

She sat, frozen in the chair, expecting him to demand her passport.

He looked up, annoyed. "That is all."

She stood, puzzled. *Why didn't he demand my passport? An oversight? Or a subtle signal to get out of France, to get out of his way?*

And if she did leave France? Then what?

And what of the paintings in the railway locker?

Was he setting a trap?

Prisoner's Dilemma

PRISONER'S DILEMMA! The phrase popped into her mind as she walked back to the hotel. Something from college. A philosophy class? Or psychology? Or that class in Game Theory in third-year?

No matter. It was exactly on-target here. Prisoner's Dilemma was a classic thought exercise. Suppose you and your cohort have done something wrong. Or are set up to seem that you've done wrong. The police haul you and the cohort in, then put you in separate cells and let you stew.

Then a cop—Bourchette fits that part exactly—comes in and offers a deal. "Tell us the truth, help us make a case, and you go free. And by the way, your friend has already agreed to help us, so if you hold out, if you don't cooperate, it will all fall on your shoulders. You'll go away for a long, long time."

What to do? Maybe the cohort has confessed, pointing the finger at you. Or maybe he talked himself clear by making up a story to dump the blame on you. If that's the case, and if you don't cooperate, then the prosecutor will throw the book at you.

But, then again, maybe that cop—again, read Bourchette—is lying. Your cohort has not confessed, and they don't have a case unless you give it to them.

So if I do what Bourchette wants, find evidence to implicate Jeremy, then he lets me off the hook.

But what if there is no evidence against Jeremy, what if Bourchette wants me to set him up? Maybe by fabricating evidence.

Then I go free, Jeremy goes to prison, and I have that on my conscience the rest of my life.

269

On the other hand, if Jeremy is implicated, as I think he is, and if I don't help Bourchette, then I'll be also be off the prison.

And it wouldn't bother Bourchette in the least that I'm innocent.

SHE FELT A SUDDEN CRAVING, and detoured to buy a gelato from a street vendor, one of the super-intense flavors—*framboise*, raspberry.

For once, never mind the calories

If, worst case—don't even think it, worst case. I might never have another chance. Do not pass go, go directly to jail, do not ever buy another gelato.

That dream from the other night, such a nice dream. I want you to know, Jeremy, that you can trust me as much as you can trust yourself.

"You can trust me as much as you can trust yourself."

But if I can't trust myself, then who can I trust?

Money in the bank

VERA FELT BETTER with the gun in her purse. She wandered through the flower market, circling around, looking back to be sure she was not followed.

She took a cab to the main post office on the *Avenue Thiers*. International calls were easiest from the phones at the post office, and more secure than cell-calls.

She was assigned a booth by the clerk on duty, and dialed her own call. Hers was one of a dozen large glass booths in a row along the side of the post office lobby.

SHE FAILED TO NOTICE the short bald man with the moustache who slipped into the booth next to hers. He had made his living for twenty years by being the sort of person others failed to notice, and she had failed to notice him watching e when she received the gun at the flower market.

He picked up the phone in his booth and dialed a few digits for the sake of appearance, but not enough to cause a call to go through. He slipped a small suction cup onto the glass; that was connected to recorder in his pocket, from which he listened by a small earphone.

He was a private detective with an agency in Nice. His firm had been retained two days earlier through an American law firm, which did not name the ultimate client. Usually it was better not to know.

His job was to follow the woman, and collect whatever information he could without raising her suspicions.

271

VERA'S CALL was to one of her banks in Geneva. After reciting the verbal code that she had worked out earlier with a bank officer, she inquired whether a promised deposit of $800,000 had been made, and was told that it had arrived a few minutes ago.

She was speechless for a moment. It seemed almost too good to be true. That was the interim payment Gawbi had promised last night. Incredibly, he had followed through. This was on top of what he and his partners had paid at the start.

"Very well, then," she said to the banker, feeling almost giddy with relief, "I shall want four transfers made from this account to other Swiss accounts."

The first, a payment of $200,000, was made to Stoddard's account in Zurich. It was less than she had promised him, but enough to buy time. Probably it would be enough to induce him to deliver more of the paintings to her. His share so far now came to $400,000.

The second payment went to Commissioner Bourchette's account in Geneva. This $200,000 was the special payment she had promised him yesterday. He had already gotten $200,000 at the start of the collaboration.

The third payment, $100,000, went to Edleigh's account: at this point, he was her only hope, and she needed to keep him working. Now he had received $200,000 in total.

THE FOURTH PAYMENT she authorized today was $300,000 to another secret numbered Swiss bank account in Geneva, one she had set up for herself. There the $300,000 joined the $700,000 she already had on deposit. By funneling the money from one account to another, and then another, she felt she had insulated it from scrutiny on the chance the French police ever become interested.

Despite the reputation the Swiss banks had for secrecy, she preferred to take no chances that any police could ever trace the route of her money. In a few days, she would go to Geneva, draw it out in Swiss Francs and personally carry the cash to three or four other banks throughout Switzerland in order to completely erase the trail. Then it would be completely secure.

ONE MILLION in her account—so welcome after the deprivations of the past few years. Now she could live as she wanted.

Granted, it was a great deal less than she had planned on. If only that wretched American girl had not thwarted the first operation, at Antibes!

But the consolation was that the real payoffs could come when she sold the originals.

With luck, they would bring her upwards of $10 million, probably a lot more if she played it right. Meanwhile, the first million would keep her going.

Finally she called the number of Stoddard's cell phone. When he answered, she recited the code that meant the deposit had been completed—"I just ordered a new dress"—and gave him the name of the café where she would wait for him.

Saddle up

SHEIK MOTAR AL SENOUR, Gawbi's older, smarter brother, kept homes scattered around the globe. They gave a semblance of continuity to the life of a man who traveled a quarter-million miles or more each year. The homes could be made much more secure than hotels ever could, which was important because Al Senour had enemies around the world. Beyond that, they were good investments.

Two of the homes were in the Middle-East. In Hong Kong he owned an apartment building, and retained the penthouse for himself. He kept a townhouse in London's Belgravia. Another home was a small chateau outside Paris. He had a 14-room apartment stretching over three floors of a secure building in Geneva. He did much of his American business from a horse farm in the hunt country of Virginia a short helicopter ride from Washington. A penthouse on the Upper East Side was his home in New York.

But now all this was in jeopardy. He had extended himself to finance a Russian venture that was now in trouble. He had to come up with a payment due in three weeks—it was only $50 million, but it was money he did not have now. A default would set the house of cards tumbling.

The message originating with the detective in Nice came when he was in a meeting in London. "You will find this of particular interest," his Special Assistant said, gliding into the room.

"Particular interest" was their code for highest priority.

Al Senour smiled at each of the others around the table, begging him for their most kind indulgence while he scanned the memo.

"Saddle up," he said to his Special Assistant when he saw the message. "We'll go there."

"Saddle up," a phrase he had picked up during his dealings in Texas, meant to fuel and service Al Senour's Gulfstream so it was ready to go.

Coming from a robed Arab, it always drew a laugh. Sheik Al Senour liked the people he negotiated with to laugh: laughter eased the tension, and diverted their attention wait for him.

Double measure

WHEN VERA FINISHED her calls, she left the post office and crossed the street to a small café not far from the train station, a place where she would be nicely anonymous, just one of hundreds passing through each day. She ordered another coffee and croissant, and a copy of *Nice-Matin*.

Nothing new on the art thefts. Good news.

Or was it? Were the police moving quietly now, drawing closer and closer?

She called the waitress over and whispered that she would like a large glass of orange juice with a double measure of vodka. She resented the smirk that passed across the girl's face, but said nothing. She kept her hands in her lap so the waitress wouldn't see how badly they were shaking.

A little *apéritif* would calm her nerves.

It would help her think, and now she had to think as never before.

BY THE TIME she saw Stoddard enter the post office to make his own calls she knew precisely how she would handle it.

When he came out, he crossed the street and took the table beside hers. She studied his face as he walked toward her, but it revealed nothing. "Well?" she whispered at last.

"It's not enough, not what you promised," he said without looking at her. "But I'll go with it for now, just to get the show on the road. Drop some coins on the floor as you leave."

She reached in her purse, as if to pay the check, and tossed a handful of coins to clatter across the floor.

Stoddard bent over and helped her pick them up. "Airport," he whispered as he slipped her a slip of paper with the coins.

The receipt carried the combination code for a locker holding the remaining paintings taken in the operation at Le Trayas, the ones he had held back yesterday until he was paid.

She took a cab to the airport. When the driver pointed out that she didn't have luggage, she told him she was meeting a friend coming in from London. Once there, she passed a few minutes walking around the terminal, making sure Stoddard hadn't set her up.

At last she went to the lockers, her heart pounding, mouth dry, legs weak with fear. Her fingers trembled as she punched in the code, and it took three tries before she got it right.

The bag of paintings was lighter than she had expected.

She caught another cab back to the hotel. Once in her room, she double-locked the door and braced a chair against it, then opened the bag. Perfect! Everything was here

She was beginning to feel in control again.

She hurried to an elegant small boutique in the Pedestrian Zone and bought a $1000 Italian leather bag to hold the delivery to Gawbi. With people like that, appearance was everything.

She used the special cell-phone and called Peter Edleigh, hoping that he would answer. When he did, she instructed him to bring the copies he had finished to the hotel. "I must make a delivery as soon as possible, ready or not," she told him.

"One always hates to raise the topic of money, but . . ." he responded.

"The deposit is in your account, I assure you."

"Then I assure you I will bring the products to you . . . just as soon as I check with my banker to be sure the money has indeed been deposited."

Broken china

WORD GOT TO Freddie Marchand about the expensively-dressed woman who had been so eager to buy a black-market pistol. Freddie was desperate for a success; his life depended on it. Without a success, they would come for him again, and this time the trip up the mountain would be real, not a sham.

There would be no second chances. He knew he had only hours to show some real progress. Maybe this was the lead that would save him.

He traced the story of the woman buying a gun to Robert Dutois, a small-timer on the fringe of the *Milieu*.

Robert was flattered at the attention. But he had received cash from the woman. He had thrown away her phone number, and didn't know anything about her beyond the fact that she had been sent by Jean-Yves Vourquerre, an antique dealer with a little shop over by the port. "*Un pederaste, un pied-noir*," he added. A homosexual. A child of the French *émigrés* who were forced back to this country from Algeria with the exodus of '62.

Marchand took Raoul Darterre along when he called on Vourquerre.

Raoul was known as "Boom-Boom" in the streets because of a couple of enforcement jobs he'd done. Boom-Boom looked the part, stupid and brutal, with a smashed nose slanting across a pitted chalk-white face. His face tended to make people cooperate.

Marchand went in alone, as if browsing. He was wearing a pearl grey suit, no tie, sunglasses. Jean-Yves looked up from his desk to ask if there was anything he could do to help, then went back to his papers when Marchand shook his head.

Marchand found a porcelain vase, a fragile creation covered with delicate painted flowers. "How much?"

278

Jean-Yves rose to come over. "Ah, that is a truly exquisite piece, dating from around 1730. It–"

Marchand let go of the vase, and it shattered on the floor.

When he heard the signal, Boom-Boom burst into the shop and slammed the door shut, flicking the lock and pulling the shade.

Marchand grabbed Jean-Yves by the shirt and jammed a stubby automatic into his chest. The trick was to establish dominance so quickly that there could be no thought of resisting.

That was all it took. Jean-Yves told them everything they wanted: Vera's name, where she was staying in Nice, her background.

Jean-Yves talked not so much from fear as from anger, knowing that Vera had betrayed him by using his name with the gun-seller after she had promised not to.

Marchand knew he was on the right track at last when he heard of Vera's involvement in the art world. He had Jean-Yves put in a call to her at the *Hotel Palais-sur-Mer,* but she was out.

Marchand allowed Jean-Yves to lock up the shop before they left, pointing out that this was a special favor to him. Then they went to wait near Vera's hotel, where they would have a clear view of everyone entering and leaving.

"THAT'S HER!" Jean-Yves said as Vera climbed out of a cab, carrying a canvas bag.

Minutes later, he again pointed out Vera, now leaving the hotel. Marchand rolled out of the car and followed her to a small expensive boutique in the pedestrian zone.

She emerged carrying what was clearly a ridiculously-overpriced leather bag, and he wondered what she was up to.

Conflict

EMILY WALKED SLOWLY back from the meeting with Bourchette, torn. She had her passport, she could leave France. At least *attempt* to leave. But, very likely, Bourchette was having her followed. Running would be read as an admission of guilt.

Jeremy's words in the dream kept echoing in her mind: You can trust me as much as you trust yourself.

She had taken a couple of courses in psychology. Sometimes dreams were just silly exercises in cleaning out memories. But other dreams conveyed deeper truths that the sub-conscious was bringing across to the conscious.

Am I really trustworthy? she asked herself.

I am loyal, very loyal to my friends.

But I demand loyalty in return. And I'm not flexible on that, not at all. Not any more. Never again.

Porter cheated on me, and that was that. End of engagement.

Bill Bridges conned me, held out a carrot and then snatched it away. And I was gone.

What about Jeremy? Did Jeremy really betray me? He did fail to tell me the police had stopped him the night of the Cape Martin robbery: that was not good. But then he claimed he had no idea that they had seen him as a suspect. How much can I believe?

Could Jeremy trust me as much as I feel I should be able to trust my friends?

He didn't quite say it, but it's obvious enough that Bourchette wants me to sneak into Jeremy's room and go through his things for something incriminating.

Snooping through a friend's things isn't a very trustworthy act.

Sure, I could say that the police forced me to do it.

But is that really an excuse? The police made me do it, the devil made me do it.

The reality is that I'd be doing it to save my own skin. Is that the act of a trustworthy friend?

And if I find nothing incriminating in his room, then what? If I tell that to Bourchette, will he move on from Jeremy as a suspect?

HER CELL-PHONE RANG. Was it Mother calling to say she was okay? Sabitaille finally returning my call?

That same woman's voice, the woman at the police station: "This is the office of Commissioner Bourchette. He says to remind you that the clock is ticking."

Snooping

JEREMY'S CAR was still gone when Emily got back to the hotel. Not that she had expected he'd be back.

No one was at the front desk. Was that good luck? Or a trap waiting to be sprung?

She spotted the key-card for Jeremy's room in the message-box next to hers. She glanced around; no one in sight. She pulled open the little gate, stepped behind the counter and snatched both key-cards in one quick motion.

Roche came running. "Mademoiselle, you had only to call out and I would have—"

"I only needed my key," she said, forcing a smile.

She walked up the winding staircase, her heart thumping, her mouth dry. No sign of the chambermaid. She unlocked her own door first and dropped her bag on the table, then closed her door, leaving it unlocked, just in case.

She slipped the other key-card into Jeremy's door. The lock clicked. What if he were in the room and the key-card she used was a spare? That would be awkward.

But he wasn't there. She slipped the card into her pocket, then locked the door from the inside.

She was not surprised that the bed had not been slept on, and that only one towel had been used. That confirmed her suspicion: When she heard him leave last night he was leaving for good.

His clothes still hung in the armoire: three shirts, a couple of pants, some shoes at the bottom.

The shirts were all well-worn, one already frayed at the collar. She checked: they were all good brands, L.L. Bean and Brooks

282

Brothers. Strange, to drive an expensive sports car, yet wear tired, worn-out clothes.

She pulled open the drawers by the bed, and the drawer of the table. Empty.

A Bible on the desk. And not a standard-issue Gideon hotel Bible. This Bible had Jeremy's name embossed on the cover. She was surprised that he would carry a Bible. Then she was angry: just another part of his cover story.

She took a tissue and lifted the cover. A letter in an envelope, along with a photo: some people standing in front of a small airplane. Most of the seven people were black: one a small child in her mother's arms, two other slightly older children, another woman, and two white men. She looked closer, and realized one of the men was Jeremy, with hair and a beard longer than now.

The letter had been typed on an old machine with a bad ribbon, undated, and bore no return address. The envelope was missing.

```
Dear Jeremy,
    We   thought  you  would  like  the
enclosed  photo,  taken  the  day  you
left  to  go  home.  As  you  well  know,
it  is  not  easy  to  get  photos  printed
here,  hence  the  delay.
    On  behalf  of  the  mission  and  the
people  here,  we  want  to  thank  you
again  for  your  wonderful  gift  of  the
Cessna,  and  for  the  many  months  you
spent  here  with  us.  As  a  fellow
pilot,  I  learned  much  from  you,  but
remain  impressed  by  your  piloting
skills  and  your  courage  in  flying
```

```
when lives depended on it, fearless
at the risk of your own.
   Good news: Imbwa, who you flew out
on one of your last missions for us,
survived, as did both of her babies,
fraternal   twins,   both   boys.   She
named  one  of  them  Jeremy  in  your
honor.  Life  goes  on  even  in  the
midst of constant death.
```

She couldn't make out the signature.

She slipped the photo and letter back into the Bible, and stood in place, stunned, mystified.

It was clear, perfectly clear, but it made no sense. Gift of a Cessna? A Cessna was an airplane, that much she knew. Did Jeremy donate an airplane to some African mission, then come to the French Riviera to recoup his money by stealing art?

Not likely. But possible.

Have I made a terrible mistake? Maybe he really is the great guy I believed he was at first.

But to donate an airplane? How much is a Cessna, even a single-engine model? A hundred thousand? Two? More than that? Jeremy is what? 30 at the most, so where would he have come up with that kind of money to donate? Donate, and then still buy himself a BMW to tour around Europe?

It didn't make sense. Could it all— the letter, the photo, all of it— be some bizarre, elaborate cover-story?

She froze when she heard voices outside the door.

Then she relaxed: it was the German couple in the room down the hall.

But it made the point: there was no time to waste, the sooner the better out of this room. She quickly went through the pockets of the shirts and trousers. Nothing.

Only one place left to look: the room safe, buried in the wall over the bed. Four buttons, to punch in sequence. But what sequence?

She began with the combination on the safe in her room: 1-2-3-4. Nothing. 4-3-2-1. No luck. 2-3-4-1, then 3-4-1-2. Still locked.

The door-lock tinkled. This room. She rolled under the bed, making it just in time to see the shoes of the chambermaid coming in.

Better the chambermaid than Jeremy. But every minute was a minute closer to Jeremy's return.

If, that is, he ever would return.

She heard the chambermaid do some perfunctory cleaning in the bathroom. Then she rolled a vacuum into the room and did a couple of swoops under the bed. Emily rolled back against the wall to get out of the way.

But something blocked her, something was between her back and the wall.

Finally, the work finished, the chambermaid left and locked the door.

Emily rolled over, still under the bed, and felt something. A canvas bag with a zipper. She felt around the edge: whatever was inside was soft.

She rolled out from under the bed and pulled the bag with her. Time was running, but this was crucial. This was probably the point of the whole exercise.

And probably not good news.

She heard the bumping and scraping of the chambermaid working next door, in her room.

SHE TOOK A DEEP BREATH and unzipped the bag. It held what she guessed it would, and hoped it wouldn't: a rolled painting. She took a quick glance at it. Whether it was one of the stolen paintings she had no idea. But if not, then why would Jeremy have hidden it under the bed?

Or why wouldn't he have taken it with him when he made a run for it last night?

She replaced the painting in the bag, then slid it back under the bed, baffled. *Was it real? Was it one of the stolen paintings? Who put it there—Jeremy? Or someone trying to frame him?*

Was that what Bourchette had really been after in that strange meeting just now?

"I am offering you an opportunity to save yourself. Do you want to do that?"

"I'm not sure what you're saying."

"You are a civilian, not a police officer, and a trusted friend of Mr. Hog. You can find out things and pass on the information to us. Discreetly."

"What kind of information?"

"I think you know that very well. If not, then you will recognize it when you see it."

You will recognize it when you see it. As in a painting hidden under his bed.

She felt sick, her legs weak. She dropped onto the bed. Her mouth was dry. She was panting fast, as if she'd been jogging.

THERE WAS NOTHING more to do now, just wait for the chambermaid to get out of the way so she could go back to her own room.

And then what? Call *Commissaire* Bourchette and say, "Come and get it. I've found what you need."

And what would Bourchette say? "Ah, Mademoiselle, I am so grateful for your assistance. You are free to go."

Maybe he'd say that. More likely, "Ah, Mademoiselle, so now you have confessed that you are an accomplice to the crimes. I have won, and you have lost. Too bad, you should have known better. I am one never to trust."

ONE!

Maybe that was it! Just plain one. As in 1-1-1-1.

She went back to the wall safe and punched in 1-1-1-1. It clicked open. Nobody had ever reset the factory default.

She heard the chambermaid close the door to her room, and stood, holding her breath, wondering what to say if the maid dropped back to bring an extra towel.

Instead she heard the rolling of the cart and vacuum across the tile floor to the small elevator.

She swung the safe door open, almost afraid what she'd find. The painting under the bed was incriminating enough: What else had he stashed in this safe?

Three thick manila envelopes bound together with a rubber band.

She pulled off the band and slid the contents of the first envelope onto the table.

An American passport. She checked the photo: Jeremy, no question of it.

But the name on the passport was Jeremy *Hough*, not Jeremy Howe!

Then she thought: maybe it *is* his name, after all! "Hough" could be, probably was, pronounced "how." And Bourchette had pronounced it "hog", once even "hoog". It was the first time she'd seen his name in print, she had just assumed Howe, without thinking.

No wonder she couldn't find any real matches for him online.

An address in Massachusetts, a suburb of Boston—that was consistent with the slight New Englandish accent.

She did a quick calculation from the date of birth: age 29, so he was about ten months older. About what she'd guessed.

She moved on to the second envelope. A wad of Euros, on quick count a bit over four thousand. In the third envelope, American bills, about $3000 worth.

It made no sense: if Jeremy had made a run for it last night, why would he leave his passport and this much cash behind? $7,000—a lot to walk away from.

She slipped the cash back into the envelopes, replaced the rubber band around them, and slid them into the safe.

That was when she saw some things at the back of the box. The cloth wallet he'd worn hooked to his belt; in the wallet some credit cards and a bit more cash. Photos: a man and woman. She guessed it was his parents, there was a resemblance. A man, maybe his brother. A woman, early 30s from the looks. His sister? Wife?

But if he was leaving, why would he leave his passport, wallet and cash?

Then she realized: there was no drivers' license in the wallet.

Which meant—at least suggested—that he had taken the license with him, along with the car keys, but left all this cash and his credit cards and other papers. Odd.

SHE WAS FITTING the wallet back into the safe when she realized there was still one more item wedged against the side.

She pulled out a stiff maroon packet, stamped in gold: an Irish passport, complete with golden harp and the words "Eire Ireland Passport."

She flipped it open. A different photo, but still unmistakably Jeremy. Same date of birth. And same spelling: Hough.

Inside, multiple entry stamps: France, several countries in Africa, Greece. But not the United States.

Odd.

No, beyond odd. Bizarre.

So he had both American and Irish passports. Twin passports, so to speak: same name, same dates and places of birth for both. But the Irish seemed the most used, judging from the immigration stamps.

SHE HEARD THE DISTINCTIVE SIGNAL of her cell-phone next door, the first movement from Beethoven's Seventh—her theme for this trip.

But who was calling? Mother? Sabitaille? Bourchette?

There was still one final item to be checked, one she was reluctant to tamper with: his tablet computer. If she turned it on, then he'd know she'd been snooping.

If, that is, he ever came back.

She opened the cover; a moment later she was looking at a photo of herself smiling, leaning against his BMW in front of the Hotel Eminence.

She blinked in astonishment. *Me? It can't be me! Jeremy hadn't taken a picture like this. I never posed for this picture!*

She looked again.

Now she saw it differently.

The photo was *almost* her. Almost. But not quite. Not her hair-style. Not any of her clothes. And now that she looked more closely, it was not Jeremy's BMW. It was a BMW convertible, but this was yellow, his was blue. And this was an older model, quite a bit older, 20 years older, maybe more.

Her cell-phone rang again next door, just twice this time.

She changed the angle of the screen to get a better view, then tapped to zoom in, suddenly realizing she'd been mistaken. This photo was not her.

This was a photo of her mother!

Of her mother, way back when she'd been here in Nice, staying at the Hotel Eminence.

And wearing a very happy smile.

Now she heard the hotel phone ringing in her room. Someone was very determined to reach her. Better check it out.

She fitted the computer and the envelopes back into the room safe as they had been, took a quick look around to be sure all was in order, then eased the door open. No one in the hallway.

She stepped into her room. The phone had stopped ringing, so she picked up and hit the button for the front desk.

"Ah, *Mademoiselle* Cederquist," Roche said when he picked up, "there is someone here wishing to see you."

"Who is it?"

"I have been asked not to say."

Surprises

EMILY LOCKED HER ROOM, then went downstairs, mouth dry, heart thumping, trying to collect herself. Whoever or whatever waiting there was not likely to be good news. Maybe some of Bourchette's people, there to search her room.

She turned the corner to the small hotel desk. A tall woman wearing a canvas sun hat stood, back turned, at the check-in desk.

Emily froze, stunned. It can't be!

"Ah, there she is now," Roche said. The woman turned.

"Mother!"

She threw her arms out and they hugged. "I've been trying to call you for an hour, since my plane landed."

"I . . . I feel I'm having a . . . a waking dream, an illusion," Emily said. "I . . . I'm stunned. What are you doing here? When did you arrive?"

"A few minutes ago. I came because . . . because I . . ." She shrugged. "I don't really know why I came, I just felt it was the thing to do. I wanted to come here again. So tell me, where's your friend?"

"My friend?" Emily said, aware that Roche, puttering with the computer, was listening. "Anyway, Mother, you must be tired. We need to get you a room."

"That's all taken care of. Though I would like to freshen up a bit before we go to lunch."

Her mother, Jennie, traveled light, so there was only a roll-on to bring up to the room. Her room was on the top floor, also overlooking the garden.

"It's just as I remembered it here, every single detail. The palms, the bright sunlight, the glowing colors. Such a wonderful change from Minnesota!"

291

"THERE IS A SPECIAL PLACE I'd like to go for lunch, if you don't mind," Jennie said a few minutes later as they were leaving the hotel. Then she stopped dead in her tracks, staring ahead. A man was climbing out of a taxi. Tall, ample white hair, for some reason looking vaguely familiar to Emily even from the back.

He paid the driver and turned to come into the hotel. He smiled at them in passing, then stopped dead in place and stared at Jennie.

"Jerry!" she said, her voice muffled, sounding breathless. "I– I– I feel . . ."

"Good Lord!" he said. "It *is* you! *Jennie! Jennie Thorpe! I can't believe it!*"

They hugged, hard, for a very long time, then pulled back to look at each other, still holding on. "This is the most incredible coincidence. Not a coincidence! A *miracle*!" she said, her voice strange, almost muffled. Emily had never seen her like this.

He pulled back a little to look at her. He asked, "And who is this?" He blinked, obviously surprised. "No, no need to tell me. Your daughter? Or your baby sister?"

Jennie pulled back and wiped away tears, laughing at the same time. "You always had that knack. My baby sister! Such subtle flattery. But yes, my daughter, Emily."

"Emily! *You* are Emily? I've heard so much about you!" I had no idea . . ."

"This is an old friend of mine, a very *dear* friend, from a long time ago," her mother said holding out her hands as if to bring them together. "Correction: Not an *old* friend, rather a very good friend from older times, Jerry Hough. Pronounced Howe, but spelled H-O-U-G-H." She looked at him. "You see, I remembered how to spell it, after all these years."

"And how! To echo one of our equally very old jokes."

He turned to Emily. "I am stunned. Blown away—on all levels, not just running into Jennie here, but that you—*you*—are Emily! Under the circumstances."

She held out her hand, finding it all too hard to take in so quickly.

He took it. "I'm Jerry Hough, Jeremy's father. I've heard a great deal about you. What an incredible coincidence that you two should bump into each other. *Here*, of all places!"

Emily stumbled back, the pieces, obvious as they were, now falling into place.

"Though that's not our real names, perhaps Jeremy told you?"

"Not his real name? No, I . . . I don't think so, I'm not sure what you mean." She felt dazed. First her mother, now this.

"I'm not really Jerry, it's just the name I took, and he took Jeremy. The real name we share is Jeremiah, old family tradition. Tradition, but sounds archaic these days."

Emily nodded, at a loss for what to say.

"Well, I'd better get checked in," he said. "Where's Jeremy?"

That's something a lot of people would like to know. Including the police. "I'm not sure."

"Well, when you find him we'll all go to lunch. I think Jennie and I can agree on the perfect place," he said, glancing at her at her as he wheeled his bag into the hotel.

EMILY LOOKED at her mother, saw the tears of joy streaming down her face, and hugged her even harder than before. "I think I'm getting the pieces of the story you never told me about your wild and wicked days on the Riviera."

"Happy days, yes. Not so very wild and wicked. He—Jerry—wasn't wearing a wedding ring, was he?"

"Jeremy said his mother . . . his mother was . . . had passed," Emily said, then wished she could pull it back.

"Ah! There you go, jumping to conclusions. I wasn't even thinking in those terms! . . . Or *was* I?"

They settled at one of the tables on the hotel's front veranda.. "So I— It's all happened so fast, 12 or however many jet-lagged hours ago I was back in Minneapolis making an impulsive decision, and now here I am in the best place in the world, with you, and now Jerry shows up. I must be dreaming, tell me I'm not dreaming!"

"You're not dreaming, Mother. It's real."

"So when am I going to meet Jeremy?"

"Mother, it's a long story, and—"

"You haven't broken up with him, have you?"

"The fact is, I don't know where he is. I haven't seen him or heard from him since last night, and his car is gone. I don't think he spent the night here in the hotel."

"Did you two have a spat?"

"A misunderstanding, sort of. But there's more to it than that."

EMILY'S PHONE RANG. She checked the number. It was not Jeremy's number. Not a number she recognized. Bourchette calling for results? She let it go.

The bag! That bag with the painting under Jeremy's bed!

But— But Jeremy wouldn't have left it there, Jeremy is clean, he's not an art thief, I just met his father.

That bag had to have been planted there!

And I was set up to betray him to the police!

Who set me up? Why? Doesn't matter. What does matter is that I move that bag out of his room. Fast. Before the police come looking.

"Emily, what are you thinking?" Jennie said. "I'm the one who should be off in another world, with jet-lag and now all this, but it's you who's drifting off on a cloud. Why?"

I can't leave it there. But what can I do with it?

Put it in my room? But Bourchette will come looking there, too.

"Mother, I have to go upstairs. For just a moment."

"But Jerry will be right back."

"It'll give you two time to chat."

GOOD NEWS: in the excitement of bumping into her mother, she hadn't turned in the room key-cards, so she now had three of them in her pocket—her own, Jeremy's, and her mother's.

The solution was obvious: for the short term, move the bag with the painting from Jeremy's room down the hall to the room her mother had just taken. If—if, heaven forbid—the police came, they would never look there.

And if they did? What then? Then they'd point out she had just checked in and . . . and a previous occupant must have left the paintings there.

Not a perfect solution, just the best option until . . . until something better came along.

Tunnel of deaths

THE OLD MILITARY TUNNELS in the mountains behind Nice—Vera had mentioned them in their early reconnaissance trip.

She had learned of the tunnels decades earlier, as a teen-ager living on the Riviera. There had been the stories of how the spooky old tunnels and the abandoned military buildings nearby had been used by the *Milieu* to hide stolen goods . . . and bodies. Just spooky legends, all of her friends said. But they never went up there after dark, and then only in large groups.

Now the area, and the winding roads leading up to the old fortifications, was popular with hardy bicyclists . . . and with couples looking for a quiet place where they could go and not be seen. But still no one ventured up there after dark.

VERN BILLY HAD SEEN THE AREA last night for the first time, when they brought what Derham termed their "special cargo." He ended up drawing the short straw as the one of them to stay up there overnight, just in case. At least they'd left him one of the cars to sleep in. But no weapon, just a hunting knife.

Nor had anyone mentioned to Vern Billy the legends of the special use the *Milieu*—local version of the Mafia—made of the area. But he knew, nonetheless, in a deep way that penetrated to his core, that this was not just a spooky old place, but a place infused with the echoes of some very dark, evil happenings. He'd been in combat, he'd endured the hours before combat, the hours of not knowing whether he'd survive. This was worse: here there was no starting point, no clear enemy.

He felt a little sorry for the poor bastard they'd locked in the cell back in one of the tunnels. He didn't want to think what that must be like back there—no light, no food, no water. No sense of what was to come next.

What was next for him? Derham hadn't said, but it was pretty clear what that would be. Nothing.

Tomorrow, if nothing changed, Derham would phone and say come on back down and leave the guy there. And that would be it. Leave him there till somebody else found him. Most likely dead, dried out like one of the old Egyptian mummies he'd seen on a TV show a while back.

He'd asked Derham: The guy's locked in there, all tied up, not going to get away. So why do any of us have to stay? He got no real answer, just a kind of half-assed hint that Vern Billy took to mean the paintings are hidden up here in one of the other tunnels, and tomorrow's the day the Colonel picks them up, and then pays us off.

Didn't make a lot of sense, didn't even sound true. But you didn't argue with that crazy bastard Derham. Not if you wanted to live another day.

Too bad for the guy in the tunnel, but no way was Vern Billy going in there tonight. He had some food, some beer. And the hunting knife. And the Vietnamese necktie he always carried with him, just in case. Something he'd learned from his Daddy and never forgot.

VERN BILLY WAS NEVER SO GLAD to see a morning come. He waited till eight o'clock, figuring the others would be coming up by then. The car radio wasn't any use at all—all in fucking French, and he didn't speak a word of French. Other than what some waitress had taught him: "oon bee-yayer"—one beer.

297

He had four beers left, and some bottled water, and the rest of the candy bars. Hellova bad mess for survival rations. Eat the candy, drink the beer, get sick, barf, start all over again.

He decided to give it another hour. And then another. And then it was noon and he'd been asleep for he didn't know how long.

ALBERT LEROUX was a city boy, unused to mountains and rugged country, and he wanted to get the hell off this damned mountain. He'd been here since yesterday afternoon when he followed the Americans to the tunnel. He hadn't signed on for this kind of job. Tell him to torch a restaurant because the owner hadn't kept up his protection payments, or to rough up some guy who was cheating on a deal— that he was happy to do, that was what he did, and he felt good about doing it well.

But this shit, sitting up here in the wild playing goddam soldier, watching to see what happened, that wasn't his thing. Truth was, the place scared the hell out of him.

It was spooky enough as it was, just being so dark and lonely all night long, no lights, no sounds, just rock and wind and goddam stunted trees.

But worse was the way the place was haunted. He'd been up here a dozen times or more on a "settling of accounts," and as he sat there all alone in the night, all the faces came back to him, just as if they were really there haunting the place.

Damn Marchand for coming up with this one! Damn the whole idea of the paintings!

At least he had a mobile phone so he could keep in touch. That and a sleeping bag that his buddy Favoire had brought up for the night, along with some food, wine, water, cigarettes, and a pair of binoculars.

He phoned in at midnight when the first car came up, the BMW convertible, followed by the other car, the one they'd been using. "Stay there," Marchand had said.

"How long? What about somebody else taking a turn," Leroux said, but Marchand had already clicked off.

He had hidden the car in a side trail a hundred meters down the mountain. It was tempting to jump in it and go, get the hell away from here. But he knew what would happen to him if he cut and ran. He'd been part of enough settling of accounts up here, and never wanted it to happen to him.

IT WAS ONE in the afternoon now, and fog had moved in to shroud the area. It felt cold without the sun. He had a swig of wine and lit a cigarette. He was running low already–gone through most of three packs in what? A little over 18 hours.

He saw someone emerge from the mouth of the tunnel. Leroux dug out the binoculars. It was the skinny guy with the shaggy hair, the one they called Vern Billy.

Leroux turned away for a moment to light another cigarette. When he looked back, Vern Billy had disappeared. He shifted over to get a look at the tunnel. Still no trace of him.

A minute passed, then two. His skin tingled now, and he had the sense he was being watched. He felt something, a presence, that meant him harm.

The images of the men he had seen dying up here would be forever burned into his mind. Men he knew, men he had worked with.

Leroux had been born a Catholic, but he'd gotten away from that. Now he didn't like to think of how many sins he had piled up on his record, how many killings. But there was no going back, once you join the *Milieu*.

The terror he was feeling made him realize he still believed in the old stories about the spirits of the dead, the ones who had died suddenly, violently, roaming the earth, puzzled, confused, terrified, wondering what had happened to them.

Leroux felt the spirit of the dead ones watching him, and his flesh crawled in terror. Superstition, he tried to convince himself. But he knew something was there. Something was watching him, something angry, malevolent.

He grabbed his pistol and spun in a full circle. He saw nothing.

He looked back at the entrance to the tunnel. Nothing.

He pulled another cigarette out to light it from the stump of the one in his mouth.

So quickly did the thing come over his face that there was no time to find a target, even to pull the trigger.

The gun dropped, for he needed both hands to pull away what was cutting into his throat, blocking his air.

He screamed with the little breath he had left, then his world went black.

"NEXT TIME DON'T SMOKE, ASSHOLE," Vern Billy said. "It ain't good for your health. He loosened the wire slightly, the Vietnamese Necktie his daddy had called it when he taught him how to use it. "Who the hell are you? Why're you here?"

At first Vern Billy thought the man had died of fright, because his skin was so white. Then he figured the guy had only fainted. He eased the cord and slapped him till he came to. It took couple of minutes to convince Leroux that he was still alive. Leroux spoke a little English, just enough

He refused to talk at first, but after a couple of minutes of the cord loosening and tightening he was willing to say anything, just to keep the air flowing into his lungs.

The *Milieu*—who the hell ever heard of them? Vern Billy wondered. Then he understood—the local version of the Mafia, only here it was Corsicans, not the Italians like at home in the States.

That made sense—of damned course the locals would want to muscle in on a good thing, the stolen paintings.

Once he'd gotten the information he needed out of Leroux, Vern Billy wasted him and cleaned out his pockets: a good wad of money, and car keys, just like he'd said.

Then he shoved the body into a clump of shrubbery. He sure as hell didn't owe that bastard a burial.

NO TIME for fooling around now. Get the hell out of here, get the hell home.

He thought about looking for the paintings that were stored in the tunnel. Maybe liberate just a few of them, then he'd really be set for life.

But were there really any paintings there? Most likely not, just another damned lie.

And if they were, probably were booby-trapped . . . at least that was what Derham had sort of said. But that lying sumbitch, that was probably just another crock of crap.

But suppose they were booby-trapped, so what? He'd been through the army demolitions training like the others. They couldn't come up with anything he didn't know how to work around.

Then he thought: Suppose I grab them. Then what do I do with them? I don't have an idea in hell on where to go to sell them. And if I get stopped with them, then I haven't got a chance.

Just get the hell away from here.

There was that other issue: the other guy locked up in there. Vern Billy thought about it, then figured it wasn't his problem.

TIME TO HAUL ASS, he decided. Cut your losses, get away while you can. He went back to the car, downed one beer to settle his nerves, then tossed the rest of them along with empties behind some rocks.

He fired the engine, spun it around and headed down the mountain.

This felt even better than when that old C-17 lifted him out of Afghanistan. He gunned the little car down the mountain, forgetting how rough and steep the road was. The first hairpin came as a surprise. He nearly made it, tires shrieking, the car's body leaning almost to the turnover point.

But in the last feet of the turn, the front wheel skidded into the low stone guardrail. The car's center of gravity rolled, and it slowly somersaulted into the void.

The car fell 80 feet, rolling gently through the air, Vern Billy screaming "Shitgoddam!" over and over in frustration.

It hit for the first time on the roof, breaking his neck. He died instantly.

The car tumbled another hundred yards down the mountainside, rolling, bucking, sliding, shedding debris—glass, doors, wheels, even the gas tank.

It came to rest, nose down, wedged against a pine tree.

Double game

VERA HAD A LIGHT LUNCH—salmon, salad, and a small bottle of white wine—brought up to her room.

Then she sat wondering what was keeping Peter. She had told him to bring what he had immediately, and that was nearly two hours ago.

At last her phone rang. It was Peter, calling from the lobby. "They won't let me come up with the bags, not until you call down to tell them it's all right."

"No, it's best if the boy just brings them up. You did bring both sets?"

"*Both* sets? I have only the—"

"I mean your copies and the originals."

"Yes, both. But I'm perfectly capable of carrying them up."

"No, it's best if we don't see each other now. Not till we get back to London. Then we shall celebrate."

"But we need to talk, settle where things go from here."

"Yes, yes, but not now. Just give them to the boy. It's best if we're not seen together. Go back to the cottage. I'll come and see you tonight, then we can talk." If all went well, she'd be safely across the border into Italy by early evening.

"But what about the next batch? I need to get working on them as—"

"Go back to the cottage, Peter. I'll call you."

AFTER THE BELLMAN delivered the bags, Vera fixed herself a celebratory vodka-tonic, then unlocked the bags and spread the paintings around the room to admire, placing the originals and the copies side by side.

Peter's forgeries, good as they were, were crude by comparison with the originals. But crude only to a trained eye, she thought. A layman, certainly fools with as little taste as Gawbi and his lot, would never know the difference.

She would bring the originals to a bank vault now. Then she would bring the copies down the coast to Cannes to deliver to Gawbi Al Senour. He would never know the difference. Never, that is, until he tried to sell them.

But he wouldn't live long enough to try to sell them, she assured herself. She had convinced him that he must hold them at least ten, better twenty years, for safety. Stupid playboys like Gawbi, addicted to fast cars and drugs and alcohol didn't have long life-expectancies. Gawbi and his co-investors would be dead long before ten years were up.

They would never know what she had pulled. And if they did happen to live that long, they would never find her.

She wandered around the room, admiring her collection. They were such exquisite pieces, so absolutely marvelous.

Her only regret was that she could never sell any of them on the open market. They were worth, conservatively, fifty million dollars. But on the underground market she would be lucky to get a tenth of that. Still, over the years, she would do well enough.

Too bad the original plan fell through—damn Emily Cederquist for intervening at Antibes!

TIME WAS SLIPPING AWAY. It was time to get the originals safely out of harm's way, time to deliver to Gawbi and get it over with.

She fitted the forgeries into the new leather bag. Appearance counted for so much in the art world, she had learned. If she treated these fakes with all the respect the originals deserved, Gawbi would be that much more certain to accept them as genuine.

The fakes in the bag of velvety glove leather, the originals in an anonymous cloth bag.

Gawbi gets what he deserves. Ignorance is bliss. Art really is whatever you can get away with.

She refreshed her vodka-tonic, then put in a call to Gawbi in Cannes, and set up a meeting for five o'clock. "You'll be delighted with what I have for you," she told him.

Then she packed her clothes. At five she would deliver to Gawbi. A couple of hours after that she would be safely out of France, safely across the border in Italy.

Last night

LAST NIGHT, after the strained dinner with Emily, Jeremy had closed his door, troubled by her attitude. For no reason he could come up with, she had been distant, even wary, from the start of the evening. Not just wary—more like seething with hidden anger.

But why? Was it something he'd done? Was she annoyed that he'd had to go off that morning?

He'd been brushing his teeth when the room phone rang. The hotel night manager: "Monsieur, I regret to disturb you, but a gentleman is here saying there is a problem with your car, and that you should come down now and see to it."

"The gentleman said he would be waiting outside," the night manager said when Jeremy came downstairs. "He is like you, an American, so you will not need anyone to translate."

His BMW was parked in the hotel's small fenced-in area. It was dark. The man stood in the deeper shadows by the car, a skinny wiry guy, shorter than Jeremy. "I think you oughta take a look at this, y'know?"

Jeremy wished he'd borrowed a flashlight from the hotel.

The man bent over and pointed to one of the tires. Jeremy stepped over to take a look. He felt another man move in behind him, someone he hadn't seen. Bad news. He tried to break free but was trapped between two cars and two men.

"There's a knife in my hand," the one behind said. British accent. "You cause any troubles, I slice your bloody throat and you bleed to death right here. You understand that?"

Jeremy felt the edge of the blade against his neck. "You want the car, just take the keys."

"Reach into your pocket and take out the keys and hand them to my friend there, use both hands, put them out where he can see them, you understand that?"

Jeremy did. The skinny guy pocketed the keys, then pulled out a roll of duct tape and spun it around Jeremy's wrists. The man behind had moved the knife from his neck; now he felt the blade breaking skin around his ribs.

"Good boy, smart lad. Now we're going to back up and walk over to that car over there, the white Citroen, and you're going to climb into the back seat with me. Got that?"

"Just take my car," Jeremy said. "You don't want me."

"It's you we want. For a little while. Cooperate with us and then you go free."

THEY SHOVED him onto the floor of their car; the British guy rode in the back with him while the skinny American drove. The Brit taped his ankles together, then pulled more tape around his eyes and mouth. It was hard to breathe.

He had no sense of where they were going: through the city for a while, working with the traffic. Then the air changed— cooler, fresher—and he sensed the car was winding up into the mountains behind Nice.

Time passed, maybe twenty minutes, maybe an hour, it was hard to know. The car left the paved road and cut across gravel and rough terrain, and then the atmosphere changed again. Now it was damp, dank. He had the sense they were in a cave.

Reunion

THEY WAITED FOR JEREMY till one o'clock, then left word at the front desk and headed for the restaurant they both were eager to revisit.

It was no surprise to Emily that this was *Le Petit Jardin*—the restaurant in the garden of the old hotel nearby, the site of that awkward dinner with Jeremy last night.

I can't believe this," Jennie said, "to think that after all these years I'm really back here. And here with you, Jerry. And with Emily, who wasn't even born until . . . until years afterwards. How time gets on! Sorry, I'm just babbling on, I'm still in shock."

"This place hasn't changed, not a bit," Jerry said.

"I do so want to meet Jeremy," Jennie said. "You have no idea where he is? Have you tried his cell-phone? He *does* have a phone, doesn't he?"

"His phone is in his room at the hotel," Emily said, realizing as she spoke the questions that would be coming.

"He left without his phone?" Jerry said. "That's not like him. I have been trying his number, no answer. But why would he leave it behind?"

"Are you sure? Are you sure he left it?" Jennie asked.

"Actually, I was checking his room just as you arrived."

"Ah, I see," Jennie said. The question hung implicit in the air: Are you two sharing a room?

"I, uh . . . I borrowed the key—the key card—from the front desk. I was getting very concerned about him, why he hasn't been seen." Getting very *concerned that he was setting me up.*

"TELL ME ABOUT JEREMY," Jennie said to Jerry.

"What's to say? Second son, dropped out of school to put full time into setting up his business. Correction: he didn't really drop out, rather, took a leave of absence to do a tech startup. Last year he and his partners sold the business, then Jeremy went off to do his good works. Now I expect he'll be resuming classes in the fall, finishing up. Or maybe in the winter, I haven't had a chance to talk about it with him."

"It's none of my business, I know," Jennie said. "But what was his business, the tech startup business he set up?"

"The apple farm, that's what they called it."

"An apple farm?" Emily burst, immediately wishing she had kept quiet.

"No, that was the joke, mostly the family joke. It wasn't apples he grew. It was apps. Apps— applications, mostly for Apple computers, but some for other operating systems, as well. He did very well. *Extremely* well, he and his partners."

"He never told me that, never mentioned anything about that."

"Didn't you ask what he did for work?" her mother asked.

"He was . . . well, elusive. He didn't want to talk about it. He said that he was who he was, not what his work was."

Jerry laughed. "That's him, for sure. Anybody else who'd done half as well as he had, by that age especially, would be broadcasting it far and wide. He is inclined, as the saying goes, to hide his light under a bushel."

Emily and Jennie held back, desperately wanting to know, but not wanting to seem inquisitive.

Jerry finally filled the silence. "You do know about the App Farm?"

Jennie shook her head. "I don't know much about Jeremy, only the little I've heard from Emily, and she obviously didn't know all that much."

"Then I suppose it's left to me to tell the family secrets. Jeremy and some friends set it up, ran it part time while they were still in school, then it grew and they took leaves of absence to run it full-time for a couple of years. Then they were bought out, for truck-loads of money. But don't let on I told you that part."

"I'M VERY PROUD OF HIM, as you can imagine. Not just for what he accomplished, so young—not yet turned 30. But more because of what he's done with his good fortune. Very generous, if a father may say so."

He looked at Emily. "You do know about his work—his *adventures*—in Africa?"

She shook her head. Only a hint from the letter she'd found snooping in his room, something about a Cessna he had donated.

"His mother—his late mother—had spent several stints working in African missions. She was a doctor, and that was her calling. She died, in Africa. An accident. In her memory, Jeremy—after his business was bought out—bought a Cessna, a small airplane suitable for the conditions. He arranged for it to be delivered to the central mission, then spent six months working with them. He was an accomplished pilot, you probably know that."

Emily shook her head. "I didn't know that." *Seems I didn't know much at all about him . . . and most of what I thought I knew was wrong.*

"But—alas, there's a but. The powers-that-be there, in what passes for the government, had him arrested on trumped-up charges, then expelled from the country."

"When was that?" Jennie asked.

"A couple of months ago. From there, he went on to spend some time recuperating in London—he'd caught some intestinal bug. Then he bought a car and took a trip to clear his head before he goes back and finishes his degree."

"His degree? Where? What's his major?"

Emily cringed. Mother was being snoopy in the ways of mothers.

"Stanford. In the business school. He has about one more semester to finish his MBA."

JERRY LEFT THE TABLE, saying he'd be right back.

Jennie leaned forward, conspiratorially. "All this. . . It's beyond my comprehension. To be back here after all these years, a place that's never been far from my thoughts, that's enough in itself. Then add in running into Jerry here, it's like a . . ."

She shook her head. "I shouldn't say like a dream, that's too hackneyed. But it makes the point. And then for you to have met his son, a wonderful young man, it seems, and—"

She broke off when the first notes of Sinatra's "Strangers in the Night" played. She looked over. Jerry stood by the restaurant bar, grinning.

Then they came together and hugged, tears streaming down both their faces.

For Emily, the moment was broken by the sounds of the hee-haw klaxons of police cars, a *lot* of police cars, coming from all across the city.

Were they headed for the hotel? Was Jeremy about to be arrested?

Afternoon in the park

VERA WAS THE KEY—Derham was convinced of that, and he'd been in the Palm Garden across from Vera's hotel from seven that morning. He'd come this far and he damned well intended to walk away with something for his efforts, something he could live on for the rest of his life.

Eventually it would break open: either Vera would get delivery of another bag of paintings, or she'd lead him to someone else. That's when he would move in.

He had followed her to the flower market and saw her exchange with the man at the café, and it was clear enough to him that she had bought a gun.

He followed her from there to the main post office, watched her make the call, then saw her meet with the Colonel at the small café.

By now, Derham knew the Colonel's real name, Roger Stoddard, though hadn't yet figured what to do with it.

Then to the airport to pick up the bag—had to be some of the paintings—looking all the while for an opportunity to move in and grab them from her. But the chance never came.

Now morning had blended into afternoon. He bought a chocolate bar from a vendor. Despite the heat and his thirst, he drank nothing; he was determined not to leave, not even long enough to use a toilet.

FREDDIE MARCHAND had been waiting for two hours in the hot sun near the entrance to Vera's hotel. Despite the heat, he still wore the jacket of his pearl-gray suit: it covered the pistol stuck in the waist-band of his trousers.

Hot as it was, he was prepared to wait all day if that's what it took. Anything was better than standing up on *Mont Chauve* waiting for the *garrote*, and he knew this was his last chance.

Boom-Boom was across the street in the car, ready to move out as soon as they had the paintings.

Jean-Yves Vourquerre sat in the back seat of the car, his legs taped together so he couldn't get away. Marchand would figure out later what to do about him—let him go? or silence him? It depended on how things turned out.

VERA WANTED to get out of French jurisdiction as soon as possible. She had booked a seat on the evening train to Milan, would spend the night in Italy, then go on to Geneva in the morning.

By the time she checked out of the hotel, she was floating in a comfortable vodka haze in which all seemed manageable.

She left her suitcases with the hotel Concierge, ready to pick up on her return from Cannes and the delivery to Gawbi Al Senour.

She kept with her only her purse, and the two bags of paintings: the expensive leather bag with the fakes to deliver to Gawbi, and the originals Edleigh had delivered earlier in a cheap nylon suitcase.

Before going to Cannes, she would stop at a bank long enough to deposit the bag of original paintings in a vault. She would leave them there until things had quieted down, perhaps a year or so, then would begin selling them off quietly, one by one.

SHE STEPPED OUTSIDE and signaled the doorman for a cab. He saluted her, and waved a car to move up from the stand at the end of the block.

The *Cote d'Azur* was superb in its way, she thought, looking through the tall palms to the blue sea. In time, once she was sure it was safe, she would come back and live here. Now, at last, she would be able to afford it.

But not in Nice, she would most definitely not live in Nice. Nice was common. The area around St. Tropez was interesting, but too full of nouveau riche film-makers and industrialists and Arabs and Russians and all the others of that sort.

Perhaps she would buy a villa in Grasse, where the interesting people lived.

A hand smashed across her face, shattering her reverie. She stumbled back, jolted by the blow, and collapsed against the glass wall of the hotel, blood gushing from her nose.

As she slid to the ground, she realized that the leather bag was gone, pulled from her hand. She screamed and pointed at the man in the light gray suit now walking quickly to the Palm Garden across the street, carrying her leather bag. But the doorman saw only the blood on her face.

She pulled herself to her feet and tried to run after him, but her legs were rubbery from pain and alcohol, and she stumbled only a few steps before falling again.

Tears of rage and frustration welled out of her now to blend with the blood, dripping onto the $1200 dress she had bought a couple of days earlier, the first uncalculated tears she had shed since early childhood.

WHEN VERA APPEARED with the leather bag, Freddie Marchand knew that his life depended on pulling it off perfectly. If he failed, there would be no way to explain how he could have been so close without getting the paintings.

He moved in behind her, working out his moves. He slammed the back of his hand across her face, then grabbed the new leather bag and ran for the car waiting across the street.

Boom-Boom saw him coming and fired the engine.

Marchand threaded his way between the passing cars, their fenders missing him by inches.

He was a dozen steps from the car when he saw the man, a blond giant, racing toward him. His eyes told Marchand that he knew what was in the bag.

Marchand panicked. He turned and ran into the park, forgetting Boom-Boom and the car. Marchand was not one for exercise, had not run since childhood, and his soft Italian sandals slipped on the pavement.

He made it to the grove of trees by the fountain. Then the bag of paintings tripped him up, and he fell. He scrambled to his feet and pulled his pistol from his belt.

But it was too late. The big man grabbed the gun and the bag of paintings. Marchand, aware that failure meant death, lashed out with his feet, catching the big man behind the knee, knocking him down. Marchand dove for the bag, then felt a river of fire slice through his chest, and he saw again the face of the chemist, the first person he had ever killed. An expression of twisted satisfaction played over the chemist's face.

Satisfaction. And anticipation.

DERHAM grabbed the bag and Marchand's gun, a .38, and paused an instant to reconnoiter the best way out of the park.

The handful of people around the fountain stood stunned, immobilized.

The Promenade was busy at this time of day. He'd go there, blend with the crowd.

He didn't see the car cutting across the grass of the park until it was nearly upon him. When he did, he emptied the clip into it, but the slugs hit only glass and metal.

Boom Boom's car hit him with full force and threw him twenty feet through the air. His head slammed into a stone wall and he was dead.

BOOM-BOOM slammed on the brakes, skidding on the grass. He jumped out, grabbed the leather bag, and threw Vourquerre out onto the grass. Then he floored it and cut across the park to the *Place Massena*, scattering chairs and people.

The square was jammed with late afternoon traffic. He swerved around a bus, and headed the wrong way down a one-way street to the Promenade.

He didn't hear the klaxon until he was turning onto the Promenade. The police car slammed into the side of the car, killing him instantly.

THERESA MULLARVEY AND MATT GILLIGAN watched it unfold from their spots in the Palm Garden. They had spent the day, positioned separately, ready to follow Vera de Cochin-Jessup.

Matt phoned her as she was about to punch his number into her cell-phone. "I think it's time for us to disappear, don't you agree?" he said.

"It's a very good time now, while there's so much turmoil about. Meet you at the train station in thirty."

"And our friend?"

"He got us into this, let him get himself out of it." She'd had quite enough of Johnny McDevitt.

Multiplying troubles

VERA REALIZED that the bag-snatcher had taken the leather bag filled with Peter's forgeries. That meant she still had the originals! What incredible good luck!

Then she heard the gunshots in the park, and knew it was a disaster. Her only hope was to disconnect herself from what was happening in the park.

"I'm afraid I made a very silly mistake," she told the hotel manager. "The man didn't take my parcel, after all. I had only this one bag. He must have stolen a bag from someone on the Promenade and bumped me while trying to escape. Because I fell and hurt myself, I naturally assumed he had taken my bag. But it was definitely not my bag that he took. No, not my bag."

The manager wanted to call the house physician to look at her nose, but she refused, saying she was late for an urgent meeting. She quickly cleaned herself up, washing away the blood, and changing to fresh clothes from her suitcase. The nose was beginning to swell, and the eyes were sure to blacken, but for the moment she looked presentable, with sunglasses.

She decided it was best to take all of her suitcases with her now. That would break her connection to the hotel and the scene in the park.

She gave the cab driver the address of the bank where she'd earlier arranged a large safety-deposit box.

It was only when she was standing on the sidewalk outside the bank that she grasped another problem. The set of copies that Peter made were gone, stolen by the bag-snatcher in the park. Those were the paintings she had planned to deliver to Gawbi.

319

But now they were gone, and she had only the originals which Peter had just returned. If she put them in the bank vault, then she would have nothing to deliver to Gawbi.

The easy way out would be to hand these originals over to Gawbi and then get away.

Never! Gawbi was a fool.

But she had to deliver something.

Or did she? Why not make a run for it?

But she couldn't leave France with these paintings now—there would be too much risk in crossing the border.

Yet she couldn't very well abandon them. The paintings in this shabby suitcase were worth millions of dollars, even on the black market.

Then it came to her: Stall Gawbi for a few more days, time enough for Peter to dash off another set of copies.

A gypsy woman with an infant on her shoulder came up, hand out for some coins. Vera lashed out with the bag, feeling satisfaction and release as it slammed into the woman's thigh, knocking her and the baby to the sidewalk.

Expensive leather bag

COMMISSIONER DE CASTARET was on the scene within minutes of the shootings in the Palm Garden, and he was standing nearby when the hotel doorman identified the woman with the stolen bag as Vera de Cochin-Jessup, who was staying in Room 420.

A few minutes later, the uniformed police produced Jean-Yves Vourquerre, who Boom-Boom had dumped from the car, moments before his fatal crash. Jean-Yves' account clinched it: Vera had spent her life in the art trade, and had come to him requesting help in finding a weapon. Almost certainly she was involved, perhaps was even the brains behind the operation.

"But we don't want to alarm her," de Castaret said. "Nothing to the media, just spread the word quietly to the men that we want her for questioning. Make some calls to see if she's settled in another hotel. Get a description, as she may be using another name. Put someone at the rail station, and the airport. Yes, and the cab drivers, as well. See if they can give us a lead."

THE EXPENSIVE LEATHER BAG, apparently the focus of the shoot-out in the park, was found in the car beside the body of Boom-Boom. Detectives of the Judicial Police opened it as soon as the bomb squad cleared it. When they saw the paintings, they called de Castaret.

By the time de Castaret arrived, they had compared the paintings with the inventory of the various thefts, identifying these as the ones stolen from the museum at Le Trayas.

De Castaret directed that Commissioner Bourchette be informed of the recovery, as well as the Director of the Museum. Bourchette had left the Judicial Police office an hour earlier and could not be reached on a secure telephone line, so was informed by police radio.

The police transmission was picked up by a reporter for Radio-Monte Carlo, and was on the air within minutes as a news bulletin.

Ironically, by the time that news was broadcast, the Museum Director arrived with one of his specialists. The specialist, intimately familiar with the paintings, declared them forgeries. "Quite good copies, to be sure. But forgeries, nonetheless."

"Are you certain?"

He took a pen from his pocket and touched the corner of one of the paintings. "*Regardez*. The paint is soft, it is barely dry, only days old, not decades."

ANNOYED BY THE LEAK to Radio-Monte Carlo, de Castaret directed that Bourchette be informed of this latest development only when he arrived back in Nice.

Under no circumstances were the forgeries to be mentioned in radio or telephone messages. That way there would be no more leaks, as only the Museum Director, his specialist, de Castaret, and two of his men knew that the shoot-out had been over a bag of fakes.

Gone forever

VERA CHANGED CABS to erase her connection to the scene in the Palm Garden, and checked into a small hotel she knew in Cimiez, one of the quieter, more exclusive areas of Nice.

She phoned the cell number Gawbi had given her at the party, intending to tell him that something had come up and she would not be able to make the delivery today at five, after all, but would be in contact in a day or two.

A woman answered. She sounded young and stupid. "Gawbi? He's not here. He's gone away."

Vera was stunned. Barely an hour ago he had agreed to be there to receive the paintings. "Gone away? Where?"

"I don't know. He went with some guys, they came and he went."

"What guys?"

"Who knows?"

"When will he be back?"

"Who knows?"

"I'm Vera de Cochin-Jessup," she said. "Certainly he left a message for me."

"No message. Maybe if you leave your number, maybe he'll call you back. You know how Gawbi is."

Her anger rising at Gawbi's lack of consideration: So very typical of those people. "Well, tell him I called. It's urgent that I talk to him. He knows why."

SHE SLAMMED the phone back onto the receiver.

But, as she thought about it, perhaps that would be better. With Gawbi away, she would have more time to work things out.

323

If Gawbi was not here to receive this set of paintings tonight, that gave her a window of opportunity to run for it. In a day, before he realized she was gone, she could be half-way around the world. He was too stupid ever to find her.

Ah, but what about those "friends" he'd brought in to put up some of the money? She wished now that she had taken the trouble to learn more about them. They might be as stupid and weak as Gawbi, or they might be dangerous people.

There was one other possibility. She punched in the number of Peter Edleigh's cell phone. No reply. That was odd, he was supposed to have it with him at all times. She tried again. Still no reply. Probably the fool had let the battery run down.

She called the hotel front desk, telling the clerk she needed a taxi. It was there in minutes, and she directed it to Edleigh's cottage in the hills.

He was out, and his car was gone, but it was clear that he was still living there.

She wedged a note in the door. "Urgent. Must see you. Here, about nine tonight. V."

AS SHE RODE BACK to the hotel Vera heard the news accounts of the shoot-out in the park.

Three dead. The bag of paintings in police custody. They would find, soon enough, that they were just forgeries. It was a mess. A disaster. The trembling began, soft quivering in her fingers at first, then spasms that shook her legs. The cab driver looked back at her in the mirror and asked if she needed to go to a hospital.

Once the police found what had been in that bag, they would become very interested in the woman who had first said it was hers, then changed her mind.

"Vera de Cochin-Jessup, of Washington, D.C." the hotel would tell them.

She could never again be Vera de Cochin-Jessup. That person, that life, was gone forever.

But it would be even worse when word got out that the paintings in the bag were forgeries!

Gawbi and his friends, dense as they were, would soon realize that the paintings she had promised him were all fakes, so they had shelled out millions for worthless canvas. They would be the laughing-stock of the world.

If only things had gone according to her plan, it would have been twenty years before anyone realized what she had pulled.

Now it would be less than twenty-four hours.

Then they would come looking for her.

Pete the Sweet

THE NEWS THAT THE PAINTINGS recovered in the park were all forgeries had been kept within the police ranks, and Radio Monte Carlo and *Nice-Soir* remained unaware.

It had been a very long day, and Bourchette was tired and frustrated. And increasingly fearful that all was falling apart. Now this—forgeries! That damned woman and her damned games!

The office was crackling with activity. First had been the shoot-out in the park. Then the discovery of the leather bag full of paintings. Finally the discovery that the paintings were, ironically, after three deaths, only forgeries.

Pierre Doucette, a Detective on the Special Brigade, appeared at Bourchette's door. "We need to talk, old friend," he said, closing the office door.

Doucette and Bourchette had known each other nearly three decades, since Bourchette had been stationed in the *Departement Alpes-Maritimes* around Nice in his early years.

Though they were now several ranks apart, they had in common the fact that they were both parts of an endangered species. Both were of the old order, "Neanderthals," in a police establishment increasingly dominated by the younger "New Wave" people like de Castaret.

Pierre Doucette had another, more personal reason, for disliking de Castaret. A couple of years earlier, before his promotion, de Castaret had conferred the nickname "Pete the Sweet" on Pierre Doucette. For months Doucette had been puzzled by it, as he knew no English.

Finally someone pointed out that "Pete the Sweet" was a play on words on his name, Pierre Doucette. The word Doux—not far from Doucette—translated to English as sweet, and Pierre to Peter.

The nickname stuck, and every time Doucette heard it he was reminded of de Castaret's mocking arrogance. So de Castaret had more education, that didn't make him a better detective, it just taught him how to play politics and get ahead. It was his type to laugh at hard-working cops who had paid their dues. Doucette was determined to get de Castaret back before he retired.

But time was running out, as both he and Bourchette were only weeks away from retirement.

"There's something interesting you should know," Doucette said, sitting and leaning close enough to whisper. "De Castaret, he's hot on the trail of something new, something related to the woman from the hotel, the one with the leather bag."

"What about her?" The effect of the news on Bourchette surprised Doucette. It was almost as if he seemed frightened. That was strange.

Doucette repeated the scuttlebutt he had picked up in the hallways. As he spoke, he saw that Bourchette was becoming increasingly agitated, though he was trying to disguise it. Doucette assumed it was the usual anger from the conflict between the police generations.

"Why was de Castaret getting involved?" Bourchette snapped. "This is my case. Paris has priority, he knows that."

Doucette shrugged. Even the edges of his mouth echoed the shrug. "I don't know why, but now de Castaret is in it. I suppose it's that shooting in the park. This relates to that, he thinks. Besides, you were out when the shooting happened and he took charge."

WHAT HE HEARD from Doucette made Bourchette even more aware of how desperate his position was. If de Castaret found just one loose thread, then there would be no way of holding back the investigation.

The key was Vera. She had been very stupid today, drawing attention. She should have just kept her mouth shut and let the paintings go. Accept it as a necessary loss.

But, leave it to Vera, she had to create a scene. Now they were all in the soup.

The police already had her name and address from the hotel registration. Now a discreet all-points bulletin was out for her.

First option was her little collection of sleeping pills.

Second option, if they caught her before she could end it, then she would talk. She would sell Bourchette out, sell everyone out, for a lighter sentence for herself. In a year or two she would be back on the street, but there wasn't a chance in hell of a *Commissaire Principal* surviving even a month in prison. If the people he had sent away didn't get him, the guards would make his life hell.

The memo he had written to the files should have been insurance enough. If things had gone according to plan, he could have used the memo to cover what he had done: it would give a plausible explanation for why he opened the Swiss account, for why he had met with Vera.

But it would not stand up if Vera started talking. Then the memo itself would be even more evidence against him, proof that he had planned his betrayal far in advance.

He had to silence her before she started talking. There was no other solution. But where *was* she?

Watchers

THE LITTLE COTTAGE seemed even more forlorn at night. A few other buildings in what had once been a neighborhood remained standing, but they were abandoned and dark. Most of the hillside had already been bulldozed, and only rubble remained. Clearly, this would be the last season for what had been a cozy relic of other decades: by next year another high-rise would have consumed the area.

Emily parked at the base of the hill and walked up, keeping to the shadows. Only two of a dozen street lamps were still working. She approached the house from the side, moving through the shrubbery.

Lights were on in every room of the cottage, though the French shutters were drawn. By peering through the slats of the shutters, she got a view inside.

It took a second to recognize the man inside: The man she had seen at the café with Vera, the man to whom Vera had slipped the code to the locker at the rail station. The same paunch, the same flowing hair, the same slept-in look. But now his face was tense and drawn. He looked frightened.

He disappeared into another room, and returned a minute later, his arms full. Rolled paintings! Later, when it was all finished, she would see in *Nice-Matin* that his name was Peter Edleigh.

Emily watched, hypnotized, as he fitted the rolls reverently into three large suitcases, her mind clicking, generating an action plan. The first step would be to immobilize his car by draining the tires. Next would be to—

329

A hand closed over her mouth, the fingers pinching off her nose. She felt cold steel at the base of her skull. "It's got a silencer. A wrong move and you're dead, understand?" American accent.

He dragged her back from the house into the remains of a vineyard. She tried to resist, but he was too strong. Her air passages were blocked, her lungs screaming for oxygen. She felt herself suffocating, the brown curtains of unconsciousness closing in.

He released his grip on her nose, and she sucked in the sweet night air. "I'm going to ask you some questions," he said. "If I let go of your mouth you're smart enough not to scream, aren't you? If you do, I'll waste you, understand?" His fingers closed off her nose again.

She nodded, desperate for air. He moved his arm down and pinioned her around the neck, the gun still against the base of her skull.

"That guy in there. Who is he?"

"I don't know his name. Apparently he's a friend of Vera's—he's working with her."

"How do you know that?"

"I saw her pass a locker combination to him."

"That was when you stole the paintings from her?"

"How do you know that?"

"She told me. Answer my question." He pinched her air off for a moment.

"Yes, but I don't have the paintings now. They were stolen from me."

"Then why're you here, why're you interested in this guy?"

"I don't know how he fits in. He's connected somehow with Vera, and I'm trying to find out how. Now you answer me: where is Jeremy?"

"Who?"

"My friend Jeremy."

"He's my friend, too, and I'll take you to him, soon as I finish a little business with the guy inside"

Before she could resist, he'd wrapped duct tape around her wrists, locking them behind her, then wrapped her ankles

Corpse

THE POLICE CAR that had been behind his turned off onto a side street, and Johnny McDevitt continued to Peter Edleigh's cottage, following the map Theresa Mullarvey had drawn yesterday.

Maybe he'd find something there, maybe not.

He was the last of the Irish team still here: Theresa and Liam Clancy had disappeared, made a run for it, hoping to save their own necks. Bastards!

He parked down the hill from the cottage, and headed up on foot, taking with him a flashlight and a tire-iron.

He froze when he saw two cars ahead, parked in the shadow of a forlorn stand of pine trees. He moved closer. The first car was empty. He tried the doors: locked. The engine was still warm.

The other was a small Renault. A rental, he guessed, from the code stuck onto the back window.

What was going on?

The cottage was dark. He circled it to approach from the back. He peered in the blinds, but saw nothing. He tried the front door. Locked. He went around to the back, and found the door ajar.

He stepped inside. It was even darker inside, and it brought back fears from childhood. He forced himself to push on. He couldn't run away.

But he knew that what he was feeling was more than just fear of the dark. His flesh crawled, and knew that he was not alone in the house.

Death!

He was in the room with Death! He sensed it, he knew it. A finger pushing softly on a trigger, a knife already catapulting silently through the air toward him. Death coming to him.

His impulse was to turn and run, to get away from this cold enveloping presence. But it was all collapsing now, this was his only chance.

He forced himself forward, a step at a time, the tire-iron in one hand, the flashlight in the other.

He tripped and fell forward. His face hit cloth and flesh.

He reacted on instinct. He rolled away, lashing out with the tire-iron. It hit hard, and he heard a crack—bone snapping? But there was no cry of pain, not even a grunt.

He slashed again with the iron; it sliced through the air, hitting nothing.

Something scraped along his leg; he scuttled away across the floor, swinging the tire-iron as a shield.

A rhythmic creaking overhead.

He felt chills washing over him. He flicked on the flashlight, knowing what he'd find.

The body swayed gently on a rope, a swollen tongue sticking out of a blood-blackened face frozen in a rictus of pain and surprise. The eyes bulged obscenely as if shocked by what they had seen across the barrier.

A man, no one he recognized, had stood on a chair, then kicked it away to begin his journey to death. It was that chair that tripped McDevitt.

But had it really happened that way? Or had someone strung the man up, someone who was waiting there in the darkness, ready to kill again?

He swept the room with the flashlight beam. He saw an open door, leading to other rooms.

His instincts told him not to go through that door. But he had to.

Too late

McDEVITT STEPPED through the open door of the cottage. As he did, he saw the flash of a pistol shot, and the old training kicked in: he dropped to the ground and scrambled behind the cover of a table.

The flashlight slipped out of his hand and rolled away across the floor. In the flickering light, he saw the hanging body gently quivering behind him: the bullets had found a target.

He dove through the back door and ran for the cover of the grape arbor in the dark yard.

A minute later, a woman stepped through the door, his flashlight in one hand, a small pistol in the other. She staggered on the top step, then fell down the three steps.

He ran over to grab the gun she had dropped. She reeked of alcohol.

"You're too late," she said, her voice flat, her words slurred. "He already got the paintings. Killed Peter, and took the paintings, the originals and the copies. All of them."

"Who?"

"I watched. I saw the whole thing through the blinds. It was horrible. He was stringing up poor Peter when I arrived. There was nothing I could do. Not with this little gun. There was no point in trying. I'd only be putting myself at risk, too."

"Who did it? Who're you talking about?"

"Stoddard."

"Stoddard? Seriously? You two were in this together from the start."

Her head snapped around. "How do you know that?"

"We've been watching you from the start, from Washington."

335

"Oh God," she moaned. "From the start."

"Vera de Cochin-Jessup, *Galerie Vera*. From the start. Now looks like it's all come to an end."

"Who are you? Why . . . why were you watching us?"

"A team, that's all you need to know. Our plan was to let you do the work and then grab the proceeds. Looks like somebody already did that."

"Your accent. It's Irish, is it not?" She laughed hysterically, and the laugh phased into coughing, then sobbing.

She was on the edge of hysteria. And drunk. He let her calm a bit, then asked, "You said copies? Are you telling me they were forgeries?"

She looked up at him, her eyes barely focusing. "What does it matter now? It's ruined, all of it."

The story came flowing out, disjointed, barely coherent. She had agreed to find buyers for the paintings Stoddard's team stole. Found some rich young Arabs with more money than intelligence.

She recruited an old friend, Peter Edleigh, to forge some copies of what they planned to steal. She had scouted out the museums with him, pointing out which items to target.

Stoddard had not known about Edleigh and what role he was to play. That was her own little deal on the side with Edleigh, potentially worth far more than Stoddard's original plan. A way to have her cake and eat it too.

The plan was to sell the paintings to Gawbi Al Senour. Sell them, yet keep them: pass the forgeries to the Arabs, and keep the originals for herself.

She advised the young Arabs to store the paintings for ten or twenty years, think of them as a long-term investment. Hold them and let the values go up. Then they could sell them on the underground market.

In twenty years, of course, the silly fools would finally get the joke. By then there wasn't a chance they'd be able to find her, of course.

In any case, odds were they'd all be dead by then, anyway. Revolutions, wild driving, drugs, whatever. Stupid playboys didn't have long life expectancies.

That was the plan.

"But I found today that Peter had been double-crossing me, from the very start. I hired him to paint for me a nice set of copies of some of the items that would be stolen. He did that all right, he made me my copies to pass on to Gawbi. That way, I'd have the copies to pass on to Gawbi, and I'd have the originals. But now I realize that Peter painted *another* set of copies which he kept them for himself. He was a genius in that way. He had no talent of his own, but he could imitate so perfectly.

"No!" she burst, her body suddenly convulsing as she realized the deeper truth.

She tried to stand, but her drunken legs wouldn't support her. She tried again, then gave up and pounded her fist into the soil. "No, no! It can't be, it can't be true! Damn him! He double-crossed me! *Me!*"

She was silent for a moment, then looked up as if remembering where she was. "It's worse than I realized. Far worse! When I saw Stoddard take the paintings tonight, I thought that Peter had simply painted himself another set of forgeries, and those were what Stoddard was taking. That was bad enough. But it's worse than that! The fact of the matter is that Peter kept the originals and gave me two sets of forgeries! One was a little better than the other, so I'd believe one was the original. And I fell for it! Damn him, poor Peter! He's so talented . . . *was* talented. To be able to fool me with two degrees of forgery. Oh damn!" The "damn" came out as a wail.

She tried again to stand. Again her legs gave way, and she rolled back onto the ground. "Now, after all the trouble and all the risks I took, all I have are forgeries."

"Stoddard has the originals?" McDevitt asked. "Where would he go with them?"

"If, a very big if, these were not another series of copies, then he would take them to the tunnel, of course, where I told him to store them."

"What tunnel?"

"The old gun tunnels, of course, on *Mont Chauve*."

"Where is that?"

She flung a hand through the air. "Back there, somewhere, behind Nice."

McDEVITT FORCED himself back into the cottage to look for a map. He tried not to look at Edleigh's body swaying from the ceiling, but his final terror seemed to pervade the room.

He found a Michelin map of the area around Nice, and shook Vera awake.

"Leave me alone," she said. "I'm ill, I need to rest."

"Too bad. I need to know where Stoddard went, the tunnels where he stored things."

"*Mont Chauve*, I told you. Now leave me alone."

"Show me on the map."

"No, never."

He flashed the light on the pistol he had taken from her, then held the gun to her temple. "Show me on the map!"

"Shoot me, it doesn't matter now. If you don't shoot me, then I'll take my little box of pills, and . . ."

"I won't kill you, I'll just wound you and leave you for the police."

He grabbed her purse and dumped it on the ground. The little bottle of sleeping pills rolled across the dry earth. He grabbed it. "I know what you have planned with these. Tell me what I need or I'll take these pills and you'll spend the rest of your life in prison."

"Oh God, you would do it! I will show you, yes. But you must give me back my pills, do you promise?"

She traced the route north from Nice, then onto a smaller road that passed through a village, then onto a still smaller route, that even on the map was nothing more than a sequence of hairpin turns climbing a mountain. She knew the spot, the spooky place with the abandoned military tunnels, because she had pointed it out to Stoddard as a place where he might store things safely. The locals stayed away from it.

Hoax

A COMPUTER SCAN turned up that Vera de Cochin-Jessup had a reservation on the night train to Milan, made through the travel agency in the *Hotel Palais-sur-Mer*.

Bourchette went to the station alone: He would convince Vera to come away with him by saying that her name was on an alert list at the border. Then he would shoot her, claiming that she had attacked him.

He got to the railway station early, and spent the time scanning the platform. It was crowded with backpackers on their way to Italy. But there was no Vera.

There was one scruffy man waiting for the train, a man who seemed to be dripping blood from his leg. But that was no concern of Bourchette's.

That was California, trying to find a way out of France before they caught Derham and the others. Get away now, he'd told himself, and there was a good chance he'd never be caught, never linked to this. And he sure as hell would never get mixed up in anything like this again.

BOURCHETTE HAD THE TRAIN HELD while he went to check the seat she had reserved. It was empty.

He returned to headquarters. As he walked in, his old friend Doucette—Pete the Sweet—pulled him aside again, and began to talk of a fatal auto accident.

"I'm not interested in that, my friend," Bourchette said. "I have too much of my own to deal with at the moment."

"Ah, but it's very relevant. And I think you and I are the only ones who understand how. Let me tell you: This afternoon, while all the others were focused on the shootings in the Palm Garden, I heard on the scanner of a Renault found wrecked off the road to *Mont Chauve*, with one dead driver, male, unidentified. They brought the body down and fingerprinted it as an unknown. But the papers on the body identified him as American, and a former soldier at that. He still carried his expired Army ID card."

"Yes? So?" His mind was still focused on how to locate Vera before she got away. Or was picked up by other police.

"I don't either, exactly. But what was an American doing on *Mont Chauve?* You remember it from your days here, don't you?"

Mont Chauve. One of the rugged mountains—the Maritime Alps—that loomed behind Nice, even in summer often shrouded in mist. Used as artillery bases in both World Wars. "Remind me." His instincts were suddenly telling him to listen now, that Doucette was onto something important.

"The old military tunnels up there on the top," Doucette reminded him. "That's where the *Milieu* like to hide what they steal. Hide bodies, too. Remember now?"

Bourchette dropped into a chair, ideas beginning to fall into place. "Any word on the whereabouts of the woman? I forget the name," he asked, hoping his anxiety didn't show. "The one whose bag Marchand grabbed?"

"Nothing. But did you hear? The bag of paintings Marchand stole from her, they were all forgeries. Fakes, every single one of them."

"Forgeries!" Bourchette forced himself to take a couple of deep breaths, fighting off the sense that the earth was about to

341

open up beneath. "Forgeries? Are you sure? Why was I not informed?"

Doucette nodded. "That's what I hear, though de Castaret tried to keep it quiet, even from us."

THERE WAS STILL A CHANCE, Bourchette tried to convince himself. Be the first to find where the art was stored, and anything Vera said against him would be ignored. After all, there was still his memo back in the safe in Paris. That would cover him, provided that nothing else went wrong.

Provided, too, that Vera wasn't around to talk.

Mont Chauve. It was a long shot. But his only hope now. He raced to his car.

He was in the car, pulling into the street, when de Castaret came running after him. "Bourchette! Bourchette! Telephone! The Minister is on the line!"

He left the car where it was, engine running, and raced back into the building. But no one knew of any call from Paris.

He looked for de Castaret, but he was gone. The bastard! A hoax, now of all times!

Long day

JEREMY had spent the night and day imprisoned in a tunnel atop *Mont Chauve.*

The men who had grabbed him outside the Hotel Eminence— the two Americans and the British guy— had locked him, still taped hand and foot, in a room carved into the rock. It may have been a cell, back when the place was military. Or maybe a weapons closet. A rusty old iron gate barred the entrance.

He had tried to free himself until sleep overtook him. The voices were silent when he woke and he began again. Pulling his hands free was hopeless: there were several rounds of duct tape.

He set about working the tape against the rock walls, but it was exhausting with his hands behind, and he had to break often to keep from cramping.

His eyes had acclimated to the darkness, and he sensed daylight way down at the entrance.

They had given him no food or water, and he was woozy. He wondered, more and more as the hours passed, whether anyone would ever come.

HOURS LATER–it was hard to mark time—he called out for something to eat, something to drink. No response.

So he was on his own. His head ached, his mouth was sandpaper dry, and now he had no expectation that anyone would come back for him.

He still had made no real progress on the tape around his wrists: The rock was just too smooth to abrade.

343

Hours later, the little light faded in the tunnel. He had spent the day alternately working on the tapes that bound him and then sleeping—he was weak from hunger and thirst. He pulled himself, snake-like, around the room again, looking for one sharp edge he could use. Nothing.

He got a better idea: He'd been thinking only of rock. There had to be something sharp on the iron gate. There was, a broken piece, but it was both too high and too low. Too high to use while he was on the ground, but too low if he stood. He managed a sort of crouch, an exhausting position he could tolerate it for only a minute or so at a time.

Finally he felt the last fibers split. He was able to pull his arms around to the front. They cramped at once, though soon eased. He unwrapped the remnants of tape from his wrists, then went to work on his ankles.

Once his muscles had loosened again, he pushed against the rusty gate, hoping the old lock would give. Bad news: They had strung a chain and new lock, holding the door and metal frame together.

He rattled the rusty door. It stayed solidly attached to the wall. He moved to the far wall and ran the couple of steps to throw himself against the bars. The door held. He tried again, and again. At last, he felt some give. Another dozen tries and the rock crumbled around one hinge, and he was free.

IT WAS DARKER THAN NIGHT in the tunnel, and no telling what obstacles, maybe booby-traps, lay ahead. After a couple of wrong turns down side tunnels, he got a hint of fresh air ahead.

He had no idea where he was. The coastline spread out below, a carnival of lights stretching from Italy on the east to far behind the airport on the west, but so very far down. It would hours, maybe a whole day to walk . . . provided he didn't take any wrong turns. Would he have the strength? He was thirsty and hungry, and very weak. He hadn't eaten since that strained dinner with Emily last night.

He wandered the barren rocky summit for a while, trying to get a sense of where the road was. It was a littered junkyard, with old auto parts, old washing machines, seats.

He found his car, camouflaged at the entrance to another tunnel by a mass of the stunted trees and shrubs that seemed native to the area.

Why had they left it here?

Probably for the same reason they had left him in the tunnel: To get him and all traces of him out of the way, to make it seem that he had run away. To buy time enough to slip out of France.

In a day or a week or whenever, the car would be found. Only then would they go looking for an owner. Or maybe whoever found it would just drive it away, and there'd be no clues to send anyone looking in here for him, dead or alive.

He felt his body sway with weakness . . . and with awareness of just how close he had come.

It was not a mirage, not an illusion, it was his car, no doubt of that.

He bent over and felt behind the rear bumper, praying that it hadn't fallen off. It had not: the spare key was still in place.

He unlocked the driver's side, then popped the trunk, already tasting the food he'd carried from Germany: mineral water and a jar of mixed nuts.

He slumped into the car seat and gobbled the nuts, pausing to guzzle water from the water bottles.

Once he felt some energy passing through his body, he twisted around in the seat and turned the key. The motor started. He hit the button and rolled back the top, a kind of celebration: He was breathing fresh air after a day locked in a cave! He was alive and free!

HE FORCED HIMSELF out and began clearing away the pile of dead limbs that had been arranged to camouflage the car.

He froze when he heard the rumble of a car coming up the rocky road to the summit. Were the men back? He fumbled around in the dark and grabbed his tire-iron from the trunk, then ran to the shelter of one of the old stone military buildings.

The car came into sight around a rocky outcropping, headlights off, guided only by parking lights.

The car went directly to the mouth of the tunnel, the tunnel, flicking on the headlights once inside.

He heard a door open. A man's voice. American. "Get out. End of the line."

"How do you expect me to do that?" a woman responded.

Emily! What was she doing up here?

Jeremy moved closer, slowly, carefully, the tire-iron ready. He felt weak from lack of food, but pushed on. He *had* to. For Emily.

The man was pulling something out of the trunk—a body. Emily. He reached down and cut the tapes that bound her ankles, then grabbed her arm and pulled her into the passenger seat. He turned the car around fast, and Jeremy recognized it was a BMW, nearly the same model as his own, though this was a sedan.

Then backed into the tunnel.

Why? Jeremy wondered? To load something? Or to kill Emily and dump her body?

He froze in place when he heard the sound of another car coming up the gravel road. He turned and ducked back to the cover of the old army building.

Forbidding

McDEVITT FINALLY MADE IT to the summit of *Mont Chauve.*

He drove the last segment to the tunnel slowly, lights off, then backed the car off the road, nose out, ready to leave in a hurry.

The view from the mountain was spectacular, with the whole panorama of Nice and the Bay of Angels spread out before him. The mountain, Vera told him, had been an artillery site during both World Wars, and he could see why. It commanded the coast for miles in each direction. The military had cut tunnels through the rock of the mountains, miles of tunnels. Somewhere in them Stoddard had hidden the paintings—at least according to what Vera had said back at the cottage

But could he believe anything she said?

Mont Chauve, she had also told him just before she passed out again, was where the *Milieu*, the local gangsters, go to do their assassinations— "a settling of accounts," they call it. "Don't be surprised if you find yourself in the middle of one of those events. Then they'll kill you, too." She sounded glad.

He popped the trunk and took out his tire-iron.

He still had the little gun he took from Vera, with eight bullets left in the clip. Too small to be much real use, but better than nothing.

The odds were not good: a tire-iron, and a half-empty little pop-gun against a bunch of commandos. Or a bunch of French mobsters. Or Russian mobsters. Or all of the above.

But there was no choice: either pull this off, or go to prison for decades.

At least he had the element of surprise in his favor.

348

JEREMY, hiding behind one of the old stone buildings left behind by one of the armies over the years, watched McDevitt approach the tunnel, though he had no idea who he was.

Clearly, the stranger wasn't police: No smart policeman would go into a tunnel alone. He'd call for backup.

He knew Emily was in the tunnel: He had heard her voice, and he knew she was in trouble. He had to do something to help her.

This man, whoever he was, was an opportunity, something to distract the one who held Emily. It was the best he was likely to get.

THE TUNNEL WAS DARK AND FORBIDDING, chilly, smelling of decay. McDevitt forced himself in, the memory still vivid of stumbling against the hanging corpse in the dark room of the cottage.

He heard sounds ahead in the tunnel, the echoes distorted by the rocky walls. He moved on. The tunnel divided, with a spur cutting off to the side. A car was parked a dozen yards down this side tunnel. Its headlights were on, illuminating the tunnel ahead.

He saw the American woman, Emily Cederquist, standing with Stoddard. Her arms were bound behind her.

Where were the others on Stoddard's team? Had they deserted him? Or had he killed them?

JEREMY CREPT along the tunnel behind McDevitt.

He saw Stoddard's car further ahead. The trunk was open. Emily was in the passenger seat.

A man emerged from a side tunnel, cursing. "They're gone! Somebody got them!"

The man ahead—Johnny McDevitt—sprinted the final steps to the BMW and shouted, "Hands up, Stoddard! I've got you covered!"

Stoddard, visibly stunned, complied. "Who the hell are you? How do you know my name?"

"Doesn't matter. Where are the paintings?" Jeremy sensed an Irish accent. Irish? Why Irish?

"Gone, that's where. Somebody got there, cleaned them out."

"Then that's your loss, isn't it? What about the rest of them? I just talked to Vera, she doesn't have them, says—"

"You— you're the guy at the pub, the Irish pub, back in Washington! How the hell did you—"

"We've been following you, me and my team."

"That's how you heard about Vera! Goddam it!"

"Vera told me. She told me I'd find you here."

"Where in hell did you see her?"

"Up at the artist's cottage? The forger--you killed him?"

"We're running the same track, you and I. Maybe we should team up."

"Team up? Sure, just remember I'm the one with the gun and you're the one with the paintings. Tell me about the American girl, the one that— "

"She knows who I am, now she knows who you are."

"What are you going to do about her?"

Jeremy had crept forward, the echoing voices covering the sound of his steps. He was a yard behind McDevitt when his foot turned on a loose rock. McDevitt spun, gun ready. Jeremy swung the tire-iron. It caught McDevitt a glancing blow on the side of the head. He fell backward, the gun dropping onto the rocky floor.

Jeremy got to it an instant before Stoddard. He raised it. Stoddard backed away.

"I don't know how to use this gun," Jeremy said. "Don't make me nervous, it might go off by accident. Now back up. Back. Back. Back."

He checked McDevitt, still motionless on the ground.

He stepped around the car, keeping his gun on Stoddard, and opened the passenger side. Emily looked up at him, disbelief blending with amazement in her expression. Then joy.

He got the tape off her wrists quickly, keeping Stoddard covered. McDevitt remained motionless.

When she had freed her ankles, Jeremy said to Stoddard, "Okay, here's the deal: I've got the gun. Come after me, and I'll shoot, and in this tunnel the bullets will ricochet around till they find you. Got that?"

"I got it. Just go," Stoddard said. "I won't bother you. All I want now is to want to get away from here, that's all I want now."

"Don't believe him," Emily said.

Precipice

THEY RAN FOR HIS CAR, glad for fresh air after the dankness of the tunnel. The sky had lightened now. Dawn was near.

Jeremy's car coughed once, then caught, and he pulled out yards ahead of Stoddard BMW.

The road was a twisting bumping ribbon of gravel, then ancient asphalt, threading its way along the edge of a precipice, cutting briefly through a stand of trees, returning again to run along the cliff-side. The curves were sharp, the angles varied, making it hard in the dim pre-dawn light to know what was ahead.

Stoddard flicked his brights on and off; the glare in the rear-view mirror was blinding.

Jeremy hit the brakes when he saw the road ending abruptly at a low stone wall. Then he spotted the pavement dropping away sharply to the side—the start of a hairpin turn.

He spun the steering wheel to follow the bumpy road as it twisted downward in a stomach-wrenching dip. The nose of the car flashed out over empty space. The tires slid across the loose gravel on the road-surface.

The road straightened, and he accelerated for a couple of seconds before another stone wall loomed up, another hairpin.

He hit the brakes again. The car slid as if on ice before the tires caught. The car careened around the corner, inches from the edge.

He made it through a dozen hairpins, then found himself racing through the single street of a village. The roar of the engine echoed in the stone corridor formed by the ancient buildings lining the roadway.

A black cat dashed into the road, then stopped, frozen with fear before leaping out of the way.

The road flicked left, right, left again, looping downhill. The speedometer nudged 60, then 70 for an instant between hairpins.

Just past a tight bend, two farmers rode side-by-side through the dawn on motor-bikes. At the sound, the farmers peered back over their shoulders, their bikes wobbling crookedly in the road. There wasn't time to stop. He swerved past on the narrow shoulder, raising a cloud of dust, missing the bikes by inches.

Emily turned, drawn to the inevitable. The cyclists, their fists raised at Jeremy, teetered out of control as Stoddard's BMW rounded the bend and came on fast, neither slowing nor swerving, its horn splitting the dawn. The cyclists rolled into the ditch as he shot past.

The windshield erupted into a lacy cobweb of cracks, centered around a tiny hole below the rear-view mirror. "He's shooting at us," Jeremy said, flicking the steering wheel back and forth, sending the car veering from side to side, making it a harder target.

Emily grabbed the gun they'd taken from McDevitt and fired, but the car hit a bump, and the shot went high.

They went through another pair of hairpin turns. Their lead on Stoddard widened. But he was picking up speed again.

As they rounded another bend, she spotted a big logging truck rolling down from the hillside above to intersect with their road. "Truck!" she shouted, unable to get anything else out.

Jeremy flicked the wheel to pass it on the left, but the truck cut straight across the road without slowing. He swerved farther to the left. His arms felt strangely weak, the hands barely able to grip the wheel. The car skirted the edge of the pavement, the tires scrubbing against the low curb.

They squeezed past, the nose of the truck a paint-width away. The driver blasted his air horn.

The car did a 180-degree turn, tires squealing.

Time stopped as they spun, and the car slid relentlessly in an arc carrying them to the precipice.

At last the car stopped at the edge of the road, inches from the edge. The engine stalled.

The truck, its long body filled with logs, was stopped now, completely blocking the road.

The driver, a stocky man in workman's blue, jumped down from the cab, cursing and shaking his fist at them. He turned and froze as Stoddard's car appeared around the bend, headed at him.

There was no way out. Stoddard braked hard, the tires shrieked, but too late. The car passed under the body of the truck in an explosion of grass fragments, then emerged with the windshield and top sheared off. It rolled another few yards, before coming to a gentle stop at the side of the road.

Rising sun

EMILY AND JEREMY sat in silence for what seemed a very long time. They watched as the first rays of the rising sun touched the top of the mountains. They listened as a rooster in the valley crowed, the call taken up by the birds in the trees around. They watched as the truck driver stumbled over to collapse against a tree. They waited for movement in Stoddard's car.

Finally, Jeremy took the pistol and reached for the door, feeling strangely numb. Disconnected.

He moved toward Stoddard's car at a half-crouch, the pistol at arms' length ahead, ready for action.

Out of the corner of his eye, he saw the truck driver look up, and chuckled at the double-take as the man spotted the gun, then blessed himself and ran back up the road.

Jeremy approached the car slowly, ready for the trap. Stoddard would rise suddenly, gun blazing. But he would be ready and get him first.

He saw now with a kind of clarity he had never experienced before, a sense of being in the scene, yet simultaneously above it, watching himself. The scents of the fresh morning struck him with extraordinary intensity. His vision seemed preternaturally sharp, attuned to the subtle nuances of light and color.

What's happening to me? Is this what happens when you die? Or when you're about to die?

STODDARD'S HANDS still gripped the wheel at three and six o'clock, his body upright in the seat. Thick dark blood oozed out of the stump that had been his neck.

His head rested upright on the back seat, facing Jeremy, a puzzled expression in the open eyes. The eyes blinked twice, then faded into blankness.

Jeremy turned and walked back to the car, his body strangely light. He had been here before, not just once, but many times. From somewhere off to the side, he saw himself returning to his car on countless other mornings, and watched each of his steps reflected through an infinity of mirrors.

He saw Emily watching him, a little older than he remembered, and he saw the two kids playing in the back seat, a boy and a girl. But he couldn't remember their names.

He bent and kissed her. "Great kids, aren't they?"

She frowned. "Kids? What about Stoddard?"

"Nothing to worry about. He lost his head, that's all." He laughed for an instant, then fell forward onto the ground.

She climbed over the door to get to him. A bright red stain spread from his head to blend with the gravel of the road.

Blue light

A BLACK RENAULT rounded the bend, tires squealing, blue light flashing on the roof. Police.

Thank God, Emily thought, they'll have a first aid kit.

The car slowed, then stopped beside her. She ran over to it, but froze when she saw the large black pistol pointed at her. Commissioner Bourchette sat behind the wheel. He was alone.

He climbed out, still holding the pistol on her. "So it's all over?" he asked, almost conversationally. "What happened?"

"Jeremy's been shot. He needs medical help."

"What happened?"

She told him. Bourchette nodded, and walked over to Stoddard's car, peered into the passenger compartment, then snapped open the trunk and looked inside. He closed it, and walked back to her. He was still holding the gun on her.

"You've done a good job, good police work. I congratulate you."

"Yes, thank you. But, please, call an ambulance! Jeremy's bleeding to death."

"Back away," he said, waving the gun. He bent to examine Jeremy's prone figure. "He'll live. Briefly."

She felt terror surge through her as she grasped the implication. Briefly. "What do you mean?"

He walked backwards to his car, holding his gun on her. "You've done too well. You know too much. I can't let you live."

Several seconds passed as she absorbed what he had said. The air shimmered in the morning gold of the new sun. "You're going to kill us?" She had been through too much to give up now. Stall for time. Look for an opening.

357

Bourchette grunted.

"You've been part of this all along, haven't you?"

He shrugged.

Bourchette, she realized, was inventing a plausible excuse for shooting them. That was good: he'd be distracted. Jeremy's hand still held the gun. Could she could get to it in time?

"Both cars are full of paintings," she lied, stalling for time, "and I know where there are still others, up where Stoddard has been hiding them. Millions of dollars worth. You can have them all. But if you kill Jeremy and I, you'll have to turn the paintings in. Let us go, and we can hold them for you. Imagine what it would be like—"

"I'm going to give you a chance," Bourchette interrupted. "I'm going to let you run. I'll count to three before I shoot."

"To make it look like I was trying to escape? I'm not stupid."

She measured the distance with her eyes. Three paces to where Jeremy lay. Figure at least a full second to find the gun, grip it, aim, and fire. Say two seconds total, with luck. That's five seconds total.

But Bourchette was a cop, he'd trained with guns, he could get a shot off in a second. Still, he might miss. It was her only chance.

"One."

She dove for the gun. The sound of the shot came before she had taken a step.

Vacuum

HER MOVEMENT SURPRISED BOURCHETTE. He had expected her to run away, not toward the car. Now he could say he thought she was going for the gun. He raised his pistol to cut her down.

He felt something touch his ear. Pain. His vision blurred.

He saw a small boy in knickers, stocky even then. Laughed at in school. Bertrand the Bear, they had called him. "The image of your father," his mother said often, without enthusiasm.

His father sold vegetables in a street market in Paris, a squat powerful man, always short-tempered.

He saw his father as he was then, and realized how alike they were. In a sudden flash of warmth, Bourchette understood now it had been exhaustion that made his father forever angry, even on those Sundays when they went to the Bois de Boulogne. Six days every week he was up before dawn to buy the vegetables at the big markets at Les Halles, working until late in the evening to clean up for the next day. It was a grueling life, he realized, with a feeling of love he never before had felt for his father.

A wild blitz of colors and sounds. Events cascading past, each momentary, yet unrushed.

He hadn't wanted to do it. He would have been content enough with his retirement pay. But Vera had done her research, found where he was vulnerable, and exploited it. First the offer, the bribe. Then the threat. Cooperate, or I will destroy you. No pension after all those years. Prison, instead.

Mazzeli, Coutane, Diverment—three of his triumphs. Important cases, ones that had made his reputation. But cases where he'd had to shade things, doctor some evidence to get the right results. They were guilty enough, but the evidence was weak. Doctoring the evidence was part of the game, something you had to do sometimes to let justice work. Even the criminal *Milieu* recognized that the flics played to win, never mind the rules.

But that was then, another era. Things were different now. Just a year ago the reformers had nailed Roncalla, another *Commissaire Principal* months away from retirement. Twelve years he got, though he only lasted three months in prison before someone put a knife in him to settle an old score.

The images blurred again, a panoply of colors and memories that cascaded upon each other.

Then abruptly a deafening silence. A vacuum. No sounds, no sights. But his mind functioned, and he wondered what was happening to him. Was this death? But why?

It cleared, and he found himself looking down on himself, the stubby body that was sinking to the pavement, blood gushing out of the head.

He saw de Castaret climb out of his car. The bastard had been in the back seat! The story he'd told of the phone call from Paris, that had been a diversion to get into the car! *Merde!*

He watched de Castaret tuck the pistol into the shoulder holster, then stumble to the side of the road to be sick.

The sound, the sense, the feeling then was of being swept up into a vacuum: noise, then darkness and silence.

Helpful

VERA PASSED OUT AGAIN when McDevitt left the cottage. When she awoke, she was deathly sick.

Finally, she managed to stumble back down the hill to her rental car, trying not to think of the sight of Peter Edleigh's blackened face, and his body swaying from the ceiling of the cottage. If she hadn't arrived late, then she would have been hanging there beside him.

It was three in the morning, and she managed to get the car back to the little hotel in Cimiez. She found an empty parking space, and pulled in nose first. She was too tired and too sick to be bothered with trying to straighten it out.

When she stepped out of the car, a man in a black suit materialized from the night. He was dark-skinned, mustached. An Arab, she realized.

"Sheik Al Senour would like to speak with you for a few moments," he said.

She didn't have the strength to resist. The man took her arm and escorted her to a black car. It was empty. The driver made a call on the car phone, then drove ten minutes and they rendezvoused with a metallic blue Rolls-Royce. The man helped her into the Rolls' back seat.

She recognized Sheik Motar Al Senour from his photos. He greeted her with a wide smile. "A supreme pleasure to meet you," he said. "Please, sit a moment so we can talk."

As soon as she was in, the car pulled away from the curb and moved quickly and silently through the deserted streets.

Sheik Al Senour touched a button, and a panel in the seat-back ahead opened. "Perhaps a coffee? Or your favorite vodka-tonic?"

She took one of each. The hair of the dog. Her mouth tasted vile, and hoped the smell of vomit and alcohol wasn't on her breath.

Al Senour made the drinks, pouring himself only some tonic water. He handed her a glass, then touched his own to it. "To a successful future endeavor."

"Of course," she replied, stunned. This was the last thing she would have expected from him. "To the future."

"Time is short, so please permit me to move directly to the point."

She was surprised by the confidence and precision of his speech in contrast to that of his brother Gawbi. His accent was crisp and vaguely British upper-class. This was a man she could do business with. Even though he was an Arab.

"I understand you have been helping my brother Gawbi in certain art investments."

She had to set the glass on the tray because of the quivering in her hands. He waited for a response. "Yes, yes, I have."

"Very interesting investments, they are."

Again he paused, and she felt drawn to respond. "Potentially very profitable, particularly in the longer term."

"Extremely unique pieces, I understand."

The silences were devastating. Obviously he knew something of what had happened, but she didn't know how much. He was giving her no clues at all, just sitting back, toying with her.

"Thank you," she said for lack of a better response. "I considered Gawbi a very special client and gave particular attention to his account."

362

"Yes, certainly you did. A very special client, particular attention, yes, that is true." Al Senour was smiling and nodding as if in gratitude for what she had done. But his eyes did not smile. They were dark impenetrable eyes. Strong. Hypnotic.

"But there are some problems now," he continued.

When she tried to respond, he waved away her words with a flick of his fingers. "My dear Vera, let us be direct. We both realize that Allah was less than bountiful in bestowing intelligence on poor Gawbi. I know the game you were playing. I know that you got him and his friends to finance the art thefts, to the extent of over two million dollars, with more to come. More than one of those millions has stuck to your own fingers, mostly in some Swiss accounts."

He handed her a typed sheet, and she saw her account numbers and even the phone codes.

"How did you—"

Al Senour ignored her interruption and continued, "But you had expected to make your real profit later."

He smiled and reached over to touch her hand reassuringly. "I know these things. I have been following your game for quite some time. But I admire you nonetheless. You are a most clever woman."

"Thank you," she said.

"You can be very valuable to me, worth much more than a few dollars. One can always replace money, but there is forever a shortage of truly talented people."

"Oh?" He is a very attractive man, Vera was thinking. So much energy, charisma, intelligence. He wasn't like other Arabs, dirty, disgusting, uncultured, vile men. Al Senour was different. Al Senour was world-class.

She would agree to whatever he said. Then, in time, she would manipulate him to her own ends, as she managed with all the others.

"But first we must get you out of France while these tiresome police investigations continue. Incidentally, enrolling and then blackmailing Commissioner Bourchette was a master-stroke."

"You know everything, don't you?"

"But you made mistakes, serious mistakes, you and Stoddard. It never occurred to either of you that someone might be on your tail. My people were there almost from the start, as soon as I heard how much money Gawbi was going through. But there were others behind you, as well. Were you aware of that?"

"Others? What others?"

"The French counterpart of the Mafia—what do they call it? —ah yes, the *Milieu*. The money drew them like sharks. And you were oblivious to them all."

"The *Milieu*? How would they—"

He handed her an early copy of the morning's *Nice-Matin*:

SHOOT-OUT IN PALM GARDEN LEAVES THREE DEAD.
Police Search for Mystery Woman.
Possible Link to Art Thefts

"Your companions in this venture, the commandos, they are dead. The police would naturally like very much to arrest you so they can claim they broke the case. The authorities were embarrassed by the affair, and you can be sure they will make a show of prosecuting you. It will not go well for you, not well at all, you understand."

"Oh God! Stoddard got me into this! He forced me to help him!"

"It is important to get you out of France quickly. You can be of no value to me in a French prison."

"Yes, yes, I can be very helpful to you."

He handed her a bag from the floor. "Put that on."

She pulled out a *djellabah*, a flowing Arab gown.

"Wear that. It is your ticket out of France. And on to London."

"London? Oh, yes, yes, London would be wonderful."

WHEN THE ROLLS PULLED UP beside Al Senour's Gulfstream at the Nice-*Cote d'Azur* airport, the French customs and immigration agents were already waiting. It was a special courtesy for the wealthy Arabs who passed frequently through the airport. They processed the exit stamps for the Sheik, for the veiled woman who accompanied him, and for the dozen other members of the retinue.

The crew had already completed the pre-flight preparations, and within minutes the plane roared out over the sea.

The attendant drew some drapes, and Vera had a compartment by herself. They brought hot towels, then food. She slept.

She woke hours later when her ears popped. They were landing. She checked her seatbelt. She was strapped in, very tightly. She reached back, but there seemed to be no buckle, no way to release the tight belts that held her around the waist and chest.

The plane banked, and she looked out the window, eager to see the soft green of England and safety.

Sand. Endless miles of desert.

She spotted the note taped onto the seat back in front of her. It was in a man's handwriting, heavy and bold:

```
Madame de Cochin-Jessup
   You defrauded my brother and
others of more than two million
dollars, and were planning on taking
even more.
   You were unwise to use a verbal
bank code without regard to who was
listening to your conversations.
Thus we will be able to recover what
you have in your Swiss accounts,
leaving us even in the financial
sense, and you with nothing.
   But much more important than the
money is the dishonor you have done
my family, and that affront demands
justice. I have an important friend
who finds western women attractive,
particularly those with your
maturity and sophistication. He is a
civilized man, and you will be
reasonably comfortable with him for
a year while you work off the
consequences of your actions.
   He is a man of honor, true to his
word, and you can be sure that a
year from today you will be back in
London. You will receive an
honorarium from him. You will be
```

free to write a book of your experiences. Of course, you will need to be discreet in what you write as the authorities will still be extremely interested in the affairs you engineered in France.

Motar Al Senour

Incidentally, my people found and disposed of the vial of sleeping pills in your purse, so there will be no early exit for you.

SHE SCREAMED UNTIL they came with a needle to quiet her.

Telling the story

EMILY SPENT THREE HOURS with the police that morning, telling and retelling her account what had happened. The questions went over and over the details from that first night in Antibes to the final scene on the mountain road.

Bourchette's gun had been fired, which corroborated de Castaret's account of why he shot: to save Emily and Jeremy.

They had the bodies of two Americans: Roger Stoddard and Vern Billy Blodgett, both of whom died near the tunnel. Both had been American soldiers.

They had the paintings found in the trunk of Stoddard's BMW. They had also found the body of Albert Leroux thrown into bushes nearby, a known low-level member of the *Milieu*, and of course the body of Raoul Darterre, also known as Boom-Boom, another member, an enforcer, who had died in a very visible collision with a police car near the Palm Garden. And they had the body of Bertie Derham, a former British soldier, who, after a gun-battle in the Palm Garden, had been struck and killed by the car driven by Boom-Boom

They had the body of Peter Edleigh, a known art-forger, found hanging in his rented cottage.

In the interrogation, Emily mentioned the painting that she had found under the bed in Jeremy's room, the bag that she had moved to her mother's room to keep it away from a police search. They threatened her with a charge of tampering with evidence, but she realized that was a bluff. They dropped it an hour or so later.

Unspoken was the shared awareness that that painting had almost certainly been planted by someone working for Bourchette and the shadowy woman with whom he had been collaborating. That was something the police did not want to come out in the news. It was most likely Vera, but they could not be sure.

Unspoken also was the deeper reality that the police really had no idea how all of these strands had come together—the art thefts, the forgeries, the Americans, the British soldier, the local *Milieu*. But it didn't really matter: the authorities had a story that satisfied the news media, and probably the public, and the paintings had all been recovered.

JEREMY WAS RELEASED from the hospital that afternoon. He had not been shot, as it turned out; instead had fainted from dehydration coupled with the stress of the chase down the mountain. The blood Emily saw had been from a bloody nose that happened when he fell.

Jeremy's father, as well as Emily and her mother, had been at the hospital when he was released, ready to drive him back to the hotel.

But two detectives arrived and said it was *tres important* that Jeremy come to the *Commissariat Generale* on the *Avenue Dubouchage* and answer a few questions. Their manner made it clear that if he didn't come voluntarily they would take him anyway.

After an hour, they let him go back to the hotel for the night, on the understanding that he would remain in Nice for another session in the morning. To ensure that, they held his passport.

THE MORNING'S INTERVIEW was a repeat of the first; apparently his answers were consistent with what they had already turned up, and the atmosphere eased. Because de Castaret had been involved in Bourchette's death, he and his men were quarantined from any involvement, so *Commissaire Principal* Daulfroux and three subordinates had flown down from Paris to take over.

After the first hour of interviews, the officers and Jeremy loaded into two cars and drove back up to the tunnel.

By this point, they already knew most of the story. A forensics team had already scoured the area, and found the body of Albert Leroux, hidden in shrubbery. They recognized him on sight as one of the grunts in the local *Milieu*. It seemed clear enough that he had been sent by Marchand (now dead), and likely killed by one of the Americans, most likely Vern Billy Blodgett (now dead in the car crash further down the mountain) .So that closed a couple of aspects of the case.

Vera de Cochin-Jessup had disappeared from the area, and both of her links—Peter Edleigh and Roger Stoddard—were now dead for reasons having nothing to do with her—one by apparent suicide, the other a victim of his own reckless driving.

Which simplified the case further, and progress could be reported to the media, and with luck the media could be persuaded to forget that *Commissaire Principale* Bourchette had been shot under mysterious circumstances.

Jeremy told them of a man with an Irish accent who had followed Stoddard into the tunnel, but there was no sign of him there. The police informally wrote that person off as perhaps a delusion resulting from Jeremy's 24 hours without food or water.

After scouring the tunnel, and all the tunnels leading off the main, the police team had found no traces of the remaining stolen art works, primarily the ones taken at Le Trayas.

Which left the question of where those paintings had gone. But there were a lot of stolen art works floating around the world, and a lot of obscenely rich people, particularly South

American drug dealers and Russian Oligarchs and the like, all ready to pay for tangible wealth. No doubt that was the case here.

Tant pis. Too bad for the insurance companies, but the police had done their job.

THE POLICE DROPPED JEREMY back at the hotel in early afternoon, along with his passport.

Emily was waiting with news: Monsieur Sabitaille, the *Nice-Matin* reporter, was eager to hear their side of the story.

They met him at the same café in the *Nice-Etoile* office complex as before. He'd brought a photographer; this time Emily had taken the time to brush her hair.

As had the police, Sabitaille talked them through from the beginning: that first night at the Picasso Museum in Antibes, how they happened to cross paths, how she happened upon Vera and the gang members, Jeremy's kidnapping and ordeal in the tunnel.

He was fascinated by the coincidence that Jeremy and Emily met at the same hotel in Nice as their parents had three decades earlier, and even more by the synchronicity that the parents had happened to come back to that same place, at the same hour. "I guarantee you, that will be a story in itself, and all the ladies and men of a certain age all over the world will read it and feel very good, and perhaps shed a few tears of joy for how well it has turned out for them."

"AH, THERE IS ONE OTHER MATTER," Sabitaille said at the end. "As you perhaps know, most of the stolen pieces of art were covered by one insurance company, a British firm, as it happens. Representatives of that firm contacted me, and asked me to pass on an invitation to you both for a lunch with them tomorrow. Off the record, and please don't quote me, but they have arranged a reward for your help in recovering some of the paintings.

Emily and Jeremy looked at each other. Sabitaille was surprised by the strange expression that flashed in her eyes, then was gone.

"*Pourquois pas*, if you'll pardon my French," Jeremy said. "Why not?"

She nodded. "But I understand that not all the stolen pieces have been recovered. Is that still the case?"

"*Oui*, that is the case," Sabitaille shrugged. "But it could have been much worse if you had not been here to do your part in stopping them."

Business lunch

A CHAUFFEUR-DRIVEN ROLLS arrived at the Hotel Eminence at eleven the next morning, and took Emily and Jeremy to the Hotel Negresco, the 5-star old-line hotel on the *Promenade des Anglais*. Its rococo white stucco front suggested a palace; its pink onion dome a Russian cathedral.

The manager of the hotel met them at the door, accompanied by two of the doormen dressed in 18th Century costume, and escorted them to a private dining room overlooking the sea.

The Managing Director of the British insurance company was fiftyish, balding, stuffy in manner. Over a glass of sherry, he told them that he had flown in that morning from London by private jet, and would be flying on to Barcelona as soon as "this little affair" was finished.

With him were three other younger men, interchangeable in their vested grey suits.

During the lunch, he gave a detailed account of a fishing expedition to Scotland. Whether it took place the previous week or a decade earlier was not clear.

AT THE END OF THE LUNCH, one of the retainers handed Emily and Jeremy sealed envelopes, then shook hands with them. The Managing Director and the others were gathering their briefcases to leave.

Emily slit open her envelope, to the obvious distaste of the grey-suited man.

The envelope contained a check for $10,000. On the back of the check, above the space for the endorsement, was a release.

373

Acceptance of the check terminated any claims that she might have against the insurance consortium. Jeremy's was the same.

"Ten thousand dollars isn't enough," she said. "Not *nearly* enough. We recovered art for you worth several million dollars, according to the news accounts. The check should be for ten percent of that—at least ten percent. That's two million, which is a very great deal more than this $10,000."

The grey-suited man shook his head. "That's utterly impossible. Absurd."

"How can you say that?"

"In the first place, you did not actually recover the art, not at all. At best, you merely played a role in determining the identity of the perpetrators. Thus, technically-speaking, you are owed nothing, so these checks demonstrate good-will on our part."

"You know very well that's legalistic nonsense," Jeremy said. "If it hadn't been for us, you would have recovered no paintings, and very likely the art-theft gang would still be pulling other jobs."

One of the assistants shrugged, "No matter. We have offered you a reward, even though we were by no stretch legally bound to do so. That is company policy."

Emily noticed the Managing Director slipping out a side door. She ran after him, and caught him in the hotel lobby. "Somebody left a few zeros off our checks," she said.

He brushed her aside. "We must leave now, running late for a meeting in Barcelona. Price-Jones will deal with you."

"That's not good enough. We recovered the art. We saved your firm millions, at least $20 million, according to some media accounts. Others suggest it was double or even triple that."

"Very well," he nodded and turned to the grey-suited man who had given them the checks. "See to it that the rewards are doubled."

"Ten percent of the recovery. Nothing less," Emily said.

The Managing Director smiled, smug, supercilious. "What an extraordinary figure. Ten percent? I say!" He laughed, looking around at the others. They joined in the laughter.

"Ten percent," Emily repeated.

The Managing Director's laughter stopped. A crowd had circled the group, drawn for a glimpse of the pair of young Americans who had broken the art theft ring. "We would certainly like to be more generous, but we have fiduciary responsibility to our shareholders, you must understand that."

A television camera crew ran into the lobby, apparently drawn by a tip that the young Americans were there. The producer nodded to someone in the crowd. Emily glanced over and saw Sabitaille of *Nice-Matin*. Good for him.

"Ten percent. That's the norm," Jeremy said.

A cold smile. "Do you perhaps have anything in writing from us agreeing to ten percent? Something signed by an authorized senior person?"

"Ten percent is the normal reward. It's the custom of the industry."

"Even if it were, we couldn't afford it in a case like this, a situation of such magnitude. Moreover, there is still a great deal missing, many paintings have yet to be recovered, so our group is facing millions in losses. We simply can't afford to give you any more. We are a business firm, after all, not a charitable organization."

He was visibly uncomfortable with the crowd overhearing the conversation. "Clear these people out of here," he told his subordinates. One snapped his fingers and beckoned to one of the hotel's security guards. The guard turned away.

"Tell me," Emily said. "You say that not all the paintings have been recovered? Do you have any leads?"

The Managing Director cleared his throat. "At the moment, not yet. But our people are very close to them now, I understand. In any case, we must leave now for an important meeting in Barcelona."

"Just how much are those paintings worth—the ones still missing?"

The Managing Director looked to one of the subordinates. "It's difficult to say, as it depends so much on the market at the time."

Jeremy turned to Emily and winked. "*Nice-Matin* and other media outlets have published estimates ranging from—"

"What does it matter what nonsense they publish? In any case, whatever efforts you may have put in were totally unproductive."

"What does it matter? The fact is that if the missing pieces are not recovered, then your consortium will be obliged to pay out a very great deal of money to museums and private individuals."

"I'm totally confident that we will ultimately recover everything."

'And if you don't manage to recover everything?"

The television crew had the camera in place, and the sound man held a big boom microphone overhead, catching the conversation.

The Managing Director's eyes blazed, though he attempted to smile for the camera "Well, er . . . One supposes. If all efforts at recovery, er, are unsuccessful. That is our contractual obligation as insurers, and we would of course do right by our clients."

"I'm asking that same question another time: Are you prepared to pay a percentage of value for their recovery?"

The Managing Director glanced at one of the other men, a puffy man with milky-white skin and curly reddish hair. "Mr. Portman-Hollingsworth has been more than gracious. I suggest you take the checks and be on your way."

"You said you'd double that amount," Emily said.

"Very well, yes."

"No, no, that's not enough, nowhere near enough" Jeremy said. "Isn't it normal practice in your industry to pay ten percent of value, sometimes twenty, depending on circumstances?"

The man with the red hair shrugged, his nose tilting back. "We have been through all that. The paintings have already been recovered, most of them. We refuse to bargain about—"

Emily smiled, and tilted her own head back, echoing the body language. "Some have been recovered—mainly because Jeremy and I led you to that little cottage in the hills above Nice, as well as to what was in Stoddard's car. We did get them for you by our efforts in following the leads. You know that, and I think the television audience will know that as well."

She turned to the camera and said, "The insurance group has generously offered Jeremy and I $20,000 for our work in recovering millions of dollars worth of paintings."

Someone in the crowd laughed, then others took it up, and someone shouted out "Cheapskate bastards! Like all insurers!"

Emily raised her hand and the crowd went silent. "The fact is, you're trying to weasel out of paying the reward for—"

"'Weasel'? I say, what an extraordinarily archaic word," the red-haired man said. "But I don't like the implication of it, not at all. It implies—"

"There are paintings still missing, I understand," Emily said again, making sure the TV camera had a clear shot at her as she spoke. "Suppose, hypothetically, those could be located. If so, would it make sense to your firm to pay twenty percent of value for those?"

A look passed among the insurance men. Then the Managing Director said, "Do you know where those paintings are?"

Jeremy laughed. "I can honestly say that I don't know where they are."

The Managing Director smiled for the camera, raising his hands in a gesture of good-humored exasperation. "I say, if you don't know where they are, then why are we having this absurd hypothetical discussion?"

"Because you don't have any idea where they are, and I just might, hypothetically-speaking, be able to locate them," Emily said. "But in the light of how cheap, chintzy, and disreputable you have already proven yourself—" she paused, hoping the reporters and camera-men got that clearly.

"Given the history of how you've already tried to cheat us, we would insist on a formal agreement in writing to that effect. Twenty percent of value for recovery."

"We would, er, of course, be open—"

Emily smiled and pointed to the camera. "Please, Mr. Managing Director, look at the camera and say that. Put it on record, so the whole world hears you. Twenty percent?"

"ARE YOU SUGGESTING—" the Managing Director began. Then he interrupted himself. "Yes, you are, aren't you? You do have the paintings, is that correct?"

Emily smiled, and spoke slowly for the benefit of the assembled media. "I did not, repeat *not*, say that I have any paintings. Not at all, let me make that very clear. But if you were to ask me if I happened to know where one of the group had hidden certain items, I might say yes."

The Managing Director pulled the others around him in a huddle, and they moved into a corner.

After five minutes, the Managing Director hurried out to the Rolls waiting at the front door, his way through the crowd cleared by hotel staff.

The first assistant, the one who first offered them the checks, came over to them, distaste evident on his face. "We find your squabbling over money most distasteful, and ethically questionable, as well. Nonetheless, under duress we do agree to pay the twenty percent you ask. Provided of course that you can deliver what you suggest."

Emily fingered the slip of paper bearing the code to a locker at the rail station in Nice. "Then I suggest we meet at the office of Monsieur Sabitaille at *Nice-Matin* an hour from now. I'm sure he'll be pleased to help . . . and will be very interested to hear the outcome, as well. We'll bring you what information we have, and I suggest you bring a suitcase full of cash."

NOTE TO READERS

If you enjoyed *Infinite Doublecross*, I'd appreciate your posting a short review on Amazon.

Acknowledgements

Many thanks to all who contributed to this book, including beta readers, editors, idea and information contributors, and to the inn-keepers who provided lodging, input, and, not to forget, food.

I appreciate the insider views on art theft and art security given me by two professionals in the field who I had the privilege of meeting at a conference on art theft a very long time ago, when the idea that has become *Infinite Doublecross* was, as the saying goes, "just a gleam in my eye":

- Donald Mason, who spent nearly a dozen years of his FBI career investigating art theft, and is the author of *The Fine Art of Art Security.*
- Gilbert Raguideau, who headed France's Central Office for the Repression of the Theft of Art Objects.

Special thanks to Monique Gignoux for her guidance on my usage of *la langue et les choses francaises*, (though any errors are my own).

Special thanks also to Marguerite Eisinger, for sharing her insights as an early reader, particularly one with her career experience in art museum operations.

And very special thanks to my wife, Susan, for advice and input along the way, for the interest she shares with me in the unusual topics addressed here, and by no means least, for her tolerance of the piles of notes and discarded drafts!

About the author / Other books

Michael McGaulley, J.D., is a lawyer and management consultant. He is a graduate of the Cornell Law School, admitted to practice in New York, Virginia, and the District of Columbia.

His consulting clients have included the Foreign Service Institute of the U.S. State Department, various other federal departments in both the civilian and military sectors, and private companies such as Xerox in the United States, Canada, and Europe; Bank of America; Kodak, and others. This work gave him the chance to see how organizations and the individuals within operate on both the visible and sub-surface levels.

Blogs and websites include:

- MichaelMcGaulley.net
- Sales-Training-Source.com

Or check out the Michael McGaulley Author Page on Amazon

Michael McGaulley

CAREER SAVVY PEOPLE SKILLS SERIES

Book #1

Am I Asking
THE RIGHT
QUESTIONS?

How to Focus on
What Matters Most

Career Savvy People Skills
Book #1

Michael McGaulley, JD

"You've got to be aware of the games that are being played. You don't have to play the games yourself, but you do need to recognize when they are being played against you." Like it or not, the reality is that games, probes, and subtle competitions—and not to forget office politics! —are facts of life in most organizations. *Smart Questions* provides the tools for looking through to what's really going on in situations, on spotting the "real rules", on focusing on what really matters and staying out of unnecessary confrontations, and on selecting the best option under the circumstances—and defending it if challenged.

Book #2

MENTAL PICKPOCKETING

How to get to the
truth without
SEEMING to ask
questions

Career Savvy People Skills
Book #2

Michael McGaulley, JD

When you ask a question, *most* of the time, *most* people will do their best to tell the truth. But not always. Sometimes simply to ask a question is to give the game away because it alerts the other person to what you're really after, and hence raises a flag on what they may want to fudge, avoid, or distort. (Or even tell a fib!) **Mental Pickpocketing** introduces you to an array of methods of getting to the truth without seeming to ask questions.

382

Book #3

UN-PUZZLING
PERSONALITIES

How to Understand and
Work Better with People
and Teams

Career Savvy People Skills
Book #3

Michael McGaulley, JD

Emotional intelligence is recognized as a particularly valuable asset in today's career world. *Un-Puzzling Personalities* is based on the system developed by Carl Jung, and includes self-instructional tutorials including mini-cases, as well as application checklists and worksheets.

The system is clear and helpful in taking a fresh look at oneself, as well as in understanding how others perceive and react in different ways to events and communications.

Michael McGaulley

QUANTUM MIND TECH SERIES

Book #1

The Deeper Grail: It's not what we think it is, and not where we've been looking.
It's the most powerful force ever known, and it's waiting to be tapped--for good or evil.

It was sought by the Nazi *Ahnenerbe* or "Occult Bureau" in WWII, and now by a scruffy, brutal "army" made up of fans of Twisted Messiah, a violent, destructive, international rock group with neo-Nazi political ambitions and dark occult dimensions.

Book #2

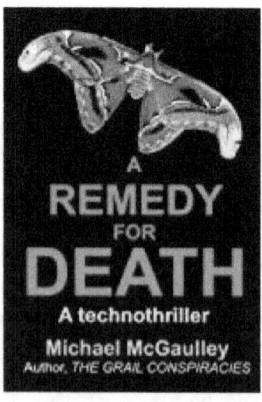

It's said that we only go around once in life . . . at least that's the way it's always been. But what if?

What if the terms of life have changed . . . for an elite, self-selected few?

What was "mere" science-fiction not long ago is a fast-approaching reality in the era of biotech and genetic engineering.

Book #3

The Alchymagic Disruptive.
Alchemy, magic, Isaac Newton, and Quantum Physics merge to form the most disruptive technology since electricity.

But it's a breakthrough that can be "weaponized" as well as "monetized" ---a discovery that governments and investors around the world are ready to kill for.

Coming Fall 2021

"INNOCENT?" INTERNATIONAL HEIST SERIES

Book #1

The South of France: Art theft, art forgery, and artful duplicity

Betrayed weeks before the wedding, Emily Cederquist takes off to France to heal.

On her first night on the Riviera, she witnesses a major art theft at the Picasso Museum in Antibes . . . and the police are convinced that she was not just a witness but a key part of the team. She finds herself caught in a tangle of duplicity, deception, and doublecross for high-stakes . . . including a guy who may be as

385

ideal as he seems, her perfect match. *Or who may be the most dangerous and manipulative of all.* **If she can't trust herself—and her instincts —who *can* she trust?**

Book #2

"I've got a racket if you've got the balls"—Jade's opening words at the club to manipulate naïve techie Dick initially into a game of squash, and beyond that into a racket that will take him to London, Amsterdam, Zurich, and finally Geneva in the course of her scheme to *"steal dirty money from the worst people in the world."*

professional advice, including counseling on any subject matter. Neither the author nor publisher accept any responsibility for any loss which may arise from reliance on information contained in this book or related website.

Some links within this e-book or related website may lead to other websites, including those operated and maintained by third parties. The author and publisher of this e-book include these links solely as a convenience to you, and the presence of such a link does not imply a responsibility for the linked site or an endorsement of the linked site, its operator, or its contents.

The publisher and author accept no liability whatsoever for any losses or damages caused or alleged to be caused, directly or indirectly, by utilization of any information contained herein, or obtained from any of the persons or entities herein above.

This book and related website and its contents are provided "AS IS" without warranty of any kind, either express or implied, including, but not limited to, the implied warranties of merchantability, fitness for a particular purpose, or non-infringement.

If you, or any other reader, do not agree to these policies as noted above, please do not use these materials or any services offered herein.

Your use of these materials indicates acceptance of these policies.

This book is intellectual property. No part of this publication may be stored in a retrieval system, transmitted or reproduced in any way, including but not limited to digital copying and printing without the prior agreement and written permission of the author and publisher.